MURDER at MERRY BEGGARS HALL

Writing as Natalie Meg Evans

Historical novels

The Dress Thief
The Milliner's Secret
The Wardrobe Mistress
A Gown of Thorns
The Secret Vow
The Paris Girl

Into the Burning Dawn
The Italian Girl's Secret
The Girl with the Yellow Star
The Locket
The Paris Inheritance

KAY BLYTHE

MURDER at MERRY BEGGARS HALL

NO EXIT PRESS

First published in the UK in 2025 by No Exit Press,
an imprint of Bedford Square Publishers Ltd,
London, UK

noexit.co.uk
@noexitpress
info@bedfordsquarepublishers.co.uk

ISBN
978-1-83501-212-3 (Paperback)
978-1-83501-213-0 (eBook)

2 4 6 8 10 9 7 5 3 1

Typeset in Adobe Caslon Pro by Palimpsest Book Production Limted, Falkirk, Stirlingshire

Printed in Great Britain by CPI Group (UK) Ltd, Croydon CR0 4YY

The manufacturer's authorised representative in the EU for product safety is Easy Access System Europe, Mustamäe tee 50, 10621 Tallinn, Estonia
gpsr.requests@easproject.com

FSC
www.fsc.org

MIX
Paper | Supporting
responsible forestry
FSC® C171272

For those who hold apostrophes dear, a note upon the title of this book:

From *A Rambler's Guide to the English Lowlands* by K. B. Rivers

Arriving at Merry Beggars Hall, a place of mighty oaks and darkling skies, I ask why no apostrophe? Should it not be Merry Beggars' or Merry Beggar's? What made those mendicant folk so joyful… the strong, local cider?

The name appears first in an Anglo-Saxon charter of AD 869 as *Beacca's Angar*, being 'the open meadow of Beacca'. Over the centuries, the name adapted to more easily roll off the tongue. 'Merry' appears first during the 15th century, perhaps a reference to the nearby parish of St Mary. More likely, it derives from *merrow*, meaning 'fat' or 'abundant' and a nod to the depth of the soil hereabouts.

Later, as I wander across neighbouring Beggars Heath (similarly unburdened by an apostrophe) I note the drier ground and conclude that if beggars ever came here to celebrate, this was the better place for them to park their wagons.

Chapter One

Suffolk, England, 1922

The last Monday of April arrived with a hard frost. Ada, Lady Hamlash, rubbed mist from the leaded panes of her bedroom window. Seeing the horse chestnuts at the end of her drive were dressed in pure silver, she murmured, 'Goodness me.'

Knotting a sturdy dressing gown over her nightdress, she hurried out of Merry Beggars Hall through the conservatory door, making her way by a series of paths to a walled garden. She tramped past white-rimed roses and dormant lavender with one fixed aim: her asparagus beds. Frost at this unseasonal time was a killer.

She inspected each raised bed and ferny shoot, removing ice-cold snails as she went. When she was satisfied there was no lethal damage to her outdoor plants, she squeezed through the door of a glasshouse where more asparagus grew under domed cloches. These were the special crowns. The glazed pots kept the light off them to produce stems that were tender and pale.

'What's this?' Amid a straight line of ivory cloches, one plant stood unprotected, its spears luminous against the rich soil at its roots. Lady Hamlash could almost imagine it shivering in its nakedness. Was her gardener descending into the dells of forgetfulness? Poor Bilney had to be well past seventy and though he had never before, to her knowledge, left a plant exposed, he was failing in other ways. How many times had she asked him to repair the glasshouse door so she might get in and out without catching her elbows? Making a mental note to mention the matter once more, Ada looked around for the missing cloche.

It was on the brick walkway which ran between the raised beds. Lifting it up, Ada's mouth fell open. Her action had revealed the face of Crosby, her butler. She slammed the cloche down, blocking out the man's appalled and fixed expression.

One highly excusable considering that only Crosby's head lay at her feet. The remainder of his person was missing.

Being a woman of stern self-discipline, Ada Hamlash neither screamed nor fainted. She took the fastest route back to the house where she rapped furiously at a side door. Only when her butler opened it and proved himself to be fully alive by wishing her a mildly bewildered, 'Good morning, my lady,' did she emit a blood-curdling shriek. A shriek that startled the rooks from the chestnut trees and echoed through the ground floor of Merry Beggars Hall.

Eight months later

Chesterfield Gardens, Mayfair, London

The second post had brought two letters: one plain, the other a jaunty lilac colour. Jemima Flowerday hesitated over which to open. Her sister Vicky passed a cup of tea across the table, saying, 'Brown envelopes rarely bode well. Better open that one first.'

Jemima did so and groaned. 'You're right. It's the children's school fees. Why have they sent the bill early?'

'Because you paid so late last time, I should think.'

Jemima read out the statement. '"In advance of Spring Term 1923, thirty-two guineas and eightpence".'

'Isn't it usually a flat thirty guineas? What are the extra two guineas and eightpence for?' Vicky demanded.

'Molly's piano lessons.'

'Why – when I could teach her?' Vicky spread her long, musician's fingers. 'Take the children out of boarding school and put them into day schools here in London. That way they'll come home every night and be pummelled into shape at a third of the cost.'

'I'm following their father's wishes. He chose Steepdale because it's one of the few schools that admits both boys and girls. It is civilised, unlike the vile institution he went to.'

'Simon didn't envisage you being left to foot the bill alone.'

This was old ground. Casting the notice on to the table, Jemima took up the lilac envelope. It was addressed to 'Fleur du Jour', her business's name. Inside, a sheet of matching paper contained handwritten lines.

'Dear Mrs Flowerday,' it began, 'I am advised by an acquaintance that you are an accomplished dressmaker, sympathetic to the needs of older clients—'

'Gosh!' Jemima exclaimed. 'A lady is offering me fifty pounds to make her three evening gowns. She's… oh… she's Lady Hamlash.'

'*The* Lady Hamlash?' Vicky queried.

'Of Merry Beggars Hall. What a bolt from the blue.'

'"Bolt" is what I advise,' Vicky responded grimly. 'As in "for the hills".'

'And miss an opportunity?' Jemima knew all about the disembodied head found deep in the Suffolk countryside. The press had covered every detail of the gruesome discovery in the walled garden. 'Merry Beggars Hall, "Beggars" with no apostrophe,' Jemima murmured, aware of Vicky's growing disquiet. 'I did wonder if the newspapers had got that wrong, but it's how Lady Hamlash writes it. She needs three gowns "in the modern mode" by Christmas Eve. She must be throwing a house party. Fifty pounds will cover the school fees nicely and leave something in the bank.'

Vicky seized the letter. 'What does one make of a person who uses a shade of writing paper favoured by schoolgirls and kept women?'

That was easy for Jemima to answer. 'Lilac notepaper and envelopes were sent to her as a birthday gift by a niece or a goddaughter, and she's too kind – or thrifty – to throw them away. Like us, she's short of money.'

'Speculation.'

'You'll discover I'm right. Lady Hamlash cannot come up to London for fittings – *ergo*, nothing to spare for hotel bills.'

As well as being a fine dressmaker, Jemima Flowerday loved studying the human mind. Saving a young colleague from an unjust charge of arson many years ago had also given her a taste for solving crime and, had she been a man, she'd have steered a course towards CID. As it was, she ran her one-woman couture business and unravelled whatever mysteries came her way. Her most recent triumph had been to unmask a milkman over-charging his customers in Chesterfield Gardens.

'Perhaps she's mean, or lazy,' Vicky suggested, meaning Lady Hamlash.

'Or afraid of recognition. Naturally, she wants me to go to her.'

'Where in Suffolk exactly?'

'Beggars Heath, near Saxonchurch.'

Vicky's face was a picture. 'One can almost hear oak boughs creaking and pigs munching acorns.'

Jemima laughed. 'It's not far from my in-laws' place, actually. If Saxonchurch is anything like the Flowerday seat, it's charmingly olde-worlde with a castle and a thatched bus stop.'

4

'And a murderer on the loose.' Vicky advised Jemima to throw Lady Hamlash's letter on the fire. 'Her butler's head was found in a greenhouse, and you want to go and poke around.'

'In a glasshouse and it wasn't the butler's head.'

'It was indeed his head!'

'I mean, it wasn't the butler's. It was—'

'Stop!' Vicky held up a hand. 'The police still haven't a clue who did it, and what if the killer lives next door, or in the house itself?'

Poor Vicky could not have said anything more likely to unleash the bloodhounds kennelled in her sister's frustrated heart. The moment tea was finished, Jemima went down to her office and telephoned Lady Hamlash.

The Weekend Sleuth

The famous weekly paper for the true-crime addict

Our roving reporter takes tea with Mrs Roland Crosby

A solemn clock ticks on the mantelpiece as the murder victim's widow serves me a slice of succulent coconut cake. Mrs Crosby bakes such fancies 'for a living', she informs me, now she is alone in the world. Despite the terrible circumstances that overset an unassuming life, Sara Crosby displays a cheer that brings this hardened hack to the brink of tears.

'Whoever hurt my Roly is the worst fiend this world ever made,' she declares from the armchair where once her husband rested his head after the day's toil. 'What he went through in his final moments is more than I can put my mind to, and I pray the police find the culprit and enact the full rigour of the law.'

When asked how she will get on with life, Mrs Crosby sits silent for a moment, then sings the opening line of the well-known hymn. 'O God our help in ages past, our hope in years to come.'

This reporter bids her farewell with a heart full of admiration and steps out into an unpretentious North London street. Here live the respectable tradesfolk we more educated people rely on, in a neighbourhood of tidy front gardens where each front porch boasts a black-leaded boot scraper and a brass house number.

This is not a place one associates with brutal murder. And yet, a man walked down this street towards his doom.

The presence of a neighbour at her garden gate leads to a second conversation. 'Madam, did you notice anything out of the ordinary the day Mrs Crosby's Roly left his home for the last time?'

The good woman answers that, 'He seemed much as usual, sir, keeping to himself, and walking with his head down, but we did see a bit of frost that morning, so it's not to be wondered at.'

The truth of Roland Crosby's fate will continue to mystify our gallant police force and tease the minds of our resolute army of *Weekend Sleuths*.

Chapter Two

It was Monday, 11 December and just four days on from Jemima's receipt of Lady Hamlash's letter. Stowing her bags and a roll of card on the rack of a train compartment, her thoughts raced ahead to her destination. At Merry Beggars Hall she would create dresses for her client while discreetly investigating Roland Crosby's murder. The police had done their best, but they lacked her singular advantage. What detective could embed himself into the heart of a household as she could, and all without raising suspicion?

She took her seat and shook out the latest copy of *The Weekend Sleuth*.

A vicar and his lady, about to join her, glanced at the vivid illustration on the front and quickly withdrew from the compartment. Jemima smiled to herself. The next two hours were a chance to read and think uninterrupted.

As the train drew away, Jemima sifted everything she knew of Roland Crosby's death. He had been fit and alive on the first Saturday after Easter, a weekend memorable for a sudden cold snap in the weather. The railings of Chesterfield Gardens had sparkled with frost and in the countryside apple blossom had withered and new lambs had been whisked into shelter.

On that day, Mr Crosby had left early for work, according to newspaper reports, but did not arrive. As was later discovered, instead of taking his usual underground train to Green Park, he had made his way to a mainline London station where he bought a rail ticket for Beggars Heath in Suffolk. A *single* ticket.

'You buy a single if you're not planning to return,' Jemima reflected as the smoky façades of the city filled her view. She pondered it as the backyards of Bow and Stratford poured past the window. 'Every report I read holds up Roland Crosby as a paragon of reliability. Not a man to miss work or abscond from a marriage either.'

Her copy of *The Weekend Sleuth* was from May, when public interest in the case had been raging. Its middle pages contained a detailed reconstruction of the victim's last known movements.

> For reasons we can but guess at, fifty-year-old Roland Crosby left his home in Finsbury Park, bidding his wife goodbye shortly after 6.30 a.m. on Saturday, 22 April. His workplace was the exclusive Bright's Club in St James' Street, SW1, where he was employed as a waiter. He did not arrive. At Finsbury Park underground station, a ticket seller recalled Crosby purchasing a third-class fare, but could not say to which destination.

After that the trail went, literally, underground. Some thirty minutes later, Roland Crosby popped up at Liverpool Street, the railway station serving East Anglia. His ticket to Beggars Heath was bought at 7.26 am for the 7.30 train. He'd cut things mighty fine. A guard remembered an out-of-breath man boarding a carriage as the whistle blew, stumbling as he got on. A ticket inspector who conversed with Crosby during the first leg of his journey described him as 'terse and distracted'. A man matching Crosby's description was later seen at Ipswich station, waiting for his onward connection.

Did Roland reach Beggars Heath? 'We cannot verify that he did', the *Sleuth* solemnly declared. 'The rural station attendant saw nobody matching the victim's description.'

As Victorian streets gave way to ribbon suburbs and gathering clouds darkened her compartment, Jemima put away the newspaper and took a leather-bound journal from her handbag. Turning to a clean page, she wrote the present date and a heading: *Notes on an unsolved murder.*

Her pencil moved steadily as the train steamed on and when she raised her head, she noticed greenery through the rain-streaked window. She blinked away a church, a farm, a cluster of cottages. Still the sole occupant of her compartment, she read out loud what she'd written.

Crosby's movements in the hours before his disappearance and death are consistent with a man making an impulsive journey. To what purpose, not even his poor widow can say. We know that Mrs Crosby helped him into his coat that final morning, when nothing appeared amiss. She recalls whisking a clothes brush over the corduroy collar of his coat and asking if he'd be home for supper. 'Who knows?' he replied. It was not unusual for Roland's shifts to end too late for him to return and, in such cases, he would bed down at Bright's Club, in the staff quarters. And so, his wife was not perturbed to be retiring to bed without seeing him. However, by teatime the following day, Sunday, she was growing uneasy. Being, in her words, 'Reluctant to bother Roly' by telephoning his place of employment, she continued to wait. Only as evening fell did she act, walking until she spied a beat constable, to whom she expressed her worries. That constable escorted her to his police station, where she reported her husband missing.

The end of this harrowing drama had been reported *tedium ad nauseam*, but Jemima had written it anyway.

Roland Crosby's severed head was discovered early on Monday, 24 April by Ada, Lady Hamlash, who had ventured outside to check her asparagus for frost-damage.

The Weekend Sleuth characterised Lady Hamlash as a wild eccentric, rushing through the dawn in her nightie. It had dubbed Roland Crosby's beheader, 'The Rustic Ripper'.
Jemima had noted this was incorrect.

The head was severed by some kind of cleaver, as used by butchers or abattoir workers. No ripping involved.

She ended with questions:

Why was Roland's head placed in the glasshouse, in so ghoulish a fashion?
    Was the placing deliberate, so Lady Hamlash might find it?
    Most critical of all—

Interrupted by the ticket inspector, Jemima closed her journal and settled down to experience the journey Roland Crosby had, theoretically, completed eight months before. She got off at Ipswich, Suffolk's county town, to wait for her branch-line connection. At five minutes to midday, she passed through the turnstile at Beggars Heath. It was raining hard, the stationmaster bustling her through and hardly glancing at her ticket.
    A car was waiting.

Chapter Three

'Late Elizabethan. A gem, wouldn't you say?'

They were standing in front of Merry Beggars Hall, with the rain heavy on the gravel forecourt. It was her driver asking the question. He had a pleasing voice, though she couldn't place his accent.

'Would I say it?' In truth, she saw nothing but an ancient manor house of russet brick, its frontage veined by climbing roses cut back hard. Stone mullions divided dark windows whose glass reflected the sky. A forest of candy-twist chimneys added interest, but only two of them breathed smoke. If Merry Beggars Hall was anything like other country houses Jemima had stayed in, it would boast enormous fireplaces where nobody had thought to light an actual fire. Still, she'd better find something to admire. 'I do love Dutch gables,' she said, 'and diamond-pane windows make me think of all the Gothic novels I ought to have read. Too many of our old buildings are being pulled down these days.'

'Not *my* old buildings.' The chauffeur, who had introduced himself as Wells, gave a one-sided smile. He wore a peaked cap, a buttoned coat, boots and gaiters. 'I'm not British.'

He pronounced it *Briddish* and she looked more closely at him. He was a little younger than her, late twenties perhaps, and reminded her of her husband. How Simon had been before a German shell had done its work. She pushed the painful thought away. 'Are you American?'

'You have a good ear, ma'am.'

'I live in a cosmopolitan corner of London. I'm always meeting Americans. From New York, mostly.' Rich women, off White Star liners, needing a wardrobe refresh, fast.

'I'm from New England originally, but I migrated to New York some years back.'

'What brings you here?'

'I guess I fancied a change. Let's get you inside, ma'am.'

Jemima followed Wells into a cavernous porch, thinking, he shuffled off my question rather expertly. The short journey from the station had been completed in silence, she sitting in the rear of a black Crossley with a glass screen separating them. She'd enjoyed watching the back of Wells's head. Four years on from the end of 'the war to end all wars', any able-bodied male had rarity value. Add to that his coming from New York... he was earning an entry in her journal.

Wells knocked and as they waited for the door to open, Jemima looked back down the drive. Merry Beggars Hall was remote even by Suffolk standards, islanded in ploughed fields and two miles from Beggars Heath, which itself boasted a few cottages and a mean-looking public house. She imagined this heavy land with a hard frost on top, as on the last-but-one weekend of April. Could a killer have dug a grave in the unrelenting clay? No. If he had been killed here, Roland Crosby's mutilated body would likely have been dragged into a thicket. As the seasons passed, falling leaves would have made his grave.

The door was opened by a butler wearing a dress coat, high-fronted waistcoat and pinstripe trousers. The hairs on Jemima's neck tingled. *The Weekend Sleuth* had drained many an inkwell describing Albert Crosby, Roland's elder brother. His shock and grief, his inability to rationalise his sibling's fate. The likeness between the brothers had been mentioned in passing; there was a familial resemblance, in Jemima's opinion. An opinion drawn from a sketch of Roland Crosby that had appeared in *The Weekend Sleuth*. Albert Crosby was thin of face, with a long, bony nose and a receding hairline. Roland had possessed the same shaped nose and chin… perhaps he had been a little fuller in the cheeks. It struck Jemima as interesting that Albert Crosby should remain here, at his post. Perhaps he, too, was searching for answers.

Wells announced her. 'Mr Crosby, this is Mrs Flowerday.'

The butler's chin reared a lofty inch above his collar. 'The dressmaker? Take her to the kitchen entrance.' Albert Crosby glanced briefly at Jemima, then at something beyond her.

She followed his look, but saw nothing but looming chestnut trees and a leaden sky.

The door was shut abruptly.

Wells blew out his cheeks. 'My mistake – I thought you were front-hall material, ma'am. That cute hat you're wearing is fit for any drawing room.'

'A little too cute, perhaps?' Jemima flashed a rueful smile. 'Better take me to the trade entrance.'

The housekeeper was more welcoming. Wells had escorted Jemima through a kitchen garden and into a glazed lobby with a cracked tiled floor. Tapping at a door, and without waiting for an answer, he led her into a room dominated by a scrubbed pine table. A woman with grey hair plaited across her scalp sat alone there, apparently sorting through pieces of string. She looked up as Wells introduced Jemima and described their reception at the main entrance.

'Only visitors and family are admitted into the main hall. You ought to know as much, Mr Wells.'

'Sure I know,' he replied. 'Be assured, anyone who turns up with darned elbows or missing buttons gets taken round to the back. Mrs Flowerday is class and I was using my initiative.'

'You're not in America now, Mr Wells. In this country, initiative is discouraged whereas respecting the rules keeps us—'

'In line?' Wells cut in.

'Keep us from being made to feel uncomfortable, if you would let me finish.' The woman gave Jemima a mildly appraising glance. 'I'm Mrs Newson and I am the housekeeper here. Welcome to Merry Beggars Hall. Let me take your coat.'

Bidding goodbye with a slight roll of the eyes, Wells left. Jemima gratefully peeled off her damp top layer. The servants' hall was warm and – intriguingly – filled with the aroma of roasting garlic. In her experience, garlic was viewed with suspicion in the provinces. The kitchen lay alongside, screened off by a wall of frosted glass, behind which a figure in white moved fluidly. The cook at work? Jemima was looking forward to lunch.

'Wells was only doing his best by me,' she said, hoping to learn more about her intriguing new acquaintance. 'It's remarkable that he would come so far to drive a motor car through English puddles.'

'He's the gardener, really.' Mrs Newson hung Jemima's coat on a wall bracket. 'But since he can drive, he doubles up. There's not been a real chauffeur here since before the war. I'll show you to your room. No, leave that.' Jemima had reached for her travel bags. 'The girl will fetch them up.'

'The girl?'

'Dinah, the house parlourmaid. If I can find her, ever…' Mrs Newson sighed and led Jemima out into a short passageway, then

15

through a latched door into an oak-panelled reception hall untouched by modernity. Its ornately plastered ceiling was yellow from decades of candle-smoke. Four interior doors led off, each surmounted by a carved coat of arms, suggesting there were family rooms behind. At one end was the door where she had earlier been denied. Mrs Newson might believe that keeping the rules prevented every social class from feeling uncomfortable, but what if you fell between the social classes, as she did?

As Jemima had predicted, a massive fireplace yawned out the smell of damp coal dust. The smoke she'd seen rising from the chimneys must have been from the kitchen, and whichever room Lady Hamlash occupied. Would she be invited into the drawing room? she wondered.

'This way, Mrs Flowerday.' Mrs Newson led her up a majestic staircase, pausing halfway so Jemima could peer down to the hall below. 'There are back stairs,' the housekeeper said, 'but as you are a guest, you should use this staircase for coming and going.'

'A guest?' Jemima echoed as they began their climb. 'Mr Crosby has no doubt of my status, but you, Mrs Newson, you look at my attire, listen to my voice, and invite me to climb the family stairs. I suspect I will be a puzzle to you all.'

Jemima had already planned to set up her studio in a corner of the servants' hall, at that big pine table. It would be warm and put her in the hub of things. She asked when she might be introduced to Lady Hamlash.

'Her Ladyship will send for you in the hours between lunch and tea,' came the reply.

The housekeeper continued the climb. From the way she put one slow foot after the other, she was either in the early stages of arthritis or reluctant to leave the comfort of the servants' wing.

'I've given you the room where the nurse used to sleep, the one that looked after Sir Rufus while he was an invalid. Lady Hamlash's late husband, that is. There's a table to sew at and it will be private.'

Jemima shivered. Heat was supposed to rise, but she was starting to see her own breath. 'Am I being consigned to the attic?'

'There are no attic bedrooms at Merry Beggars. You'll be sleeping on the same level as myself, and Dinah too. And even Her Ladyship, though the main bedrooms are in the south wing. We female staff keep to the north side, a little out of the way, but nice and quiet.'

As the grave, Jemima reflected. This would not do. She must start as she meant to go on. 'Could I meet Lady Hamlash's personal maid, to get an idea of what Her Ladyship likes?'

It turned out that there was no lady's maid.

'My mistress dresses herself,' Mrs Newson said over her shoulder. 'I help her, if she's dining out. Not that she does often, since Sir Rufus passed. We're right thinned down here. The old gardener left, we can't keep a cook longer than five minutes, it seems. Since… you know.'

'Since the murder?' When no reply came, Jemima tried a different tack. 'Lady Hamlash resides here alone, apart from her staff?'

The housekeeper confirmed it. 'She had two sons, but only one came home from the war. He is married and resides Norfolk-way.' Mrs Newson made Norfolk sound like far-off terrain, when in fact it was the neighbouring county. 'The elder is buried in a French field, though there's a nice plaque to him in the parish church.' Her sigh implied – at least, Jemima suspected – that the wrong son had perished and the incorrect one had been spared.

They were now threading through a warren of corridors. Passages grew narrower, the doors plainer and, yes, colder, until Jemima was envisaging frost on the bedposts. Finally, the housekeeper opened a door to reveal a room with a single bed, a washstand, dressing table and chair. A sash-cord window allowed in wintry daylight. A tiny fireplace was swept clean.

'Here is your room while you're with us, Mrs Flowerday.'

If Wells had materialised, offering her a lift back to the station, Jemima would have run at it. He wouldn't, of course, so now was the moment to lay down terms.

'Where is the fire, Mrs Newson? I cannot sew with frozen fingers. And the light switch?'

'The fire should have been lit,' Mrs Newson said. 'There's no light switch since there's no electricity in the house except in the library and telephone room.'

'Electricity in those rooms only?'

'Sir Rufus had it put in, but he wouldn't have it in the rest of the house. Said it was a fire hazard. Lamps and candles are what we use.'

Candles being the greatest fire hazard of all time. Stifling a groan, Jemima said, 'I see. Or rather I won't, once the light fades.'

'I can let you have a paraffin lamp to work by.' Mrs Newson remained in the doorway. Likely, her face had never been a canvas for cheer or vivacity, but on their way up her anxiety had seemed to palpably deepen, prompting Jemima to ask, 'Do you dislike being in this room?'

'I do.' The housekeeper gave Jemima her first proper inspection since she'd taken off her coat.

Jemima sustained it confidently. She'd travelled in a plaid skirt with a relaxed waist, a sailor top and a cardigan, belted on the hip. Her own design and very 'now', though her colours were subdued, mourning for a husband lost. Mrs Newson's expression grew pensive as she took in Jemima's tight-fitting cloche hat, the swing of brunette hair beneath and the red painted lips.

'The world is changing for a certainty, Mrs Flowerday, but Merry Beggars Hall is a place apart. I hope you've brought warm under-things.'

'A blaze in the grate is what I need, Mrs Newson.'

'I told Dinah, "Lay a fire for the dressmaker lady".'

'Who is Dinah, again?'

'The girl. House parlourmaid, when the fancy takes her. Ah, here she comes.' Mrs Newson stepped aside to allow a brown-haired girl into the room.

The newcomer's cap was askew. Her black dress and white apron just about accommodated her figure. Muttering, 'There you go,' this apparition plonked Jemima's travel bags and parcels of cloth on the bed.

Jemima counted the items. 'Where is my cardboard, Dinah?'

The girl blinked sweeping lashes. 'Huh?'

'A roll of taupe-coloured card. I left it on the kitchen table.'

'Oh, I thought that were suffin' Mr Crosby were chuckin' out,' Dinah replied in an accent Jemima placed as 'farming Suffolk'.

'Mercy no! It's for me to draw Lady Hamlash's measurements on, to make a pattern for her.'

Dinah gave a kind of shrug. She was extremely pretty in a sullen way. 'I could bring it up later, I suppose.'

'You'll do it right away,' Mrs Newson cut in.

Jemima added, 'Please do, Dinah, else I can't do my job.'

While Mrs Newson instructed Dinah to bring up whatever Mrs Flowerday required, along with fuel to get a fire going, Jemima went to the window. Her heart gave a quick, irregular beat. The view was of a walled garden. *The* walled garden. There couldn't be two. It was set out like a Tudor parterre with gravelled paths between rectangular beds containing clumps of sage, rosemary and hardy Brussels sprouts. Along the far wall ran a glasshouse the

19

length of three London buses. *The* glasshouse, with its own boiler room and chimney.

This side of the hall formed one of the garden's boundary walls, giving her a prime view. How lucky, after all, to have got this room!

Directly below her window was a sloping roof which she noted as a potential escape route in the event of fire. This was something she did whenever she stayed somewhere new. She would never rid herself of the memory of flames sweeping through the London department store where she'd worked as a young girl… the panic and terror. The hysterical accusations of arson afterwards, targeting a girl Jemima knew and cared about.

Mrs Newson wrenched her from these thoughts by telling her that the roof below lay over an outhouse.

'It's a glorified tool shed, really, and it's where Wells takes his meals and shelters when it's batting down with rain. I should keep your curtains drawn, Mrs Flowerday.'

'Against Wells?'

'No, indeed. I'm thinking you won't want to look out to where the horrible thing was found.'

Jemima let a moment pass before asking, 'Do you have any idea how Roland Crosby's head came to be in the glasshouse? It seems such a puzzle.'

Beneath her tightly secured plaits, the housekeeper's brow furrowed. 'You aren't one of those journalists, are you? Lurking in the lanes, badgering us with questions?'

'I'm precisely as described, Mrs Newson.' Jemima produced her Fleur du Jour business card. 'I'm a peripatetic couturière.'

Mrs Newson turned the card and frowned. 'And what's that then?'

'A travelling dressmaker. But a curious one. Why just his head?'

The housekeeper stepped back. 'To my way of thinking there's two people know the answer to that. The poor victim and the wicked devil that did for him. If you can get an answer from either of them, you'll be doing better than any police detective they put on the case.'

A distant bell chimed one o'clock. Mrs Newson said they'd better go down. 'Her Ladyship sits down to luncheon when she hears the stable yard clock.'

Jemima had set her watch to the correct time at Liverpool Street Station that morning, enabling her to say, 'Your clock is fast by ten minutes.'

'It is, you're right. Sir Rufus made it so, to ensure his horse was waiting for him when he wanted to ride out. Her Ladyship won't have it changed. You must take your lunch now, Mrs Flowerday, so we servants can sit down to ours at half past one.'

'Am I not eating with you – or, for that matter, with Her Ladyship?'

'You will take your meals in the library while you're here.'

This told Jemima exactly where she swam within the Arctic waters of Merry Beggars Hall. Not to dine at Lady Hamlash's table, yet not expected to muck in with the servants either. It would make investigating Roland Crosby's death hard, and her time here lonely.

'Mrs Newson, on a gauge of one to ten, ten being Outer Mongolia in February, how cold is the room where I am to eat?'

'You do have an odd way of asking a question. No need to change your clothes' – Jemima was taking off her hat – 'but please hurry.'

Jemima laid her hat on the dressing table and ran a comb through her bobbed hair. She would dine in the warmth, by hook or by crook. Making a face at herself in the mirror, she hurried after the housekeeper.

Chapter Four

The library was off the great hall and smelled of musty bindings and old paper. A stone-tracery window, that wouldn't have looked out of place in a monastery, gave a view of a puddle-strewn terrace and, beyond that, rain-swept parkland. A single place setting had been put out on the reading table. Fire in the hearth there was none.

'That girl!' Mrs Newson muttered. 'I'll get her in here at once.'

Jemima laid an urgent hand on the housekeeper's arm. 'I'll eat in the kitchen with all of you.'

'Mr Crosby wouldn't like it. He's a stickler for doing things right.'

'Mrs Newson, if you insist on segregating me, I'll be on the next train out and Lady Hamlash will have no new dresses for Christmas.'

Mrs Newson fought back. 'There's plenty of local women will sew for Her Ladyship. They've been good enough in the past.'

'Fine. Ask Wells to kindly fetch the motor car.'

Mrs Newson held out for a few more seconds then huffed, 'All right then, but I warn you, Mrs Flowerday, we have a new cook.'

'Why should I mind that?'

'A French cook.'

That explained the roast garlic.

'I happen to adore French food, Mrs Newson.'

'Lucky for you,' the housekeeper grunted. '*Madame* won't cook anything we ask for and flies into a rage if anyone complains.'

Madame? How unexpected.

'Mr Crosby is forever telling her to mind her place, but does she listen? He doesn't like strangers at Merry Beggars Hall.'

'As I discovered.' Jemima looked for a light switch. Wasn't the library one of the rooms blessed with electricity? If there was one, it was well hidden.

Her gaze sweeping towards the window, she caught a movement. Wells, still in his chauffeur's coat and peaked cap, was walking past. There was something poking out of his coat pocket. A small whisky bottle? He stopped and tilted his head as though to catch someone's words. Jemima moved to the window in time to hear him say in a voice very different from his amiable New England twang, 'Go away, I'm plumb out of patience! Let me do my job.' Whoever was in his sight must have made a reply, as he came back with, 'No. No. It won't happen.'

At that moment, he turned. Whether or not he recognised Jemima on the other side of the glass, he looked vexed at having been seen.

Jemima stepped back. Mrs Newson, checking for dust on top of the fireplace, suddenly recalled that the servants' lunch could not start without her. In her urgency to leave, she knocked over a branch of candles. Minutes were lost as Jemima crawled about, retrieving them.

When they stepped into the great hall, they found Crosby the butler standing ramrod straight beside one of the interior doors. At the same moment, a door within the wood panelling opened and out came a young footman. He carried a tray laden with domed dishes and walked with a pronounced limp, his shoes clomping unevenly on the oaken boards. Behind him, and clearly out of breath, came Dinah, bearing a smaller tray with a coffee pot, cup and saucer, and a cheese platter.

'Quite a parade,' Jemima whispered to Mrs Newson.

'It's how it's done here,' the housekeeper replied. 'Everything is taken in at once to Her Ladyship, even the coffee, so we servants can eat our food without jumping up to wait on her. It is her choice to have it so.'

'You are fortunate. Not all employers are like that.' Jemima thought of her parents-in-law, Lord and Lady Winterfold, whose country seat lay twenty miles to the south of here. Both were demons for ringing the bell, keeping their staff on perpetual alert. They had been flabbergasted to discover that Jemima made her own tea, and preferred it so.

The footman proceeded into what had to be the dining room, but Dinah was stopped at the door.

With a sharp hiss that carried all the way to the library, Mr Crosby said, 'You can't go into Her Ladyship with a damp apron and cap. Where were you – outside?'

Dinah's reply was inaudible. Mr Crosby took her tray and dismissed her.

Mrs Newson touched Jemima's arm. 'I warned you. A stickler. Follow me.'

They made a dash for the servants' door concealed within the oak panelling. Dinah came into the servants' hall a few moments behind them. Jemima watched her pull off her bandeau-style cap and replace it with a dry one. Rain droplets sparkled in her hair, and Jemima only just stopped herself saying, 'It rarely pays to follow a man around. It gives them too much power.'

As Jemima waited to be invited to sit, she reflected on the secrets of the house. Her Ladyship, sequestered behind closed doors. Wells, walking in the rain with an empty whisky bottle in his pocket. Dinah, being told by him to buzz off before getting a dressing-down from the butler.

And what about the walled garden? The great, unanswered question vibrated like a sustained note on a cello. She had imagined Roland Crosby's headless body lying under a carpet of leaves in some nearby woodland, but could it be closer still? Buried in the walled garden, perhaps?

As soon as the rain stopped she would find her way there and look for signs of disturbed earth. She might even sneak into the glasshouse... though if that were forbidden territory, she would have a choice to make. Whether to abide by the rules, as a modest dressmaker ought, or break them in the style of an audacious sleuth.

Chapter Five

If Albert Crosby was irritated by Jemima's appearance at lunch, he made no sign as he took his seat at the head of the table. He was more concerned with the time. 'Between Dinah and our French cook, things have gone to pot. Her Ladyship received her lunch six minutes late.'

'Now, now, Mr Crosby.' Mrs Newson took a chair at his left hand. Jemima was bidden to sit beside her. 'A minute here and there won't herald the end of the world.'

'I'm not talking of minutes lost, Mrs Newson. I'm talking of boundaries.'

'Indeed,' Mrs Newson acknowledged, 'but don't become like Sir Rufus, pacing after us with a stopwatch.'

Albert Crosby's lips made a thin line. 'Boundaries. The crossing of which by those who do not know how things are done.'

The footman Jemima had seen earlier limped in and pulled out a chair opposite her. He gave her a friendly nod. 'Jack Millar.'

'Mrs Flowerday, good to meet you.'

Jemima noticed how Jack sat down at an angle, manoeuvring his right limb beneath the table with both hands. A wooden leg would explain the limp. He also had a badly scarred cheek.

Catching her glance, he threw out a one-word explanation, 'Cambrai.'

He was naming a town in northern France near the Belgian border, a place of brutal fighting towards the end of the war.

She said, 'I'm sorry.'

'Don't be. I'm used to being the broken wheel.' Jack's mouth formed a frugal smile. 'So, you're the modiste from the Smoke?'

'From London, that's right.'

Jack inspected her tunic top with its square neck and bell sleeves. 'Is that what ladies are wearing now, sailor shirts?'

She told him it was called a middy blouse. 'And, yes, they're all the rage.'

'Very fetching, miss. It's quite a thing for us, having modern women in our midst. First a posh lady chef, now you.'

Crosby told Jack to curb his impudence, and chivvied Dinah, who had yet to sit down.

'Somebody's in my place,' Dinah said pointedly.

'Naturally, Mrs Flowerday takes your place, Dinah, and you must sit lower while she's with us.'

A chair scraped. Dinah flung herself down, reminding Jemima how fiercely servants protected their ranking at the communal table.

'I thought you was having your dinner in the library,' the girl accused.

Jemima noted she must remember that what she and the upper servants called 'lunch' was 'dinner' to a country girl like Dinah. Later in the day they would have tea and then, finally, a late supper.

'It was too cold,' Jemima replied. 'Sitting in an icebox hinders the creative process.'

'It's perishing cold outside too,' the girl snapped back. 'I had to fetch in more coal and go up the back stairs with a bucket for your bedroom fire.' Dinah turned to the butler. 'Which was why I got wet and was late.' She redirected her irritation to the housekeeper. 'I shouldn't have to get coal in at all. It's not my job. I had to scrub my hands to serve Her Ladyship, and Mr Crosby still wouldn't let me.'

'You must organise your time better,' Mrs Newson replied. 'And your job is whatever I say it is.'

Dinah gave her reddened hands a miserable inspection. 'We should have a village girl come in, one as will do rough work.'

Jack agreed. 'A 'tween maid, so you can keep your hands soft.'

Jemima was certain Jack had spoken sincerely, but his reward was an angry look from Dinah.

Mr Crosby cleared his throat. 'We will say grace.'

A skinny kitchen maid, surely no more than thirteen, crept from the kitchen, a steaming tureen in both hands. She bowed her cotton-capped head as Crosby intoned, 'For what we are about to receive—'

Jemima was delighted when a clear consommé was ladled into her dish, as good as anything she'd tasted in Paris during her honeymoon with Simon. She congratulated Mrs Newson for having found a real French cook. 'The true article.'

'Call her "Cook",' Dinah butted in, 'and Madame Guyen will chuck a pan at you. We got to call her "Chef".'

'Noted.' Jemima doubted Dinah had rendered the Frenchwoman's name correctly. Likely, it began with a hard 'G' as in Guy Fawkes. She filed the name in her memory. 'Will she join us?' The kitchen, behind its barrier-wall of frosted glass, appeared empty now that the kitchen maid had taken her place at the foot of the table.

'Not her,' Dinah answered. 'She eats in her room.' She dropped her voice to a whisper. 'Her and Mr Crosby don't get on. It's fish knives at dawn.'

They finished their consommé, after which the kitchen maid fetched in a smoked-fish flan and sautéed potatoes sprinkled with caramelised garlic.

'Fish, and it's not even Friday.' Dinah turned her slice over with her fork. 'Is it meant to be hot or cold? I like my food one or the other.'

Jemima knew that a French flan, or quiche as they called it over there, was traditionally served tepid. This one smelled divine, and it deserved their full attention. Plus, silence sometimes taught more than chatter. The servants who had chosen to remain at Merry Beggars Hall were not at peace. Fish knives at dawn between the chef and the butler who, between sharp rebukes, drifted into a fretful world of his own. The housekeeper, reluctant to leave the comfort of the servants' hall. A kitchen maid whom nobody had bothered to introduce.

What more had Jemima learned?

Ah. That poor, broken Jack was sweet on Dinah, while Dinah's feelings were engaged elsewhere. No sooner was the thought released than Dinah asked Jemima what she made of Mr Wells.

'He seems affable, though I wonder why a man would travel so far to become an English country chauffeur.'

'Gardener,' Jack shot out.

'Why would he cross the Atlantic to become either?' Wells couldn't be here for the money. Merry Beggars Hall breathed an air of financial distress. The staff, for all their attempts at dignity, had a darned appearance and the room they were in was crying out for a coat of fresh paint; yet Lady Hamlash boasted a cook of quality – not to mention Jemima's services.

Dinah ignored Jack's interruption, saying eagerly to Jemima, 'Handsome isn't he, though, in his driver's cap and coat?'

Jemima said, 'I suppose he is, in his way.' She had no wish to antagonise Jack, whose face had gone red at the mention of the man who, patently, was his rival. Wells's absence at table had struck her from the first. 'Doesn't he eat with you?'

'Never.' Jack's injured cheek twitched. 'Outdoor staff keep to their own.'

But what 'own'? Jemima had seen no evidence of other outdoor workers. Remembering the bottle poking from Wells's coat pocket, she wondered if he was lonely. Bored. A midday drinker? Time to change the subject.

'Has Madame Guyen worked here long?' she asked Mrs Newson.

'About a week. She's from London, like you. Lady Hamlash was anxious for a proper chef in time for Christmas, but it was hard getting anyone.'

Getting anyone who wasn't put off by the cloud of an unsolved murder and the absence of electricity, Jemima presumed.

Mrs Newson asked the kitchen maid if Madame Guyen was taking her meal in her room as usual. 'Only, I didn't see you fetch her cutlery from the dresser, Beth.'

Beth. Jemima made a mental note.

'She went out,' the girl answered meekly.

Hardly was it spoken when a white figure flitted past the glass lobby, briefly visible through the rain-streaked panes. A short while later, the opening and shutting of a solid door suggested Madame Guyen had come in through a rear entrance.

'Up to her tricks,' growled the butler.

'Most likely picking herbs for dinner,' Mrs Newson soothed.

'Nettles and thistles most like,' grumbled Dinah. 'They eat funny stuff in France.'

'That's enough,' said the housekeeper. 'Take a tray of food to her, Beth, then bring in dessert.'

After some minutes away from the table, Beth returned with a crème brûlée. Mr Crosby broke the sugar glaze on top with a spoon. It was divine and even Dinah cleared her bowl. Afterwards, as Beth rose to stack dishes, Jemima felt it was time to present herself to Her Ladyship.

Mrs Newson led the way, leaving Jemima at the drawing-room door while she consulted with her mistress. Almost at once, Jemima heard raised voices and stepped closer, the better to hear. She hoped she was not the cause of an argument. The thickness of the door frustrated her and so she turned the handle, giving a gentle nudge with her shoulder, allowing the door to open as if by accident. Through the gap, Jemima saw Mrs Newson at the open window, leaning out and sharply bidding somebody to 'Leave My Lady alone.' This part of the grounds was private, she added. 'You are out of bounds!'

Lady Hamlash must have been in the room too, because Jemima could hear somebody breathing close by in an agitated way. It was beyond her audacity to step uninvited into the room, and so she softly re-closed the door. Mrs Newson came out a minute later, looking flushed, and explained that owing to a headache, Lady Hamlash was 'unequal to a meeting at present'.

Her curiosity stirred, Jemima needed no encouragement to retire to her room where, to her delight, a fire crackled in the grate. Pulling the chair up to the window, she took out her journal. She wrote in some detail about the lunch she had enjoyed – 'Sublime, though unappreciated by the servants and seasoned with the butler's unconcealed hostility' – and added Dinah's revelation regarding fish knives. Then she pondered.

What have I learned? Dinah likes Wells, whereas he has
little time for her. 'Go away, I'm plumb out of patience!'
were the tender words I overheard. Jack likes Dinah,
whereas Dinah… dear me. Star-crossed lovers.

Had it been Dinah bothering Lady Hamlash, straying into forbidden territory in her pursuit of Wells? It seemed likely.

To call the emotions swirling through Merry Beggars Hall 'undercurrents' was an injustice to currents. It seemed reasonable to suppose that the tensions originated in the terrible shock of a murder so close and so personal. Jemima chewed her pencil before adding:

I am as far as ever from guessing how Roland Crosby
came to die, or where the rest of his body might be. As to
why he made his journey, could the simple truth be that
he came to visit his brother?

Albert Crosby's face swam into her mind's eye. Anxious, vexed, haunted. Could the brother also be the killer? Was not the first bloody story of the Bible that of fratricide, when Cain slew Abel?

It was an idea that put a temporary stop to speculation. Jemima laid her journal aside and took out her sketch pad. Working fast, she schemed out a series of evening gowns designed to flatter a lady in late middle age and was still sketching when the stable clock gave three deep chimes. At the same time, a pungent smell filtered in from outside. Pushing up the window sash, she peered down on the roof of the tool shed directly below. Tobacco. Her late father had been an occasional pipe smoker and Jemima recognised the odour.

'Virginia leaf,' she decided.

Wells emerged from the shed and her comment, 'Are you smoking?' brought his head up.

'Not smoking, ma'am, cooking.' His good mood seemed restored and he gave her a lopsided grin.

'It doesn't smell very appetising,' Jemima said.

'It isn't meant to. It's insecticide, home-brewed and deadly.'

'Deadly?'

'*If* you happen to have six legs.' He touched the peak of his cap in salute, then walked to the middle of the walled garden to stand in the drizzle. He'd changed from chauffeur's uniform into a tweed jacket and breeches, she noted, with gaiters over his boots. Two jobs, two rig-outs.

At precisely three by Jemima's watch, ten past if one went by the stable-yard clock, a woman entered the scene. Despite a felt hat pulled down over her forehead, she was recognisable to Jemima from the photographs that had appeared in the press last spring. It was Ada, Lady Hamlash.

Chapter Six

As Lady Hamlash strode towards Wells, the greatcoat she was wearing gaped to reveal woollen stockings and shoes capable of treading juice from turnips. Watching Wells again touch his cap in the prescribed English manner, Jemima guessed that a garden inspection was underway.

It crossed her mind to call out and ask Her Ladyship where the headache had flown to, but something more interesting was unfolding. A third figure had entered the garden, this one in snowy aprons. A chef's pillbox hat, a sweep of brunette hair above a swanlike neck… who could it be other than the French chef, Madame Guyen?

Lady Hamlash perceived the new arrival at exactly the same moment as Jemima and tried to walk away. But Madame Guyen caught her up and there followed an energetic exchange. Lady Hamlash boomed, 'Go away,' several times as the Frenchwoman waved her hands, eager to communicate something. Her Ladyship then tried to escape a second time, but Madame Guyen blocked her. Wells then put himself between them, allowing Lady Hamlash to flee through a gate in the far wall. To Jemima's consternation, Madame Guyen then turned on Wells, striking him while he fended off her blows with a bent elbow. She was shouting in French and Jemima picked up one unmistakable word—

'Justice!'

Leaning out over the sill, Jemima shouted in her schoolroom French, 'Ça suffit, madame!'

Instantly, Madame Guyen lowered her hand, turned and walked towards Jemima's window. She gazed upward through immense dark eyes. 'Who are you?'

Her accent was interesting. French, yet with a transatlantic nuance in the way she pronounced the 'r' sound. Very like the way Wells spoke his.

'So?' Madame Guyen was waiting.

'I'm Jemima Flowerday. Do stop attacking poor Wells. He's too much of a gentleman to lump you back. Wait. I'm coming down.'

Dragging closed the window, Jemima looked in vain for her coat. Of course, it was drying on a hook downstairs. She left anyway. A furious row yards from the scene of a sensational crime was not to be brushed under the carpet. Not under any carpet in Jemima's keeping.

But by the time she'd found her way to the garden, Madame Guyen was gone. Nor was Wells to be seen.

The pungent smell of tobacco drew her to the tool shed. Opening the door, she reeled back in a spasm of coughing. Goodness, Wells hadn't been exaggerating when he described his home-made insecticide. Six legs or two, it was foul. Jemima retreated to the far side of the walled garden until she was beside the glasshouse. Finding its end door half-open, she squeezed inside to recover her breath and escape the rain.

Or so she told herself. A shiver of excitement revealed her true motive. To stand under the moss-mottled glass of the murder scene fulfilled her principal purpose in coming to Merry Beggars Hall.

35

And it had been so easy to get inside. No padlocks on the door. No police notices warning 'Keep Out'.

Jemima began walking its length; taking slow steps to absorb every atom of its atmosphere. Raised beds each side of the brick path held an army of clay pots and cloches, but where was the famous asparagus?

'Not a ferny stem to be seen,' she remarked.

Nor was the boiler, whose chimney she'd seen from her window, pumping out any heat. Lady Hamlash's elderly gardener had left his job the day after the head had been discovered, according to a report in *The Weekend Sleuth*. Perhaps Her Ladyship had given up on her passion at the same time. One could hardly blame her.

Jemima reached the midpoint of the glasshouse where, reportedly, Roland Crosby's head had been placed. There was nothing marking the spot. The cloche that had been put over it would have been taken away as evidence. And, of course, the police would have combed this scene for any and every clue.

She retraced her steps, conscious that the light was fading and that Lady Hamlash might be asking for her. As she turned sideways to get through the doorway, she noticed a scuff on the frame. Something had collided with the white paintwork, creating a ragged dent and exposing the wood. Something shiny as a beetle's shell nestled in the dent. She prised it out and found she was holding a flake of metal. Enamel? Yes. In the light, it was not beetle black but dark, conker brown. A shiver ran down the back of her neck and a voice within her mind whispered that it was evidence. Evidence of what, exactly? That somebody, squeezing through this warped doorway, had caught a button or a gardening tool against the frame.

'You will have to do better than this, Jemima Flowerday, if you are to solve a murder,' she told herself, mimicking the voice of a long-ago and unlamented schoolteacher.

Returning to the house through the front entrance, having left the door slightly ajar on her way out, Jemima heard someone speaking. It came from a room off the great hall. The outline of electric light around a doorframe told Jemima the telephone lay behind that door.

She tiptoed closer. The speaker – almost certainly Lady Hamlash – sounded upset.

'Yes, just this moment,' she was saying in a throbbing contralto, 'running me to earth during my garden inspection, uttering the most absurd and outrageous claims. And before that, peering in at me in my drawing room. All she talks about is "justice" and she has made the wildest accusation… What accusation? No, no, I will not repeat it. I told her I will not listen. I know an imposter when I see and hear one.'

Jemima had no doubt now that she was eavesdropping on her hostess, but who was the other party?

After a pause, Her Ladyship continued, 'Dismissal without notice? I've tried. She won't go! No, really, you didn't see the look in her eye!'

Silence held for a minute and whoever was on the other end of the line must have overstepped a boundary because Lady Hamlash responded fiercely, commanding him or her to *kindly* stop lecturing her.

'I am aware that I am a gullible fool, Finchley. Letting her into my house… What? No, I did not get her from an agency, they had nobody suitable. She answered my advertisement – there wasn't time to check references. Who insisted I get a trained chef at absolutely no notice, when I would have been perfectly content… oh, fiddlesticks, you are always impossible. No, don't come over. I am too upset. I will speak to Crosby.'

The receiver was clashed back on its stand.

Jemima scooted away, getting halfway upstairs before Lady Hamlash emerged.

Back in her quarters, Jemima sat in repose by the fire, sifting through what she'd just heard. Who was Finchley, besides being a district of North London? More relevant, what 'justice' was Madame Guyen seeking?

Perhaps the most pressing question of all – now she'd seen Lady Hamlash from the front, back and side – was how she was going to adapt the new, uncorseted style of evening wear to her client's very substantial shape.

Chapter Seven

When it grew too dark to sketch, Jemima decided to take up Mrs Newson's offer of a reading lamp. Finding her way along unlit corridors with only a flickering candle to guide her, it was easy to imagine how one might meet with an accident up here. A loose floorboard… a shove in the small of the back at the head of the stairs…

She descended, gripping the handrail.

Muted light beneath a door off the hall placed Lady Hamlash in her drawing room, most likely sipping tea beside a well-tended fire.

'I'm ready for a cuppa myself,' Jemima murmured. Servants' tea in most big houses was at five and, on cue, she heard the stable clock chime. Five gongs, so ten minutes to the hour.

A door softly closed, followed by footsteps across the hall below. Swift, light, purposeful. Jemima craned to see whose feet they were, but whoever it was had closed the servants' door behind them.

Dinah, returning from another outdoor sortie?

Reaching the same door, Jemima groped at the panelling for a minute before working out that one poked one's fingers through a hole to lift a concealed latch. Honestly, Merry Beggars Hall was designed for maximum inconvenience at every level. As she entered the corridor running between the servants' hall, staff bedrooms and the back stairs, she became aware of raised voices. She found Mrs

Newson, Dinah and Jack gathered beside the pine table, listening to a tirade of French flowing from the kitchen.

'C'est une injustice, une grave injustice!' Madame Guyen, most certainly, and sounding every bit as angry as she'd been in the garden.

The next voice was Crosby's. 'Calm down, calm down,' he said, before adding provocatively, 'This is an English house, not a French theatre.'

Madame Guyen's answer: 'Pah!'

The lady herself stalked into the servants' hall and threw herself on the chair at the head of the table. Her aproned breast rose and fell, and when the housekeeper politely reminded her that the seat she was in was not rightfully hers, she repeated, 'Pah! If Monsieur Crosby wants his place of honour, let him throw me off. He wishes to throw me *out*, after all.'

'Shall we have tea and settle this nicely?' Mrs Newson begged.

'Like good, obedient English people? I shall have my coffee.' Madame Guyen placed a china cup and saucer on the table.

When Beth brought out a tray laden with everyday blue-and-white crockery, Jemima concluded that Chef liked her own things. And things her own way.

She was struck by the Frenchwoman's elegance. The length of her neck, the moulded cheekbones and sensual lips. In the light of an oil lamp suspended over the table, Madame Guyen's finger-waved hair shone like obsidian.

She must have felt the appraisal because she looked in Jemima's direction and snapped, 'Why are you following me around?'

Jemima stepped forward. 'I'm not. I've come to fetch a paraffin lamp and drink tea.'

'You are the dressmaker?' Madame Guyen took in Jemima's outfit and appreciation flared in the velvet eyes. 'The couturière, I should say.'

'Thank you. And you, madame, are a great chef.'

'Huh. Little good my talent does me here.'

Mr Crosby, who had perhaps spent the intervening minute adjusting his dignity and his tie, entered the room. His mouth turned down as he saw who occupied his chair.

Madame Guyen read him perfectly. 'You want your seat, Mr Crosby? Evict me, since it is your job, like the poodle you are. Non, not a poodle' – she gave the butler a brisk assessment – 'a skinny mastiff. One who barks, but dare not bite.'

'Madame Guyen, in asking you to quit Merry Beggars Hall, I am carrying out not only Lady Hamlash's orders, but those of her son, Sir Finchley.'

'Then you will fail.' Madame Guyen turned to the kitchen maid. 'Beth, ma petite, I need my coffee.' As Beth scurried into the kitchen, the chef's expression hardened again and she said to Albert Crosby, 'I have come a very great way to be heard.'

'You have nothing to tell this company, Madame Guyen.' Crosby raised a hand as if to press a dangerous genii back into its bottle. 'Pack your things and I'll have Wells drive you to the railway station.'

'You cannot force me to leave. You haven't the strength, *Albert*.' His name was spoken with rolling French intonation, though Jemima was again recognising the flecks of a New York accent.

'Jack.' Albert Crosby beckoned the footman. 'Take one of Madame Guyen's arms and I'll take the other.'

Jack flatly refused.

'Then fetch Wells.'

'He won't do it neither, Mr Crosby.' This was Dinah speaking. 'Mr Wells is more a gentleman than Jack is, so if Jack won't… Mrs Newson, can we have our tea before it's cold? I want to hear what Madame Guyen has to say.'

Jemima also wanted to hear what the Frenchwoman's calls for

justice entailed. The butler's reference to 'Sir Finchley' had not escaped her noticed either. A minor mystery was now solved. Lady Hamlash had been speaking on the telephone to her surviving son.

Beth returned, staggering under the weight of another huge tray on which was a canteen teapot, a small coffee pot, a jug of cold and a jug of hot milk, and a bowl of sugar cubes, white and brown.

Mrs Newson helped the girl set it down, then gestured at the chair beside her. 'Do join us, Mrs Flowerday. You may have a soothing influence. Beth, pour Madame Guyen's coffee at once.'

Madame Guyen offered Beth the porcelain cup. 'As I showed you, petite. Coffee in first, then the milk.'

Beth poured a black stream into the cup, topping it up with heated milk. That done, she picked up the double-handed teapot and moved around the table, filling the blue-and-white china cups with strong Indian tea. Jemima watched Madame Guyen take the sugar tongs, and drop a brown sugar cube into her cup. She stirred it round and round, until, with an ironic smile, she raised her cup as if toasting the butler.

'Your superior English tea is so much better than our French coffee, non, Albert?' Draining her gold-rimmed cup in one gulp, she stood up. 'You are welcome to your seat. Voilà.' She gave Albert Crosby a half-smile, which froze. She pressed a hand to her throat, gasping as if trying to clear a blockage.

Albert Crosby regarded her disdainfully. 'More theatrics?'

When Madame Guyen gripped the back of the chair, he tutted impatiently, but Jemima could see that this was no performance. The knuckles on the chair were white.

Mrs Newson saw it too. She caught the kitchen maid's sleeve. 'Beth, what's in that coffee?'

Beth shook her head and muttered something incomprehensible. 'Speak up, girl! What have you done?'

'Only what I always do. Madame showed me how to make her coffee how she likes it. Very strong and piping hot.'

'Madame?' Jemima tried to get Madame Guyen's attention, but received only a dark, unblinking stare. A rattling sound came from the chef's throat and her eyes seemed to slip backwards in their sockets. A wild thrust of her arm dashed the cup off the table and it shattered on the floor.

'Mr Crosby!' Mrs Newson shrieked. 'She's going to fall.'

Albert Crosby did not move. Jack tried to help, but his prosthetic leg caught against his chair.

It was Jemima who reached Madame as she crumpled. Kneeling, she slid her hands beneath the woman's head and looked for Beth. 'Quick, bring a cloth, a towel, something to make a pillow.'

But Beth was rooted, her expression flat with fear. Jemima took off her cardigan and folded it under the rigid neck.

The Frenchwoman was by now snatching for breath, her face waxy pale. In a voice that was hardly human, she rasped, 'He warned me.'

'Who did? Warned of what?' Jemima wiped brown spittle from the woman's lips and chin using a napkin from the table.

No answer emerged, only a desperate plea. 'Help me.'

'Dear mercy.' Mrs Newson crouched beside Jemima. 'That stink… it's all over her.'

Jemima had already smelled the odour of tobacco beneath that of strong coffee.

'Do we call the doctor?' Mrs Newson whispered.

'Yes, and a priest too,' Jemima said, though she knew from the blankness in the staring eyes that Madame Guyen was sliding beyond the reach of medicine or prayer.

Chapter Eight

The local GP was Dr Rushbrook, from Saxonchurch. Completing his examination of Madame Guyen, he gave the cause of death in a single word: 'Anaphylaxis.'

Jemima asked what that meant.

'A severe allergic reaction to some substance or other. You believe she drank coffee contaminated with tobacco?'

They were in the bedroom that had been Madame Guyen's, one of those off the servants' passage. Her body had been carried there by Jack, Wells and Jemima. It was Jack who had telephoned for the doctor as Crosby had gone up to inform Lady Hamlash of the terrible event. He was still with her, to Jemima's best knowledge. In the moments following the death, Dinah had been sent to find Wells in case the car should be needed. She'd run him to earth in the stable yard where he'd been at some task. He was with them now, standing by the wall, as if he needed its support. The house-keeper was present also, but staring into space, occasionally wringing her hands. It was Jemima who confirmed she had smelled tobacco on the dead woman's lips.

'I'm inclined to believe her coffee was adulterated,' she told the doctor. She had smelled the same reeking odour earlier that day, she said, coming from the tool shed in the walled garden. Giving

Wells a chance to comment, and hearing only his disjointed breathing, she felt she had no choice but to add, 'I suspect Madame Guyen came into contact with a tobacco-based insecticide.'

Deadly insecticide. If you happen to have six legs, Wells had joked. Not so funny now.

'Mm, my nose agrees with you.' Dr Rushbrook's fingers probed Madame Guyen's neck and lower jaw. 'Swelling of the soft tissue leading to asphyxia and death. Her forehead is pale, such as I can make out from her brunette complexion, and clammy... A textbook case of anaphylaxis. Some people are violently allergic to the evil weed.'

'It all happened so quickly.'

'Anaphylaxis is by its nature sudden and catastrophic, Mrs... er...?'

'Flowerday. Jemima Flowerday.' She had given her name to the doctor already, but didn't blame him for mislaying it. Even for a seasoned medic, the sight of a body locked in its final, horrified struggle must be deeply affecting.

The recoil of shock throughout the servants' quarters was palpable. When Wells had raced into the servants' hall, Dinah behind him, he had found Jack and Jemima attempting to lift Madame Guyen's inert form. He had thrown himself down beside her, roaring, 'What have you done?'

Jemima had not known who he was accusing in his distress. She had also heard him say, 'Marie, Marie, what did I tell you?'

Marie. The intimate use of a name, coupled with Wells's intense anguish, had caused Jemima to look at him in a new light. *He warned me,* had been Madame Guyen's dying words. There and then she had determined that Wells and Madame Guyen had not been coincidental visitors to this corner of Suffolk. They had known each other.

Wells finally spoke from his position by the wall. 'Was there the smallest chance we could have saved her?'

Dr Rushbrook considered the question. 'If treated in time with an injection of epinephrine to counter the allergic response, *if* the patient is of a good constitution, then yes, anaphylaxis is survivable. And, yes, I wish that Merry Beggars Hall were not at the end of a poorly maintained country road five miles from town.' He consulted his notebook. 'Mrs Flowerday, you estimated Madame Guyen's death occurred at five twenty this afternoon. Did I take that down correctly?'

'You did, doctor. I'm as sure as I can be.'

'Have the police been informed?'

'Police?' Mrs Newson snapped out of her stupor. 'Surely not.'

'My good lady,' the doctor said in his clipped way, 'as this is a sudden death, and Madame Guyen was never under my care, and as I act as the police doctor in these parts, I must indeed inform them.'

'But you've already explained how she died,' Mrs Newson argued in a tone of bewilderment.

The doctor was inflexible. His next call would be the police station.

'Oh, dear, dear, dear.' Mrs Newson raised her knuckles to her brow. 'Whatever will become of us?'

Nothing good, Jemima predicted. Police once again descending on Merry Beggars Hall.

Albert Crosby chose that moment to enter the room. He must have overhead the last exchange as he too challenged Dr Rushbrook's intention to call in the police.

'Once you have properly examined the deceased, I am certain you will be satisfied that her death was no more than an unfortunate mishap.'

The doctor's demeanour chilled. 'I flatter myself that I have "properly" examined her, in as much as I can without adequate light. I will issue a death certificate only after a full examination in appropriate surroundings.' The police would establish if this event was a mishap, or something more, he added. 'What noxious substance this woman imbibed – how and why – is for them to determine. In due course I will inform the coroner of the full findings.'

His challengers silenced, Rushbrook went to the washstand and poured water from a jug. After rinsing and drying his hands, he reached for his medical bag. 'I will go up and speak with Lady Hamlash.'

Crosby stepped between him and the door. Her Ladyship had already been appraised of the tragedy. There was no need to distress her further.

Dr Rushbrook was a lean man whose shoulders-back posture and meticulously barbered moustache hinted at a military past. His next words neatly expressed his belief that the butler should get out of his way. 'This is not a case of chickenpox in the servants' hall, my man. Kindly permit me to leave.'

Crosby knew when he was beaten, but it was more than his dignity could stand to allow even a doctor to walk in on Lady Hamlash unannounced. He strode away, forcing Rushbrook, who was unfamiliar with the geography of the servants' quarters, to shout for him to slow down.

In the silence following, those left in the room heard muffled weeping coming from the kitchen.

'Beth, I think.' The housekeeper sighed. 'Will you go to her, Mrs Flowerday? I'm that vexed with the silly creature. It must have been her put that stuff in the coffee.'

'We don't know that.' Jemima gave Wells a hard stare, determined that he must, now, say something.

He did not, nor did he meet her eye.

'Go to the others,' Mrs Newson urged Jemima. 'You've a kindly way about you, and any one of them might confide something useful. I'll watch over the deceased. Wash her face and hands.' She rose stiffly and went to stand by the bed. 'I did not always find myself in charity with Madame, but no woman should be laid out like this, face mucky, her clothes twisted.'

Madame's shoes, rubber-soled clogs, had been placed by the bedside cabinet beside a second, dressier, pair of shoes. The sight of two feet exposed in black cotton stockings, a fine darn alongside one of the big toes, filled Jemima with pity. Madame Guyen – Marie – was a defiant woman laid low, her fine eyes imprinted with the last, terrified, seconds of her life. Some might hold this death to be convenient. To Jemima, it felt brutal, pointless and desperately sad.

When he had arrived, the doctor had asked Jemima to remove Marie's apron. She'd hung it at the foot of the bed, and it was there still, splashed with brown stains that matched those on the napkin she'd snatched earlier to mop Marie's chin. The napkin was on the floor, where it had been dropped as Jemima helped carry Marie in. Picking it up, she put it with the apron.

'Don't wash her, Mrs Newson. The mess on her clothes is evidence, as is everything in this room.'

On the bedside table were a few items displaying the victim's personal tastes. A slim, hardback book, *Delphine*, by Madame de Staël, a pressed dwarf daffodil marking the place she'd read up to. There was a hair slide, a pot of face cream and a small, brown bottle which Jemima opened. She put her nose to its rim. Pineapple.

'I think this is bromelain,' she said. 'My sister Vicky keeps some in her handbag.' Bromelain was an antidote to bee stings. 'Vicky's terribly allergic—' The significance of what she was saying struck home. 'Madame Guyen was prepared for allergic reactions. Mr Wells?'

'Mrs Flowerday?'

'Did you know she kept bromelain with her?'

Wells left the room.

'You don't mind staying here alone?' Jemima asked the housekeeper. She was angry now, convinced Wells had withheld information from Dr Rushbrook.

'It's not the dead I fear,' answered the housekeeper. 'It's the living ones who have no heart that frighten me.'

Leaving Mrs Newson to keep vigil, Jemima went out into the passage and followed the sounds of weeping.

Chapter Nine

The kitchen maid was not present, but Dinah was, and the sobbing was coming from her. Jack was seated at the servants' dining table with her, holding her hands. The tea things had been cleared. Wells, leaning against the dresser, was regarding the two indoor servants inscrutably. At Jemima's appearance, he asked if the doctor was still with Lady Hamlash.

'As far as I know. I believe he is her family doctor and will have helped her through other, equally difficult events.'

Wells nodded. 'I imagine he is administering something to calm her nerves. There is always something of the kind in his medical bag. One thing you should know about Lady Hamlash, she doesn't like bad news.'

'One can hardly wonder at it. She endured her husband's illness, then widowhood and the loss of her elder son in the war. Followed by Roland Crosby's murder and now the death of someone in her employment.' One could not but feel a little sorry for Ada Hamlash, despite her intention to evict Marie Guyen. That thought led to another.

'D'you think Sir Finchley will come over?' Jemima asked. 'He must feel his place is at his mother's side, as head of the family.'

Jack answered from his place at the table. 'Course he's head of the family. Sir Finchley inherited the title when his brother died. That's the way it goes.'

Jemima replied that she understood the rules of inheritance and that Jack had mistaken her meaning. 'I was wondering if he would make the journey from Norfolk.' She was impatient to lay eyes on Sir Finchley Hamlash, who had spurred his mother to get rid of Marie Guyen. 'Where in that county does he live?'

'Next door to His Majesty,' said Jack with a facetious twitch of the lips.

It was Wells who explained. 'Sir Finchley's estate borders Sandringham Castle, the King's country seat. Lady Olivia, Sir Finchley's wife, is daughter of an earl and moves in the highest circles.' He paused, then added, 'You don't seem adequately impressed, Mrs Flowerday.'

Jemima replied that he might consider her impressed. 'Indeed, over-awed.'

'Under normal circumstances, very little would induce Sir Finchley to show his face here,' Wells continued. 'Lady Olivia considers it too damp and, since he married, Sir Finchley has found his childhood home ever more intolerable. Steeple Court – their Norfolk place – has electricity on every floor, and heating, would you believe?'

Jemima could not miss his ironic tone and remarked, 'I know you Americans think we dwell in a medieval hinterland.'

'It's what makes you so charming. Why install electric lighting, telephones and hot running water simply because they're available?'

Dinah, perhaps feeling neglected, gave a gulp of misery, drawing the attention in her direction.

Wells spoke quickly and quietly to Jemima. 'Since you like to know things, Mrs Flowerday, I can tell you that Sir Finchley isn't in Norfolk right now. He and his wife are guests at a house party not three miles from here.'

So the telephone call she'd overheard had been a local one. 'Then he has no excuse not to come,' she said.

'He'll come, be sure of it. My advice is to stay out of his way. Sir Finchley is a cargo train when it comes to the social graces.'

Jemima asked him to explain.

'A freight engine. Sounds the horn, but rarely applies the brakes.'

She thanked him for the warning and then recalled why she had come to the kitchen in the first place. 'Where is Beth?'

Jack jerked up his head and scowled at Wells. 'Hiding in the scullery. He made her cry.'

Wells gave a slight shrug. 'I'm angry. I know I shouldn't be, but if Marie – Madame Guyen – died of an allergic reaction to contaminated coffee, somebody put it in her cup. Accident or not, it can only have been Beth.'

Jack fired up. 'Hear that? Who boiled up that poison in the first place?' He fished an iron key from his pocket and waved it menacingly. 'I've locked your tool shed, Mr Wells, so you can't go chucking that mixture away before the police get a look at it. Then we'll see, won't we?'

Such rage bloomed in Wells's eyes, Jemima feared he might do the footman harm.

She tapped him sharply. 'War-wounded, wooden leg,' she hissed. 'Get a grip!'

Wells stared back at her, his gaze brimming with the despair she'd heard in his voice at Marie's side. Without another word, he went out, slamming the doors of the lobby as he went, making the panes rattle. They heard his boots scrunching along the cinder paths between the herb beds.

'Where will he go?' Jemima asked.

'To hell, with luck,' Jack muttered. 'Or to his cottage. One or the other.'

Dinah batted Jack's hand from hers. 'You keep your nastiness to yourself, Jack Millar. If you say any more about Mr Wells poisoning Madame Guyen, and they hang him, I won't forgive you.'

'And I won't forgive *him* if he points a finger at poor little Beth,' Jack came back hotly. 'Who else could have dosed the coffee but him? Beth's got no reason to. And it's tin, Miss.'

Jemima had turned to leave, but something beside a chair leg caught her eye and she crouched to pick it up. She was recognising it as a piece of a china cup when Jack's comment impinged. 'Sorry – what's tin?'

'My leg.' Jack rapped his prosthetic limb. 'Sir Finchley had it made for me, 'cause the last one clumped and got on his nerves when I was waiting at table. Don't you heed what Wells says. Sir Finchley isn't all bad. He was on the Western Front alongside me and his brother. Foreigners such as Wells don't know what it was like there, but they should.'

Jemima straightened up. 'I know, Jack. I understand.' She was holding a piece of Madame Guyen's gold-rimmed cup which had smashed where she was standing. Holding it to her nose, she smelled a trace of coffee and – unmistakably – tobacco. Slipping it into her skirt pocket, wondering where the rest of the cup had gone, she went in search of Beth.

The scullery was an annex behind the kitchen furnished with stone sinks and galvanised buckets. The sight of a draining board stacked with damp crockery made Jemima cry out. A little mound of china segments gleamed from their recent dip into warm water frothed up with baking soda. Marie's broken cup had been rinsed of its evidence. Even the tea and coffee pots had been scoured out.

'You've washed up. You shouldn't have, Beth. The police needed to see the tea crocks left as they were. Why?'

Beth's eyes were swollen half-shut, tear trails on her cheeks. 'I don't rightly know.'

'Who told you to do this?'

Beth stammered, 'It were nobody. It's what I always do.'

'I'm sure I said—' Had she? Or had she just thought it? 'Don't touch anything that could be evidence.'

Beth repeated, 'It's what I always do.'

Even more unsettling than sparkling crockery was the sight of Madame Guyen's apron and cap soaking in warm water. The napkin Jemima had used and left on the end of the bed was there too. Bending over the bucket, she smelled Reckitt's Blue. Marie Guyen's bedsheets and coverlet were immersed in a second bucket.

'You don't normally do the laundry, I imagine, Beth?' Jemima said coldly.

'No. Mrs Revell come in and do that, but it's not her day.'

'And, of course, it couldn't wait. Did Mrs Newson bring it in and tell you to soak it?'

'I don't know.'

'Oh, come on, that won't do.' Whatever Beth lacked intellectually, she made up for as a thorough laundress and washer-upper, Jemima reflected. The police would now struggle for evidence of either wrong-doing or accident. 'Was it Mrs Newson's orders, or someone else's?'

Beth looked past Jemima. The housekeeper was standing in the scullery doorway. Had she heard?

If she had, she gave no indication, informing them in a shaky voice, 'The doctor's gone, and now PC Trowse has arrived from

Saxonchurch. I knew his mother, and him too, when he was tossing his rattle out of his cot. He wants to see us all in the servants' hall. Beth, you come with me. Mrs Flowerday, kindly wait in the library. The PC will speak to you once Mr Crosby has explained everything that happened.'

Mr Crosby explain everything that happened? A redder rag was never waved before a more goaded bull. Jemima pushed past Mrs Newson, reaching the servants' hall in remarkably few strides. There, she introduced herself to the youthful bobby seated at the table with the words, 'I am Mrs Jemima Flowerday and I was the closest witness to Madame Guyen's murder.'

The astonishment on the faces in front of her alerted her to her gaffe. Too late. It was said.

Murder.

Chapter Ten

The shockwaves settled, by which time Mrs Newson and Beth had joined them. Fresh tears showed on the kitchen maid's cheeks.

PC Trowse waited until everyone was seated before asking if this was all of them, the whole staff. It was all the indoor staff, but Wells was absent. Dinah had been sent for him a few minutes earlier and had returned claiming she couldn't find him.

'Then I'll get started.' PC Trowse took a notebook and pencil from his tunic front pocket. Despite Jemima's stringent objection, he was determined to take only Mr Crosby's evidence, due to 'Him being a man and most likely to know what went on and me not wanting to get misled by ladies disagreeing with each other.'

With a swift, exultant glance at Jemima, Albert Crosby gave his account of Marie Guyen's death. The constable noted down his words with a stubby pencil and his verdict when all had been said and written was, 'It's a rum 'un all right.'

'No doubting it, we are looking at a tragic accident,' Albert Crosby said in a deliberate contradiction of Jemima's opinion. 'If young Beth made a mistake, I still see no need to involve authority further.'

'Well…' The police constable chewed his lip. A decision seemed to be hatching inside his skull.

Beth began to cry again, burying her hiccups in her hands. Jemima trained a basilisk stare on PC Trowse, hoping to nudge him to a decision. It seemed to work.

'I'd like to use the telephone, if I may, Mr Crosby, and put a call in to Ipswich. To CID.'

Albert Crosby shook his head. 'No need, no need.'

'CID is Criminal Investigation—'

'I know who they are,' Crosby snapped. 'We had them here before after my brother's... after his death. Closing off rooms and stamping in and out.' Anxiety drew deep lines from the butler's brow to his chin. 'Where's your authority, young Trowse?'

In reminding them of the constable's inexperience, Albert Crosby had blundered.

Trowse folded his arms. 'CID knows the proper line of enquiry from henceforth.'

Jemima let out her breath. How often had she dreamed of rubbing shoulders with real, paid detectives? Never had she imagined it would happen in such harrowing circumstances. The only thing she could do for Marie Guyen was set the facts in front of those with the power to investigate. Let anyone attempt to gag her.

'In my view,' she said, 'there are unanswered questions around Madame Guyen's death, not least the substance that killed her and how it got into her system.'

PC Trowse went off to make his call. Jemima also found a reason to leave. She was cold and wanted a cardigan from her room, the one she had placed under Marie Guyen's head having vanished. In the great hall she saw the electric light flicker on in the telephone room and heard the constable requesting the operator connect him with Suffolk Police headquarters.

She paused a moment. The footsteps she had heard crossing the hall the last time she came downstairs had come from the telephone room. Jemima traced a line with her eyes. From that door to the one into the servants' hall was perhaps twelve fast steps. She tried it herself. It was fourteen, executed at a pace somewhere between a walk and a bustle. They had been feminine footsteps she'd heard, which opened the possibility that a woman had been instrumental in getting toxin into Madame Guyen's cup.

Chapter Eleven

It was nine in the evening and very dark before a motor-car engine cut through the dried-pea rattle of rain on the windows. PC Trowse had mounted his bicycle some hours ago, heading back to his police station at Saxonchurch. The rest of them had tried to settle to their various chores. Jemima, anxious for some kind of mindless occupation, had insisted she peel vegetables to help Beth.

Lady Hamlash had taken her supper on a tray in the drawing room. Mr Crosby retired to his butler's pantry with a plate of food. He needed to pen an order to the wine merchant, he said. 'Since Christmas will happen, come what may.'

Jemima and the others ate their supper of cold ham, boiled carrots and potatoes at the servants' long table in a silence so profound that whenever a knife or fork scraped, everyone jumped. Conversation was limited to expressions of shock and disbelief.

'But five hours ago, poor Madame was as alive as any of us.'

'Speaking one moment, gasping for breath the next.'

'How could she not have smelled the stuff in her coffee?'

'*Allergic*, the doctor said.'

That word – 'Allergic' – was passed around the table. Jemima was explaining what the doctor had said about anaphylaxis when headlights threw a jack-o'-lantern gleam on the glazed lobby. She jumped up, saying, 'I think CID has arrived.'

Jack went to inform Mr Crosby and they returned together. The butler announced that he would go alone to admit the detectives. 'If – *if* – any of you are called to give your evidence—' he began.

'If?' Jemima interrupted.

'Evidence?' Mrs Newson gasped.

The butler was determined to complete a sentence '—then it is your duty to say nothing. The police won't want to listen to five different accounts.'

'You hear that, Jack Millar?' Dinah hurled at the footman. 'They won't want your lies.'

Jack responded that he would tell the truth, 'without perjury.'

Without prejudice, you mean. Jemima kept the thought to herself, wondering if Jack's subconscious mind was working his tongue.

'All will be well, all will be well,' Crosby muttered as he went out.

Anxious minutes passed, everyone's eyes trained on the door connecting the servants' hall to the passageway that led to the great hall. For this reason, the stamp of boots on the tiles of the lobby and the entry of a hulking figure in civilian clothes, had everyone turning like a startled Greek chorus. The man who walked in from the kitchen garden was clad in brown from his rain-spattered homburg hat to his open coat and shabby tweed suit. He stared at each of them in turn. His eyes – brown, unsurprisingly – rested for an extra moment on Beth, who looked close to fainting.

'Ladies,' he said, with a polite nod to Jemima and Mrs Newson.

Jack planted himself in the newcomer's path, sharing his weight between his good leg and his tin one. 'I know you,' he said. 'You're pretty.'

Jemima shook her head at the footman. Unwise, mocking a man twice his age and breadth. She realised her error when Jack continued speaking.

'I cleaned your boots, Sergeant Pretty, when you were here investigating Roland Crosby's death. Big boots, a right bother to polish. Your old mum lives on the same street as mine.'

'*Detective* Sergeant to you, lad,' came the reply. 'Sit down, if you please. While my detective chief inspector speaks to Lady Hamlash, I want to know what you good people saw and witnessed today.'

'Oh, we're not to mention anything,' Mrs Newson said nervously.

'Says who?'

'Mr Crosby.'

Her comment coincided with the butler's return. Unwittingly, or perhaps not caring, DS Pretty pulled out the butler's empty chair and plonked himself in it, shrugging off his coat. Dinah had banked up the stove and the room was warm.

'I, on the other hand, wish to hear everything,' DS Pretty announced. 'I shall question you all in turn about the events of this day.'

'You may address your questions to me,' said Albert Crosby. He had declined to sit and stood ramrod behind Mrs Newson's chair.

'I shall speak to you all in turn, and kindly do not interrupt.' Pretty took out a notepad, pulled a pencil from its spine and looked up at the pendulous ceiling lamp. 'Don't you have a better light?'

It was Jemima who fetched the table lamp Mrs Newson had put aside for her and lit it for DS Pretty. He thanked her.

'Being as you're on your feet, ma'am, I will ask you first what you witnessed of the death of Miss Guyen.'

'Guy*en*.' Jemima couldn't bear Marie's name being mispronounced. The doctor had also mangled it. 'And she is – was – *Madame*.'

Pretty made a note, licking his pencil end twice. If a boiled Clootie Dumpling could have come to life, it would have looked like DS Pretty, with wide jowls and pockmarked cheeks, and it would speak in the same ponderous way. She suspected, however, that to dismiss this man as a fool would be a gross error.

'So, miss. Tell me what you saw.'

'I'm *Mrs* Flowerday. I will start my account from a few minutes prior to Madame's collapse.' Jemima described coming down the stairs in search of a lamp and a cup of tea, and reaching the great hall at precisely five minutes to five.

'You can be that precise?'

'The stable clock chimed when I was on the stairs. Five chimes mean ten to five.'

'It took you five minutes to descend a flight of stairs?'

Jemima explained. It was dark, she was unfamiliar with the layout of the house and had come down cautiously. Also, she had stopped to listen as someone hurried through the shadows below her eyeline. As she had later established to her satisfaction, the footsteps had emerged from the telephone room.

'Footsteps belonging to someone in this house?'

Jemima hesitated. If she gave her opinion, every female under this roof from Beth to Lady Hamlash would be in the frame as a potential purveyor of poison. Though, actually, did she know beyond doubt they had belonged to an inmate of Merry Beggars Hall?

'Mrs Flowerday?' DS Pretty was waiting.

'I beg your pardon. As I mentioned, I had no lantern and darkness had fallen. I'm afraid I couldn't possibly say whose they were.'

'And then what?'

Jemima described fumbling to open the door in the panelling, coming into the servants' hall to find Dinah, Jack and Mrs Newson at this table, listening to an argument between Madame Guyen and the butler. She pointed to the panels of textured glass that screened the kitchen. 'From behind there.'

'What was the nature of this argument, Mrs Flowerday?'

'That's irrelevant,' Albert Crosby barked. 'How would she know, if she wasn't present?'

'You'll get your moment, Mr Crosby,' Pretty said in his unruffled style. 'Mrs Flowerday?'

'I believe it revolved around Her Ladyship's desire to dismiss Madame Guyen.' Jemima described Marie Guyen flouncing in from the kitchen to appropriate Mr Crosby's seat. 'Where you sit now, Detective Sergeant. I would describe her mood as defiant and volatile.'

'Vola-tile.' The word was recorded.

'She'd been given her marching orders and she was upset.'

'Well she might be,' Jack chimed in, with a hard glance for the butler. 'You can't turn someone off with no notice, and I don't like being told to manhandle a woman.'

'I said no interrupting, young man.' However, DS Pretty jotted down Jack's comment. 'Mrs Flowerday, do you believe, or do you *know*, that the French lady was being turned off? There's a big difference.'

Jemima acknowledged the difference. 'Mr Crosby made no attempt to disguise the fact and Madame Guyen accused him of acting as "Lady Hamlash's poodle" only she changed that to "mastiff", calling him "a skinny one".'

'"Skinny one".' DS Pretty made careful note.

Jemima dared not look at Albert Crosby. She then described the telephone conversation between Lady Hamlash and her son. 'Which I accidentally overheard when returning from a jaunt in the garden.' She glossed over the fact that she had purposely lingered, the better to hear. 'Her Ladyship was agreeing with Sir Finchley – her son – that the cook must be got rid of.'

'"Got. Rid. Of",' wrote DS Pretty. 'Right, you, lad—' He pointed his pencil end at Jack. 'Confirm who told you to manhandle the French lady.'

'Mr Crosby. He wanted me and Wells to take an arm each and lug her out to the car.'

'I did not use the word "lug",' Crosby objected.

'Wells being?' Pretty asked.

'The chauffeur,' Dinah said eagerly.

The same time as Jack muttered, 'The gardener.'

They glared at each other.

'Wells is both,' Jemima explained. 'The servants double up here, as there aren't enough of them.'

DS Pretty sniffed. 'Most of us would be satisfied with an occasional one. So, Mrs Flowerday, back to you. What happened next?'

'Madame Guyen came in for her coffee, saying she would go nowhere until she had received justice.' Jemima paused for Pretty to ask, 'Justice for what?' He did not, so she continued. 'Mrs Newson told Beth to pour Madame's coffee. Beth had made tea in a big pot, and a smaller pot of coffee for Madame as per normal.'

Pretty looked around. 'Which of you is Beth? You?' He jutted his chin towards the child-servant, whose head was bent so low her hair-parting shone in the oil lamp's gleam. 'Well, dear?'

Beth's shoulders shook.

To spare the child, Jemima described how Madame Guyen had instructed Beth. 'Coffee in first, then heated milk, the way she liked it.'

'Anything else poured in?' Pretty's pencil hovered.

'Madame added a cube of sugar to her cup, using the tongs.'

'Sugar from the common bowl… Mrs Flowerday?'

Jemima had fallen silent, her inner gaze sliding back to five o'clock tea at this table. Beth had brought the sugar bowl on the tea tray, along with the teapot and coffee pot and the jugs of milk. The tongs had been balanced on top of the sugar bowl. In that moment, Jemima knew. *She knew.* She snapped out of her trance.

'Yes, the same bowl. Detective Sergeant, I have an idea that what killed her—'

Jack, listening with growing impatience, interrupted saying, 'We know what killed her. It was that muck Wells brewed.'

DS Pretty moved his attention from Jemima. 'What muck would that be, lad?'

'His tobacco mix. He boils it up in his shed. Nasty stuff, like creosote.'

'You saw him slip some in the victim's coffee?'

'Well…' Jack wilted under Pretty's pugilist stare. 'Not exactly.'

'What does "not exactly" mean?'

'It means no,' Dinah shot out. 'Jack don't know anything, but he hates Wells, so don't you listen to a word he says. I reckon he did it himself, out of spite.'

Pretty held up a cautioning palm. 'Now, now young miss, laying false information is a criminal offence. Think before you speak.' He turned back to Jemima. 'At what point did Madame Guyen show signs of being unwell?'

Hiding her frustration at not being allowed to reveal what she believed was the mode of murder, Jemima answered the question. 'She drank down her coffee and the effect was almost instantaneous. She went from speaking to collapsing within a minute. Jack is right, tobacco is to blame. I smelled it on her as I crouched beside her.' She presented Pretty with the segment of china cup she had rescued, and the little, brown bottle from Marie Guyen's bedside table. 'This shard is the only piece of Madame Guyen's cup that hasn't been washed. The bottle contains bromelain, an antidote to bee stings and other allergens.'

While the sergeant scrutinised the bottle, removed its cork stopper, sniffed it, she described in more detail Marie's collapse, the change in her breathing and the pallor of her skin.

'Mr Crosby was asked urgently to telephone for the doctor, but it was Jack who went.'

This time, she gave Mr Crosby a direct glance. He did not notice, seeming intent on the shadows cast on the ceiling by the oil lamp.

'What time was that?' DS Pretty was putting the bromelain bottle into a box. Presumably as evidence. He did the same with the piece of gilded china then angled his pencil to record Jemima's answer.

'I gave the time of death to Dr Rushbrook as five twenty p.m. I have no reason to change that estimate.'

'You are very certain, Mrs Flowerday.'

She told him why. 'When I took off my cardigan to place it under Madame's head, I glanced at my watch. The position of the hands is engraved on my memory.'

The detective issued a faint growl, which she took as approval.

'Does anyone disagree with Mrs Flowerday?' He looked from one servant to the next, like a spider choosing which silk-bound fly to eat. Nobody objected to Jemima's timings. 'Where is the chauffeur-fellow, then?' Pretty demanded. 'Where is Wells?'

In his cottage, most likely, came the answer.

'He lives within these grounds, or outside?'

The gardener's cottage lay alongside the boundary wall of the park, within the curtilage of the hall. 'By the north gate,' Mrs Newson supplied timidly.

'I'll get him.' Jack levered himself up.

'Best you don't,' warned Mrs Newson, explaining to DS Pretty, 'Jack's tin leg gets stuck in the cinder path when its wet.'

Dinah offered.

'No, you don't, Dinah. For most likely we won't see you again for an hour. I'm not at all sure you did a proper search last time you went to fetch Wells.' The housekeeper sighed towards Beth, then said, 'I suppose I had better get him.'

'I'll go,' Jemima said firmly. 'If somebody can lend me a torch?' She would have liked to hear the servants' witness statements, but smoking Wells out of the gardener's cottage was an equally tempting prospect. Jack's accusations sounded exactly what they were; a jealous man lashing out. But there was no doubt Wells had possessed the means of killing Madame Guyen, if not the motive. If CID decided Jack had a point, a net would close around the American. Would that be justice?

Jack found her a torch and offered to come with her. 'Country-dark is different from London-dark, Mrs Flowerday. It's that much deeper. So is Mr Wells, and I don't mean that as praise.'

She assured him she'd be fine. Jack's heart was in the right place, she decided. Pity Dinah didn't see it.

Chapter Twelve

In the glazed lobby, Jemima picked an oilskin coat off a hook and thrust her arms into its sleeves, dropping its hood over her head. The garment swallowed her. Jack hadn't exaggerated the deepness of the night and, despite her torch, she veered off the cinder path, tripping over almost at once. She got to her feet, brushed soil off the coat and pointed her torch beam down. She'd fallen over a severely pruned rose whose stems were speckled with something gritty, as was the soil around them. Beth had emptied the tea and coffee pots right here. Perhaps she always did. It was commonly believed that cold tea kept bugs off roses and coffee strengthened their roots.

Jemima knelt down, giving the earth a good sniff. It smelled exactly as soil should, with perhaps a hint of horse manure. No reek of tobacco, so unless the rain had washed the smell away, the toxin that had killed Madame Guyen had not been in her coffee pot. It bolstered Jemima's conviction that the toxin had got into Marie's cup by another means, and she was glad now that she'd been prevented from speaking her thoughts out loud in front of the servants.

She continued on her way.

Jack's directions had been to stay on the cinder path, past the coal bunkers, 'to the park boundary, following the North star, like the three wise men'. The stars were invisible on this dank and cloudy night, proving that Jack couldn't resist a joke, even in a crisis. Jemima stayed on the path until a glimpse of lamplight between partly closed curtains signalled she was approaching a dwelling. It was a cottage, built into the park's boundary wall, with an unembellished front door and a single window to one side.

At her knock, the door was hauled open with aggressive speed.

'What are you doing here?' was hurled through the space.

Jemima cleared her throat. 'Summoning you to the house, Mr Wells.'

'Oh, Mrs Flowerday.' Wells was instantly his amiable self. 'Beg your pardon, ma'am. I thought you were Dinah.' He blinked at her coat. 'She wears that garment to go out in the rain to fetch coal. More than once she's leapt out at me while wearing it.'

'Jack would gladly be in your shoes.'

'Hm. Please, come out of the night, into the warm.'

Jemima stepped into a living room that was just large enough to contain a well-worn armchair and a side table. Wiping her shoes on the mat, she took an unhurried look around. Interesting. Wells had no personal possessions, unless they were upstairs in what was probably the solitary bedroom. The only homely note was a blaze within a tiled fireplace, the flames feeding on wedges of paper. Wells didn't strike her as a man who would burn books, so what was going up in smoke? He followed her gaze, but gave no explanation, asking instead about the car that had arrived a short while ago.

'Sir Finchley and his lady, all in a fuss?'

'No, CID,' she replied, adding that Sir Finchley had not yet arrived. 'We have a DS Pretty taking notes in the servants' hall. His superior is with Her Ladyship.'

'I see. Friendly?'

She couldn't comment on the senior officer, but as for DS Pretty,

'I'd call him thorough. He's unpicking the events leading to Madame Guyen's death, one witness at a time.'

'They'll blame me,' Wells said bitterly.

Jemima saw no point in stoking his fears, but the suspicion she'd caught him destroying papers prompted her to ask, 'Was it you who ordered Beth to wash the tea things?'

He began a denial, but gave up at her look. 'Yes, it was. I knew how it would be once Jack got his knife into me.'

'Tampering with evidence is likely to strengthen feelings against you.' Jack's suspicion of Wells was not altogether unjustified, she was starting to think. With that in mind, she pounced. 'How long had you and Marie Guyen known each other?'

Wells looked wary. 'What makes you say that?'

'As you observed when we first met, I have a good ear. Marie's French accent was strong, but came with a twang I'm familiar with. New York. It showed in the way she pronounced "Coffee".' Jemima reminded Wells of their first conversation. 'I asked what brought you here and you said, "I guess I fancied a change." But, really, the idea that two New Yorkers would fancy an identical change in the same rustic bolthole insults the most average intelligence. Unlike the sheets and the crockery, it won't wash, Mr Wells.'

'You're putting two and two together and arriving at fifty, Mrs Flowerday.'

'Not so. You and Marie were on first-name terms.'

'We're American, it's kinda how we are.'

'"Marie, Marie, what did I tell you?"'

As she echoed Wells's words at Marie's deathbed, he flinched. He quickly recovered, however.

'I can't be responsible for things I said in a moment of distress.'

'I don't doubt your distress,' she agreed. 'Your words indicate a previous conversation. An exchange of views. A meeting of minds.'

When Wells advanced no more than a shrug, her patience snapped.

'I don't need to be a detective to know that her death shocked you because you foresaw it. By coming here, Marie put herself in danger, and when you saw her lifeless you realised she'd met the fate you'd feared.'

'Two and two still doesn't make fifty, ma'am.'

'You and Marie were in cahoots. Don't deny it. Was it her search for justice that connected the two of you?'

Until this moment, Wells had kept a polite distance, but the use of the word 'justice' triggered a change. He picked up a brass poker. A step brought him so close, Jemima could see the evening stubble on his jaw and individual eyelashes as he blinked. Pushing a hand into the deep pocket of her coat, she curled her fingers around the torch Jack had lent her.

'That's quite a leap, Mrs Flowerday.'

'Not so much,' she answered nervously. 'Marie repeatedly sought out Lady Hamlash, to the point of peering at her through her drawing-room window, I now realise, and ambushing her in the garden. Will you tell me why?'

Clearly, he would not.

She glanced at the fireplace. 'You are burning the evidence that links you.'

'Just clearing clutter. I'm a tidy soul.' When Jemima went to look more closely, Wells gave an exasperated cough. 'Don't get too close, you'll scorch your cheeks.'

But something in the fire had caught her interest: a woollen cuff knitted in slip-stitch rib, in burgundy and coffee-coloured yarn. Over the course of an evening, Jemima had watched her sister creating that very cuff, Vicky being as deft a knitter as she was a pianist.

'Mr Wells, why are you burning my cardigan?'

His instinct for denial melted in the face of her indignation. 'I'm sorry.'

'I laid that garment under Madame's head, and it got stained. Why else would you burn it? You've done everything you can to hinder a police investigation and that includes persuading Mrs Newson to launder the linen Marie was in contact with. Was it to get rid of the smell of tobacco? Someone helped Mrs Newson lift Marie's body to get the sheets off the bed. She couldn't have done it alone, even if she'd wanted to.'

After a charged moment, Wells admitted it all. 'I walked around the rear of the house after I left you with Jack and Dinah, and went back into Marie's room. Mrs Newson was grateful when I suggested we begin the clean-up.'

'You took advantage of her.'

'I played to her natural instincts to cleanse and purify. It comes down to this, Mrs Flowerday: I don't want to hang for something I didn't do.'

'You'd prefer Beth was implicated?'

'No, of course not. Poor kid.' Wells placed the poker on the hearth, and a hand on Jemima's arm. 'I forgot myself a moment ago. Did I scare you?'

'Not in the least.' Actually, she hadn't liked the poker so close to her head, but she kept her composure. 'I'm not a broken flower, Mr Wells.'

'Neither was Marie, but courage is not always helpful.'

'You're admitting that you knew her?'

'I guess I am.'

'Then I will tell you something in exchange. I know how that substance—'

The door burst open and Dinah hurled herself in. The sight of

Wells's hand on Jemima's arm brought a kind of hiss from her throat. 'I guessed it! What are you two doing? What kept you?'

Jemima responded first. 'Hello, Dinah. Did DS Pretty send you?'

Dinah answered without looking at Jemima, all her fervid energy for Wells. 'Mrs Newson thought you'd lost your way, but Jack said, "I bet Wells is making eyes at Mrs Flowerday" so I came and Jack was right. Now my feet are soaking.'

'So they are,' Jemima agreed, noticing the damp shoeprints on the boards, criss-crossing the ones she had left. Dinah's prints were broad, nothing elf-footed about the girl. 'I'm wearing the coat you like to use. Would you like it back?'

Still without looking at her, Dinah said, 'The other detective wants to speak with all the upper servants, including Mr Wells.' Finally, she turned to Jemima. 'And you.'

Jemima went out, switching on her torch. She doubted DS Pretty had included her within the roster of upper servants. That snub had the ring of Albert Crosby about it, or Dinah's spitefulness, but it didn't matter. What mattered was that she was about to face a detective chief inspector, a man empowered to call Marie Guyen's death an accident or something darker. She would choose her moment and divulge her theory to him. She had added two plus two and reached a solid four.

She expected Wells and Dinah to follow her out, and when they did not, she turned back. Confused by the dense silence from within the cottage, she crept to the window. Through the gap in the curtains, in the sallow lamplight, what she saw made her blink in disbelief.

Dinah and Wells, locked in an embrace, Dinah's damp hair loose around her shoulders. They were kissing as if the world were falling apart and they had only moments left to live.

Chapter Thirteen

Jack and Beth were alone in the servants' hall when Jemima returned.

Jack looked up, then past her. 'Just you, then, Mrs Flowerday?'

'Dinah is helping damp down Mr Wells's fire,' she said, taking off the oilskin coat. 'Is everyone else in the drawing room?'

Jack confirmed it. Sir Finchley had arrived within the last twenty minutes. 'He came alone from Brabberton Manor. That's where he and Lady Olivia are staying. I'm not wanted and Beth can't be left, considering what's lying not far away.' He meant Marie's body, her death having come too late for the undertaker to collect. Besides, the detectives would wish to view her in situ. 'What did you mean, Mrs Flowerday, "Damping down the fire"?'

'Exactly that. Wells had over-piled the burning coals.' Jemima was keen to get away from the emotions disfiguring the young man's face and went to join the others.

DS Pretty stopped her at the drawing-room door.

'Her Ladyship kindly requests you remove your outdoor shoes, madam. There's been enough traipsing in of wet footprints, she says.'

Jemima obliged, placing her neat, T-strap shoes beside a porter's chair. Had she known she'd be going out, she'd have changed into her walking shoes.

As she waited to be admitted, a piano note rang out from behind the closed door. A lifetime of being Vicky's sister had given her an acute ear. 'Tonic A,' she murmured.

'I'll take your word for it,' Pretty answered. 'Seems we've come all this way in the dark to tickle the ivories. In you go, DCI Bullace expects you.'

'Bullace?'

'My superior. Is the driver-fellow on his way?'

'If you mean Wells, he knows he's wanted.'

'Bullace' was a new name to Jemima. *The Weekend Sleuth* had acquainted her with a DCI Lidney who had led the investigation into Roland Crosby's death. Lidney had not solved the crime, and one could only imagine his feelings when Scotland Yard was sent in to pep up the hunt for the killer. Perhaps he had been promoted into early retirement. Replaced by Bullace... pronounced Bull-Ace. The name manifested a policeman of the most dogged, unsentimental kind.

She stepped at last into Lady Hamlash's domain and basked for a moment in the glow of a blazing fire. No stinting on coal in here. Her second impression was that she would struggle to get a quiet word with the detective chief inspector: she had added herself to quite a gathering.

To one side of the fireplace stood Albert Crosby, his hands behind his back. A pace behind him was Mrs Newson, the narrow lace of her cuffs forming accents against her dark skirt. A stranger sat in one of the two fireside armchairs. This must be Bullace, Jemima surmised, judging by his morose expression. He was younger than she'd expected, though metal spectacles and a receding hair-line lent him a studious air. A suit of mossy tweed added to the impression of a young man heading for premature middle age.

He gave Jemima a brisk glance, then turned away to stare crossly at Lady Hamlash who was at the piano playing gentle scales... Lady

Hamlash and a tall, elegant man standing at her shoulder, appreciating her finger work. No country tweeds for him, but a suit of grey barathea, the glimmer of a watch chain relieving the plainness of a tailored waistcoat. He leaned past Her Ladyship to play the scale of A major in a fluid run. Here at last was the son and heir, come to support his mother in her hour of distress. With his patrician features and sandy-grey hair falling over his brow, Sir Finchley Hamlash was older and – yes – more appealing than she'd anticipated.

Lady Hamlash played the opening bars of 'Keep the Home Fires Burning' while her companion added a one-handed harmony. It was a charming domestic scene, but unsettling, given the circumstances. Feeling that her arrival ought to have been acknowledged by now, Jemima cleared her throat. The occupant of the armchair gave her a second look, his spectacles catching the glint of the fire.

'Who are you, then?' he demanded.

'I am Mrs Flowerday, Detective Chief Inspector, and you wished to speak to me.'

Braced for an apology, she was taken aback when he responded, 'Who the devil d'you imagine I am?'

The home fires were abruptly extinguished and Lady Hamlash rose from her seat.

'Finchley, whatever your habits in your own abode, here good manners prevail. Mrs Flowerday is the dressmaker I told you about and is daughter-in-law to Lord and Lady Winterfold. Greet her civilly.'

As Jemima scolded herself for falling into lazy pre-judgement, the scowler in country tweeds rose awkwardly from his seat. So, *this* was Lady Hamlash's son. The figure leaning against the piano, regarding them all with hooded fascination, must be DCI Bullace.

'No offence taken,' she said, returning Sir Finchley's handshake. 'I hope your journey was tolerable. You've come from the neighbouring parish, I believe.'

'Finchley and Lady Olivia are staying at Brabberton with the Courtney-Leveretts,' Lady Hamlash informed her. 'They keep a larger staff and there are radiators in the bedrooms, can you imagine it?'

Jemima nodded politely, her mind on local geography. Brabberton Manor, she seemed to recall, was the station before Beggars Heath when travelling from Ipswich.

'I too must apologise, for being so remiss in my welcome today, Mrs Flowerday. What must you think of me? I had no notion you were related to the Winterfolds, until my daughter-in-law telephoned a short while ago and I mentioned you. Lady Olivia goes up to London often and knows who is who.'

'I don't trade upon my connection to Lord and Lady Winterfold, Lady Hamlash,' Jemima said firmly. 'It has no bearing on my professional status.'

'Even so, I apologise for not receiving you sooner. It has been a day beyond my capacity to describe.'

Jemima could well believe it. All was not well with Ada Hamlash. At some point, Her Ladyship had changed into an afternoon dress of tawny-brown wool with dogtooth-check cuffs and collar. She must have thrown it on because the buttons down the front were wrongly fastened. She seemed quite distracted, yet her movements were lethargic. Wells had implied that Dr Rushbrook was in the habit of giving Lady Hamlash 'something for her nerves' when he called. Judging by the dilation of Her Ladyship's pupils, that 'something' was barbiturate.

Wells came in, provoking Sir Finchley to suggest that they jolly well get on with things. 'I hardly need say that Lady Olivia will be anxious if I'm back late. She wasn't all that happy I drove myself. The Silver Ghost is not built for rustic potholes.'

'You can always stay over,' Lady Hamlash said. 'Mrs Newson would air a room for you.'

Jemima detected a shiver from Sir Finchley. 'Thank you, Mother, but the point of owning an expensive motor is that one can get back to one's glass of port before the servants have retired.'

Jemima was not shocked. Rudeness was so commonplace these days, one did not clutch one's lapel when encountering it. She satisfied herself by reflecting that her eleven-year-old son, Tommy, behaved a great deal better in company than Sir Finchley Hamlash.

DCI Bullace fished a gold hunter watch from his waistcoat pocket and said, 'I wonder if we could pull up seats in a semi-circle so I can ask my questions without feeling I'm addressing a half-empty lecture hall. Lady Hamlash, will you mind?'

Lady Hamlash looked to her butler. Crosby inclined his head, though his, 'Very good, Inspector,' suggested he found the idea as vulgar as it was alarming. They fetched chairs from every part of the room and set them out in front of the fire. All sat down, except Crosby, who stood behind Her Ladyship's chair. Jemima sat at the furthest extreme, claiming to dislike being so close to the hearth, but really so she could observe Wells.

He'd come in with his hands in his pockets, a touch of false swagger in his walk. Was that kiss lingering in his thoughts and on his lips? He leaned forward to catch Jemima's eye. She returned a chilly stare. Charming liars were the worst, in her opinion.

DCI Bullace chose the piano stool for his perch, placed at the opposite end of the semi-circle to Jemima. Beside him sat Sir Finchley and the order after that was Lady Hamlash, Wells, Mrs Newson and finally Jemima. DS Pretty had remained outside the door.

Bullace opened the proceedings. 'The coroner has been informed of an unnatural death and will ask for a post-mortem on the body of Madame Marie Guyen.' Bullace pronounced the deceased's name correctly, to Jemima's approval. 'My job is to establish whether there was foul play.'

A straight talker. Jemima's approval grew. She might eventually forgive him for misleading her with his louche air and for wearing his jacket unbuttoned.

Bullace continued. 'With the exception of you, Sir Finchley, all here present were under this roof at the time of Madame Guyen's death. Correct?'

A general murmur confirmed it until Wells spoke. 'I was not in the house, leastways, not under the roof.'

'Where were you?' asked Bullace.

'In my cottage eating lunch, followed by a catnap as the rain was too heavy for working outside, and Her Ladyship wasn't needing the car. After that I went to the old coach house. There's a boneshaker bike in there I've been wanting to repair for a while. It's where Dinah found me, after... after Madame Guyen collapsed.'

'Thank you, Mr Wells.' Bullace stared at the backs of his hands. Then, abruptly, he went to the door, rapped twice and called, 'Pretty, exhibit one, if you please.'

A squat, green bottle was angled around the door by DS Pretty. Bullace held it up for them to see, then passed it to Sir Finchley. 'Inspect it and hand it on.'

Jemima noticed how swiftly Wells relinquished the bottle to Mrs Newson when it was his turn. It looked like the one Jemima had seen in his coat pocket as he walked by the library window. When it reached her, Jemima read the embossed maker's mark on the glass: James Buchanan & Co. Ltd, Distillers.

A whisky bottle, full almost to the maker's name. The way the liquid moved told her it contained something more viscous than Scotch. Briefly leaving her seat, she took the bottle to Mr Crosby. Bullace, who was studying their reactions in a lazy kind of way, invited the butler to remove the cork and smell the contents.

'Tobacco and tar,' was Crosby's verdict, accompanied by a grimace of disgust.

'Let the company have a sniff, Mr Crosby, if you please.'

One after the other, they inhaled the noxious contents, keeping their noses at a distance, except Sir Finchley who jerked his head back.

'Damn and blast, what is it?'

Wells answered, 'It's the insecticide I made this lunchtime.' His swagger had been replaced by palpable anger. 'I could have said so and spared Sir Finchley a choking fit. What's the purpose in this, Officer?'

'Call me Inspector.' Bullace recorked the bottle and placed it on the mantelpiece. 'The doctor gave his opinion that Marie Guyen died from allergic shock, having swallowed a mixture containing tobacco and its toxic constituent, nicotine. My first purpose is to establish the presence in this house of a liquid capable of causing death to a vulnerable person. Since I have your attention, Mr Wells, can you confirm that this bottle does indeed contain a solution of nicotine?'

'It's made from tobacco which contains nicotine, so yes, obviously it does.' Wells was making no effort to conceal his vexation. 'Lady Hamlash's old gardener passed on the recipe. Bilney was keen I should keep making his special bug-killer, claiming no proprietary brand could do the job as thoroughly.'

Bullace leaned towards Lady Hamlash. 'Do you concur, ma'am?'

Her Ladyship had fallen into an abstracted state and Bullace had to repeat his question. 'Oh, yes, quite so,' she gasped. 'Bilney invented it after we suffered a plague of spider mite the year before war broke out, when we lost all our precious hoyas. We never had an outbreak after that.'

A huff of irritation escaped Sir Finchley. Was he thinking of the comforts of Brabberton and his glass of port… or did he find his mother's plants a dead bore?

Bullace asked Lady Hamlash how she used the mixture.

'From a spray canister,' came the answer.

'I mean, is it diluted, or used neat on the plants?'

'Goodness, never neat. Bilney supplied the tincture ready-diluted, in that bottle. He wrote out the recipe before he left and I gave the bottle to Wells on his first day.'

Wells confirmed it. 'Bilney's note was a bit of a scribble. I mean, he wanted to be gone and wrote it in a hurry, but I deciphered it. The bottle was to be refilled whenever it ran low, to his exact recipe.'

'Winter is the time to spray,' Lady Hamlash explained earnestly to the inspector. 'All crevices, floor to ceiling, the panes of the conservatory as well as the plants, their pots and soil. Tiny creatures lay eggs everywhere, you would be astonished.'

Jemima wondered where the conservatory lay in this rambling house. They generally faced south-east which, if her orientation were correct, would place it on the other side of the telephone room.

'You've never taken ill from this tincture?' Bullace asked Lady Hamlash.

'Never. One must kill overwintering pests and discourage mildew. Perhaps you are unaware, but fungal attacks increase in the colder months.'

Bullace thanked Lady Hamlash before asking Wells to list the ingredients and his method for making it.

'Sure. Take a tin of tobacco, add water and boil it in a pan over a flame for an hour, then strain off the juice. To that add tincture of common elm and a pint of coal-tar. The apothecary in town stocks both. Boil it all up some more, until you have a quarter-pint of brown liquid or are ready to pass out, whichever comes first. It should have the consistency of thick treacle.'

'And then?'

Wells continued without falter, 'You add a quarter-pint of water to the neat tincture and bottle it.'

'Let me be clear. You mix your raw tincture with equal parts of water?'

Wells hesitated, as if to check his memory. Then he nodded. 'Correct, sir.'

Bullace regarded the whisky bottle thoughtfully. 'If I were to pour some, would it be diluted as you describe, equal measures of tincture to water?'

'It would,' Wells agreed emphatically, 'unless somebody tampered with it.'

Bullace let that pass. He asked Wells if the liquor came from the batch he had made that day.

'For sure. Her Ladyship informed me a few days ago that she was running low and on my way to the train station to pick up Mrs Flowerday today, I bought the ingredients. After returning the motor car to the garage and changing my clothes, I went to my shed and put a batch on to boil. Prior to my lunch break, I fetched the empty bottle from the conservatory.'

'That very bottle?' Bullace pointed to the mantlepiece.

'Haven't I already said so? I'd left the mixture simmering over lunchtime, and by two this afternoon, it was done. I let it cool, then replenished the bottle, which I returned to the conservatory.'

'At what time?'

'About four in the afternoon, or a little before. I walked around the side of the house and noticed the sun sinking behind the conservatory roof. I'm going to say three fifty p.m.'

'Where exactly did you place the bottle, Mr Wells?'

As if mocking the inspector's desire for detail, Wells answered, 'On a slatted shelf, right-hand side of the conservatory as one enters, next to a ball of gardener's twine and Her Ladyship's spray canister.'

Jemima mentally put herself back in the library shortly before one o'clock that afternoon. Wells had walked past, bottle in pocket, so that part of his story rang true. He had called out to a figure invisible to Jemima: *'Go away, I'm plumb out of patience! Let me do my job!'* Dinah, jealous because she'd sniffed a connection between Wells and Marie? If, as he said, he'd returned the full bottle to the conservatory at three-fifty p.m., the mixture had been sitting on its shelf an hour before Jemima had heard mystery footsteps in the great hall. Dinah, armed with the means of killing her rival? The housemaid's unrestrained passion for Wells might have provoked her to a desperate act. Yet Jemima had studied the girl's shoes while in Wells's cottage. Dinah's footwear was low-heeled and round-toed, and unlikely to create the lightweight patter seared into Jemima's memory.

The inspector next produced the bromelain bottle Jemima had passed over to Pretty, saying, 'Did you know Madame Guyen had an allergy, Mr Wells?'

Wells's pause was infinite, but it was not lost on Jemima. Nor, she suspected, on Bullace.

Wells said, 'It's mine, not hers. It was in my pocket when I heard she'd collapsed.'

'Do you always carry bromelain?' Bullace sounded intrigued.

'Always. I react badly to bee stings. When you're gardening you prepare for such things.'

'Even in winter?'

'All year round.'

'Did you know Madame Guyen was a fellow sufferer?'

'Sure. She wasn't bothered by bees, though. It was cigarettes in her case.'

'Tobacco, then. You'd discussed it?'

'It came up, yes. We chatted. Marie Guyen was French, from

Paris, but had lived some years in New York, as have I. We had a lot in common.'

'I see.' Bullace asked Wells why the insecticide was not labelled. 'One would expect some kind of warning on something so potent.'

For the first time in this room, Wells betrayed remorse. 'I guess so, but that's how Bilney bequeathed the bottle to me. You will back me up, ma'am?'

He looked to Lady Hamlash, who nodded.

'We never labelled it. Indeed, why should we?' she answered. 'I alone tend to my conservatory plants and know the contents of every bottle and box on my shelves.'

'Damn stupid, though,' Sir Finchley grunted. 'Lady Olivia labels everything, even the jam on the sideboard at breakfast though it's invariably apricot or gooseberry.'

'I will learn my lesson,' Her Ladyship answered heavily. 'I will label every poisonous substance from now on.'

Bullace asked her if she had used the liquor on her plants that day.

She had not. 'I hardly spent any time on my personal tasks, because of that woman.'

'*That* woman?'

'Madame Guyen, Inspector. Pestering me with—' She stopped as her son violently cleared his throat and turned to him. 'You know it was so, Finchley. It doesn't mean I'm not sorry for what happened to her, but she was a thorough pest. You said so. In fact—'

Sir Finchley interrupted again. 'Mother, restrict yourself to the inspector's questions or this night will never end.'

'Perhaps Wells can answer my next question.' Bullace gestured at the bottle. 'Any missing?'

Wells answered fervently, 'None.'

Bullace leaned forward. 'Think hard, Mr Wells.'

'None. At. All. Sir.'

'Mm. Did you decant *all* the liquor you made into this bottle?'

Wells's teeth clashed. Anyone could see he hated these questions. 'I poured out as much as I could and scraped the residue on to the muck heap. It's disgusting stuff and I don't want to have to make more any time soon.'

Sir Finchley, shifting on his chair, grumbled, 'Can we get back to the matter of how the devil that revolting substance ended up in the woman's coffee and why she chose to drink it down?'

'I have asked that myself.' Mrs Newson spoke at last. 'But you see, there was no hint of tobacco at the table, or in the cup Madame Guyen brought in with her, nor in the coffee as it was poured out. Even Beth would have smelled something amiss. The girl swore absolutely that she made the coffee "As Madame liked it, as Madame showed her how". I believe her. In simple tasks, Beth is reliable as clockwork.'

'Except that your clock is habitually ten minutes slow,' Bullace commented. He then invited the housekeeper to state where this was leading.

'I'm not quite sure, sir, only that the dreadful smell rose up after Madame fell.'

'You were all at the servants' kitchen table, yes?'

Mrs Newson said yes. She was there, with Dinah, Mrs Flowerday and the footman, Jack Millar.

'And this girl – Beth—'

'Beth Noaks. She's not the cleverest, but she never puts a foot wrong if she understands what is wanted of her.'

Never puts a foot wrong. Such as washing up the crockery and soaking bed linen in suds of Reckitt's Blue… Jemima mulled on it and thought, I must find my way to the conservatory and view the famous slatted shelf. She might then work out if a person could slip in there, decant tobacco tincture from the bottle – just a smidgeon – before returning, like a Corner House Nippy, to the kitchen. If not Dinah's footfall then Beth's? The kitchen maid wore clogs, similar to Madame Guyen's. Jemima had checked. She might have slipped them off, of course, and changed into a daintier pair of shoes. As might Dinah have done.

Jemima glanced at Mrs Newson's feet. The housekeeper wore old-fashioned, button-up boots. Small and narrow. Could Mrs Newson scurry, afflicted, as she seemed to be, with arthritis? And what about Lady Hamlash? Jemima had already noted how broad her hostess's feet were. So much so, she must have had difficulty buckling on the brocade evening shoes she was currently wearing. Ada Hamlash was certainly no Nippy and had most likely been here in the drawing room when Jemima heard the footsteps. It was a conundrum if Jemima was determined the culprit had to be someone in this house. But what if somebody – a woman – had slipped in from outside?

She pictured Marie Guyen flouncing in from the kitchen, fresh from her argument with Albert Crosby. Beth pouring Madame's black coffee into a china cup with a gold-leaf rim, and after that the heated milk. *As I showed you, petite. Coffee in first.* Marie Guyen raising her cup to her lips…

Sir Finchley had asked how the 'revolting substance' had got into the cup. This was the moment for Jemima to reveal her theory. She got to her feet.

'DCI Bullace—'

A commotion outside the drawing-room door cut her off. They heard DS Pretty shouting, 'You can't go in. Stand back, lad. You too—'

The door was flung wide and Dinah hurtled in. Throwing herself to her knees beside Wells, she shrieked, 'I did it! I killed Madame Guyen!'

Chapter Fourteen

As Dinah's confession rang out, Jack Millar rushed in. Rather, he half-fell over the threshold, DS Pretty hanging on to his jacket.

'Don't listen to her,' Jack cried. 'She's mad for that swindler. She'll say anything. She didn't kill anybody.'

'I did it!' Dinah roared. 'Where's the detective inspector, the proper one? I want to confess.'

Bullace raised Dinah to her feet. 'I am DCI Bullace, and you are…?'

'Dinah Pullen. I work here.' Dinah's cap was half off, her hair dishevelled.

'So I perceive. What are you confessing to, young lady?'

Mrs Newson belatedly acquired some energy, crying, 'Don't say any more. I mean it, Dinah, or you'll be in such hot water, there'll be no dragging you out.'

Dinah was beyond the reach of wisdom. 'I poisoned the Frenchie because she was a wrong 'un, going on about justice and tormenting Her Ladyship. I didn't mean her to die, I just wanted her to fall sick and leave. I'll go to prison, I don't care. Just don't listen to what Jack says 'cause he hates Mr Wells, and he'll do anything to get even with him. That postcard he's found means nothing.'

'Postcard?' Bullace moved Dinah aside. 'You, are you Jack? What is she talking about?'

Jack was holding on to DS Pretty for support, either because his prosthetic leg was giving him pain, or its fastenings had come adrift. From his pocket, he pulled a scorched rectangle. 'I had a poke around in that rotter's cottage. This was in the grate, with the other stuff he tried to burn.'

The inspector took the fragment. 'A postcard sent from London, by the looks of it. Did you read it?'

'Course. I can read!' Jack's cheeks flamed. 'It's from Madame Guyen, telling Wells she was coming to Merry Beggars Hall and he couldn't stop her. Read what she put, Inspector, and you'll see!'

It took Bullace a minute to read what was legible on the back, during which Dinah's ragged breathing was the loudest sound. Wells looked on with contempt, but Jemima saw his fingers curling and uncurling. Between him and the door stood the bulldog bulk of DS Pretty.

Bullace proffered the card to Wells. 'You read it out to the company, as it's your property.'

Wells flatly declined. 'I am not on trial.'

Jemima stepped forward, aware that through his intransigence, Wells was backing himself further into a corner. 'Shall I?'

'Mrs Flowerday, do, I beg you,' DCI Bullace replied.

The date written, presumably, in Marie's hand was readable when seen directly under a lamp. November 24. The postcard had been sent just over two weeks ago. 'It's from the something-something hotel,' Jemima said, 'W2. That's West London.'

'I suspect we all know, Mrs Flowerday,' said the DCI.

There were a few lines of sloping scrawl in the space provided for a message. Jemima started reading what remained visible. '"Dear Kenneth, I have gained the post of chef at Merry Beggars Hall—"'

'Who is Kenneth?' Lady Hamlash interrupted. She had watched the uproar between her servants in bemusement, clearly unable to follow the cut and thrust of accusation and confession.

'I am, Your Ladyship,' Wells said.

'Really? Is it a Scotch name?'

'Irish, ma'am, originally.'

'I didn't know you were Irish.'

'*Originally*, ma'am. I'm American.'

'Mrs Flowerday?' Bullace's good nature showed the first, faint crack.

Jemima read on. '"—and will join you there as I am sick of paying you for no result."' Jemima could no longer conceal her disappointment in the man she had liked on sight. 'Not only did you know her, she was paying you. Why and how much?' she asked Wells.

'Mrs Flowerday, you are not the detective in the case,' warned Bullace. 'Read, but do not analyse.'

She continued. '"I arrive on December 4, mid-morning. Bring the car to the station."'

Bullace invited comment from Wells, who shook his head.

Jack made full use of the hesitation. 'You don't have to be a detective to see what's what. He knew Madame and she was paying him. Your fancy-piece, was she, Kenneth?'

'Remember where you are, Jack,' the butler admonished.

Jack took no heed. 'He didn't want her here, course he didn't, 'cause he'd found other fish to fry. But she came anyway, so he got rid of her. That's all you need to know, Chief Inspector.'

Bullace cut in drily, 'We need to know a very great deal more than that, young man.'

'Not when you hear what else I have to say. When I knew what had killed Madame, I went to his shed, where he sits half the day—'

'That is not true!' Wells looked ready to lash out.

Bullace frowned, inviting Jack to finish what he was saying.

'I took the pan he cooked that stuff up in and what was left in the bottom was enough to kill a dog.'

Bullace let this sink in. 'A moment ago, Mr Wells, you assured us you had scraped the pan clean.'

'I did.'

Jack sneered. 'Minute she got here, poor Madame was a goner. Why else burn that postcard?'

DS Pretty had slipped out at some point, and now returned carrying a saucepan so bent and blackened, it reminded Jemima of the pots one saw hanging over Romany fires on Epsom Downs, on race day. A stench invaded the room.

'Thick as molasses, sir,' he said to his superior.

Wells looked punch-drunk. 'I cleaned it out, at the midden heap, with a trowel. Go check… I swear it.'

'Take it away.' Sir Finchley looked close to retching.

Bullace snatched the pan from his deputy, strode to the nearest window, hauled the curtains aside and raised the sash. He flung the pan outside then faced the room; he too snatching for breath. He also looked furious.

'DS Pretty, arrest Kenneth Wells on suspicion of the unlawful killing of Madame Marie Guyen.'

The next few seconds were pure chaos. Wells, evading Pretty, snatched the whisky bottle off the mantelpiece and hurled it into the fireplace, where it smashed in a ball of flame. Concentrated coal-tar being highly flammable, the carpet ignited. Sir Finchley, Crosby, Bullace and Pretty raced each other to stamp out the flames.

Jack, shoved aside by Pretty, fell to the floor. On her way to help him, Jemima saw the fringing on one of the armchairs had caught light. She snatched a cushion and beat out the flames. Lady

Hamlash seized another cushion and came to help, though she mostly bashed Jemima's arms and shoulder. Dinah, meanwhile, screamed at a pitch that reminded Jemima of her daughter, Molly, playing a piercing note on a school recorder.

DCI Bullace shouted for everyone to stand back. 'The fire is out. Dinah, whatever your name is, cease your noise.'

It was at least a minute before Dinah fell silent.

It was only then they discovered that Kenneth Wells had gone.

Chapter Fifteen

In the great hall, a blast of icy air implied the route Wells had taken out of the house.

The door to the telephone room stood open. Following Bullace and Pretty, still in her stockinged feet, Jemima discovered her hunch had been correct. The telephone room was tucked between the great hall and a spacious, high-roofed conservatory. It was too dim to see much, even with the telephone-room light on, but it was obvious its door stood open to the elements. Wells had to be heading across the country park.

'Secure the cars,' Bullace ordered Pretty. 'I wouldn't put it past the rascal to try that means of escape.' Finding Jemima behind him, he made a gruff sound. 'Mrs Flowerday, have the butler call Saxonchurch police station, tell them we've a man on the run.'

Jemima conveyed the message to Crosby. The call was made while the detectives searched the grounds, checking their vehicle was locked, and Sir Finchley's Rolls Royce Silver Ghost also, before securing the garage where Lady Hamlash's car stood. That done, they invaded Wells's cottage. Jemima followed, stopping at the threshold and peering in through the open door.

She doubted Wells had risked going back. His jacket and cap were gone from their hooks, but it was likely he'd worn them to come over to the house, perhaps leaving them handy in the great hall. After a search, and the confiscation of a passport and wallet Pretty discovered in the bedroom, the detectives returned to the main house. There, DCI Bullace split the men into two groups to scour the building from top to bottom. His team consisted of Crosby and Sir Finchley. Pretty had to make do with Jack.

Bullace's search party came downstairs having found no sign of the runaway.

Pretty and Jack returned from the servants' wing with an identical report.

'Any cellars here?' Bullace asked.

'Blocked off years ago, after they flooded,' replied Crosby.

Sir Finchley proposed that Wells would by now be on the open road. 'Heading for the railway station. Good riddance. This family has endured scandal enough.'

'Murder is murder,' was Bullace's reply. He was short of breath and shorter of patience.

'Until a post-mortem is conducted, that is pure speculation,' Sir Finchley countered, adding for reasons not entirely clear, 'the Chief Inspector of Constabulary is a personal friend of my father-in-law.' He announced his intention to return to Brabberton Manor and gave his mother a perfunctory kiss on the cheek.

Shortly after, they heard the throaty purr of his car.

Bullace ordered DS Pretty to have Wells's description telegraphed to all local police and railway stations. He then suggested the ladies should go to bed. 'DS Pretty will remain.' He indicated the porter's chair by the front door. 'He will keep guard until he's relieved in the morning. I bid you a gentle good night.'

After a nip of hot brandy in the servants' hall, Jemima went upstairs behind Mrs Newson. The housekeeper hauled herself up, exhausted beyond the power of speech. Dinah led the way with a lantern. The girl had tried one last time to claim the murder of Marie Guyen, but DS Pretty, returning from the telephone room and a call to police headquarters, had growled, 'Leave it be or I'll arrest you for wasting police time.'

The three women parted in the north-wing corridor, each to their room. Jemima had the furthest to go, and the shoes she'd put back on downstairs felt cold and damp. Since the lantern went with Dinah, she fumbled in complete darkness and found her door only after trying to get inside a linen closet. Her bedroom was frigid. Imagine, seventeen hours ago, she'd been on her way to Liverpool Street railway station, excited at the prospect of an adventure. Hoping to earn a neat fifty pounds.

Shutting her door behind her, she eased off one shoe, then the other. A floorboard creaked. She sensed movement behind her, but before she could even gasp a hand clamped over her mouth and an arm came across her body.

'Not a sound, Mrs Flowerday, because I have a knife and my God darn fingers are shaking so badly, they might just slip. Stay calm and do as I say.'

Chapter Sixteen

'Do as I say' translated as 'Sit down, turn on your torch and don't speak.'

'I don't have a torch,' Jemima whispered, feeling for the edge of her bed. 'It was Jack's and I gave it back.'

'God darn,' Wells muttered.

'So you said a moment ago.'

'Shush! D'you have money?' She heard him clear his throat. 'Mrs Flowerday…?'

'Am I to speak or not?'

'Answer the question.'

'A little.'

'Shush!'

She whispered, 'A little.'

'This is no joke, ma'am.'

'I'm perfectly aware of that. A woman lies dead and you, the prime suspect, are holding a blade to my throat. Or so you claim, though I cannot feel it.'

'A gardener will always have a pocketknife on his person,' Wells said huskily.

'But you aren't a gardener, are you? Nor, I suspect, a cold-blooded killer.'

'You are right.' Wells stepped back. 'You don't think I harmed Marie?'

To be frank, her opinion had spent the night fluctuating. 'Perhaps not, but that you're a liar – definitely.' Now seated on the edge of her bed, Jemima found her confidence. 'You swore you had no friendship with Marie, but were in her pay. You claim Dinah pesters you, yet you are clearly engaged in a passionate liaison with her. Oh, don't,' she snapped, cutting off his denial.

'Dinah. What the devil was she up to, confessing in front of the household?'

'Saving your skin, I imagine. She's in love with you.' Jemima felt the dip of the mattress as Wells sat down next to her.

'I can't help what she imagines, Mrs Flowerday.'

She told him not to insult her intelligence. 'I saw you kissing her, so unless you were giving her mouth-to-mouth resuscitation from a standing posture, I'd say you were sending distinctly mixed messages.'

'Okay. Okay. But it's not what you think.'

Jemima snorted. 'Said every false man from the days of Adam.'

'Shush! Listen, I'm no seducer. No murderer either and I'm damned if I'll go to jail or be strung up to appease an embittered footman and a maidservant suffering romantic hysteria. Same goes for a DCI with his eye on promotion to Scotland Yard.'

'How do you know DCI Bullace is aiming for Scotland Yard?'

'Because they all are. Just as you'd love to work for a Paris fashion house.'

'I don't in the least wish to, but let's not talk about me. What will you do now, Mr Wells? You asked me for money, so I presume you have rail travel in mind?'

He shifted position and she sensed his defeat. Without his passport, he was stuck on these shores. Without his wallet he was stuck full stop. Wells was not dressed for winter travel and his jacket smelled of smoke, tobacco and tar.

She said, 'I would like to help, but I have to know who I am helping.'

'Fine.' If he nodded, she couldn't see. 'You were right. Marie and I knew each other in New York. We came to England together, and she was supposed to hole up in London, not turn up here. There's more to do on her behalf, and for that I need to be free.'

'To achieve justice… will you tell me what that is?'

'Please don't ask, Mrs Flowerday. Do you need any more proof how dangerous curiosity can be? Be content to know that Marie was a nurse in the war and in a field hospital, she met the love of her life. That love did not prosper and there is an account to be paid. There's still more to do, vital work, and I have to get clear. I'd sure appreciate a loan as they'll be staking out my cottage.'

'They've already searched it.'

He gave a '*tsh*' of frustration. 'Jack will be lurking behind a bush with a pitchfork, I don't doubt, having already painted a picture of me slipping a lethal dose into Marie's coffee pot.'

'It was never in the pot.'

Her self-assurance hit home. He asked, 'You know, or you're guessing?'

'When is the pivot-point when a guess becomes a certainty? I know how it happened.'

A creak from the other side of the bedroom wall silenced them. After a moment in which they hardly breathed, she muttered, 'Mice.' Old houses like this always settled at night while the mice who dwelt within their walls did the opposite. Jemima was telling Wells about the footsteps she'd overheard crossing the hall prior to Marie's collapse, when the sound came again.

'What room is next door?' Wells whispered.

'The laundry closet.'

Again, they held their breath and Jemima reflected how loud one's heartbeat seemed to be at moments like this.

The tension galvanised Wells to action. 'I have to get on a train. Give me what money you have and I promise, on my honour, I'll pay you back.'

In the darkness, Jemima located her purse, knowing that by advancing him even a shilling, she was aiding and abetting a suspected murderer. Despite her vexation with Wells, she sensed a case being built against him. An unjust one. She put two pound notes and some silver into his cupped hands. 'I must keep something back to tip the servants when I leave.'

'For their good nature and obliging ways?'

'Don't be unfair. Why should they welcome strangers, considering all?'

In a jingle of coins, Wells dropped the money into his jacket pocket and Jemima thought about the oilskin coat she'd benefited from, wondering if she could fetch it for him without disturbing DS Pretty. She was about to voice the thought when they heard low voices coming from the direction of the main stairs. Male voices.

'Help me, Mrs Flowerday,' Wells breathed.

A paralysing panic crept across Jemima, as she'd experienced many years ago in the London department store where fire had broken out. She'd been working there, the most junior of apprentices, sent up to count gloves on the third floor. As alarms rang and smoke billowed up the stairwell, she had found herself trapped. She had shut herself in the stockroom with the gloves, a decision that would have been fatal had not a strange clarity seized her. As if she'd stepped out of her own body, she'd pictured the outside of the building and seen her salvation. Knocking down a tower of glove boxes, she'd uncovered a small window. A stouter woman would never have got through, but fourteen-year-old Jemima had managed to wriggle on to a parapet from which she was plucked to safety.

The memory still had the power to terrify, but it got her moving. With the voices just yards away, she groped for the bedroom door and turned the key, locking herself and Wells in. Moving to the window, she levered up the sash, gasping at the inrush of freezing air. Wells was at her side.

She said, 'Your tool-shed roof is six feet below.'

Whispering, 'Pray for me,' he swung his legs over the sill. Jemima heard the desperate scraping of boot soles on icy roof tiles. A moment later, a thud proved that he had made it, one way or another, to the ground.

To Jemima's relief, the crunching of those same boots on loose stones and a dark shape moving through the walled garden assured her that Kenneth Wells was making his second escape of the night. She reflected on the choice she'd made, though not for long.

A fist bashed against the door, DS Pretty's voice shouting, 'Open up!'

Jemima juggled her options. Escape likewise? Get into bed and feign sleep?

In the end she chose the best protection from the charge of helping a wanted man. Feminine frailty.

DS Pretty and Albert Crosby joined their weight to force the door open. No easy feat as Mrs Jemima Flowerday lay curled up against it, apparently in a dead faint.

Chapter Seventeen

'The scoundrel could have murdered you in cold blood.' Mrs Newson placed a cup of tea in front of Jemima.

It was her third cup of the morning. Wrapped in a shawl, she was keeping up the pretence of a terrified survivor. Pale cheeks and heavy eyelids required no acting.

After Mr Crosby and DS Pretty had found her, a truckle bed had been set up for Jemima in Mrs Newson's room. Sleep, so needed, had evaded her as disjointed images raced past her inner eye: Marie Guyen's last moments; Wells hurling a bottle into the fireplace; the shock of finding him waiting for her in the dark. And just as she was slipping into the sweet abyss, a thought had her sitting bolt upright. Two deaths at Merry Beggars Hall could not arise out of pure chance. They must – *must* – be connected. But how?

As she drank her sweet tea, she wished Mrs Newson would fall silent. A vain hope.

'When I came out of my room to see DS Pretty and Mr Crosby outside your door, I won't deny it, Mrs Flowerday, I expected I would be looking at the second corpse of the day.' The housekeeper shuddered. 'I never imagined Wells capable of attacking a lady.'

'He didn't,' Jemima said for the third or fourth time. She might as well have saved her breath.

'Goes to show, you cannot judge by a person's looks. Poor Jack is no Greek statue, but he's trustworthy as the day is long, and you should remember that, young lady.' The last comment was for Dinah, who was present.

'I hope Mr Wells is miles away,' Dinah responded.

'I don't see how that can be, unless he's learned to fly,' Mrs Newson came back. 'A person can only run so far on a winter's night.'

Jemima privately agreed. During the early hours, the temperature had plummeted, bringing a penetrating frost. Wells could have reached Beggars Heath or Saxonchurch easily enough, but he'd find all the railway stations as far as Ipswich under guard. Staying on the road, catching a ride in a dawn milk lorry, might be his best hope.

'Mr Wells is a proper gent. I know that better than anybody.' Dinah leaned her knuckles on the table, knuckles that were dusted with grey. She'd been sent to sweep the drawing-room carpet and scour the fireplace of all traces of last night's conflagration. A mutinous light shone in her eye, until Jack came in with news that a horse-drawn hearse was pulling up outside.

'For Madame's body.'

The following minutes took on a grim character, the servants standing with their heads lowered as the pall was carried out. Madame Marie Guyen was covered with a sheet.

Before the hearse was beyond the park gates, Jemima overheard Albert Crosby informing Mrs Newson that she must clear out Madame's room. 'Sir Finchley's orders, communicated privately to me before he left last night.'

Jemima put her foot down. 'That room holds evidence and, for another thing, Madame Guyen's possessions belong to her next of kin, and until they are contacted you are responsible for safeguarding them, Mr Crosby. Ignore me, and I shall seek out DS Pretty.' When she'd come into the servants' hall a short while ago, Pretty had been gulping down a large cup of tea. He had certainly not resembled a ray of sunshine. So close to capturing Wells that second time, he had the air of a man who knows that while his brain might still be athletic, his body is not. He'd since gone out again to take a turn around the park, 'To unrumple my muscles after a night in that cussed chair,' as he put it, though most likely to search for footprints.

The consequence of Jemima's interference was that Marie Guyen's bedroom was locked with Jemima and Mrs Newson as witnesses, the key added to the collection that hung from the housekeeper's belt. The butler muttered that he hoped Mrs Flowerday was satisfied.

'On this occasion, I am.' Jemima hesitated. From somewhere fairly close came a rhythmic thud. It sounded like somebody pumping a wooden dolly in a wash tub. 'Is the laundress in today?'

She was told no, it was Beth they could hear, doing the sheets. 'I'd prefer you leave her to it and come back to the warm, Mrs Flowerday. I don't know why' – Mrs Newson sighed as they returned to the servants' hall – 'but the sight of a hearse makes me want to reach for the teapot.'

At this moment, DS Pretty came in from the kitchen garden, stamping white frost off his boots, and gladly accepted the offer of another brew. 'It's cold enough out there to freeze treacle.'

Jemima had drunk her fill of tea, but joined them at the table, content to sit and observe. As tea was poured, the milk jug passed around, she pictured Marie Guyen as she had been yesterday, seated in Mr Crosby's chair, declaring, 'I have come a very great way to be heard.'

Picture it. The gold-rimmed cup, coffee in first then hot milk, Beth pouring. A brown sugar cube dropped from the tongs by Marie herself. *Splash*. Beth, plodding clockwise around the table, filling teacups one after the other. *The Weekend Sleuth* liked to tease its readers with philosophical notions of motive versus opportunity. Did one trump the other?

Mrs Newson could have acquired a miniscule amount of the fatal tincture from the conservatory and got it into Marie Guyen's coffee here at the table, but where was her motive?

Beth had brewed the coffee unsupervised, but she was a guileless child and anyway, had reason to like Madame, who was kind to her.

Dinah, with less opportunity to acquire the poison, had the strongest motive in her love for Wells, if she had discovered his prior relationship with Marie.

Wells himself lacked obvious motive, but had all the opportunity in the world.

Mr Crosby? He had motive aplenty. He also had free access to the conservatory where the tincture was stored and had been in the kitchen while the coffee was being made.

Lady Hamlash also had motive in spades and could go in and out of the conservatory as she pleased. She could not, however, enter the servants' wing without provoking a kerfuffle. *If* Jemima factored in the footsteps she'd heard as she came down the stairs, she could rule out Beth, Dinah, Mrs Newson, Jack, Mr Crosby and Lady Hamlash.

And since she was certain how the poison had got into Marie's cup, this process of deduction ended back at Wells – whom she believed to be innocent – or she must consider the involvement of somebody outside this house.

Dinah shuffled her chair closer to Jemima's and said in a low voice, 'I know what you're thinking.'

'I doubt it, Dinah.'

'You're thinking you've got away with a pack of lies.'

'Have a care.'

Dinah's eyes glittered feverishly. 'It's a cock-and-bull tale, you being knocked *on-conscious* by Mr Wells. I know you're telling fibs. You had your eye on him from the start.'

'My dear girl, not every woman turns giddy at the sight of a peaked cap and button-up jacket.' As the glittering gaze narrowed into malice, Jemima sighed. 'Oh, well, it's your heart to pierce upon the thorn. How I ended up on the floor of my bedroom is a perfect mystery to me.'

Dinah leaned right into the air Jemima breathed. 'Did you know Beth and I had to sleep in the same room last night?'

Jemima wasn't sure where this was leading.

'Normally, little dim-witty sleeps down here since we've always had women-cooks to keep an eye on her. She can't be down here now with only Mr Crosby and Jack for company, so Mrs Newson put her in my room.'

'That's understandable.' There was nothing unusual in two maid-servants sharing a room.

Dinah's lip curled. 'She wet the bed.'

'Oh, how awful for her.' The energetic pummelling at the wash tub took on a new significance. 'Still, I'm not surprised, considering what the poor child witnessed and suffered yesterday.'

'Awful for me too! I had to fetch new sheets.'

Dinah paused, and Jemima now realised where this conversation was going.

'The linen closet,' Jemima said. It lay right next to her room. 'Come.' She beckoned to Dinah to follow her out into the passageway. Moving a safe distance from the door to the servants' hall, she folded her arms. 'You overheard me talking.'

Dinah nodded fiercely. 'With my Kenneth. I was getting fresh sheets and I heard you saying you know who killed Madame Guyen.'

'Those weren't my words. I said I knew *how* it happened.'

'I heard Kenneth ask you to help him and that's why I stopped where I was and didn't shout out. You let him out the window, didn't you?'

Jemima insisted she had no memory of last night.

Dinah sniffed. 'It's obvious to me who put that nasty stuff in Madame's coffee.'

Jemima was all ears. 'Who, in your opinion?'

Dinah strung out the moment. 'I bet you'd like to know.'

'Only if you wish to tell me. Ha, let me guess. It's you, confessing again.'

Dinah flashed a contemptuous look. 'No point doing that now Mr Wells has gone. I'm accusing you, Mrs Flowerday.'

'Me?' Jemima had not anticipated this.

Dinah had forgotten to lower her voice and the servants' hall door had opened. DS Pretty had stepped out into the passageway. Whatever was said next would be heard by him and everyone still at the table. Dinah kept talking.

'You could have got into the conservatory and found the bottle of tobacco-stuff. Dead easy for you to have poured some into the coffee pot afterwards.'

Mm. Only, I know the coffee pot is innocent, Jemima thought. Aware she was now playing to a very alert audience, Jemima answered in her clearest voice, 'When Madame choked, I was sitting four feet from the head of the table. I'd have had to practically spreadeagle myself to meddle with her coffee.'

Dinah played a countermove. 'But what if Madame drank her coffee too fast, and it made her faint. You ran to her side and while she was out of her senses, you spilled tobacco-juice into her mouth and killed her.'

Actually, that was rather ingenious. Jemima's opinion of Dinah rose several notches.

Not so Mrs Newson's. 'Dinah Pullen!' The housekeeper squeezed past DS Pretty. 'Speak such slander in my hearing again and I'll send for your father to fetch you home.'

Dinah said she wouldn't mind a bit if someone took her home. She denied it was slander. 'She' – she meant Jemima – 'was leaning right over Madame and afterwards went trotting about the place, muddling up the evidence.'

'I was trying to conserve evidence,' Jemima protested. 'If it comes to it, Mrs Newson could have done what you have accused me of. But why on earth would either of us wish to kill a cook? What would I have against a woman I had not set eyes on before that day?'

'You come from London, don't you?' Dinah folded her arms with the air of a criminal barrister who has landed his point.

Mr Crosby emerged just then from his private room, and catching the reference to London, his gaze shifted between Dinah and Jemima. 'What's going on? It sounds like business as usual at Billingsgate fish market.'

Dinah jerked a thumb at Jemima. '*She* comes from London and so did Madame Guyen. Your brother did too, Mr Crosby. That's three in all and it's a well-known fact, there's no such thing as coincidence.'

'Well-known fact, is it?' DS Pretty reached into the conversation. 'Go on then, make your point, young miss.'

Dinah didn't hesitate. 'Two of them are dead while she's right as ninepence. You should take Mrs Flowerday in for questioning.'

Jemima gaped at Dinah in awe. In the wee hours of the night, she had conjectured that the deaths were linked, but this girl had steamed ahead of her. It was blindingly obvious. *London.* There wasn't time to think it over, as Jemima was being regarded by her audience with varying degrees of uncertainty. She held out her wrists. 'If you agree with Dinah, DS Pretty, put on the cuffs. I am ready.'

'No need at all,' the sergeant replied. 'A police constable found me a few minutes ago, as I returned from my perambulations. A post-mortem is taking place on Madame Guyen as we speak. So how about we all hold off making accusations until we get the results?'

Mr Crosby wholeheartedly endorsed that. He went out with the intention of informing Her Ladyship of the inquest, only to come back within a minute to say that the telephone had rung for DS Pretty. 'Your chief inspector is holding on the line.'

Pretty went out and returned as Jemima helped to remove the tea things. He was followed by Crosby, and he looked very grave. He said to Jemima, Mrs Newson and Dinah, 'You may wish to be seated, ladies.'

Jemima felt a sinking sensation. *They've caught Wells. He's for it, and so am I.*

Everyone waited as DS Pretty rocked on his heels, once, twice, summoning words.

'Not an hour ago, the stationmaster at Beggars Heath noticed an object on the railway track, on the upline. He found evidence of' – Pretty cleared his throat – 'of an unfortunate incident.'

'Incident?' Mrs Newson queried in a voice of dread.

'On the railway, yes.'

'This is no use,' Jemima burst out. 'Better to say nothing if you won't give the facts.'

'Mangled flesh on the rail.' DS Pretty said it fast then nodded apologetically at Mrs Newson, who had lost what little colour she had regained in the last hours. 'The stationmaster retrieved a man's tweed jacket, blood-stained, in the pocket of which was two pounds, seven and sixpence, and a receipt for coal-tar and common elm tincture, made out to Mr K. Wells—'

Dinah's screams filled the room.

Chapter Eighteen

Once brandy had been administered and Dinah's distress reduced to a low keening, DS Pretty gave his professional opinion. Wells must have been trying to board the 3 o'clock milk train on its way through Beggars Heath. 'It trundles through to Ipswich, then on to London.' The coaches carrying the churns had slatted sides and it was not unknown for foolhardy types to grab on for a free ride. 'But with it being so cold…' Pretty left the rest to their imagination. 'Local bobbies are walking the track, searching for further remains.'

'Will charges against Wells now be dropped?' Mr Crosby asked.

'He was never formally charged.'

'What about Madame Guyen's death?' This was Jemima asking, and the tremor in her voice was unfaked. She should have made Wells hand himself in. Should never have loaned him money. The thought of him clinging to a frozen railway car, unable to get a foothold, was harrowing. 'If you've lost your chief witness, what of her?'

'Her inquest will be opened by the coroner,' Pretty explained patiently. 'Opened and adjourned while we continue our investigation, Mrs Flowerday.'

Jack limped in, bringing the whiff of silver cleaner. From the streaks on his apron, he'd been polishing cutlery. His sanctuary, the boot room, was next to the laundry.

'Something's missing, has anyone noticed?' he said.

'If this is a tasteless reference to Mr Wells, we have just heard,' Jemima said curtly.

'Eh?' Jack looked genuinely bemused.

'He's dead, so now you've got what you want!' Dinah hurled at him.

'What? Who's dead?' Jack demanded. 'I was asking, has anybody noticed that the stable-yard clock hasn't chimed?'

The question felt trivial to the point of insensitive, until Jemima realised this wasn't another example of Jack's facetiousness. Thinking about it, she hadn't heard the clock since five o'clock yesterday. 'Or should I say, ten to five. Why would that be?'

"Cause it was Wells's job to wind it,' Jack answered. 'It always has been the gardener's last task of the day, before the light goes. By four thirty, it's too dark to see, so he should have wound it by the time Madame took bad. And where was he?' He answered his own question. 'Hiding away, mending that old bicycle.'

Nobody contradicted him, and Jack continued eagerly, 'Fixing his means of escape, on account of him knowing full well what was about to happen.'

'Show me that bicycle, lad,' Pretty commanded. 'If it's still there. Stay here, the rest of you, and don't chatter among yourselves. Mrs Flowerday, now you've had chance to recover your nerves, I require a statement from you regarding your last sight of Mr Wells, in your room, last night.'

She inclined her head. 'Of course. What I can remember.'

After Pretty and Jack left, Jemima asked if she might relight her bedroom fire. 'I might as well get on with the work I came here to do. At some point, I shall need to measure Her Ladyship and have a private conversation with her. No, don't trouble Dinah.' Mrs Newson had been about to chivvy the girl to fetch the coal scuttle. 'I'll find what I need. I know how to light a fire.'

Mrs Newson wouldn't hear of it. 'Moving about will do Dinah more good than sitting with her face stuck in a handkerchief. Dinah, I don't know what you think you were to Mr Wells, but you'd best face facts, he's gone.'

What Dinah was to Wells. Good question. Jemima mulled over it when she was once again in her bedroom, looking out over the walled garden. Was the girl an amusement to pass the time or his accomplice? Jemima couldn't deceive herself; she had enabled Wells to go freely to his death under the wheels of the milk train. And if, as Jack stated, Wells had been planning his departure ahead of Marie's death, the shadow of suspicion reattached itself to the American. Never had Jemima felt less the canny sleuth and more the clumsy meddler. It was with the utmost difficulty that she fixed her mind on the fabrics and trimmings for Lady Hamlash's evening gowns. Mrs Newson had promised to speak with Her Ladyship and set a time for Jemima to take measurements.

Searching for a pencil in her pocket, Jemima found the postcard Jack had retrieved from Wells's cottage. In the chaos of last night, she'd forgotten she still had it.

'"November twenty-fourth the something-something hotel, W2."'

It felt strange, reading the words of a dead woman to a dead man. Though, in the light of day 'something-something' was clearly 'The Royal Darnley Hotel'. Jemima knew the place. It was on Inverness Terrace, off Bayswater Road, opposite one of the gates into Kensington Gardens. She and Vicky had been there a few times to meet an old friend for tea. Rereading Marie Guyen's cryptic message, Jemima tried to form a picture of the sender's relationship with the recipient.

It began 'Dear Kenneth' – so first-name terms. She had got the chef's job at Merry Beggars Hall, Marie said. Was that a surprise to Wells, or even a shock? The message was too brief to reach a conclusion but there was no ambiguity over the fact that Marie was paying Wells and was tired of getting nothing for it. What exactly had she been paying for? All Jemima could reasonably extract was that Wells and Marie had enjoyed – was that the right word? – a complicated, mutually dependent relationship. Had Marie threatened to cut off the money, spurring Wells to violence? That felt unlikely, since a man in the pay of someone generally wishes that person to stay alive. Wells had no striking reason to want Marie Guyen dead. But were they friends or lovers? Bound by passion and jealous natures? Or was it business only?

Jemima was shaking her head over the unanswered questions when the stable-yard clock chimed twelve. Jack must have taken over the job of winding it. She checked her watch. It was dead on midday; he must have decided the ritual of 'ten minutes fast' had outlived its use. She was on the verge of going down to see if Lady Hamlash was ready to receive her, when a knock at her bedroom door pre-empted her.

It was Dinah. 'Her Ladyship says she'll see you now, Mrs Flowerday.'

Jemima picked up her sketchbook and workbag. In silence, they made their way down. As they crossed the hall, Dinah pacing ahead, Jemima attuned to the girl's footsteps. Clomp-clomp, two red herrings, unlike her own contact with the floor. Jemima's glacé leather shoes, kept for best and for indoor wear, had a narrow heel and a leather sole.

'My word,' she breathed. 'If I had to accuse anybody of flitting across this hall in the interval before Marie Guyen's death, I would point at myself.'

Two days ago, she'd have laughed. She was not laughing now.

As Dinah raised her fist to knock at the drawing-room door, it flew open and a woman strode out. Younger than Lady Hamlash by many years, she waited for Dinah to scuttle backwards and bob a curtsey before saying, 'Her Ladyship's fire is getting low. More coal needed.'

Jemima heard Dinah say, 'Very good, Lady Olivia.'

Aha. Lady Olivia Hamlash, the daughter-in-law. Jemima's skilled eye appraised Lady Olivia's outfit: a suit of Scottish tweed, better cut than was usual for the English upper classes. A silk blouse, a brooch at the neck inset with cloudy diamonds which struck the correct chord for this hour of the day. All the shine was in the lady's red-blonde hair. Curling irons and glycerine, Jemima surmised, applied by an experienced maid. Lady Olivia wasn't beautiful, but the label 'handsome' might be applied.

She accorded Jemima a slight nod as she walked past her towards the door hidden in the oak panelling. She knotted a headscarf under her chin as she went and she was accompanied by a discreet hint of gardenia.

Rapping against the servants' door, Lady Olivia called out, 'Crosby, fetch my coat. I am ready to leave.'

What was the place they were staying at... Brabberton Manor? One stop up the line from Beggars Heath though of course, Lady Olivia would have been driven here in comfort. Jemima watched, amused despite everything, as Sir Finchley's wife admitted herself into the servants' quarters, loudly demanding, 'Anybody there? I don't have all day. My coat!'

Jemima predicted she'd reappear accompanied by a chauffeur, who would look forlorn at being deprived of his second cup of tea. When the lady came out alone a few minutes later, buttoning up a duster coat, Jemima thought – surely she doesn't drive herself? They have a Silver Ghost, hardly a lady's motor.

Defying Jemima's assumptions, Lady Olivia fished a pair of leather gauntlets from her pocket and pulled them on. Without introducing herself, she called across to Jemima, 'I'm sitting down to a game of bridge at eleven. The cards detest unpunctuality. You are staring at my coat?'

Jemima admitted it. 'It seems rather heavy and I'm wondering if it hampers your feet on the car's pedals.'

'You are entirely right. It's a horrid coat, but I stupidly left my caped silk one in the London house. There was a tear to mend – I could have asked you, couldn't I? You're the dressmaker, yes? Lady Winterfold's daughter-in-law?'

Dinah coming out with coal dust on her apron saved Jemima the need to reply.

Lady Olivia clapped her gloved hands at the maid. 'Open up. Quick-quick.'

Dinah dashed to get to the front door ahead of Lady Olivia, and Jemima tried not to gasp. Lady Olivia's impatient footsteps were a duplication of those she'd heard yesterday as she came down for tea. She craned forward, taking a mental photograph of the fast-departing shoes. They were dyed-black kidskin and with each planting of the wearer's foot, they made a brushing sound followed by a metallic click as the heel went down.

Brush-click, brush-click. *You were here yesterday at ten minutes to five, Lady Olivia Hamlash.* Jemima had not only worked out the method of killing, she had identified the killer. It was time to seek out DS Pretty or his boss.

Not at this moment, however. Closing the front door on Lady Olivia, Dinah shot Jemima a look of reproof. 'What are you waiting for, Mrs Flowerday? Her Ladyship expected you five minutes ago.'

113

Chapter Nineteen

Her Ladyship sat by the fire, though not in the armchair whose fringes had been set alight the night before. That one was pushed up against the wall, draped with calico. Ada Hamlash got to her feet, giving the impression that, far from waiting, she had slipped into a semi-slumber.

'Oh, Mrs Flowerday. Good morning. I do hope you slept.'

Jemima gave a disingenuous nod. Her mind was still whirling. Lady Olivia, slayer of Madame Marie Guyen? It felt too Gothic, and yet, as she had boasted to Wells in the car, she had a pitch-perfect ear for sound.

'What an unutterably dreadful day,' Lady Hamlash was saying. 'First the cook, now my chauffeur.' Wells's ill-fated attempt to board a moving train had evidently been explained to Lady Hamlash. 'When I said my prayers last night, it was with the hope there would be no more tragedy here. Poor young man.'

Jemima agreed. One blow after another. Privately, she wondered how this woman would cope with a daughter-in-law as a potential murderess?

'I found Wells most congenial,' she added, feeling she ought to say something.

'Oh, yes, and so polite. Americans often are, you know. So, so shocking. What must you think of us, Mrs Flowerday?'

Jemima mentioned her encounter with Lady Olivia. The firing of a powerful motor car engine at the front of the house took Lady Hamlash to the window.

'There she goes, dear Olivia, off to join her bridge four. She came to call and brought me some jam.' Lady Hamlash indicated a pot on one of the nesting tables beside her chair. 'Not her own making, though it has managed to be rhubarb even so.'

'And she's her own chauffeur,' Jemima observed, adding in a throwaway fashion, 'I imagine she can come and go as she likes. She could call here at any odd hour.'

'Yes, but generally she does not.' Lady Hamlash stepped away from the window. 'Olivia and I share few common interests. When Edgar wrote home that they were engaged, I was resigned, but not jubilant. Perhaps I shouldn't say this, but you have a face that encourages confidences, Mrs Flowerday.'

Edgar... the son who had not returned from the war?

Jemima said, 'Surely, you mean it was Sir Finchley she became engaged to?'

'I mean Edgar. Olivia was to marry my elder boy only she found herself bereft, as did so many wartime fiancées.'

'I had no idea.' With a start, Jemima recalled Wells telling her how Marie had nursed during the war and in a field hospital, where she'd met the love of her life. Had that love perhaps been Sir Edgar Hamlash, creating a bitter rivalry between Marie and Lady Olivia? If Lady Olivia had been here yesterday, with or without Lady Hamlash's knowledge, she had the opportunity and now, a clear motive for harming Marie. Knowing better than to ask straight out, Jemima took an oblique approach. 'It's unusual, even these days, to see a lady driving herself. But what freedom it must bring. I'm envious.'

Lady Hamlash batted this away. 'My daughter-in-law operated an ambulance at the Front, so our lanes hold no dread for her. Added to which, the Silver Ghost has no starter handle.' Jemima must have looked baffled as Lady Hamlash explained, 'No need for a brawny forearm on a cranking handle. The motor starts from the dashboard, though Finchley insists on taking the wheel when they travel together, explaining the finer points of driving to her as they lurch along. Shall we start?'

'Of course.' Jemima took a tape measure from her workbag. 'Are we remaining here, Lady Hamlash, or would you prefer to retire to your room?'

'No, far too cold upstairs.'

Measuring Lady Hamlash took almost to the 1 o'clock lunch hour. During her department-store career, Jemima had risen to become a senior fitter in Ladies' Town Attire and in that time, she'd learned a vital rule: Look twice, measure thrice, say nothing. Helping her client undress to her undergarments uncovered an elastic-fronted corset extending from Lady Hamlash's bust to a point halfway down her thighs. Jemima had departed from her motto and suggested removing it.

Her Ladyship had declined, saying, 'I like my clothes made to my daytime shape, not the one my body assumes when I'm in bed.'

'But you wish for the latest mode, and the new shapes require no heavy underpinning.'

'But *I* require heavy underpinning,' was Her Ladyship's quelling response.

Jemima noted all the measurements from shoulder to hip. After Lady Hamlash was dressed again, she pulled up a small table and shared her design ideas.

'I see no need to put you in black. I favour midnight, mauve and malachite.'

Lady Hamlash took this in. 'You mean dark blue, purple and green?'

Jemima smiled. 'Touché. Insets of embroidered velvet and lace at the neck, wrists and hem.' She turned a page in her sketchbook. 'The ideas I've drawn out are bang up-to-date, waists dropped low, hems at mid-calf. I want your new gowns to be comfortable as well as flattering.'

A frown corrugated Lady Hamlash's brow. 'I don't think I have dressed for evening and been comfortable since I came out of the nursery.'

'Times have changed,' Jemima said gravely. 'We are no longer martyrs to boning and lacing. We can inflate our lungs, drive motor cars, even dance without being in agony.'

Lady Hamlash began leafing through the sketchbook and Jemima took the opportunity to take a turn around the room. The walls were peppered with botanical prints, but curiosity drew her to the grand piano where, last night, she had noticed some framed photographs. Three men, two of them in uniform.

By balance of probability, they were Lady Hamlash's late husband and her two sons in happier days. In one picture a gent in a top hat and a huntsman's coat sat astride a thoroughbred. That had to be the late Sir Rufus Hamlash, he of the stopwatch and clock-tampering habit. In a second picture, the same man was seated in a lounge whose ceiling was supported by pillars. His starched collar and a sweeper moustache dated the picture to the High Edwardian era. The portraits either side were of young men in army officer's uniform. Jemima bent forward to make out the insignia on the cap badges.

'Suffolk Regiment.' Lady Hamlash had come over quietly. She

pointed at the right-hand picture. 'My late son, Edgar Vivyan. Wounded in action. He succumbed to his injuries a few days before Christmas, 1917.'

'My deepest commiserations, Lady Hamlash. He was very handsome.'

'Wasn't he? That one—' Lady Hamlash indicated the left-hand portrait, 'is Finchley, whom you have met.'

It was a slimmer, younger Finchley than the one who had been rude to her in this room. With his barbered moustache and the peak of his cap covering the over-large forehead, he was not much less dashing than his brother.

'Captain Finchley Hamlash?' Jemima ventured.

'Lieutenant. Edgar was raised to the rank Major before he died.' Lady Hamlash sighed. 'Edgar was not only the elder, he was the cleverer and the better horseman. Nicer, frankly, in all respects. Names have such power, don't they? Edgar and Vivyan are my family names, whereas my younger son was baptised after a location in London where my late husband's family owned land. Poor Finchley.'

Not exactly *poor*, Jemima reflected. Finchley Hamlash had survived the war, inherited the title and bagged an earl's daughter. A second-hand match, but even so, it was a modern-day fable of the tortoise and the hare. She looked again at Edgar. To give him his full honours, Major Sir Edgar Hamlash, deceased. Chiselled jaw. Deep, soft eyes. A faint, knowing smile. A reaper of hearts, then reaped in his turn?

'This, I presume, is the late Sir Rufus?' Jemima pointed to the Edwardian gentleman seated in a club chair alongside a gilded pillar.

'It is. In the lounge at Bright's of St James's.'

Jemima's pulse gave several hard beats. 'Sir Rufus was a member there?' Bright's Club was where Roland Crosby had worked as a waiter.

'All the men of this family are given membership of Bright's on their twenty-first birthday.'

Jemima could not believe what she was hearing. Sir Finchley Hamlash and Roland Crosby had spent time under the same roof and must have had more than a glancing acquaintance with each other. Had the police made that a line of enquiry, or had she made a stunning discovery?

Lady Hamlash cleared her throat. 'What do we do now that you've taken my measurements?'

Jemima dragged her thoughts back to the task in hand. 'Create patterns and sew toiles. Those being try-outs made from muslin which can be hacked about to your taste. Any thoughts on my designs, Lady Hamlash?'

'Yes. I'll take all three.'

Heavens. Jemima expected to spend at least a day moderating her ideas. That was the usual way. You spent a few hours designing, then twice as long compromising. She hid her relief that her fifty-pound fee had not evaporated. 'You require the gowns by Christmas Eve, Lady Hamlash – or sooner?'

'By the twenty-third. Can you?'

'I will make sure of it. You are aware, I must return to London and have the dresses made up there. There isn't time for me to do it without help, but before I leave, I will have fitted you to perfection.' Jemima glanced towards the fireplace, where the single armchair looked, to her imaginative eye, like a creature deprived of its mate. 'I presume you won't be spending Christmas here, after everything?'

Lady Hamlash seemed surprised by the question. Her Christmas plans would unfold as they always did, she informed Jemima. 'My son and daughter-in-law will join me for their first Christmas as man and wife.'

'They are quite recently married, then?'

'They wed last July. Olivia's parents, the Earl and Countess Rivers, chose the day, and it was the hottest of the year. The church was stifling. Finchley was nervous as a flea and red in the face. There was a moment I thought he might pass out at the altar.'

'Goodness.' Jemima could hardly imagine that the relative newly-weds would aspire to hang their stockings on the frozen bedposts of Merry Beggars Hall. They must dream of spending their first Christmas elsewhere. *Anywhere*. Fearing her thoughts might show, she said hurriedly, 'You have no cook. Won't that present a problem?'

'Crosby is seeking after a replacement,' Lady Hamlash replied. 'He is writing to his sister-in-law to ask if she can make herself available.'

It took a moment for the penny to drop and, this time, Jemima couldn't conceal her astonishment. 'You refer to Mrs Sara Crosby? The late Roland's—'

'Widow. Indeed. She has filled in for us before and is familiar with the kitchen. If she can come, it will make things so much smoother.'

Dead woman's shoes. Jemima smothered a shudder, and said, 'I didn't realise Mrs Crosby was professionally trained.'

'I'm not sure she is,' Lady Hamlash answered, 'but I have never found her wanting. She fits the description "Good, plain cook" well enough.'

Jemima recalled the interview with Sara Crosby in *The Weekend Sleuth*, the widow revealing her intention to soldier on, hinting at the mental suffering that follows a violent bereavement. She had stated, vis-à-vis her husband, 'What he went through in his final moments is more than I can put my mind to.'

It was remarkable – admirable, even – that Sara Crosby would contemplate coming to the place where the grisly remnant of her husband had been found. Did she need work so badly, or was she driven by a desire to know more, to investigate, to uncover?

Perhaps Lady Hamlash had discerned Jemima's previous thoughts, because she said abruptly, 'I am quite sure that Finchley and Olivia would prefer to spend the festive season at their residence in Norfolk, or with friends, but I have always kept Christmas at Merry Beggars Hall and have suffered too much loss and disruption in my life to tolerate change, now, at this stage. As I tell them, one day I will be gone. Until then, humour me.'

As she packed up her sewing bag, Jemima found the courage to ask the question that had accompanied her into this room. 'Did Lady Olivia drive over yesterday, by any chance?'

'Of course not. Why do you ask, Mrs Flowerday?'

'I thought I saw lights,' Jemima said vaguely.

'Finchley drove over late, but alone. You met him here.'

'Yes, I did. Just, I thought I heard a car at around four thirty. Perhaps I imagined it.'

'I rather think you did. If either Finchley or Olivia ever have anything to tell me, they invariably telephone. The Courtney-Leveretts have four telephone rooms at Brabberton, all with comfortable chairs and fireplaces, can you imagine? Olivia would not drive the Silver Ghost here on a whim. Nobody squanders petrol in these narrow times, Mrs Flowerday.'

Jemima accepted the rebuke. 'How far away is the Courtney-Leveretts' place?'

'An hour across country on horseback, fifteen minutes by car and five by train. You seem inordinately curious, Mrs Flowerday.'

'Let me explain: I'd like to leave a business card there, on my way home. Ladies who entertain lavishly are potential clients.'

'In which case, take the train from Beggars Heath. The house is a hop and skip away, Brabberton station having been built to serve its needs.'

Jemima mulled on this as she closed the drawing-room door behind her. There was just time before Lady Hamlash's luncheon parade for her to whip into the library and lay out her drawing equipment and cardboard, ready for making patterns later. Perishing as it was, the library was ideal as the table was large enough for her to lay out all her tools and the room stood separate from both the family and the servants' wings, making it intensely private. At some point during her interview with Lady Hamlash, Jemima had resolved to share her theory on the manner and means of Marie Guyen's death with DS Pretty. But how did one go about inviting a police detective to meet one secretly?

After sharpening her pencils over the empty fire grate, Jemima slipped upstairs to comb her hair in time for servants' lunch.

The soup Beth brought to the table was not a patch on Madame Guyen's consommé, but mopped up with bread and cheese, it did as fuel. As she sat facing the glazed lobby, it was Jemima who exclaimed as the first snowflakes of winter floated down. 'And more to come, judging by the colour of the sky.'

DS Pretty had not joined them at the table, giving Jemima time to lose her nerve about confiding with him. Perhaps she ought to test her theories first, as he would undoubtedly challenge her when she named her suspect. As an inventor might prove his flying machine by launching himself off the white cliffs of Dover, she might discover how easy it would be for Lady Olivia to have left Brabberton Manor, accessed the conservatory here and appropriated the tincture stored on the slatted shelf.

Getting up, Jemima declared her intention to go for a walk.

'Good Lord, why would you want to do that?' Mrs Newson asked. It was the unspoken response of everyone around the table.

Jemima picked a white sugar lump out of the bowl and slipped it into her pocket saying, 'In case I need sustenance, like Scott of the Antarctic on his expedition.'

'Better take two lumps, then,' quipped Jack.

Mrs Newson looked ready to weep. 'Please have a care, Mrs Flowerday. You don't know these lanes and byways. Another fatality, my heart will give out.'

Chapter Twenty

A bracing twenty-minute walk brought Jemima to Beggars Heath station. The stationmaster she'd encountered the previous day was on duty, though markedly less cheery. He tipped his hat.

'Afternoon, madam. Excuse the official presence, but this is owing to an unfortunate incident.'

He meant Wells's death, of course. She purchased a return fare to Brabberton Manor and recognised PC Trowse guarding the gate to the platform. Other police officers milled about behind him. She had timed her arrival well, her train drawing in almost at once. After a delay while a policeman spoke with the driver, they were away and Jemima enjoyed a blissfully warm five minutes before the wheels changed rhythm and the brakes squealed.

She was the only passenger getting off at Brabberton Manor. The platform was deserted and peering in at an office window, she had no expectation of finding anyone on duty. To her surprise, she saw a uniformed figure hunched over a desk, apparently playing a game of patience. When she tapped on the glass, he sprang up and opened the door.

'Walk straight through, madam.'

'Don't you wish to see my ticket?'

'Not particularly, being as you look like the kind of lady that remembers to buy one.'

Jemima moved away from the smell of alcohol on his breath. His uniform had seen better days, the collar mis-buttoned. Still, this job must offer little incentive to be either smart or alert. She presented her ticket anyway, saying, 'Did a lady come through yesterday, between three and four in the afternoon, travelling to Beggars Heath?'

'What kind of lady?' the attendant asked after some moments spent cogitating.

'How many kinds of lady are there? Tall, fine posture.' Jemima raided her mental image of Lady Olivia. 'Possibly wearing a driving coat and leather gloves.'

The man gave it more thought. Jemima noticed that he gripped the doorframe. There'd better not be an emergency on the line as he'd be of little use.

'No,' he said at last.

'No lady travelling yesterday?'

'No travellers all day. Not one. It was quiet.'

'I see,' she said crisply, aware that a minute of her life had been wantonly wasted. 'Thank you, Mr—?'

'Deacon, madam. Sydney Deacon, stationmaster of this parish, scholar, gentleman and sometime acrobat.'

Answer to a bartender's prayer, more like. She asked the way to Brabberton Manor.

Sydney Deacon pointed. 'Five minutes with your eyes closed, you'll walk smack into it.'

Jemima crossed the station yard, taking care on the icy cobbles. Choosing a left turn, she walked along a lane until she saw chimneys through the leafless trees. A pair of iron gates flanked by stone pillars appeared soon after, between hedges of clipped bay. Beyond the gates, an avenue led towards shrouded grandeur. Here, the

Courtney-Leveretts held sway, and Sir Finchley and his lady found sanctuary from the chills of Merry Beggars Hall. Or was that a cloak of convenience, hiding a darker intent? The telephone call between Lady Hamlash and her son had raised the prospect of Marie Guyen's removal. Marie had been dead two hours later.

If Lady Olivia had done the deed, she hadn't taken a train. Not if the tipsy stationmaster was to be believed. Lady Hamlash had insisted that her daughter-in-law was nowhere near Merry Beggars Hall yesterday – but could Lady Olivia have entered the house by stealth? Or with Lady Hamlash's collusion?

Jemima peered through the iron scrolls of the gate, resigning herself to the probability that she had come out in the cold for no purpose. But as she turned away, she saw something poking between the snow-tipped leaves of the hedge. A flower, its yellow petals diaphanous as old lace. She recognised the pressed daffodil she'd seen marking the place in Marie Guyen's bedtime reading. Suspicion fired up. Lady Olivia must have taken it from the bedside table not two hours ago when searching for her coat. What else had she taken? Digging a hand into the hedge, she withdrew Madame de Staël's *Delphine*. The book had been ripped along its spine, pages torn away.

'Vandalism,' Jemima gasped. 'Isn't murder enough?' Fighting the urge to march up to the manor and confront Lady Olivia, she put the flower inside the book and stowed them both in her coat pocket. One day, somebody who cared for Marie Guyen should have them.

Roiled with emotion, Jemima breathed herself calm. If her goal was now to solve two killings, she must apply cool logic, not rage. Think. If Lady Olivia had not driven to Merry Beggars Hall yesterday, and hadn't taken the train, she must have walked.

With an hour of daylight left, Jemima orientated herself and set off to follow what she now firmly believed was the route of a killer.

Chapter Twenty-One

It soon became obvious that no lady could have walked this route in kidskin shoes. Even in sturdy town shoes, it was a challenge. Crossing the first of many iron-hard fields, and with the snow thickening, Jemima slithered and slipped. Twice, she went over on her ankle. If Lady Olivia had walked these field paths yesterday to adulterate Madame Guyen's coffee, she must have worn boots. Nothing ruled out her changing into lighter-soled shoes on arrival, of course, but Jemima suspected she had wildly underestimated the walking distance between Brabberton and Merry Beggars Hall.

The sun was sinking as Jemima crossed the park and saw the leaded panes of the library window glossed with gold. The conservatory, which fitted around the south-east corner of the house, shone like molten amber and she headed towards it as to a beacon.

She reached it to find the door locked. A hunch made her pull aside a steel boot scraper and there it was, an iron key which fitted the lock. Leaving the door ajar, Jemima stepped into a space smelling of greenery and moist soil. Where was the slatted shelf on which Wells had placed his fatal tincture? She couldn't make out much with the dying rays of the sun piercing the glass. She walked around, stroking the ribbed leaves of Lady Hamlash's precious hoyas. She identified the shelf by the balls of gardener's twine and copper watering pots arranged on it. No sign of the tincture, as the police would have seized it as evidence, but going up on tiptoe to sniff, she detected an odour of tobacco and tar.

'Imagine,' she said to herself, 'you are Lady Olivia. You have got here at great physical risk and are looking at a bottle full of a substance you know will create a violent allergic response in your victim. But how to get it into her system…?'

Jemima took out the sugar cube she'd pocketed earlier. She'd resisted eating it on her walk. 'You uncork the bottle and place the sugar lump on top.' She mimed doing so. 'In one slick movement, you upend the bottle for the count of one, two, just enough to soak the sugar. You re-cork the bottle and put it back. Nobody will notice that the liquid has sunk a hair's breadth. You wrap the sugar lump in a scrap of cloth, or a handkerchief, so it won't drip on your clothes and give you away by its smell. You know something about allergies because you drove an ambulance in the war. You rubbed shoulders with nurses and doctors and know how little of a trigger-substance is required—'

But wait. There was a weakness in her theory. How would Lady Olivia know of Marie Guyen's particular allergy? Jemima racked her brains, unwilling to abandon a hypothesis she had invested in so heavily. What did the two women have in common?

It came to her at once. London. Lady Olivia had mentioned leaving her favourite driving coat behind in her London home. Could the two women have met in town, and gained knowledge of each other? It was possible and, as *The Weekend Sleuth* often propounded, possibility and probability existed at each end of the same spectrum. Assume it was so.

Jemima carried on playing out her theory. Again pretending to be Lady Olivia, she wrapped the supposedly-poisoned sugar cube in an imaginary cloth. Now what?

'Your next task is to plant the cube in such a way that your victim will take it, but *only* your victim.'

'Something of a random hope, wouldn't you say, Mrs Flowerday?'

Jemima froze. The comment had come from the open door of the conservatory. DCI Bullace stood on the threshold with his back to the darkening sky.

'Did you follow me?' Jemima managed to ask.

'Not exactly. I saw your approach and came out to see where you might end up. I was intrigued.'

'You crept up on me as silently as a pillar of smoke.'

'A notable talent of mine.' He came inside and closed the door. 'May one ask... other than trespassing on a crime scene and tampering with evidence—'

'I haven't tampered,' she insisted. 'I conjured items in my imagination. Of course you will want to know why.'

'I confess to a passing curiosity.'

'I know how the poison got into Marie Guyen's coffee.'

'Splendid. Tell all.'

She knew he was being ironic, or sarcastic, or probably both. However, the temptation to display her insight proved too much. 'It was driving me distracted, how Madame Guyen could have imbibed poison accidentally. The answer became obvious. It was no accident.'

'You've already called it murder, my sergeant tells me.' Bullace walked behind Jemima, stopping at the door to the telephone room. 'Lady Hamlash might come in to talk to her plants at any moment, so let us take your theory directly to its conclusion. Your imaginary culprit has dripped a potent insecticide onto a sugar cube and must now "plant it". You have a theory as to how it was done, Mrs Flowerday, and I have ten free minutes.'

Jemima found herself suddenly tongue-tied. It was one thing

129

to speculate privately, quite another to have one's great idea put to the test. But DCI Bullace was waiting, amused, irritated, but also unable to hide a sliver of curiosity. It was enough to propel Jemima on.

She gestured to the door where he stood. 'The culprit leaves, on tiptoe. It is coming up to five in the evening – later than it is now – and it's entirely dark outside.'

'Show me.' Bullace opened the door and gestured for Jemima to precede him.

In the telephone room, the buffer zone between the conservatory and the hall, she pressed the light switch. An unshaded bulb flickered and came on, illuminating a room just large enough for a small table and a chair. The telephone itself sat on its cradle, plaited brown wire snaking to the skirting board. An address book lay open at the letter 'R'. 'Rushbrook, Dr' was the only entry on that page.

With no reason to linger, Jemima led the way into the hall, choosing the shortest route to the servants' door. Bullace, striding behind, asked if they were going to the servants' hall.

'No. Direct to the kitchen.' Jemima opened the door within the panelling and walked swiftly down the passageway, taking them past the butler's quarters and Marie's locked bedroom. A door at the end, on the left, admitted them to the kitchen.

They found Beth seated at a table, methodically buttering scones for tea. The girl did not perceive them until Jemima asked where the kitchen pantry was, at which Beth jerked in surprise and dropped her knife.

'The – the door behind you, there.' The girl pointed towards a narrow plank door.

Jemima thanked her. She lifted a latch and found herself staring down three white-painted steps. The pantry was a simple room with a mesh-covered window, and shelves for cheese, cold meats and butter. Everything that needed to be kept fresh.

The sugar bowl was present and Jemima added the sugar cube she'd kept in her palm, saying, 'Marie Guyen absorbed toxic tincture from sugar which she herself stirred into her cup. She thought she was adding a brown cube, but—'

'She added a white one, stained brown with tobacco,' Bullace finished for her. It was he who reached up to a high shelf and took down two large Tate & Lyle boxes to inspect their contents. One contained white cubes, the other brown. 'I see what you're saying, Mrs Flowerday. But why didn't she notice? Why didn't Marie smell it as it went into her tea?'

'Coffee,' Jemima corrected. 'She despised tea as a vice of the English and drank only coffee. Very strong. The steam rising from her cup would have masked the odour.'

'Have you considered that the contaminant might have already been in the cup?'

Jemima answered that she had considered it and rejected the idea. 'Madame brought her own cup to the servants' hall and nobody could have squeezed brown liquid into it without her seeing. She was a highly individual woman. Her preferred cup, her coffee made to her precise liking. Milk in second, always. She wouldn't tolerate anything out of place.'

'What of the girl?' Bullace meant Beth. 'Could she have done it?'

Jemima spoke very softly. 'You will hear Beth variously described as dim, slow, simple, yet she liked Madame Guyen. From my short observation of them together, Madame was patient with her, called her "petite". The others aren't so gentle, though Beth takes pains to get things right and dreads being in trouble. That, I believe, makes her a most unlikely attacker.'

131

Bullace raised another flaw in her argument. 'Murderers like certainty and too much is random in your hypothesis. Had Madame Guyen taken a white sugar cube, she would still be alive. One of the other servants could have taken the brown-stained one and died in her place.'

Having recovered from being caught acting out her suspicions, Jemima's brain had regained its agility. 'It's not random, Chief Inspector. Nobody puts brown demerara sugar into tea, but we all like it in coffee. Marie Guyen was the only one at that table to be served coffee and whoever planted it would have known. But the crucial point is that the tincture did not kill Marie.'

'I beg pardon, Mrs Flowerday, the doctor himself—'

'It wasn't the tincture.' Jemima remained deferential but firm. 'It was the severe allergic reaction it triggered that was fatal. Only Madame Guyen was ever in any danger.'

'Being allergic to tobacco,' Bullace said slowly. 'Wells mentioned her intolerance of cigarettes, didn't he? He took bromelain to her bedside, hoping to save her, though of course by then she was dead. She expired where she fell, beside the tea table.'

Jemima was determined Wells should not be convicted for having a common remedy on his person. 'Wells did not take bromelain to her bedside with the intention of saving her. He happened to have it in his pocket, and produced it as a last-ditch attempt to help her. It proves he knew her fatal weakness, but doesn't prove intent to harm. Others could also have discovered the weakness.'

'Well, who?'

Jemima hesitated.

'Don't be coy, Mrs Flowerday. You're too far in.'

'Lady Olivia Hamlash.'

Interestingly, Bullace looked sceptical but not appalled. 'Was

Marie Guyen on such close terms with Lady Hamlash's daughter-in-law that she'd have discussed an allergy?'

Jemima admitted she didn't know.

Bullace asked her who else she had in her sights. 'Having ruled out Wells and the kitchen maid.'

'Nobody.'

'Oh, come, don't disappoint me.'

'Nobody,' Jemima repeated. After all, she alone had heard the killer moving towards their victim, but now was not the time to describe footsteps, or the process by which she had eliminated every other member of the household. 'If I were in charge of this investigation, I would interview Lady Olivia.'

Bullace raised a stern finger. 'But you are not. As a police officer, I am entitled to my suspicions. As a civilian, you're on a slippery path towards slander.'

He walked up the pantry steps, and in the kitchen spent a while looking along the shelves and into cupboards, his height giving him an advantage. He ran a hand along the iron range and opened its oven doors, shutting them afterwards. Beth watched, clutching her buttery knife. Jemima observed too and wished she knew what was passing through the man's mind.

Bullace sought her eye. 'This has been an interesting conversation. Let us continue it in private.' He took her to the library, closing the door behind them. 'Well, Mrs Flowerday, you have shown me how poison might have been delivered to Madame Guyen's cup and how she came to swallow it. You *haven't* convinced me who did it. As far as I am concerned, Kenneth Wells is still my prime suspect. Eight times out of ten, victims know their killers.'

'I am not an apologist for Mr Wells,' Jemima declared, conscious that she had been exactly that on several occasions. 'But you seem so fixed on his guilt, despite him having no obvious motive, whereas

133

the Hamlashes actively wanted Marie Guyen out of this house. But Marie wouldn't budge.'

'And so they conspired to kill her. Is that your opinion?'

'It is a suggestion you should take seriously,' Jemima answered. 'Lady Olivia, as a loyal wife, acted to advance her husband's interests, planting poison.'

'I have shown you how it could be done.'

'So you have.' Bullace regarded her inscrutably before saying, 'From my experience of twenty-five years, I can count the motives for murder on the fingers of one hand. The most prevalent being financial gain.' He raised fingers as he counted. 'Sexual gratification, pardon my bluntness, comes next, followed by intense jealousy and a desire for revenge. Occasionally, murder is done for self-protection. Finally, some rare, deranged persons kill for fun. Ridding oneself of an inconvenient domestic seems an inadequate motive for a crime for which the penalty is death. It hasn't escaped my notice, Mrs Flowerday, that you enjoy being an amateur detective.'

It didn't sound like a compliment.

'I was born with a curious nature,' Jemima said cautiously.

'You imagine nobody sees or notices what you're about.' Bullace walked to the library window whose Gothic tracery was now filled with night and took up a stance that held no invitation for her to join him. 'You flatter yourself they look at you and say, "genteel dressmaker" while you pursue your covert interest.' He turned to her, as she had not moved from her place. 'While that secrecy may keep you safe, it causes you to miss vital – may I say, obvious – facts.'

'Such as?' She felt stung by the comment.

He tapped a pane. 'I was in here when I saw you walking up through the park. Standing as I am now, staring out. You did not see me as the sunset had made a mirror of the glass. Yesterday, you reported seeing Wells on the terrace at three minutes past one—'

'Yes,' she agreed. 'He spoke with somebody I didn't see. I told you exactly that.'

'Ah, but if only you had asked who else was out there at the time. That is my point, Mrs Flowerday. Constrained by a need for concealment, you fail to ask the critical question in any given circumstance. You fail because you have no choice.'

'Mrs Newson was present, and I didn't feel I could push open a casement window and ask Wells who he was talking to.' By saying this, she had proved Bullace's point, she admitted to herself. It was chastening none the less. Wanting to drive the subject away from her shortcomings, she asked archly, 'When you saw me, did you take me for a ghostly monk?'

'No. I thought you were Mrs Flowerday wearing a charming hat. Will you explain what took you out in such uninviting weather?'

Seeing her only chance to rise in the chief inspector's estimation was to open up her thinking, Jemima explained her train ride to Brabberton Manor and her trek back again. 'It was to prove that somebody could come on foot from there and enter this house unseen.'

'But I saw you.'

'You were in here, and you said yourself, few people ever are.'

'True.' He sat down, elbows on the table, fingers laced together. 'Why slog all the way to Brabberton? Why not to Saxonchurch or Beggars Heath?'

'Sir Finchley and his lady are guests at Brabberton Manor.' From her coat pocket, Jemima took the ruined copy of *Delphine*. 'I first saw this on Marie Guyen's bedside table, and yet…' She described plucking it from a hedge not two hours ago, and how that tied in with the appearance of Lady Olivia that morning. 'She had called on her mother-in-law, and I watched her go between the drawing room and the servants' hall. She must have removed the book then, only to discard it at the gates of Brabberton Manor. In my *amateur* opinion, Inspector, that implies hostile feelings towards the deceased.'

Bullace didn't speak for long seconds. 'You are sure it is the same book as in Madame Guyen's room?'

Jemima showed him the pressed daffodil bookmark. 'There cannot be two of these in the world.' She had no choice but to jump into a dark pool and discover if it had a bottom or not. 'Lady Olivia Hamlash stole a dead woman's property and I will swear on oath that it was she, wearing kidskin shoes, whom I heard scuttling across the great hall yesterday, minutes before her victim died.'

Bullace let another few, dry seconds pass. 'Are you aware who Lady Olivia Hamlash's father is, Mrs Flowerday?'

'Yes. She's the daughter of Earl Rivers.'

'*The* Earl Rivers of Walsham, and rarely is a definite article so loaded with influence. He is also Lord Lieutenant of the County of Norfolk.'

Jemima's confidence had risen and rose further at this suggestion that Bullace also had feet of clay. 'If a peerage scares you, there is little I can say.'

'Oh, don't turn Bolshevist on me,' he snapped, though with a twist of amusement in his tone. 'You make frocks for wealthy women. Would you march into a client's drawing room and tell her she is too short, too fat, too old?'

'Of course not.'

'In the same vein, I cannot arrest Lady Olivia Hamlash on your circumstantial evidence of her being here yesterday, wearing particular shoes, and this morning borrowing a book.'

'Stealing a book.'

'Borrowing. You cannot prove intent.'

'I shall remind you of that when you next impugn Mr Wells.' Another silence fell until DCI Bullace asked her to explain again, 'Why would Lady Olivia want to harm her mother-in-law's cook?'

'To protect her husband and his family interests. Marie was pestering Lady Hamlash, demanding justice.'

'Justice for what?'

'I have no idea, but I heard her demanding it of Lady Hamlash in the walled garden. Wells was present and Marie was angry with him too. He, by contrast, was patience itself.' Jemima described the telephone conversation she'd overheard shortly after between Lady Hamlash and her son. 'Her Ladyship was complaining how Marie was constantly pestering her for an audience. We have both experienced Sir Finchley's irascible temper.'

'That does not a murderer make. Murderers are often… what was your observation of Wells? "Patience itself".'

Despite all I've said, Jemima reflected, you have shut your eyes and ears. 'What a shame your favourite suspect is dead,' she said curtly. 'You are convinced Wells is no more?'

Bullace nodded, implying he had no doubts. 'The train he tried to board was checked at its destination in London. There was blood on the wheels from the mid-section all the way to the guard's van at the back. Wells held the key to Marie Guyen's fate, but you wrong me by saying my mind is shuttered.'

'I did not say that.'

'Your face said it.' Bullace was staring at her as he might at a library shelf, reading the spines to see which book would offer the most information.

Jemima presumed that, by now, DS Pretty would have shared

137

Dinah's accusations with his superior. By defending Wells, had she implicated herself further? Noises from the great hall provided a reprieve.

'Half past four,' Bullace said, glancing at his fob watch.

Footsteps could be heard, accompanied by the clink of silver and china. Lady Hamlash's tea was passing by.

Jemima said, 'Were you to open the door, you would see a parade headed by Mr Crosby, with Jack and Dinah following with the best porcelain and a single biscuit on a salver.'

'And so we come full circle.' Bullace rose. 'Tea is brewed and a woman dies, and the following day, more tea is brewed.' He picked up the torn novel, saying he would add it to the evidence chest. 'Cease your investigations, Mrs Flowerday. It is neither helpful nor healthy.' He made to leave.

'Will you follow up on my suspicions?' Jemima had no idea if, by divulging her theories, she had helped or hindered the course of justice. 'Or do you believe that because Lady Olivia is well connected, she cannot also be capable of malice?'

DCI Bullace gave a last, deep look into her eyes. 'Firstly, the cause of Marie Guyen's death is still open. Secondly, what I may professionally think is none of your business.' With that, he left.

Jemima let some moments elapse before returning to her room, dissatisfied with herself and with DCI Bullace. She hung up her coat, having shaken it out. Tomorrow, she would return to London. She had intended to visit Inverness Terrace and the Royal Darnley Hotel, a short walk from where the seamstress who would make up Lady Hamlash's dresses lived. Now she thought, why bother? If her logic was unsound, her suspicions dismissed as merely meddlesome, what was the point?

Jemima refreshed her appearance, changing her wet and muddy town shoes for the glacé leather ones, and made her way downstairs in the gloom. Lord love him, couldn't the late Sir Rufus have allowed one electric light on the stairwell? The stable clock chimed five as she lifted the latch to the servants' door and a thought hit like an outlaw's arrow. This morning, she had watched Lady Olivia Hamlash stride up to this very door and open it without the slightest hesitation. It proved that Lady Olivia, for all her apparent dislike of Merry Beggars Hall, knew her way around. A spark flared. Jemima doused it. No more sleuthing today. She had tea to drink and dresses to make.

DCI Bullace had elected to join the servants' tea. Jack was speaking and as Jemima sat down she realised the footman was remembering the day at Cambrai when Major Sir Edgar Hamlash, his battalion commander, was wounded by a German shell. A splinter moved in Jemima's heart. Jack could have been describing her husband Simon's experience at the Battle of the Somme.

'The rotten thing exploded twelve feet away,' Jack was saying. 'The blast got the major square in the neck and face. We crawled from our dug-out, and he tried to keep going, shouting, "Come on, lads".'

Simon's next-in-command, writing to Jemima afterwards, had said much the same. 'He kept going forward, you never saw a man so fixed on his purpose, as if the pain were nothing'.

Keep going forward. The words attached themselves to Jemima like the war service medal she kept at home, in a box. Beth filled her cup, the teapot spout dipping. When Jemima tried to take a sip, her cup seemed to be made of lead. It clinked as she set it back on its saucer.

'Mrs Flowerday, are you all right?' Mrs Newson looked alarmed.

'I'm – I'm sorry.' Jemima pushed back her chair and hurried out. DCI Bullace must have followed because she heard him calling her name when she was part-way up the stairs. She kept going.

After an hour lying on her bed, she went down again and spent the interval before supper in the library, drawing out her patterns, cutting out her muslin toiles. It was while she was working at the library table that she came across the pressed flower from Marie Guyen's book. It must have fallen out when Bullace took possession. From her pocket, she withdrew the postcard Marie had sent to Wells.

A flower and a singed, sepia view of the Royal Darnley Hotel. In her coat pocket, wrapped in a scrap of muslin, was a ragged flake of brown enamel. When looked at dispassionately, her gathered evidence was nothing but jackdaw's pickings. 'Do the job you are paid to do,' she advised herself and threaded a needle with white cotton.

Later, having sewn up the toiles, using big stitches that would be simple to unpick, she sought out Mrs Newson, and asked if Lady Hamlash could be prevailed upon to see her again briefly. 'It would be helpful to fit these pieces to her at least once before I leave.'

'I'll send a note in with Crosby, at dinnertime,' the housekeeper promised, adding, 'You did look bad earlier, my dear. I'm afraid we were thoughtless, speaking about things perhaps you'd rather forget.'

'They can't be forgotten as I live with the consequence every day,' Jemima replied harshly. She collected herself. 'Thing is, Mrs Newson, I don't wish to forget. I want to be able to tell the children what happened to their father, when they're older. I'm only sorry if I made Jack feel in any way responsible.'

'It was the chief inspector who got him talking. Speaking of which—' Mrs Newson handed her a fold of paper with her name on the front.

Bullace had written her an apology, for allowing a teatime conversation to develop along lines 'that so clearly distressed her'.

If my manner towards you appears churlish or cold, regard it as concern for your wellbeing. You are intrigued by the mystery of an unsolved case. I was here last spring, assisting DCI Lidney, and can assure you that the reality of murder is cruel, and brands the soul. I have no wish to be called back to investigate a <u>third</u> killing.

A third killing. He had underlined it. A slip of the pencil? Bullace could not have written anything more likely to reignite Jemima's desire for answers. It told her that he also believed that the murders of Roland Crosby and Marie Guyen were linked. What was the common thread? Dinah had unwittingly identified it in her clumsy accusations: London. Excited, agitated, Jemima went back into the library and located a railway timetable.

Tomorrow, she would go home and her investigation would switch to a new scene.

Chapter Twenty-Two

Jemima woke the following morning with her determination undiminished. She'd managed an hour with Lady Hamlash the previous evening, and as a result had made alterations to her toiles which she had stayed up to finish. Three ghostly muslin forms draped the end of her bed. It was only just growing light and going to her window and drawing back the curtains, she gasped. Heavy snow had fallen overnight and as she looked out over the walled garden, she could barely make out the shapes of the raised beds and other structures. She would have to walk to Beggars Heath for her train, as there was no chance of a lift, Wells being no more.

At breakfast, she asked if there was such a thing as a taxi in these parts, only to be met with smiles.

'Not a sniff of one, Mrs Flowerday,' said Mrs Newson. 'Mr Crosby could ferry you, though.'

The butler, in his place at the head of the table, spreading marmalade on toast, did not take the bait.

'You can drive, Mr Crosby?' Jemima prompted.

'I can,' he said. 'During the war, I learned to drive a grocer's van, doing my bit. However, today is not convenient, with the police still coming and going. I may be able to take you tomorrow.'

This didn't suit at all. Jemima was eager to get home, and on the trail of Madame Guyen and her life before she came here. And to get the toiles to her seamstress, of course. Walk she must, wrapped up to the nines and with her bags.

Salvation arrived when the postman stomped in through the glass lobby, a letter in his bag for Mr Crosby. The butler glanced quickly at the postmark before abandoning his toast and leaving the room. He returned minutes later, saying, 'You are in luck, Mrs Flowerday. The letter was from our replacement cook. She arrives on the 10.58 this morning and requires me to pick her up.'

'Goodness,' Mrs Newson said. 'You only wrote off to her yesterday afternoon, Mr Crosby. That's a fast reply.'

'I did not write, I telephoned the grocery shop in London where my sister-in-law purchases her goods,' Albert Crosby explained. 'A boy took a message round, and Sara got a letter into the final post yesterday.'

Of course, Crosby's sister-in-law had spent time here previously, cooking for Lady Hamlash, and would likely know how far the station was from the house.

'She's getting off at Beggars Heath?' Mrs Newson queried. 'Only, last time, Mr Crosby, you picked her up from Ipswich because she hadn't the heart to travel on a local train, and have people stare at her.'

'Her letter states Beggars Heath. Thankfully, people have stopped staring,' the butler replied with asperity.

All this was fascinating, but the timings were off for Jemima, who had planned to catch the 11.07 train from Ipswich to London. Convenience won out. 'I will ride with you, Mr Crosby,' she said, 'and be ready to leave by, shall we say, ten-thirty?'

After the butler left and they were again alone, Mrs Newson sighed. 'I do wonder at Mrs Sara Crosby being so eager to return

143

here. Do you ever feel a desire to visit the place your husband fell?'

'Go to the battlefields of Normandy?' Jemima gave it consideration. 'No, never.'

Mrs Newson nodded. 'It does strike me as odd. Still, we are all different, and Mrs Crosby has her way to make in the world. We widows must take what is offered.' Jemima had nothing to say to that and the housekeeper continued. 'Well, it's a relief to know we won't have to wrestle with Beth's under-cooked potatoes any longer and we'll be served good English fare.'

'I daresay Mrs Crosby rarely bothers a garlic?' Jemima suggested. 'Lady Hamlash described her as a good, plain cook.'

'It's what she is.'

Jemima rather regretted leaving just as Sara Crosby was coming. The piece in *The Weekend Sleuth*, which she'd reread on the journey down, had pricked her curiosity, whisking her into that modest, North London sitting room for tea and coconut cake. Would 'a good, plain cook' meet Sir Finchley and Lady Olivia's exacting standards, though?

'She does well enough,' Mrs Newson answered when Jemima asked. 'Her cakes are light as a feather and she has a nice way with a roast joint. It'll be a pleasure to sit down and not have to listen to Dinah complaining.'

Jemima was ready to leave by ten, bags packed and parked in the great hall. With time to spare, she took the opportunity to resolve some loose ends. Returning to the servants' hall, she went into the kitchen garden, taking the cinder path. Despite the snowfall, she found the place where she'd stumbled on her way to fetch Wells from his cottage. Just to be certain, she located the rose whose stems she'd tripped over, where Beth had emptied out the dregs of the tea and coffee. Scraping back the snow, she rubbed her palms against the earth then cupped them to her nose. *Tea leaves. Well-dug soil, horse manure and coffee.* The tang of tobacco was notably absent.

Jemima straightened up and smacked the dirt off her palms. It backed up her theory that the fatal tincture had not been added to the coffee pot or slipped into Marie Guyen's cup. The piece of broken cup Jemima had retrieved from the floor in the servants' hall had carried a whiff of tobacco, however. 'It went into the cup on a sugar cube. I know I'm right.'

From there she went into the kitchen garden and, in a far corner, identified a compost heap by the ivy stems and swept leaves that were visible beneath a jacket of snow. Patches of pristine whiteness were stained treacly brown. Jemima found a broken bean pole and poked it into the stained area. It came out coated in a tarry substance which, without doubt, was the gooey remains that Wells had scraped from his pan. She remembered the tone in which he'd described doing so.

I cleaned it out, at the midden heap, with a trowel. Go check... I swear it.

She had no time to search for the trowel but would pass this information to Bullace or Pretty. She could have gone back inside then, but the glasshouse pulled her. She hesitated at the door, which was still wedged part-way open, reluctant to damage her coat by squeezing through. In the end, she turned the coat inside out, folding the collar inwards before putting it on again. Checking that she was unobserved, she sidled inside. Last time she'd been in here, rain had been falling heavily. With snow on the roof, it was like entering an igloo, the windowpanes etched with ferny shapes and frozen cobwebs. Her breath formed a light fog in front of her as she paced the length of the building, looking for changes in the messy arrangement of cloches and pots. She detected none. Almost certainly, nobody had been in here since she herself, two days ago.

Unwrapping the flake of enamel she'd extracted from the doorframe on her last visit, she stopped under a roof pane where daylight penetrated, and held it up. Bullace would dismiss this fragment as of no importance, but Jemima disagreed. The flake could have come off a button. Or become embedded in the doorframe by someone manhandling a gardening implement through the door. Then again, whoever had left Roland Crosby's head here last April had to have transported it in some kind of container. If the door had been in the same half-stuck state last spring, they might have caught its edge on the frame.

'If I were taking a severed head onto a train,' Jemima mused, 'I'd use something robust with a padlock. Such as an army provisions box.' Like the one Simon had taken to France on mobilisation, filled with chocolate, marmalade, sugar and tea. His had been khaki green, with his initials printed on top in white. 'What about a deed box,' she said to herself, 'the kind found in lawyer's offices?' They were lockable and anonymous. One often saw clerks on trains and buses, balancing them on their knees.

It fascinated her that while so much had been written of the murder at Merry Beggars Hall, nobody had seemed to consider the practical matter of bringing a head to a remote country house. Perhaps it took a woman's mind…

It had been found early on Monday, 24 April but had likely been placed the previous day when Bilney, the gardener at the time, was enjoying a day of rest. That weekend had been notably cold, with a hard frost in the early hours of Monday morning. Jemima had discovered for herself that the servants here liked to stay indoors when it was inclement, with only Dinah making reluctant forays with her coal scuttle. Jemima's conclusion was that it would have been relatively easy for Roland's killer, that Sunday, to gain access to this glasshouse without being seen.

The police had done a thorough search of the gardens and grounds and were satisfied that the rest of Roland Crosby's body was not there. But of course, there were many square miles around of field, ditch and woodland that could not be searched.

Feeling chilly, Jemima got moving again. The glasshouse walkway was constructed from bricks in a herringbone pattern and, from her extensive reading on the case, she knew the police had discovered no footprints. No tell-tale fingerprints either; but then, it being so cold, the perpetrator would have been wearing gloves. She stepped off the walkway onto one of the timber-edged beds, her feet making no impression because the soil was frozen. It would not have been frozen at the time of Roland Crosby's murder as the boilers would have been in use, coddling the asparagus plants. This would have been one of the warmest spots at Merry Beggars Hall. The killer would have left imprints in the soil, unless they'd had the foresight to brush the soil smooth when they stepped off.

The head had been positioned... here. As on her last visit, Jemima stopped at the midpoint. It had been laid down, eyes staring up, and covered with an asparagus cloche.

Selecting a large, cream-coloured one at random, she stood holding it. 'I wouldn't want to look into that face,' she said to herself. 'I'd have put my box or bag down on the bricks and removed it with my eyes shut. I'd be wearing gloves bought for the purpose. I'd position the head and select a cloche which I'd slam down on top as fast as I could. I'd want to get away as swiftly as possible too. First, though, I'd check nobody was about.'

She stared out into the motionless garden, but the glass was too misty to give her any detail. 'If I had come during the day, I would make for the lane. I might have a bicycle parked nearby, or I would slip away into the fields. If it were night, I'd melt into the darkness and perhaps cut through the park as I did earlier. Where would I be aiming for?'

The railway.

The ticket inspector on duty at Beggars Heath had reported nobody arriving or departing that weekend who had caused him to look twice. Could a local person be the culprit? Or had the killer alighted at another station? Brabberton Manor, for instance? Where had Sir Finchley and Lady Olivia been on the penultimate weekend of April?

She stepped off the frozen soil with one of her laces coming undone. Bending to retie it, she saw, wedged between two bricks, a short nail with a round head. It was a shoemaker's nail, the sort that secures a leather upper to a sole. She had seen the same kind of nail in the clogs Beth wore and those that Marie Guyen had been wearing at the moment of her death. Jemima had picked up those clogs, putting them next to Marie's bedside cabinet. She recalled the darn to Marie's stocking, where a nail working itself loose could have rubbed a hole in the fabric.

'No – you're putting two and two together and making five.' Jemima did not want to embrace the disturbing idea that Marie Guyen might have come into the glasshouse and walked its length, for any other reason than curiosity. Marie Guyen, Roland Crosby. One the killer of the other? Wrapping the nail along with the enamel flake in its muslin square, and placing it in her pocket, she found her dressmaker's notebook and turned to a clean page. Taking the pencil from its spine, she listed the points where Marie Guyen and Roland Crosby's lives might intersect. She wrote fast, as she was growing conscious of the time.

LONDON
The railway
Merry Beggars Hall
The walled garden/glasshouse
Domestic service

The last point flowed from her pencil's end. Both Roland and
Marie had been servants of a superior sort, Marie a trained chef,
Roland Crosby a waiter in a gentlemen's club. Five potential inter-
section points in the victims' lives warranted further exploration.
She closed her notebook. She hadn't wanted to consider Wells a
killer, and her mind rebelled against labelling Marie Guyen likewise.
Yet she couldn't deny that two people working together would
more easily dispose of and dismember a body than one person
working alone.

'Mrs Flowerday?'

A face the other side of the glass made her jump violently. It
was a relief to recognise Jack Millar.

'You're needed,' he mouthed through the glass. 'DS Pretty wants
you.'

She got herself through the door, ignoring Jack's question – 'Why
is your coat on the wrong way?' – and turned towards the house
in some trepidation. Why would Pretty want her? Had Dinah
renewed her accusations?

Jack caught up with her. He was holding something out. 'You
dropped this.'

It was her notebook, which had fallen open at the page where
she'd been writing. She suspected he'd read her list, and he
confirmed it.

'Know what, Mrs Flowerday? I reckon you're a journalist,
wanting to crack the case to get fame and riches.'

She denied it. Certainly, the wanting to get rich part. 'I'm curious to know who killed Roland Crosby and I'm committed to learning who harmed Madame Guyen.'

'We know already—'

'Stop it!' She was furious suddenly. Jack's arrival compounding the unsettling ideas that had formed in the glasshouse had caused her to drop a notebook that not only contained a compromising list, but also Lady Hamlash's measurements. Gross negligence. 'Before you hurl more accusations, Jack, you need to confess to laying false information.'

'What false information?'

'The compost heap,' she said. 'You refilled Wells's saucepan from the scrapings he'd thrown away so you could claim he'd kept some back. I shall ask DS Pretty to inspect the pan for bugs and traces of ivy.'

'You wouldn't do that.'

'I jolly well would. Hating Wells is one thing. Framing him for murder is quite another. It won't make Dinah love you.'

'Given up on that,' was the muttered response.

'You shouldn't. And if not Dinah, then another girl who will make you happy.'

'What girl's going to want me? Half a leg and shrapnel cheeks.'

'Lots of them will,' Jemima said bracingly. 'You're alive, you have a job and a war pension. If you heaved your chin off the floor, you'd see there are plenty of young women wanting a husband. Has Mr Crosby been wondering where I am?'

Not as far as Jack knew. 'Last I saw him, he was tying a silk scarf around his coat collar. His room door was open a little way and I could see him in front of the mirror. Vain old codger. He's only going to the station, who cares if his scarf is tied just-so?'

*

DS Pretty was waiting for her in the great hall and greeted her with, 'Ah, Mrs Flowerday, the chief inspector and I wish to search Madame Guyen's room, and we'd like a lady present. Mrs Newson is busy and can't be spared.'

Handed an unlooked-for gift, Jemima eagerly told the sergeant she was at his disposal. 'You know I have a train to catch?' She looked at her watch, adding, 'I can give twenty minutes.'

'Let's get started, then.' Pretty's face found its habitual frown lines as he took in Jemima's appearance. 'Why are you wearing your coat inside out?'

'It's how we do it in London,' she said in blithe unconcern. 'Lead on.'

Chapter Twenty-Three

DCI Bullace turned as they entered and nodded to Jemima. He was standing in front of an open wardrobe.

'She didn't bring much. Mrs Flowerday, would you glance at her clothes, give me a picture of the woman?'

Jemima got straight to work, and the task didn't take long. There were three dresses hanging up. Two black and one navy. A black winter coat. A belted jacket with bell sleeves in Prussian blue. A hip-length jumper and a couple of sporty-looking cardigans. All the clothes carried the label of Bergdorf Goodman.

'A New York department store,' Jemima explained. 'From a single glance, I'd say the clothes are last season's, and well kept. Expensive, based on French couturiers' work.'

'She had a bit of money, then.'

'She certainly chose her clothes well. I would classify Marie Guyen as a woman who bought wisely, but not often.' Jemima cast a glance to the top of the wardrobe. 'Have you looked in the hatbox?'

In reply, Bullace lifted it down. It was Japan-lacquered tin the colour of bitter chocolate, with a little key in the lock. He laid it on the bed and Jemima caught her breath. The side facing the wall was damaged, as if it had been dropped at some point. Some of the enamel had chipped and her fingers itched to take the fragment from her pocket to see if it matched. Bullace, meanwhile, lifted the lid and removed the contents.

'Surprise upon surprise,' muttered Pretty from the side of the room. 'A hatbox containing a hat.'

It was a cloche of black felt with a plain grosgrain band and it too had a New York, Fifth Avenue, label, reinforcing Jemima's view of Marie Guyen as a woman who understood that stylish clothes were an investment. 'What exactly are you looking for?' she asked.

'Whatever is here,' said Bullace. 'No point looking for what isn't, or for what you would like to see.'

Another lesson for me? Jemima took the Prussian-blue jacket from the wardrobe and held it up in front of her. Something was off-key here.

Bullace watched her. 'You like it? You approve?'

'Yes, I would wear it myself,' she said, 'but where is the second hatbox?'

'Does there have to be a second one?'

'Absolutely. Marie Guyen would wear the black hat with her black coat, but not with this jacket. She would have a second hat, in navy or a mid-blue. Or fawn, at a pinch.'

'Every day's a school day,' was Pretty's comment.

'So where *is* the second hatbox?' Bullace asked.

In London, Jemima surmised, but kept the thought to herself. The damaged hatbox disturbed her, feeding a notion that it might have come from contact with the glasshouse doorframe. Having had a little time to reflect, Jemima knew logically that this could not be so: Marie, and Wells for that matter, had arrived in England months after Roland Crosby met his fate. And yet nothing was as it seemed in this realm of shadows and mistruth. If she were to find a nail missing from one of Marie's kitchen clogs... she glanced towards the bedside table. The shoes were no longer where she'd placed them. Could they have been taken as evidence?

The real reason for her presence in the room was revealed when DCI Bullace indicated a chest of drawers. 'Please go through everything in there, Mrs Flowerday. If there are letters, papers, love tokens, I wish to know. The rest may remain private.'

Jemima started with the bottom drawer, quite prepared for the elegant minimalism she found there. Two silk scarves in winter colours. A pair of black, calfskin gloves. A pair in navy. A rain hat. In the middle drawer, she found stockings, black with cotton-reinforced heels and toes, and two pairs of caramel silk. Layers of tissue paper guarded Marie's underwear, all sensuous silk in sorbet colours. She lifted out each item, pressing the folds for anything hidden within. She found nothing. The top drawer contained some jewellery and hair-curling rags. Under a pile of laundered handkerchiefs, she at last found something to satisfy the detectives. It was an envelope in a familiar lilac colour, post-marked 'Saxonchurch'.

The detectives had got tired of waiting and were moving the bed aside to search beneath it. Jemima seized the chance to read the letter unobserved. It was a few lines only, written in a forthright hand.

Merry Beggars Hall, 23 November 1922

Dear Madame Guyen,

I thank you for your response to my advertisement for a professional cook, placed recently in 'The Lady'. I would be happy to offer you the position if you can make an immediate start. Write to this address stating your terms and indicating your intended arrival time, and I will ensure a car is waiting for you at the station.

Yours sincerely,
Ada, Lady Hamlash

23 November... The day following, Marie had sent her postcard to Wells, informing him that she was joining him, having grown 'sick of paying him for no result'.

'Interesting reading, Mrs Flowerday?' DCI Bullace was behind her, his talent for stealth again taking her unawares.

She handed him the letter. The direction on the front of the envelope was to M. Guyen, care of Wittington Chambers, Kensington High Street, London. It had the ring of an accommodation address, to Jemima's thinking. To Bullace she said, 'At least we know how Marie Guyen came to be here. She answered a classified advertisement.'

Jemima would have liked to stay and search for the clogs. The shifting of the bed hadn't revealed them. The hatbox was still in reach, however, and Jemima moved casually towards it, her hand going into her pocket to retrieve the flake of conker-brown enamel.

'Mrs Flowerday, here you are! I've been looking high and low for you.' Albert Crosby stood in the open doorway.

Goodness, her train. She'd momentarily forgotten. With a nod for Bullace and Pretty, she followed the butler out. At the main entrance, the car waited with its engine running. Once she'd stowed her bags in the back, she got into the front, ignoring Albert Crosby's evident irritation. However short, a journey was an opportunity to learn.

They drove off in silence, but to her surprise, it was not she who broke it.

Chapter Twenty-Four

Unlike Wells, who had handled Lady Hamlash's car as if born to it, Albert Crosby sat forward, gloved hands gripping the wheel. Jemima had not wished to distract him.

He gave her a start, then, when he said without preamble, 'I would ask that on your return you desist from engaging Lady Hamlash in conversation about her late son. Mention of Sir Edgar upsets her dreadfully.'

'I didn't raise the subject and she seemed eager to speak of him.' Had the butler been listening at the door yesterday, while she was taking her hostess's measurements?

Apparently not. Crosby informed her that Lady Hamlash had mentioned it to him at breakfast. 'She slept badly last night and had me telephone the doctor for more sedative drops. Her son's passing was the single worst event of her life.'

'I can understand.' Jemima promised to avoid any further mention.

Crosby hadn't finished. 'Jack tells me he came upon you in the glasshouse. May I ask what you were doing there?'

'Being nosy,' was the best she could offer.

In a surprising display of emotion, Albert Crosby took his eyes from the road to look at her. 'Can you conceive what horrors that place holds for me? To learn that you were in there, indulging in idle curiosity, is offensive and disturbing.'

'I can see it would be.'

'And what do you mean by writing lists?'

Ah. Jack had certainly gossiped. 'I write lots. I sometimes consider my life to be a list without end.'

He dismissed the flippant comment with a shake of the head. '"London. The railway. Merry Beggars Hall. The walled garden. The glasshouse." What do you mean by it?'

He hadn't included 'domestic service', so either Jack had incompletely remembered her points, or Crosby felt the description did not fit his brother.

She explained. 'My list comprised everything I know that links your brother to Marie Guyen.'

Her candour inflamed Crosby. 'I don't claim to understand where your imagination leads you,' he burst out. 'I would simply ask that you stop in the name of decency. And for your own good.'

'I can take care of myself, Mr Crosby. Unlike poor Marie Guyen, I have a family and— Oh, slow down!' A fox dashed from a ditch ahead of them. Crosby jammed on his brakes and Jemima's bags flew off the rear seat. The fox reached the opposite verge with a yard to spare and Jemima took a lesson from its narrow escape: Think before you cross this man.

The rest of the journey passed in silence. When the low, brick building of Beggars Heath station came into sight, Jemima risked one last question.

'Did you ever meet His Majesty the King?'

Albert Crosby swung his eyes to her, clearly taken aback. 'Of course not.'

'Only, Sir Finchley is His Majesty's country neighbour, if I understood Jack correctly.'

Crosby lifted his chin. 'Sir Finchley and Lady Olivia's Norfolk residence, Steeple Court, abuts the royal estate at Sandringham and they are occasionally honoured by the gracious notice of King George and Queen Mary.'

I'll take that as a yes, she thought.

'What about the weekend of 22 and 23 April?'

Crosby pulled up in the station yard, engaged the handbrake, but kept the engine running. 'What about it?'

'Where were they? And you, for that matter?'

For a moment it looked as if Albert Crosby would produce a crushing set-down, but something inspired him to answer. Perhaps it was the way she held his gaze with modest, unblinking patience.

'I was in Norfolk for part of that weekend,' he said. 'At Lady Hamlash's request, I drove to Steeple Court with an urgent menu-item for a dinner party. Significant guests were expected that evening. You may infer who I mean.'

The King and Queen, presumably. Their presence on that date could easily be checked in the court circular.

A train was pulling in, its brakes audible, steam rising above the ridge of the station roof. Jemima tried one, last gambit.

'Did you drive up on the Saturday?'

'On the Friday, if it's any business of yours. I stayed overnight in the staff quarters at Steeple Court, returning to Merry Beggars Hall in time for luncheon on Saturday.'

'At half past one in the afternoon, or one-forty by the aberrant stable-yard clock.'

'Jest you may, Mrs Flowerday, but you have never run a large household and have no understanding of the importance of exact timing.'

'You're right. Nobody cares if I take my lunch at twelve or not at all. What did you deliver to Steeple Court – what was the menu-item?' And, she added silently, what did you bring back?

A new possibility was unwrapping itself, but she didn't have time to ponder it as Albert Crosby got out of the car and walked round to open her door.

'What did I deliver?' he echoed. 'Asparagus. Merry Beggars' early asparagus is famous and Lady Olivia was most eager for it to be served at her dinner that Saturday night.'

As Jemima stepped out, the familiar station attendant came through the ticket gate, pushing a trolley on which was balanced a large trunk.

'One out, one in,' he said jovially, pausing to touch the brim of his cap to Jemima. 'The up train is a few minutes delayed, madam, so no need to rush.'

A short, stout woman came behind him and from the way she waved to Albert Crosby, this must be his sister-in-law. Jemima did her best to appear incurious. The lady was bundled up in a green-check coat with a woolly scarf wound around her neck. On her feet – Jemima wondered if she would ever lose the habit of staring past people's ankles – were rubber galoshes, waterproof overshoes.

'Oh, dear,' Jemima said as the woman came near, 'has it also snowed in London?'

Sara Crosby gave a laugh. 'Put it this way, dear, when I hid my door key under the boot scraper as I left, the blessed thing almost froze to my fingers. Snow never lingers in The Smoke. It'll be grey slush by teatime.' Her grin revealed that she had lost several teeth. Her cheeks were red, possibly from exposure to cooking ranges, and her demeanour expressed both mirth and stoic optimism. The greeting she gave her brother-in-law was as cheery as a chimney sweep's.

'Here I am again, Albert, stockpot and barrel. Glad to see you've

159

brought the motor, as I wasn't fancying a walk all the way to Misery Buggers 'All. How's Her Ladyship?'

Albert Crosby replied that Lady Hamlash was in tolerable health and would be appraised of Mrs Crosby's arrival. He trusted Sara had experienced a comfortable journey. No hug, no handshake, Jemima noted. Sara tipped the stationmaster, saying how nice it was to see another smiley face.

'You too, madam. I'll stow this trunk and fetch the other directly,' the man said.

Having thanked Albert Crosby for the lift, Jemima picked up her bags. Walking onto the platform, she found the stationmaster trying to position a large wicker trunk on his trolley. In the end, he had to tip it on its side, and as he lifted it, its lid flopped open. Out tumbled pans and cake tins, knives of various sizes, utensils, cloths and a rolling pin – which did exactly what a rolling pin should do. Jemima caught it before it fell onto the track.

Albert Crosby, drawn by the noise, came through the side gate. Seeing the heap, he muttered something about his sister-in-law, 'Bringing the kitchen sink with her.'

He had a point, Jemima thought. Sara Crosby had come prepared for a dozen Christmas banquets and must have spent half the night packing. Next to a half-bottle of brandy was a box full of cake flavourings. The bottom oven would be kept busy at Merry Beggars Hall, she predicted. She helped repack the wicker trunk. Rescuing a cotton canvas apron, shaking some flakes of snow off it, a letter dropped from its folds. A bill, picked off the mat as Sara left? It was addressed to: Mrs Crosby, 37 Cherry Hall Road, London N4.

A distant whistle told Jemima her train was coming in. She dropped the letter into the wicker trunk a moment before Albert Crosby strapped it up.

As she took her seat and her train slid away, her last view was of the station yard. Albert Crosby was loading the wicker trunk into the rear of the Crossley; his sister-in-law seated in the front passenger seat.

Jemima leaned back with a sigh. Extraordinary. Since arriving at Beggars Heath two days ago, she had witnessed a death and travelled the tracks where poor Wells's violent end had taken place. She had seen a new cook arrive. All in the space of forty-eight hours. Wait… She checked her watch. It was twelve minutes past eleven. To be accurate, forty-seven hours and seventeen minutes had elapsed since she had first walked through the turnstile at Beggars Heath and found Wells waiting with the car.

Albert Crosby had been wrong when he accused Jemima of having no appreciation of exact timing. It was the scalpel-sharp tool of the investigator's trade.

Five minutes later, the train pulled into Brabberton Manor station for a brief, uneventful stop. Jemima took out her journal, turned to the last notes she had written and added some more lines.

I have learned that on the Saturday of Roland Crosby's disappearance, his brother Albert drove home from Norfolk having delivered asparagus to the home of Sir Finchley Hamlash. 'By Royal Appointment'.

As an alibi, it took some beating. Who would dare to challenge it?

Chapter Twenty-Five

On the morning of 14 December, Jemima left her Mayfair home after a long night spent cutting out Lady Hamlash's dresses from the fabrics they'd chosen. She was on her way to visit her seamstress, who lived on the fringes of Bayswater. The fruits of her labour were in a basket over her arm.

She chose a route through Hyde Park and Kensington Gardens. There had been more snow overnight, and she'd taken a leaf out of Sara Crosby's book, putting on side-buttoning puttees to protect her stockings and shoes from the wet.

A pause had settled on London, muffled as it was under a crystalline mantle; traffic silenced and the rooks pen strokes against a white sky. Normally, walking was thinking time, but Jemima's mind was numb from the emotion of the past days. All she could think now was that Roland Crosby might have walked this same path if he'd fancied a break from Bright's Club in St James's. Had he ever passed Marie Guyen on one of her strolls from the Royal Darnley Hotel? Whether they had met, or known nothing at all about each other, was a moot point and it frustrated her that she couldn't reach a conclusion. How did DCI Bullace connect all the different threads into a coherent line of inquiry? Either he had a capacious mind, like the composer who can hear six strands of music at once, or he relied on his deputy to share the load. Or perhaps, and Jemima smiled wryly at this thought, Bullace dispensed with possibility and concentrated only on the provable.

She crossed the Serpentine by the stone bridge. Skirting the Round Pond, she exited the gardens a few degrees north of Kensington Palace. Her seamstress's address was Campden Buildings on Peel Street, which was sandwiched between Kensington Gardens and the poorer enclave of Notting Hill. Miss Price was her name and, like Jemima, she resided with a sister.

Jemima unbuttoned her puttees on the doormat as Miss Price invited her in. Her coat was whipped from her. 'Come in from the cold, Mrs Flowerday. Put your basket down by the fire. The kettle's on the stove and my sister Angela will do the honours.'

Jemima gratefully took the offered seat. The Price sisters' flat, one of many in a tenement building, was crammed with outdated furnishings and fringes, but scrupulously neat. It was a style of living Jemima and Vicky would have been restricted to had Jemima not married Simon Flowerday. She moved a copy of *The Lady* from a table beside her chair and spread out the designs for Lady Hamlash's dresses. 'Do you still advertise in that magazine, Miss Price?' she asked conversationally.

'Every month. You, Mrs Flowerday?'

'I did when I first set up in business.' *The Lady* was a renowned vehicle for recruiting domestic servants. Jemima's advertising had generated many requests for mending and darning and one unsettling offer from a Scottish gentleman of marriage. 'I favour *The Queen*,' she said. 'I also scatter business cards wherever I go. I had them redone recently. Here—' she handed a Fleur du Jour card to Miss Price.

Miss Price gave Jemima one of hers in return. It was neatly handwritten. 'Printing has become so expensive,' sighed Miss Price.

'Hasn't it just?' Though Jemima had secured the means of paying the looming school fees, money never lingered long in her purse. Her share of Simon's war pension was eaten up by living costs and while she had the use of a smart, Mayfair house, it was in her father-in-law's name and he had vetoed her request to let a room to make a little extra.

As they drank their tea, Jemima talked Miss Price through every aspect of her designs. It was an intense session, and Jemima felt the sleepless hours catching up with her. She was glad when Miss Price's sister came in, offering more tea and a slice of cake.

Though almost blind, Angela Price moved around with confidence. Jemima had noted on previous visits that nothing in the small room was ever moved or placed in her way. She watched Angela take the lid off the tea caddy, having first run her thumb down its side to identify it, then peer at the pattern on the lid of a cake tin. It had a decoration of exotic animals marching around its sides.

Jemima exclaimed, 'What a delightful object!' and was told it had been painted by a barge-woman, at the side of the Regent's Canal.

'She visits the zoo for inspiration and this is a picture representing Noah's Ark.'

Angela held out the tin and Jemima saw two zebras entering a boat, followed by paired elephants and panthers. On the lid were the entwined necks of two giraffes, their markings expressed in vivid colours.

'I have a speck of vision still,' Angela said, 'so I like things that are bold and clear.'

The Victoria sponge that came out was excellent, and it was past lunchtime when Jemima finally left Campden Buildings, her eyes adjusting to the winter light. She would return tomorrow as there were always problems to solve when the sewing began. Miss Price would send pieces out to trusted seamstresses, a bodice to one, sleeves to another, which would come back to her for assembly and finishing. By sharing the work, three evening gowns would be created to Lady Hamlash's tight schedule.

Somewhat light-headed after sitting so close to a fire, Jemima realised she was on the Bayswater Road only when she saw a street sign for Inverness Terrace. Fate? She let her feet make the choice.

Inverness Terrace was elegantly genteel, its white stucco houses benefiting from their proximity to Kensington Gardens. Go along at mid-morning, you would meet a battalion of uniformed nannies pushing perambulators, preceded by excited children.

The Royal Darnley Hotel was midway along. Its pillared front entrance boasted a uniformed doorman who advised Jemima to take care on the steps. 'Are you a resident, madam?'

'A visitor. I, er, wish to establish if a friend is staying here.' Until that moment, Jemima had entertained no fixed purpose other than to view the place from where Marie Guyen had written a postcard to Kenneth Wells. She was invited to step inside.

The hotel lobby exuded gracious comfort. Padded leather chairs, brass umbrella stands, ceiling roses and archways... she'd have thought it very grand in the days before Simon took her home to meet his parents. A stag's head gazed out over the reception desk. Curtains and upholstery were all in the Royal Stewart tartan.

A young woman at the desk asked politely if madam was wishing to book in.

'Not today. I'm a dear friend of Madame Marie Guyen.' To her dismay, Jemima faltered in speaking the name. Marie's last, rasping entreaty – *Help me* – came back full force. 'I believe she, er, has been your guest?'

165

She expected a denial along the lines of, 'We cannot give out such information'. What she did not expect was for the young woman to say, 'Sorry, I don't know anyone of that name. When was she here?'

Jemima sifted what she knew of Marie's arrival in England. 'I'm not sure when she booked in, but she wrote a card from here on November twenty-fourth. On the fourth or fifth of December, she left for the country.'

Marie had operated at a level of secrecy, replying to Lady Hamlash's advertisement through an accommodation address.

The young woman flipped back through the guest register. 'Hm. Nothing.' She gave an embarrassed smile. 'This is the Royal Darnley, madam. Might you have mixed us up with the Royal Inverness Hotel on the other side of the road? We often get confused for them.'

'This is the place.' Jemima was adamant. 'Dark-haired, dark-eyed. A French lady.'

'Oh.' The young woman's expression altered. She leaned forward. 'The lady the police were asking about, who sadly passed away?' The girl closed the register book. 'I was behind the desk when the officer asked for "Madame Guy-Anne", which is why I didn't pick up what you were saying.'

'What kind of policeman?' Jemima couldn't imagine DCI Bullace had found time to come to London.

'Scotland Yard, enquiring for a rural force. All I was able to tell him was that no "Madame Guy-Anne" had ever registered here as a guest. It was only after he'd gone that Mrs McAlistair realised who he must mean.' The receptionist explained that Mrs McAlistair owned the Royal Darnley.

'Was Madame staying here under an assumed name, then?'

'Oh, no.' The girl sounded shocked, as if masquerading at an establishment such as this was unthinkable. 'Under her legal name. Just, that name wasn't Guyen.'

'Show me, please.'

The receptionist turned the register so Jemima might read the entry for 1 November 1922. The guest had stayed in Room 12, under the name of Marie, Lady Hamlash.

Clarity leapt like an actor onto an empty stage. Either Marie Guyen was a brazen imposter, or she had married into the Hamlash family. In which case, her purpose at Merry Beggars Hall had indeed been the pursuit of justice: recognition of her marriage to Sir Edgar. With this thought, the undoubted motive for her killing struck Jemima like a bolt of lightning.

Chapter Twenty-Six

Jemima asked if she might see the room Marie, Lady Hamlash, had occupied. The receptionist didn't see why not and directed Jemima to the first floor.

'Tell the chambermaid I sent you, and she'll unlock the room for you. Lady Hamlash paid her bill until the New Year, so everything's as she left it.'

Mounting the sweeping staircase, Jemima remembered words Ada Hamlash had spoken into the telephone three days ago. 'She answered my advertisement – there wasn't time to check her references.'

Marie had secured her position by subterfuge. But why stoop to disguising herself and renting a correspondence address for anonymity? Why not drive up to the front door of Merry Beggars Hall and declare herself?

Wells would have the answer. Would have had. I suppose I asked all the wrong questions when I had the chance, Jemima thought sadly.

Peering through an open door, she spied a girl in a frilly apron running a duster over the frame of a bed with a tartan coverlet. When Jemima explained her purpose, the maid willingly put down her cloth and unlocked Room 12, echoing the receptionist's comment.

'Just as Her Ladyship left it.'

The room smelled of violet and vanilla, its source a bottle of *L'Heure Bleue* on the dresser. A more refined tincture than the one that had ended Marie's life. The dressing table was busy with little pots, diamond hair clips, a tortoiseshell brush-and-comb set. It looked to Jemima as if Marie had left 'Lady Hamlash' behind in London, arriving at Merry Beggars Hall complete with cook's whites and nailed clogs. Whatever else she had been, she had been a fine chef. 'Pastry never lies,' Jemima murmured.

A two-shilling tip ensured her as much time as she desired and Jemima began with the wardrobe. As in Suffolk, few items hung there, reinforcing the belief that Marie had sailed from New York with no intention of courting society. These dresses differed in that they carried the labels of Parisian couture houses. It didn't necessarily follow that they'd been bought in Paris, as French couturiers licensed their collections each year to outlets in New York, including Bergdorf Goodman.

Pulling up a footstool, Jemima lifted two hatboxes from the top of the wardrobe. One was fashioned from tin, finished with a layer of shiny brown Japan, the twin of the one in Suffolk. The other was cardboard and very light; something one might take on board ship as hand luggage. Inside was a straw cloche with a navy-blue lining and a matching rosette to one side. To go with the jacket at Merry Beggars Hall? The label was Reboux. *Très chic.* Too chic for the country, and suitable for spring, not winter. Jemima wasn't surprised it had been left behind. The tin box was not only heavy, it was locked, but a search of the dressing table produced a slender key. It turned out to be full of papers.

Jemima retired to a circular table, where a desk set and a blank notepad suggested that, here, Marie had written her letters. A rack bearing the hotel's coat of arms held a stash of postcards featuring the Royal Darnley Hotel in sepia. The same cards as the one Jack had rescued from Wells's fireplace. It was a chastening thought, Marie using *this* pen and *that* ink to advise Kenneth Wells she was joining him. Wells had been thoroughly against her leaving London, as her final words had proved. *He warned me.*

Jemima began to empty the hatbox. The first items were bills and receipts, including Marie's paid-up account from the hotel. Jemima next found two tickets issued by the White Star Line for a voyage from New York, calling at Southampton and Cherbourg in Normandy. The tickets were dated mid-October, with a return journey booked for January 1923. Marie had sailed first class, Wells in third. Jemima took that as a signal that they had categorically not shared a cabin.

A bill from a hotel on Place Vendôme, Paris, in October for a single room, suggested that Marie had stayed on board to Cherbourg, travelling onward to Paris. Had Wells disembarked at Southampton, making his way to Suffolk alone?

There was a receipt from No. 9, Rue Matignon, Paris, for the Reboux hat, dated November 1. Jemima blinked at the price before remembering to divide the figure in French francs by eighty. Even so, that little hat had cost more than her children's school fees. Clearly one got rich being a French chef in New York.

Rich though she may have been, a union between Marie and Sir Edgar Hamlash would have been viewed with suspicion by his family and his set. Having married well above her own station, Jemima knew full well how women like her were viewed among the English upper classes. Gold digger. Upstart. Fortune-hunting shop girl, in her case. Her first encounter with Simon had taken place in 1909 when Simon had come into her department store, gallantly accompanying his great-aunt to Ladies' Town Attire on the fourth floor. Jemima had approached, asking if she might be of assistance.

The great-aunt had peered at her through opera glasses, saying in a carrying voice, 'My, you're a bonny little thing.'

'Honestly, Auntie.' Simon had apologised to Jemima, adding, 'Can't take her anywhere.' A few days later, he had come in alone and passed her a note, inviting her to meet him at the Lyons tea shop in Piccadilly.

With a heavy sigh, Jemima continued digging through the papers.

A passport, issued by the United States, belonged to Marie Guyen Hamlash. Born 23 July 1886, in Paris, France. It made Marie thirty-six at the time of her death. The small photograph was instantly recognisable, and the document stated her height and hair colour along with other physical details – 'Forehead: High. Nose: Straight'. Occupation was given as 'Restaurant proprietress, New York'.

In a nutshell, Marie had been an American citizen of French origin, with the title of Lady Hamlash.

Jemima was about to set the passport aside when a line inserted in different-coloured ink caught her eye. Eight words that changed everything: 'The bearer is accompanied by her child Vivyan'.

Sir Edgar Hamlash's full name had been Edgar Vivyan. Jemima had learned that from his mother. It was the final clincher. Marie and Edgar. Man and wife, parents to a son. Where was the child now? At home in New York, or here in London? The burning question was this: how much did Ada, Lady Hamlash know? Had she known she was mother-in-law to Marie, grandmother to a child?

The last item of interest to Jemima was a letter in a shade of writing paper 'favoured by schoolgirls and kept women', to quote her sister Vicky. The letter was brief, brutally so, and revealed a profound deception at the heart of Merry Beggars Hall.

Jemima knew she ought to go to the police, put this letter in their hands and divulge everything she had found out today.

And she would, she assured herself. She would contact DCI Bullace, once she'd shown these words to one whose judgement she trusted above all others.

Chapter Twenty-Seven

The world had completed seven revolutions since an envelope of the exact same lilac shade had crossed the tea table at 17, Chesterfield Gardens, W1.

Last time, it had been Vicky passing it to Jemima. Now, the action was reversed. 'Read it, please, and give me your honest opinion.'

'Has Lady Hamlash written already?' Vicky put her spectacles on, peering down at the letter her sister had given her. 'I thought you were returning in a few days anyway.'

'It isn't addressed to me. Read the envelope.'

Vicky did so, out loud. '"Wittington Chambers, Kensington High Street, London. To be handed to the French person calling herself Lady Hamlash." Calling herself? How rude.'

'I checked Wittington Chambers and as I thought, it's an accommodation address,' Jemima explained. 'They handle letters addressed to all kinds of people. It's what's inside that matters. Read it.'

'Certainly not.' Vicky laid it on the tea table. 'It would be unconscionable.'

'I'm investigating a murder. Double murder, potentially.' Jemima didn't need her sister to point out that in removing the letter from the hotel, she had acted unethically. 'I was the last person Marie spoke to. She didn't want to die, Vicky, and now I know she has a son, I understand her terror in those last moments. Imagine, if it were me, wondering how Tommy and Molly would survive.'

'They'd do fine, as I'm their guardian in the event of your demise. Though I daresay it would be gloves-off with your father and mother-in-law.' Vicky tapped the envelope with a fingernail, telling Jemima that she *must* take it to the police.

'I mean to, but please read it, Vicky, because I need your wisdom. It's not as if you'd be steaming it open. Poor Marie can no longer speak for herself.'

With clear reluctance, Vicky yielded, making a face as she took the writing paper from the envelope. 'Lilac is charming in bouquets and acceptable in underwear and nowhere else.' Adjusting her spectacles, she read the letter out loud.

Merry Beggars Hall
22 November 1922

Madam,

I write to you in advance of legal action to demand that you no longer importune me by asserting your unfounded claim to be Lady Hamlash by virtue of having married my son. Such a claim is fraudulent and demeans my son's character. I have borne this for too long. Should it come to my attention again that you are passing yourself off as my daughter-in-law, my solicitor has instructions to take the matter to court. Any further letters you may send will be returned, unopened.

Ada Hamlash

Vicky lowered the letter. 'Your Marie was pretending to be a Hamlash, I take it?'

'Not pretending. It's the name in her passport. She married Sir Edgar, in France, I suspect. He died there of his injuries in the winter of 1917. Recognition of the marriage is the justice she was seeking.'

'She left it rather a long time,' was Vicky's caustic response. 'The war's been over four years.'

It was a good point. It was a long time to wait, Jemima admitted.

'Doesn't that rather hint at fraud?' Vicky suggested. 'You know, somebody reading the casualty lists in an old, British newspaper and thinking, "Here's a chance of some easy money"?'

'Hardly easy, coming all the way from America,' Jemima countered. 'Anyway, I've seen her passport. It proves she was who she says she was.'

'You can fake a passport.'

'How many have you faked? Marie *is*, rather *was*, Lady Hamlash, Edgar's widow, with rights to a financial interest in her late husband's estate, on behalf of their son.'

'Why didn't she claim her rights before?' When Jemima gave no answer, Vicky tried a different tack. 'When did Marie come to England?'

'October, docking in Southampton at the end of the month, staying on board to Cherbourg – or so I speculate as she was in Paris at the start of November.'

'Hm.' Vicky sounded cagey. 'A jaunt to Paris implies somebody getting their money's worth from a liner ticket. Where in France did they marry, she and Edgar?'

'Good question.' And not one that Jemima could answer. 'Edgar fought with the Suffolk Regiment and took part in the battles around Cambrai. My father-in-law could tell us the exact week that regiment was mobilised, but let us say it was some time in 1915, or early 1916. At the tail-end of 1917, Edgar was severely wounded.'

'They could have married in England or France,' Vicky said. 'A sight of their marriage lines would tell you the place.'

Jemima agreed, adding, 'Wells could have said more.'

'Ah, yes, Wells.' Vicky had heard Jemima's full account of her time at Merry Beggars Hall. 'The handsome American who must be innocent because… remind me… he possesses honest blue eyes?'

'Innocent because he wasn't in the house when Marie died and wasn't in England when Roland Crosby was butchered. You realise I think the two killings are linked?'

'I realise it,' Vicky said wearily.

'Wells's liner ticket bears the same dates as Marie's. They arrived together and would have sailed back together.'

'Married fraudsters, perchance?'

Jemima gave a dry laugh. 'Marie had a stateroom. Wells's ticket was one up from steerage. It would be a strange sort of marriage.'

'Not if they were playing their roles to the hilt.'

'Oh, Vicky!'

'You like me to test your thinking. What use am I if I squawk "Aren't you clever?" like a trained parrot?'

Jemima acknowledged the point. This was why she consulted her sister. Why she trusted her. 'I can see why you think Marie's claim was a charade. Only, wouldn't it be an awful bother to swindle a dowager in England, travelling across an ocean at great expense when there must be richer pickings in New York?'

Vicky allowed this to be so, but on one matter she was immovable. 'You must hand in this letter. What if there *is* a child, in limbo and in distress?'

'I'll post it to DCI Bullace this afternoon,' Jemima agreed meekly. 'I've a call to make first.'

'A call where?'

'SW1,' Jemima answered, without adding any more detail.

Vicky picked up and put down her cup. Their tea had gone cold. 'If your deductions are correct, once Marie revealed her identity and the existence of a son to Lady Hamlash, she was marked for murder.'

Jemima felt a shiver. Wells had known it and now he too was dead.

'I know why you do this, Jemima.' Vicky had risen to relight the spirit kettle on the dresser. 'It's to take your mind off Simon and—'

'Not at all,' Jemima cut in fast. 'I find it fascinating, is all. If Marie were legitimately married to the late Sir Edgar—'

'Their son is the rightful heir to Merry Beggars Hall.' Vicky placed a silver kettle on the flame. 'Edgar was the elder and primogeniture can be overset only by Act of Parliament. If it was known there was a little boy, Sir Finchley—'

'Would not be Sir Finchley,' Jemima finished. 'He would be plain Mr Hamlash. He wouldn't own Merry Beggars Hall. He would have the burden of running the estate for his infant nephew without the pleasure of the title.'

Vicky asked a question that brought a profound chill to the cosy room. 'Is the child in danger?'

'I hope not.' Something Wells had said before he escaped through her window came into Jemima's mind. *There's still more to do, vital work...* 'Before she died, Marie stated that she had come "a very long way to be heard". It's obvious, isn't it?' Hers and Vicky's eyes met, agreement reached like a plain handshake. 'Who had most to lose if she made her claim public?'

'Sir Finchley Hamlash. His mother, and most particularly his wife.'

Jemima agreed that here was a cogent reason for Lady Olivia to resent Marie Guyen. 'A husband's demotion might cost them their social position in Royal Norfolk.'

'Social death,' Vicky agreed, though a moment later, her innate cynicism sprang back. 'It's all too Gothic. I'm as susceptible as anyone to a gripping yarn, but I say the balance of probability is still that Marie's death was a tragic accident.'

Vicky topped up the teapot from the steaming kettle. A moment later, as she lifted her freshly filled cup to her lips, Jemima shouted, 'Don't drink that!'

Vicky put her cup down hurriedly. 'Why not?'

'I dropped in an adulterated sugar cube when you weren't looking.'

'You certainly did not. Don't be an idiot.'

'You're right,' Jemima agreed. 'But if I had, would you want people going round saying it was a tragic accident?'

'You have a sinister way of making your point, Jemima. You're going back to Merry Beggars Hall? I suppose that's a redundant question.'

Jemima said she had to return, to fulfil her commission and be paid. 'Miss Price will have the dresses ready by the 18th, mid-morning, and I'll take the afternoon train to Suffolk.'

An emotion closer to fear than resignation put shadows in Vicky's cheeks. 'What if it's your head next, left under a flowerpot?'

'Asparagus cloche. It won't be.'

'The children will be home this time next week. Shall I tell them that their mother is off gambling with her life?'

'Vicky, dearest, I'll be back in time to meet them off their train.' Jemima gathered up the tea things and took the tray down to the kitchen. As she washed up she thought of Beth doing the same chore, several times a day, every day.

After she'd dried up and applied lanolin cream to her hands, she retired to her little office, opened her journal, put the day's date and wrote:

'With Vicky's collaboration, I have established a motive for Marie Guyen's death, which points to Sir Finchley Hamlash and those whose fortunes are tied up with his.' That being his wife and perhaps his mother. 'On Monday, December the eleventh at a little before five PM, somebody entered Merry Beggars Hall and set in motion events that would lead to the deaths of Marie Guyen and Kenneth Wells.' Jemima crossed out 'Marie Guyen', and wrote, 'the younger Lady Hamlash.' She continued: 'Thus removing the threat she posed to Sir Finchley's possession of the title. It is probable to my mind that Lady Olivia Hamlash delivered the substance that caused Marie's fatal seizure, and possible that one or more servants at the hall are under Sir Finchley's influence or in his pay. *Nota bene*, Albert Crosby's alibi at the time of his brother's disappearance involves a visit to Sir Finchley's Norfolk estate. Wells's death was certainly accidental but let me commit to paper my belief that Marie's demise and that of Roland Crosby stemmed from the same murderous hands. In this belief I am joined by the Detective Chief Inspector in charge of the case. If I were him, I would put Albert Crosby's alibi through the wringer.'

'I'm off. Be good.' Vicky called out as she passed Jemima's door. She was on her way to give a piano lesson at a home in Chesterfield Gardens. Jemima listened for the front door to close before going upstairs to change for outdoors. Into a sturdy shoulder bag went her purse and various props she would need in the hours ahead. She left a note for Vicky, saying she'd be home by six. Buttoning on her puttees at the front door, she left the house.

On Berkeley Square, after a twenty-minute trudge through snow that was fulfilling Mrs Crosby's prophecy of turning into dirty slush, she dropped a letter addressed to DCI Bullace into a post box. He would receive Lady Hamlash's threat of legal action against the other Lady Hamlash, anonymously, by morning.

She flagged down a taxi, giving the driver an SW1 address.

The man repeated it back to her as she got in. 'Bright's, St James's Street, Madam? They won't let you in, I can tell you that much.'

'I don't need to go in. Drive on, please.'

Chapter Twenty-Eight

The polished black door of the exclusive gentlemen's club was guarded by a porter in top hat and white gloves. He politely informed Jemima what the cabbie had already told her: ladies were not permitted over the threshold of Bright's.

Jemima was prepared. Dabbing eyes reddened with a fingertip of rouge, she pulled an envelope from her bag. It was a plain, white one from her desk. 'Then would you deliver this to a gentleman who comes here?'

'Who might that be, madam?' Clearly, she was not the first forlorn female to attempt to get a message to a privileged member.

'Sir Edgar Hamlash.'

The porter reeled back a hair's breadth, telling her it was quite impossible. 'Sir Edgar was killed on active service, madam, and his name is inscribed on the Board of Remembrance in the members' billiard room.' Glancing at the envelope still clutched in Jemima's hand, he sighed. 'You are not the first lady writing to him.'

Jemima feigned shock. 'Who, when?'

'I'm not at liberty to say who, but it was a year ago. I recall the postman bringing it as I fixed a Christmas wreath to the door. It was sent from America.'

'America—' Jemima almost gave herself away by asking too eagerly, 'Do, please, say who sent it.'

'I couldn't possibly. One of the club servants took charge of it, to pass on to Sir Edgar's family, having a brother in service with Sir Edgar's mother.' The porter stopped. The shock blooming in Jemima's face had required no acting.

That club servant had to be Roland Crosby, but dare she demand proof?

Seeing Jemima open and close her mouth, the porter said gently, 'You'd do best to put whatever all this is behind you, madam.'

Settling back into her charade, she dabbed away another fictitious tear. 'I wish I could. I – I have poured my soul into this letter.'

'Very well,' the porter said, one kind heart to a distressed one. 'Sir Edgar's brother pops in when he's up from the country, so perhaps I could pass it to him.'

'Sir Finchley's a member here too?' she asked, wide-eyed, though she'd been told that all Hamlash men received membership at the age of twenty-one.

'He comes in when he and his lady wife are in town.' White kidskin fingers took the letter and Jemima walked away, her handkerchief pressed to her face until she was certain she was no longer being watched. At some date in the future, Sir Finchley Hamlash would receive an envelope containing nothing at all.

From St James's, she walked to Piccadilly where she called at her bank. Waiting in line to withdraw money, she wondered why the police had given so little weight to the fact that Sir Finchley Hamlash and Roland Crosby had rubbed shoulders in Bright's Club, one as a member, the other as a waiter. Bullace's predecessor must have been aware of it. Bullace himself must know. She concluded they had chosen not to push the point. 'Ye shall not ruffle titled feathers' being a well-known police motto. But had they known that a letter sent from New York to Edgar Hamlash – and who would have sent it if not Marie? – had fallen into Roland's hands?

Vicky might accuse her of leaping to conclusions, but here was an unarguable link between Roland Crosby, Marie Guyen and the Hamlash family. With a couple of bank customers still ahead of her, she made a quick journal entry.

I can classify both Marie Guyen and Roland Crosby as threats to Sir Finchley Hamlash. Marie, as mother to the true Hamlash heir. Roland because he may have opened the letter entrusted to him. If that letter contained an account of Marie's marriage and the birth of a son, he would be in a position to expose a scandal.

The beauty of this explanation was that it did not require Marie to have met with Roland at all. Jemima could dispense with ideas of them rendez-vous-ing in Kensington Gardens or by the Serpentine. All it required was Marie's letter to have been opened and read by a man inclined to act in a self-interested way.

Imagine this… Roland had exerted pressure on Sir Finchley. Picture a waiter sidling up to a seated figure in the members' lounge of Bright's Club, bending to whisper into the ear above a starched and laundered collar.

'May I have a quiet word, Sir Finchley?'

A quiet word, repeated more and more loudly until it became coercion and the victim felt he had no choice but to rid himself of the man

'I need to break into their world,' Jemima said to herself. 'I need to discover if blackmail took place. But where do I start with that?'

*

The following morning, Jemima made her scheduled visit to Campden Buildings. Miss Price was out, expected back in fifteen minutes. Jemima accepted Angela's offer of tea and while it was being made, entertained herself by riffling through copies of *The Lady*.

Jemima could imagine Marie flipping through in just the same way, her eye snagging on a familiar name in the classifieds at the rear: 'Lady Hamlash requires a good, plain cook for the Christmas period, immediate start.' Wells had planted himself at Merry Beggars Hall a month prior and Marie had seized this chance to join him. Had she curled her lip at emulating a 'plain cook'? Probably. But a free pass into the house that had always been denied her could not be ignored.

'I bet she posted her application in ten minutes' flat,' Jemima said to herself.

How soon after Marie's arrival had Lady Hamlash discovered that she had invited her nemesis into her home?

'One lump or two, Mrs Flowerday?'

The arrival of tea and Miss Price's return from her errands curtailed this stream of thought. An hour was spent inspecting the progress of the gowns. Miss Price had drafted in three outside hands, women who worked fast and to a high standard. Jemima was confident her deadline would be met. It was decided that a taxi should collect the gowns from Miss Price first thing on Monday, and deliver them to Chesterfield Gardens, boxed for Jemima to take to Suffolk.

As she got up to go, the copy of *The Lady* she'd been looking at slid to the floor.

'Were you reading the piece on Lady Olivia Hamlash?' Miss Price asked. 'It was in a September issue.' She located it and read it out. '"Following her marriage, Lady Olivia Hamlash has formed a society to be known as The Gentlewomen's Cricket Supporters' Club." It's a bit of a mouthful, but they watch matches together,' Miss Price said, 'and she holds teas at home afterwards. In her garden, very select.'

It wasn't a surprise to discover that Lady Olivia liked cricket, being a woman who reached outside the feminine sphere. Her appearance was inscribed in Jemima's memory: driving coat, tan leather gloves with incongruous, kidskin shoes.

'What's their London address?' she asked. Lady Hamlash had referred to a London home, as had Lady Olivia. The doorman at Bright's had implied it too. 'Near the cricket ground, I suppose?'

Miss Price had no idea. 'Take the magazine, Mrs Flowerday. I've done with it. May I impose on you to take some of my business cards also, to pass on to your clients? I don't believe I will be trespassing on your territory.'

Jemima agreed readily, promising to leave them where they might gain Miss Price the best clients. It was a few minutes past two by the time Jemima was on her way, walking down the stairs of Bayswater underground station. A low rumble presaged her train's arrival, and she hopped on without checking its destination. Sitting down, opening the magazine Miss Price had given her, she turned to the piece on Lady Olivia.

The information she was seeking was contained in the middle paragraph, and Jemima silently thanked the writer for being so gushingly clear about it.

> The Hamlashes' town residence occupies a pleasant position in St John's Wood, where stands a magnificent cedar, casting shade upon Lady Olivia's summer teas. Her beloved cricket ground is close enough to hear the ageless crack of leather upon willow.

The next station – Paddington – arrived, its name imprinted on the tile-glazed wall, and Jemima felt the hand of fate at work once again. All in a hurry, she'd taken a train terminating at Edgware Road instead of going in the other direction. When she got off three stops later at Baker Street, a vague plan had been fired into shape.

Yesterday, she'd wished she could peer into the masculine worlds of Roland Crosby and Sir Finchley Hamlash, suspecting it to be beyond her scope. By chance, another doorway had appeared; that of Lady Olivia Hamlash's London home.

Chapter Twenty-Nine

From Baker Street, she took the Metropolitan Line and got off at St John's Wood Road, asking directions to the cricket ground. Halfway down a broad avenue she felt the hairs tingle at the back of her neck. She paused outside a residence called Cedar House, where grey-green boughs soared above the roofline, and thanked the animal instinct that had brought her to the right place. She let herself in through the gate and, ignoring the front porch, went down steps into a railed area and knocked on a glazed door. She recalled commenting on Lady Olivia Hamlash's driving coat in the great hall at Merry Beggars, asking if it hampered her ability to drive. Lady Olivia had agreed that it did, describing the coat she had on as 'horrid'. She had left her favourite one in the London house. With a tear to mend…'

The kitchen door opened and a heavy-set woman with rolled sleeves and a duster knotted over grizzled curls asked, 'Well, dear, what can I do you for?'

Jemima presented one of Miss Price's business cards, explaining that she'd come for Lady Olivia Hamlash's caped silk driving coat. 'It requires repair.'

'First I've heard.' The domestic glanced at the card. 'Miss Price, are you? Well, come in, let's keep the breeze out.'

Jemima stepped into a kitchen that smelled heavily of washing soda. Cupboards stood wide open, their contents spread across various surfaces. Evidently, a thorough clean-up was taking place while Sir Finchley and Lady Olivia were in the country. A leisurely clean, helped along by a steaming kettle and a currant cake with a large wedge missing from it. A maid of about twenty years old, sitting at the table, glanced up from the puzzle-book she was engrossed in. Her colleague explained Jemima's reason for calling.

'Lady Olivia's silk duster?' The maid frowned. 'That's Miss Bedgley's business, mending and the like.'

Miss Bedgley must be a lady's maid.

Jemima smiled brightly. 'Miss B. was there at the time, but it was Lady Olivia who was most concerned to have the coat repaired.'

'Oh, so you've been to… where's the place they were staying?'

'Steeple Court or do you mean Brabberton Manor? I have connections with both,' Jemima said, resisting the urge to embroider detail. It would be awkward should these women mention her visit at a later date.

The older domestic surveyed Jemima's hat and coat, in a brisk assessment of her status. 'Miss Bedgley would have our hides if we stepped into Her Ladyship's private domain, but you're free to take a look yourself.'

Jemima smiled. 'Thank you. I was told it's in the larger wardrobe, alongside the country tweeds. Or if not, it's in the boot room next to Sir Finchley's spare overcoat.'

Her confident lies earned an instant dividend.

'When you've done, Miss Price, come down and take a cup of tea with us.'

Conscious that the afternoon was wearing on, Jemima shed her coat and headed upstairs, identifying Lady Olivia's bedroom suite by its pastel drapery and the scent of gardenia. A search of the wardrobes revealed clothes from Lucile, the leading London couturière known socially as Lady Duff-Gordon. Jemima didn't find a duster coat for mending, nor did a search of the dressing-room reveal it. She turned a pair of satin evening shoes upside down. Handmade in London. What was interesting was the way their tops arched to accommodate the wearer's high instep.

'Coat, where are you?' Jemima had absolutely no interest in the garment, except that it was her alibi. Her intention was to get into Sir Finchley's study, to find evidence of contact between him and Roland Crosby. Marie's letter, arriving at Bright's Club at Christmas, 1921, had ignited something between the two men, she was certain. It was too early to say if that something was blackmail, but where there was conflict of interest, there were always traces.

So stated *The Weekend Sleuth* in every issue.

Sir Finchley's bedroom was two doors along from his lady's. Its air was impregnated with the scent of bay rum, the popular elixir for male baldness. Curtains and the bedspread were a shade of claret, the pictures on the wall hunting prints mouldy enough to have come from Merry Beggars Hall. But what she needed to find was Sir Finchley's study, where he wrote letters and updated his diary.

When she and Simon had lived together in Chesterfield Gardens, there hadn't been space for him to have his own office and he'd dealt with business correspondence at the dining-room table. Jemima couldn't picture Sir Finchley submitting to such limitations, being shooed out whenever the table had to be laid. Somewhere within Cedar House would be the master's private domain.

She went downstairs and in a boot room near the scullery, to her profound relief, there hung a caped driving coat of ribbed beige silk. A quick inspection showed its front pocket was almost torn off. Jemima folded it over her arm and returned to the main hall. She quietly opened doors one after the other. Drawing room, dining room, morning room… all opulently furnished and hung with excellent pictures. An impression was growing that this house, this life, was Lady Olivia's endowment and that the Hamlash marriage was a financially unequal one. Finchley hadn't even been Lady Olivia's first choice, now she thought about it.

The next door that Jemima opened revealed a library. In contrast to Merry Beggars Hall, its atmosphere was tolerably warm and smelled of lavender and beeswax. Eureka! To one side, an arched niche contained a masculine-sized desk, a swivel chair and a green-hooded reading lamp.

She hesitated, the weight of good manners bearing down on her. It was the memory of Marie Guyen's life slipping away in front of her that made her approach the desk, opening one of its drawers. Empty. She opened a second, a third. Also empty. The pull-out tray under the desktop contained only spare pen nibs and a lined pad without a mark on it.

'Swept clean' was the phrase that best fitted this desk. Sir Finchley had expunged all his private correspondence, perhaps before leaving for Norfolk. Running her fingertips around the edge in the hope of finding a secret compartment, she muttered, 'Finchley Hamlash, your furniture is as dull as you.'

Jemima heard footsteps on the hall tiles, then, 'Miss Price, are you up there still?'

The person asking must be standing at the foot of the stairs. Jemima looked frantically for a means of escape. She couldn't climb out of the window. If seen, any enquiry would lead straight to poor Miss Price. What possible excuse could she make for being in here?

Fear makes a person clumsy. Stepping back, Jemima's elbow collided with a wire tray, unnoticed until now. It fell from its shelf, spilling papers and letters.

'Are you somewhere down here, Miss Price?'

It was the older of the two maids, whose footsteps now drew near the library door. Scrabbling to refill the wire tray, the last item Jemima picked up was an unopened letter with the insignia of a London bank. From its weight and shape, she guessed its contents. She jammed it into the folds of Lady Olivia's coat and replaced the wire tray as the library's door handle rattled.

Jemima scuttled across the room and clambered up onto a set of steps, grabbing a book at random from the shelf, Lady Olivia's coat still draped over her left arm.

The maid came in. Seeing Jemima slightly above her eyeline, an open book in her hand, she gave a dubious frown. 'We wondered where you'd got to. I see you found the coat.'

'I did, then couldn't resist popping in here.' With a broad, apologetic smile, Jemima displayed the book's cover. 'If I could turn a magic ring this is where I would go, in a flash.'

'"Into the Amazon Basin"?' the maid read cumbersomely. 'Well I never. A week in Clacton would suit me.' Her brow cleared, as if finding Jemima to be a bookworm was disappointing but not suspicious. 'We've made a pile of ham-and-cress sandwiches, if you'd care to join us.'

Conscious she had a short lease left on the day and one more task to pull in, Jemima began to decline, when her stomach rumbled. Gadding about London in the snow whipped up an appetite. 'Thank you. Let me put this book back.'

'I daresay Lady Olivia would lend it, if you asked. This was her grandfather's collection.'

'You've been with the family a while?'

'I've served in the present Earl Rivers' household since I was twelve years old. Take the book, Miss Price, since you'll be coming back.'

'I will?' Why did the woman think so?

'After you've mended the coat.'

Such a blunder. She laughed to hide her gaffe. 'My mind was miles away.' Jemima returned the book to its place and stepped down from her perch. 'Nobody really likes to lend books,' she said as she followed her guide back to the basement kitchen.

The sandwiches were delicious, and the tea poured with them most welcome. Jemima steered the conversation onto her subject of interest.

'How do you find it, in service here?'

Lady Olivia was decent enough, she was told, if you worked to her standards, while Sir Finchley had a peevish turn of temper.

'We all know she married beneath her,' the older maid said, spreading mustard between the layers of her sandwich.

'She took second best,' added the younger maid.

'Having been engaged to Sir Edgar Hamlash?' Jemima prompted.

'That's it,' nodded the greyer of the two. 'Mortal sad, that was, him dying. After the war there weren't men enough left, were there? Doris should know.'

With a sigh, the younger maid – Doris, presumably – displayed her left hand, the stubby fingers devoid of rings.

'I daresay you wouldn't be "Miss Price" either,' the older one continued, 'but for the casualties. Only, hang on, you do wear a ring.'

Jemima had reached for another sandwich, plainly showing her wedding band.

Blunder number two. She thought on her feet. 'I wear a ring to protect myself from male impudence while travelling by bus. I understand that Lady Olivia married Sir Finchley in July.' She recalled Lady Hamlash saying so. 'Was it a London wedding?'

'No, Norfolk. They married from Earl and Countess Rivers' country seat and their Majesties sent flowers. It was in the papers.'

'A society wedding, then,' Jemima observed. Somehow, she couldn't imagine Sir Finchley Hamlash spurring the diarists of the press to much rapture, but, naturally, Lady Olivia's nuptials would have merited a mention in the society pages.

'Wanted a husband, did Lady O,' said Doris. 'Didn't like being a spinster. More tea, Miss Price?'

Jemima declined, hoping to get home before dark, where she'd take off her shoes, draw a bath and have a nip of something stronger than tea before confessing her day's work to Vicky.

On the train a short while later, rumbling towards Baker Street with Lady Olivia's coat in her guilty possession, she reviewed the letter harvested from Sir Finchley's study. The postmark showed it had been sent quite recently, and Jemima presumed that his correspondence was at some point to be sent down to the country. The letter was from the London County Bank, Hanover Square branch, and it contained a wad of used cheques. A year's worth of cleared cheques written by Sir Finchley Hamlash were being returned 'for his records'. She sorted through them. Some were made out to Bright's Club. A substantial one was to a Jermyn Street tailor. Another was to a Mayfair motor garage. There were regular payments into a Life Assurance fund, and several to a company of wine merchants. One to a Norfolk golf club. Another to the Royal Automobile Club and another—

This was what made sleuthing so irresistible, driving Jemima through the doubts and the blundering. A cheque for three thousand pounds had been made out to a payee named 'Crosby'.

Here was the twist. Not R. Crosby, but A. Crosby.

On 21 April this year, Sir Finchley Hamlash had paid a small fortune to his mother's butler, a day before the butler's brother had left London, never to be seen alive again.

Was Jemima heading straight home to her bath? Absolutely not.

At Baker Street, she stayed on the train until she reached the interchange for the Piccadilly Line. Her next destination, North London.

Finsbury Park, and the home of the late Roland Crosby.

Chapter Thirty

As she walked up Cherry Hall Road, N4, Jemima knew her sister would be looking out at the lowering light and wondering where she was. She must make this quick.

The reporter who had visited Sara Crosby had described this street as 'neat and unpretentious'. Jemima did not disagree. Behind a clipped privet hedge, the front garden of number 37 was thickly planted with myrtle whose glossy leaves each held a teaspoonful of snow. Beneath a bay window, the grille of the coal cellar sparkled with tiny icicles, no bigger than earrings. The window curtains were drawn and the effect was of a life barricaded against a messy, intrusive world. Sara Crosby would have had a surfeit of intrusion. In that spirit, on her last visit to Merry Beggars Hall, she'd asked her brother-in-law to fetch her from Ipswich, to spare her the stares of fellow rail passengers. She must be feeling more chipper these days, as she'd walked from the train just the other day, hailing her brother-in-law without a flicker of fear or suspicion.

At the station, as they traded comments about the snow, Sara had helpfully mentioned where she hid her door key. Jemima moved the boot scraper and closed her fingers around ice-cold metal. Moments later, she was inside. There was gas lighting in the front

195

passage, but she daren't use it as it would shine through the door glass, visible to anyone passing.

Upstairs first, or downstairs? She had perhaps half an hour of daylight in which to search, if she drew the curtains back. Hesitating at the stairs' foot, she thought she heard a creak from above. After an intense minute's listening, she dismissed it as the contraction of an empty house at the end of a day. To the sitting room first, she decided. Once in there, she opened the curtains and gazed around. Here, a writer from *The Weekend Sleuth* had partaken of tea and coconut cake. Jemima saw little of the domestic cheer the reporter had evoked. It was cold and everything that could be polished was rubbed to a hard shine. The armchairs were draped with linen antimacassars that were spotlessly white and smelled pleasantly. At some point, a man who oiled his hair with a mint-infused balm had sat here.

She chose the closest chair to sit in and picked up a folded copy of *The Evening News* from a side table. It was the lunchtime edition from Friday 21 April, the day before Roland Crosby had set off on his perplexing journey into Suffolk. Had it come home with him after a long shift at Bright's Club? Had he sat here reading it? That Sara had left it suggested she'd made this room a shrine to 'her Roly'.

'I don't think she comes in here very much, except to clean,' Jemima muttered.

She got up and went to a Scotch dresser in the corner. Room-pieces like this had been wildly fashionable in her parents' day, dark veneered with candy-twist insets and deep, lockable drawers. The drawers of this one were not locked.

The bottom three contained tablecloths and scallop-edged tray mats, cushion covers and embroidered hand towels. Jemima got a noseful of camphor, a smell she detested though it was the best preservative against moth. It told her these items were rarely used. Sara and Roland Crosby had no children. They did not entertain. Jemima felt a coldness in the house that wasn't entirely to do with its owner being absent.

The top drawer proved more rewarding as it held papers, including the deeds to the house which, interestingly, were in Sara Crosby's name. Jemima found letters from a doctor, which she did not read, bills from the Gas Board and two from the coal merchant, one with a November date, and another dated three days ago. A National Insurance card belonging to Roland showed he'd paid his stamp up until 24 December, last year. At which point, he had stopped. Stopped paying into a fund that would guarantee him an income should he fall ill. . . on Christmas Eve. Was that relevant? Marie Guyen's letter had arrived as the doorkeeper at Bright's hung a Christmas wreath. Perhaps Roland had discovered a better form of insurance than paying his stamp.

She found no bank statements among the papers, but it was doubtful Roland or Sara Crosby had their own bank account. Few working people did. Jemima had one because her father-in-law had agreed, reluctantly, to act as guarantor when she had set up in business.

Conscious of the fast-fading day, she searched the remaining papers, finding a post-office savings book. It was Roland's, and it proved to be a Book of Revelation. Last year, on 27 December, Roland Crosby had deposited one hundred pounds in his savings account.

A month later, in January 1922, thirty pounds appeared. In February, another thirty. March, likewise. April, likewise.

'I smell blackmail,' Jemima said to the empty room.

In May – she knew before turning the page there would be no payment. 'How do you get rid of an extortionist?' she asked out

197

loud as she replaced everything in the drawer and closed the curtains. 'You kill him.'

But why, having done that, do you cut off his head and place it in your mother's asparagus house?

She walked into a kitchen as tidy as Sara Crosby's living room. The range was recently black-leaded. Kindling, logs, matches and coal were arranged beside it in a copper box. The table was clear but for a candle in a holder and a paper pad. Jemima lowered a blind and lit the candle using the matches. The pad turned out to be an invoice book, which showed that Sara Crosby regularly sent out bills for baking cakes. She got paid quite well. The top page read: 'For making of wedding cake for Mrs Blandford and daughter. Five shillings and eightpence, payment received with thanks.' It was a carbon copy, the top sheet having been torn away for the customer. A glance through showed that Sara Crosby had kept busy the whole year, with an understandable gap in April and May. This most recent October and November had seen her baking batches of Christmas cakes for local bakeries. Jemima now understood why she ordered so much coal. That range must eat it.

She took a slow look around. Tiers of cake tins lined the shelves, in every size from base drum to snuffbox. Though Sara had 'packed the kitchen sink', according to her brother-in-law, the kitchen still contained an armoury of implements. Wooden spoons, metal strainers, cheese graters and colanders hung from hooks. The drawers held an array of knives, skewers and measuring spoons, though there were gaps, presumably because Sara had taken some with her. The kitchen cupboard stored crocks of flour and dried fruit, raising agent, food colouring and every essence imaginable: vanilla, almond, coconut, pineapple, coffee and peppermint. A great deal of peppermint oil, come to that, twelve miniature bottles. As a professional baker, Mrs Crosby would naturally buy in bulk.

Leaving the kitchen, Jemima was shocked to see how dark it had become outside. She ought to leave, but the urge to explore upstairs was too strong. In the main bedroom, she eased open the curtains, letting in the last glimmer of daylight. There were two mahogany wardrobes, the first that Jemima peered into containing two skirts, a single dress and a blouse. Sara must have taken most of her things to Merry Beggars Hall, though perhaps she didn't possess much anyway. The second wardrobe throbbed with the masculine odour of hair oil. The first thing she touched was a winter overcoat.

Had Roland Crosby owned two coats then? In her statement to the police, as retold by *The Weekend Sleuth*, his wife had whisked a clothes brush over a corduroy coat collar. The one hanging up had a velvet collar. A neighbour had reported Roland leaving early on that ice-cold April morning, wearing 'his usual coat and hat'. No reason he shouldn't have a second coat for best, though the one she was looking at didn't strike Jemima as being particularly superior. Not for a man getting thirty pounds a month on top of his salary.

There was a suit on a double hanger, of a pre-war cut. Waistcoats, casual trousers, shirts. On the base of the wardrobe was a pair of black leather Oxfords… Jemima took them out. Size ten. They appeared unpolished. She could not remember a single occasion when either her father or her husband had put shoes away without a shine you could see your face in. Perhaps Mrs Crosby's house-proud ways did not extend to footwear. Jemima was about to close the wardrobe door when, on impulse, she dug her hand into the overcoat pocket. She brought out a halfpenny, a silver threepenny piece and a small iron key. The kind of key that opens the door of an inside room.

In the other pocket, she found a train ticket. It had a clip out of the side, so it had been used once. The room was far too dim for her to identify the issuing station or the destination. Desperate to see more even to the point of risking switching on the lights, she tried to step back. Only she couldn't. A physical weight was blocking her. Faint breath touched the back of her neck and terror robbed her of speech. She tried to scream, but a hand clamped her mouth.

A voice whispered in her ear, 'What are you doing, Mrs Flowerday?'

It was the voice of a dead man.

Chapter Thirty-One

'Mr Wells,' she gasped when the hand over her mouth relaxed. She turned, and there he was, bear-like in the dim light. His brute appearance, she realised, was owing to the woolly blanket he'd wrapped around his shoulders, and the fact that he needed a shave. 'You!'

'Me, yes. The very same.'

'That was a vile trick, creeping up.'

'I needed to be sure it was you, not a neighbour or the lady of the house who might, just might, have had one of her kitchen knives on her person.'

'I cannot imagine Sara Crosby stabbing anyone, but it would have been your just deserts. However, she's in Suffolk.'

'That's handy.'

'We thought you were dead!'

'As you were meant to.'

Jemima moved towards the window, wanting to put distance between herself and the wardrobe, which was now an object of distaste. Wells stopped her. He told her she should not have opened the curtains at all.

'This is the sort of road where neighbours keep an eye out.'

'I needed to see what I was doing,' she retorted. 'I could hardly carry a wavering candle.'

'The solution would have been to come earlier.'

'Impossible, for reasons I won't go into. Will you tell me how your clothes ended up beside the railway line and your blood on the wheels of a train?'

'It wasn't my blood.' Wells sat down on the side of the bed.

Jemima, after a moment's indecision, joined him. Wells had never scared her... not entirely. She judged him to be a man of ferocious emotion rather than of violence.

'Whose blood, then?'

'You don't want to know.'

She did. She was very clear about it.

'Okay. Back to the moment I dropped out of your window. I legged it across the garden and the park, then over the fields to Brabberton Manor station. I could have got on the train from there, but as it's often left unmanned, it didn't serve my purpose.'

'I'd have thought an unmanned station would have been perfect for an escape,' she said.

'No, no. I needed the police to find evidence of my terrible accident at first light, not in two or three days' time. I needed them to stop looking for me at once, see? So I walked along the tracks to Beggars Heath.'

'That's why no footprints were found between there and Merry Beggars Hall. And the falling snow covered your escape across the park.'

'Nature was my friend, though if I'd been going to die that night, it would been from exposure.'

'You were explaining the blood.'

'You are ghoulish. I like that in you. On my way to Brabberton, I passed a turkey farm. Men were at work, in the early hours, slaughtering the birds.'

'Of course. Only a week until Christmas. Am I to understand that the blood...?'

'The killing of turkeys involves more than squawks and feathers. There was a barrel outside the barn, enough blood in it to drown a warthog. Not that one would.'

'You daubed your jacket?'

'Dipped it, ma'am. And got colder because I'm far too much the fine gentleman to have put it back on again.'

'You threw it down with a shoe and your hat by the railway line, to stage your death.'

'Yup. Dropped them a short way on from Beggars Heath station, as if I had clung to the side of the milk train for a few, heroic yards before letting go. I even scattered the money you kindly loaned me, as if it had tumbled from my pockets. That hurt.'

'But there was more than money and blooded clothes discovered,' she said. 'DS Pretty spoke of mangled flesh.'

Wells gave a grim-sounding laugh. 'Did he? Then the police must have stumbled over some unfortunate creature that perished on the tracks the same night. Much as I like detail – and if one is going to stage one's death, one should do it with gusto – hacking off a foot or a hand would have made escape impossible.'

'You boarded a train at some point, then? You must have done, to be here in London.'

'I jumped on a slow freight train and hid in the van. One shoe, no outer clothing, how I survived comes down to being New England born.' He explained, 'Winters there make winters here feel like a wet kiss from a warm aunt.'

'Where have you been sheltering?' Jemima glanced at the blanket round his shoulders, then at his feet. He wore two shoes, which appeared to match.

'There are hostels in London for stranded ex-colonials. I acquired my first night's down payment by begging outside a luxury store. A man with no jacket, wearing one shoe, inspires little pity, but those high-and-mighty doormen will bribe him to move on. The hostel has a well-stocked lost-property cupboard.' He lifted a foot, to display a round-toed workman's boot.

Jemima congratulated him on being so resourceful. 'But why are you here, in Mrs Crosby's home?'

'Why are you here, Mrs Flowerday?'

She struck a bargain. She'd tell him if he'd tell her.

She described how she'd gained entry to Marie's room at the Royal Darnley, and the friendly chambermaid who had left her alone to look through a hatbox full of papers. 'Your homebound liner ticket is among them.'

Wells thanked her for the tip-off. 'I'll need to retrieve it at some point. Go on, because you haven't answered why you're here.'

She told him, 'I'm doing what you're doing, establishing a cause for Marie's death in the greater scheme of things.' A visit to Bright's Club, a conversation with the doorman there, had set her off on a new trail. 'My mission is to show how Marie's killing is linked to that of Roland Crosby.'

'We're not on the same mission,' he said. 'I don't care about Roland Crosby. I'm pursuing the commission Marie was paying me for.'

'To prove her marriage to Sir Edgar Hamlash? I discovered her passport,' Jemima said. 'I know what brought her to England.'

The fact that Wells did not contradict her told her she had got to the truth. He said gravely, 'She was put into the outrageous position of having to prove her marriage, but she couldn't.'

'Why not?' Jemima realised she was still holding the rail ticket she'd taken from Roland Crosby's coat. She put it in her own pocket. If Wells was pursuing a different line of country, chasing a different fox so to speak, he would not be interested. 'Why could Marie not produce her marriage lines and say "here's the proof"?'

'Because she had lost them. Lost the certificate. I think I told you something of her past. She went to France in 1915 as a nurse, part of a cohort of American women volunteers, to do her bit for her old country.'

'And met the love of her life, you said.'

'Sure. A year later they married, in front of French witnesses, wearing their uniforms. The groom hadn't had formal permission, so was breaking military law. It took place in a village close to Amiens where the priest was known to be willing to bend the rules. Afterwards, Marie went back to her field hospital behind the lines, until one night, she and her fellow nurses had to evacuate their patients at a minute's notice. She left everything behind, including her marriage certificate. By the time the war was finished, the village she'd married in was rubble, the population fled, the priest with them.'

'So no way of proving her status.'

'Marie had letters from her husband stating his desire to join her in America once he was out of the army. He wrote to his 'Darling M', but at no point did he directly address Marie as his wife. Nor, frustratingly, did he use her married name on the envelopes either.'

'Oh?' The letters Simon had sent Jemima from France, after they married, were always addressed to 'Mrs Simon Flowerday'. He'd proudly written the name, he'd told her. 'Sounds to me that Edgar regretted going through with the marriage.'

The comment seemed to stall Wells momentarily. 'Oh, maybe. Thing is, it went ahead without his parents' permission or knowledge. His father would never have accepted Marie – French-American, a working woman – as a daughter-in-law.'

Familiar territory, Jemima reflected. 'How about his mother?'

'You've met Lady Hamlash. If she doesn't want to know something, you can tell her till the cows come home and she won't accept it. Did her son tell her he'd got married in France? I don't know, but Marie concluded that he'd meant to, then funked it. His father died towards the end of 1916 and with his mother liable to nervous outbursts, I guess he decided to leave it. Maybe till the war was over? Marie returned to America in the summer of '17, because she was expecting a child. She wrote to her husband who was with his unit near the Belgian border, but after a while the letters went unanswered.'

A mortar shell had exploded yards from Edgar. Jack had witnessed it, he'd told Jemima. 'Edgar Hamlash received terrible blast-injuries and died in the winter of 1917,' she said. 'Marie must have got the news at some point.'

Jemima relived the moment of opening a letter from Simon's colonel, sent from France, but delayed in transit. *Dear Mrs Flowerday, I write with the heaviest heart—*

'Marie must have known she'd been widowed, even if it took weeks for the news to reach her.'

'I guess,' said Wells.

Sketchy answers were one of Jemima's pet hates. 'What does "I guess" mean?'

'Yes, she was informed by letter in the spring of 1918 that Edgar had been killed in action.'

'Poor Marie.' To wait in hope so long.

Wells shifted uncomfortably. 'A new mother, grieving but forced to get out and earn a living… it nearly broke her. As for her heart, that family well and truly broke it a second time. Her marriage was denied. "We have no knowledge of it ever having taken place."'

'So cruel.'

'Deliberate cruelty is the worst. It's why Marie felt so humiliated, so angry. She sent letter after letter demanding to be recognised to assert the rights to her name, but got nothing back.'

'And eventually she wrote to Edgar at his club – but that makes no sense.' Timing, Jemima's private passion, reared up. 'That letter arrived four years after his death. Why on earth would she do it? Was she suffering delusions?'

'No, of course not.'

'Then why write to a dead man?' Wells sat silent so long, Jemima assumed he hadn't heard so she repeated, 'A dead man – a dead husband. Explain.'

'To get noticed,' Wells said at last. 'All the polite notes to her mother-in-law at Merry Beggars Hall were ignored or returned to her unopened. Writing to Edgar last Christmas was a desperate ruse. Marie knew by then that anything sent by her to Merry Beggars Hall, or to the lawyers' office, would be destroyed on receipt. But a letter with Edgar's name, sent to his club, would find its way to Lady Hamlash.'

'I see. Only it got into Roland Crosby's hands. Did you know?'

'I know. Marie couldn't predict that twist of events,' Wells said. 'America's a long way away, and silence is confusing. She waited for a response. Waited and waited then, suddenly, she opened a newspaper and there was the Hamlash name.'

'After Roland's head was found? Your newspapers scooped up the story, I suppose. "Horror at English country mansion". Did she decide right then that she needed to go to England and fight her cause in person?' Because Marie had not left instantly. Roland's murder had taken place in April. Marie had not sailed until October. But of course, she had a child to consider, and a restaurant to run. Perhaps she had left as soon as she could make arrangements. Wells did not contradict, and she asked what his part had been.

'Mine? To worm my way into the heart of the family and learn its secrets. See, Marie believed that at some point, her husband must have written home about his marriage. She was convinced his mother would have saved the letters. Mothers do that.'

Jemima agreed that was true. All the cards and letters sent home by her children were kept in a large biscuit tin. 'You and she sailed here, and while she stayed at The Royal Darnley, you went to Merry Beggars Hall to find written proof of a marriage. You got a job, in short.'

'Two jobs,' he answered. But that was only the beginning. Having limited access to the house, and none to the places where personal letters might be stored, his role was to prevail upon a member of the household to search for him.

'Dinah!' Jemima said. 'She was your bloodhound because she could go into any room in the house, under the pretext of cleaning.' Jemima did not add, 'Oh, Mr Wells,' but her tone conveyed it and he shifted uncomfortably.

'I lied to her, sure, but I didn't tell the foolish girl I was her sweetheart. Not ever.'

'You are a handsome and glamorous stranger, she an inexperienced girl. Of course she would fall for you. You broke Jack Millar's heart too.'

'Let him step forward then. I'm officially dead, aren't I?'

Jemima recalled seeing Wells in front of the library window, in the rain, barking at Dinah to stop pestering him. She reminded him of it. 'How could she be your bloodhound one minute and pestering you the next?'

'You're wrong, I wasn't—' He broke off. 'Let's just say, appearances can be misleading.'

'Can't they just. You told me you still have work to do for Marie.'

'I do, and for myself. If I can show the police the truth, suspicion over her death will shift elsewhere. I want to see justice done. I owe it to her. If I can, I'll track down witnesses to the marriage. She visited France when we arrived, attempting the same.'

'I know she went to France. She bought a hat in Paris.'

'Course she did, that's Marie all over. Her real purpose was to visit the village where she married, see if anybody had returned. She spent a few days staring at rubble before returning to London. She wrote to Lady Hamlash from her hotel, but I don't suppose she got an answer.'

'She did, actually.' Jemima gave Wells a precis of the legal threat she had found among Marie's papers and which she had posted anonymously to DCI Bullace.

'I wish you'd kept it for me,' he said.

'I didn't know you were alive, so how could I?'

'Good point, ma'am. Well, it explains why Marie was in such a coiled-up state of mind, carping about how much she was paying me, how long I was taking. I begged her to be patient, stay in her nice suite, to let me do my job.'

Jemima doubted that patience had been one of Marie's shining virtues. 'She saw Lady Hamlash's advertisement for a cook and it must have felt like fate. Her mother-in-law had never laid eyes on her. Nobody had in Suffolk, so here was her chance to come among them incognito and find her evidence herself. You warned her against it. And not, I think, because you wanted to carry on being paid.'

'Darn right. I told her on no account to come, but she ignored me.' *And look what happened*, was Wells's unspoken postscript.

'What now, Mr Wells?'

'I'm going to search out some of her husband's former comrades-in-arms, see if they know or can remember anything.'

'You could start with Sir Finchley and Jack,' Jemima said, pithily. 'They were in the same regiment.'

Wells gave a sniff of amusement. 'Why didn't I think of that? Oh, yes. Because the marriage was secret. I'd appreciate it if you would keep all this under your hat, ma'am. I need to stay dead a little while longer.'

Of course she would say nothing. 'Unless asked directly by a police detective.'

'Ah, you've got Bullace eating out of your hand, Mrs F. Don't underestimate your powers.'

'Don't call me Mrs F. And *you* underestimate DCI Bullace. He wants his murderer. Or murder*ers*. He wants results very badly.'

'Why hasn't he solved Roland Crosby's case, then, or found the body?'

'I put it down to an institutional blind spot,' Jemima said. 'Too much deference, too little desire to rock boats. In Marie's case, I clearly directed him towards the poisoned sugar cube.'

That grabbed Wells's attention. 'You told me you'd worked it out. You think the stuff that killed her got into the sugar?'

'It didn't "get into" anything. It was placed deliberately. Now it's your turn to tell me why you're here. You say you're not interested in Roland Crosby, so why are you in his house?'

'We both know he was blackmailing the Hamlash family. Something Dinah said about a telephone last Christmas put me on the scent. It all checks out, and I'm looking for physical evidence.'

'Of money being paid…' Jemima was conscious of a cleared cheque for three thousand pounds in her bag.

'Roland was getting thirty pounds a month,' Wells said, 'paid direct.'

'You found the post-office savings book, I take it?'

'Uh-huh. If I can find proof that the Hamlash family was paying off Roland Crosby, I might get them to admit there was a marriage. Marie wanted nothing from the family, only recognition, and I'll do my utmost to get it for her.'

She asked Wells how he had got his job at Merry Beggars Hall.

'I was staying in Saxonchurch, at The Bell, getting the lie of the land. I had an idea of calling at the hall, claiming to be researching the family name. By chance, in the tap room, I met an old, old man. Bilney, his name.'

'Lady Hamlash's gardener.'

'Former gardener. He left the day that head was uncovered, never went back. After several beers, he got to telling me that the gardener's job was going begging and "Her Ladyship couldn't find a chauffeur neither, for love nor money". I was taken on that same afternoon.'

'Lady Hamlash doesn't check references.'

'Beggars can't be choosers. Not even Merry ones.'

One last, difficult question. 'Does Marie's little boy know his mother is dead?'

Wells was silent for several seconds before saying, 'I have to finish what I started and get home.'

That wasn't quite an answer, but she derived enough from it to understand that news of Marie's death had not travelled to New York. She said, 'I need to show you something. Let's go down to the kitchen, where we can risk shining a light.'

When they were there, Jemima re-lit the candle. She placed Sir Finchley Hamlash's cheque, made out to A. Crosby, on the table.

Wells gave a whistle. 'That's—' Words seemed to fail him.

'More money than Albert Crosby would earn in ten years,' said Jemima. 'My theory is Albert's name is on the cheque because he has a bank account and his brother didn't. He was meant to pass the money on to Roland. A final payoff to a blackmailer. Look at the date on it.'

Wells held the cheque in the candle's halo and said thoughtfully, 'It was drawn up the day before Roland left London. The twopence duty's been paid, and the banker's stamp shows the funds were deposited into Albert's account on 24 April.'

The significance hit them at the same time. That was the day *after* Roland's head was discovered.

'Pretty conclusive Roland didn't get the money,' Wells said.

Jemima agreed. 'Albert Crosby received a cheque made out in his name. His brother dies, and he keeps the proceeds.' Meaning, Albert could have killed his brother for financial gain. *As Cain slew Abel.* 'Money is one of the principal motives for murder.'

'Tell me about it.' Wells made a face. 'But why dump Roland's head in the glasshouse for Lady H to find? Poor old girl, nobody deserves that.'

'It wasn't dumped. It was placed. That's very different.' Jemima took back the cheque. 'I will give this to DCI Bullace, but does it help in your quest to find justice for Marie?'

Wells didn't answer. He seemed to be listening to something. A dull rumble filled the air. It took over the room for a few seconds, stopped, then started again.

'Does the tube train run just below these streets?' he asked.

'It's the Piccadilly line up here and that's very deep.' When the rumbling began again, then fell away, they went to the front hall. Here, the noise was louder, but mixed with sounds from the street outside. Men's voices, boots up the path. The letterbox clashed and a sheet of paper fell inside. Wells picked it up as a man's throaty voice urged, 'Giddy up, lad,' followed by the scrape of heavy hooves.

'A coal merchant's bill.' Wells came to stand beside Jemima as she opened a narrow door off the hall. Together, they stared down into darkness. 'Must be the coal cellar,' he said.

She coughed as an earthy odour caught the back of her throat. Another smell found its way into her senses. Rat bait. She quickly closed the cellar door. 'Mrs Crosby only had a coal delivery a few days ago. Poor thing must be getting addled.'

They returned to the kitchen, where Wells took in the cake tins and other cooking paraphernalia. 'Maybe she puts in too much brandy when she's soaking the fruit. May I have another look at that cheque before we blow out the candle and leave?'

She left him examining it while she made a last search through the kitchen drawers. She'd noted the knives and a cleaver of the kind her father had used in the days before refined sugar, to cut lumps off the sugar loaf. There was a set of skewers, some fine as crochet needles, others much thicker. A burst of light to the side of her eye made her turn.

'Mr Wells, what are you doing?'

He was holding the cheque in the candle flame and when she ran over to save it, he raised it above his head.

'You're burning evidence – again.' She hadn't forgotten, or forgiven, the destruction of her cardigan.

'That cheque was a bullet in your head, Mrs Flowerday. A knife in your gut. If I'd let you take it back to Ada Hamlash's stately pile, next thing I'd be reading of your death in the paper.'

'They wouldn't kill me. I'm too well connected.'

'You reckon.' He dropped the charred paper into the sink. 'Time to go.'

They agreed to leave separately, she first, he in twenty minutes' time.

'You're going to track down some of Edgar Hamlash's military comrades, you said. But do you have money to feed yourself?' she asked.

'I'm good. I telegraphed my bank at home for funds.'

In the front hall, she picked up Lady Olivia's driving coat from where she'd left it and put out her hand. 'Goodbye and good luck.'

'Good luck, Mrs Flowerday, and thank you for showing trust.'

The shadows hid her blush. Many a time she had asked herself if Kenneth Wells might be a killer and only once had she answered 'Yes'. She was glad he was alive, and glad once again to feel confidence in him.

Though not so much confidence that she had shown him the key she'd found in Roland's coat pocket, nor the rail ticket. Like a poker player, she was keeping aces up her sleeve.

On a crowded underground carriage, Jemima was offered a seat by a student-type with floppy hair and a spotted cravat. When she sat down, he continued reading an Aldous Huxley novel standing up, sending flirtatious glances her way. Shattered from the accumulated events of the day, a headache sweeping in, Jemima removed a glove to put her wedding ring in his eyeline. She then settled back to gaze out of the lightless window. So much to digest from Wells's melodramatic reappearance. He was an imposter of a kind. A private investigator passing himself off as a simple-hearted American wanderer. She could not overlook his exploitation of Dinah. They were agreed on one thing, however, that blackmail lay at the heart of the Merry Beggars deaths.

She would put this in front of DCI Bullace and though she was frustrated by Wells's destruction of the cheque, the bank would have records. And she still had the train ticket. Studying it now under bright light, she discovered it was for a return journey from Brabberton Manor to London Liverpool Street. The clip to its edge suggested it had been used for the outward journey.

Could she take from this that Roland Crosby had visited Suffolk in the days or weeks before his death? She tried to figure out the significance of him having a return ticket bought in Suffolk, alongside the single ticket bought in London on Saturday, 22 April. Sara

Crosby's neighbour had mentioned to the police something about Roland returning home twice on the Friday, first at lunchtime, then much later that night. He had been at work that day, giving him little opportunity to shuttle between London and Suffolk. What if that trip had taken place some days previously, when his wife thought he was working and his employers believed him to be at home?

If so, why buy a return ticket in Suffolk when his journey would have started in London? Had it been date stamped, she wouldn't be cudgelling her brains. *Think, Jemima, think.* It was indubitable fact that Roland had bought a single from Liverpool Street on the morning of Saturday 22 April. Could he have used this return ticket to travel home again?

Except... His head had been found on Monday 24, at Merry Beggars Hall. Very well. How about: He went to Suffolk on the Saturday, took a train heading home and was murdered at some point on that journey.

It was a neat conclusion. Murders on board trains were not unheard of. She could envisage the deed taking place between Beggars Heath and Brabberton Manor, the only witnesses a sleepy ticket inspector and the birds roosting alongside the track. At the very least, this ticket showed an intention and a purpose. A possibility the police had not considered and, as such, it must be handed over.

Realising her stop was approaching, Jemima stood up in a hurry, dropping both her glove and the ticket. Her Huxley-reading admirer swooped to recover the glove for her and in the polite tussle that followed, the ticket disappeared under the feet of other passengers pushing to get off.

Chapter Thirty-Two

Monday 18 December

In accordance with their agreement, Miss Price sent the three completed dresses to Jemima on the morning of 18 December. Jemima had mended Lady Olivia's coat and posted it back to the house in St John's Wood, with the fervent hope that her description would never be passed on to its owner by the two maids. Having carefully packed Lady Hamlash's gowns in one trunk, and her own overnight things in a holdall, Jemima took a taxi to Liverpool Street Station, having confirmed by post her arrival time to Mrs Newson. In the event, she caught an earlier train than the one she'd planned on taking, and this bonus half hour allowed her to act on an idea.

Instead of getting off at Beggars Heath, she left the train at Brabberton Manor, entrusting her trunk and bag to the ticket inspector, who would have them taken off at the next stop. Stepping down onto the empty platform, the stationmaster came up to her, offering his arm.

'It's a mite slippery, madam.' It was an older man than the one she'd seen before. 'Are you for the manor house?'

'Not on this occasion,' Jemima answered. 'I wonder if I could have a word?'

The loss of evidence is a cruel thing to a criminal investigator and Jemima hadn't forgiven the young man who had tried to rescue her glove on the underground train. She had a perfect picture in her head of the lost ticket, however, and though she had hoped to see the attendant who'd been here on her first visit – Deacon, wasn't it, Sydney Deacon? – she would make the best of things.

'I got off a station early,' she said.

The stationmaster assured her she wasn't the first to do that. 'Next train stopping there is in half an hour. You'll do best sitting with me in the office, in the warmth.'

Inviting her into the station building, he pulled up a second chair to a glowing fire. Jemima sat down, observing that he must be new here.

Sitting down also, he leaned forward conspiratorially. 'I am new, you're right.' Deacon had been relieved of his post a couple of days previous, he said, 'For wholly falling off the wagon.'

'The wagon… you mean, he surrendered to insobriety?'

'Came to work drunk as a weasel at midsummer.'

'Oh, dear.'

'Told one passenger he had a face like a mangelwurzel and another that he'd heard that the town of Lowestoft had been washed away in a storm. So happened, *that* passenger was the Mayor of Lowestoft and he wasn't best pleased.'

'Mr Deacon has struggled with drinking for some time?'

Deacon's replacement nodded. 'It's in his family. They had the front step taken out at the Wheatsheaf in Beggars Heath so his old dad could roll out at the end of the night. It's bad for Sydney, though. Losing his work means he's lost his house.'

Jemima really was sorry to hear that and asked where Deacon was currently living.

'Here and there,' she was told. 'They won't have him in the alms

217

house till he's sober. And all because he came into an unexpected windfall.'

Her ears pricked up. 'Windfall?'

'Last April, Syd came into the Wheatsheaf where I was supping my half-pint and ordered a round for us all. Then another. By the end of the night, he was fit to be poured and I reckon he spent a month's wages.'

Jemima asked if he could recall the exact day this happened.

'Well… I was drinking with Fred Bilney…'

Lady Hamlash's former gardener. Jemima's thumbs began to prickle.

'Fred was muttering about the weather, how it was turning cold again—'

'With the danger of frost?'

'Quite so. He was worried for Her Ladyship's tender plants.'

If Bilney was still working at the hall at the time of this conversation, then Deacon's windfall must have arrived before the incident with Roland Crosby. Jemima said as much and the stationmaster agreed.

'Reckon it was the Friday before *that thing*. That London chap who lost his noddle… I don't need to say more, do I, madam?'

'You don't.' *That thing* referred to the weekend of 22 to 23 April, a date that had assumed apocalyptic significance. 'Did Deacon say where his windfall came from?'

'I asked, and got told to mind my own business, but I overheard him tell the landlord that he'd found a treasure and sold it on.'

'What, like a watch or a brooch? Something left on the train?'

'Something he found was all he said.'

They sat in silence for a while, as burning apple logs sighed in the grate. It was time to voice the question she'd got off the train to ask. 'Mr…?'

'Saddler, Madam. Charlie Saddler.'

'Mr Saddler, if a person bought a return ticket for London from here, and still had that ticket in his coat pocket some months afterwards, what would you think?'

The stationmaster scratched his head. 'Is this one of those riddles, like, a man is locked in a room with no way out, and only a piece of rope and a wax candle?'

'It's a straight question. The ticket's been clipped. There was an outward trip.'

'It's valid for the way back, then.'

There was no point asking Saddler if anyone had bought such a ticket on Friday, 21 April as he hadn't been working here. Sydney Deacon might know.

'What manner of establishment is the Wheatsheaf at Beggars Heath?' Jemima asked casually.

Charlie Saddler shook his head. 'It's a rough, reasty old place and they wouldn't serve a lady.'

They chatted about the weather until the next down train rumbled in. More snow, was the stationmaster's prediction.

Chapter Thirty-Three

The car was drawing up on the forecourt at Beggars Heath as Jemima walked out of the station. She'd come from Brabberton Manor on the train she would have caught had she left Liverpool Street at the time she'd originally intended.

Albert Crosby got out and opened the rear door, presumably as a way of informing her that he had no desire to have her sitting next to him on the way back.

She managed to fire one question. 'How is Mrs Crosby settling in?'

To which he replied, 'Well enough, and we are all feeling the benefit in our stomachs.'

The countryside was blanketed in white, but as the car's rear windows did not defrost during the entire drive, Jemima was unable to fully appreciate the beauty. She was dreading a return to the bedroom in the north wing and decided – I can't do it. I will take measures.

The servants' hall was snug as always and she received a pleasant welcome. The atmosphere seemed warmer, somehow, the smell of baking enhancing the impression.

Jack, bringing in her trunk and bag, said almost cheerfully, 'I'll trudge these upstairs for you one at a time, Mrs Flowerday, if that's all right. Your usual room?'

'Leave them, Jack. The trunk can stay downstairs and I'll take the bag myself.' Jemima's plan for an alternate bedroom was taking shape.

'Right-o,' said Jack, looking relieved. 'If you're sure.'

'Is Mrs Crosby baking ginger cake?' she asked, sniffing the air.

'Golden syrup, I believe,' said Mrs Newson.

'Who's taking my name in vain?' The glass-panelled door between hall and kitchen opened and a stout figure in an apron and cap came through. Sara Crosby's cheeks were fiery, her blue cotton dress sleeves rolled up to display staunch forearms. 'Good afternoon. Mrs Flowerday, isn't it? There's cake for tea, don't you worry. How was the Old Smoke?'

'London? Just that, with the streets covered in slush as you predicted.' Jemima added a wince of manufactured pain. 'Sadly, I slipped on my steps at home.'

'Ouch.' Mrs Crosby glanced down at the ankle Jemima helpfully raised. 'That's winter for you. Wretched boys on my street make slides in the ice, till it's not safe to venture out.'

The words 'my street' reminded Jemima that very recently, she had trespassed in this woman's home. She covered her discomfort, saying, 'I've had to stop my children doing that a few times.' She turned to Mrs Newson. 'Dare I ask if there's a fire lit upstairs for me?'

Mrs Newson thought not. 'I asked Dinah, only she isn't herself at the moment.'

'Not unwell, I hope?'

'No, it's this.' Mrs Newson took a newspaper off the dresser, showing Jemima its front page. It was the local news. 'Fresh Tragedy hits Merry Beggars Hall' ran the headline and it referred to Kenneth Wells. 'Youthful stranger to our shores believed slain in train accident.'

221

Sara Crosby sighed in sympathy. 'Not that I met the young man, but what a shame. They have to say "believed slain" as no body's been found—' She stopped, bit her lip, because she could have been commenting on her husband.

Jemima pictured herself sitting on Sara Crosby's bed, Wells beside her, the two of them pooling evidence of the blackmail carried out by this woman's husband.

Jemima put the newspaper aside. 'Poor Dinah.'

The girl herself came in, nodding mutely when Mrs Newson reminded her it was almost time for Her Ladyship's tea. 'And afterwards, you're to make up Mrs Flowerday's bedroom fire. It gets dark so early now.'

Everyone glanced at the clock, and agreed, it did, and a bustle ensued. Finding herself alone, Jemima lit a candle taken from the dresser drawer and walked out into the passage alongside the servants' hall. She reckoned Albert Crosby had retired to his private room and listening at his door, she heard a chair creaking and a pen-nib scratching. A glance inside the room opposite showed it had been allotted to Mrs Crosby. Jemima recognised the dark-green coat on a hook.

A few paces on, a sly turn of a door handle, verified that Marie Guyen's old room was now unlocked. Marie's chocolate brown hatbox was still on top of the wardrobe.

The last-but-one room off the passage was the cubbyhole where Beth had slept until nightmares drove her upstairs. The last room was the enclave where Jack cleaned the shoes and polished the silver. Jemima next accessed the laundry room, her candle revealing ironing tables against the wall and a line of smoothing irons standing nose-up on a shelf. The door to the exterior was unlocked and Jemima stepped out into the dark chill, her candle lighting up a yard laid with snow-covered brick. On the far side stood a washhouse.

Though her teeth began to chatter, she resisted the temptation to retreat inside. Walking through a gate, she entered the stable yard where tyre tracks told her that Mr Crosby had driven the car through not long ago. She saw the Crossley in what must once have been an open-bay coach house. A bicycle was propped up against a wall. It must be the one Wells had been working on when Dinah had alerted him to Marie's collapse. Had he mended it as a means of escape, or simply because he wanted to keep busy, and it was there?

A further gate led into the gardens at the rear of the house where a flight of steps took her onto the terrace. She passed the library window, continuing to the conservatory whose door was now locked. Nor was the key under the boot scraper. She suspected Bullace had seen to that.

The wind picked up, snuffing out her candle. Now miserably cold, Jemima continued right around the house, passing the drawing room whose curtains were closed – a pencil of light between them. She trudged around the front, past the porticoed entrance, past the dining room, round another corner into the kitchen garden and back into the servants' hall by way of the glazed lobby.

Thankful to return to the warm, she took off her coat. 'So now I know all the ways in and out of this house. A person could go from the great hall to the outside using the servants' corridor. They could do it without setting foot in either this room or the kitchen,' she muttered.

When Jemima had sat down for her very first lunch here, Dinah had been sent to knock on Marie Guyen's bedroom door, but before she could do so, a figure in chef's whites had darted past the window. *Likely picking herbs for dinner*, Mrs Newson had speculated. Had Marie in fact been circuiting the house, looking for a way to get Lady Hamlash's attention? *Running me to earth during my garden inspection… And before that, peering in at me in my drawing room*, Lady Hamlash had complained later to her son on the telephone.

'Marie, Marie, you should have let Wells do his work. He'd have found your proof in time, if such proof exists.'

Beth came in to set the table for tea, gawping because she'd caught Jemima speaking out loud. Jemima helped the girl lay out place mats and, when the moment felt right, asked what had become of Marie Guyen's chef's whites. 'Her apron and cap.'

'Don't know.' Beth placed blue-striped cups onto blue-striped saucers.

Distantly, the stable-yard clock chimed five. Jemima looked at her watch. The clock was still at the correct time.

'Did the laundrywoman take them?' she asked.

Beth muttered, 'I done them.' A pause, then, 'She pinches me.'

'The laundrywoman? You must tell Mrs Newson.' Jemima took the sugar bowl off Beth's tray, balancing the tongs on top. 'Who cleaned out Madame Guyen's room? It looked newly swept when I peered in a moment ago.'

'What room?'

'The one down here, where she slept.' Jemima could quite understand why people lost patience with Beth. 'Did the police give permission?'

'It was Mrs Crosby.'

'Mrs Crosby asked for the room to be cleaned?'

'No. Madame's apron. She had me cut it up for cloths.'

This was useful information and a lesson too. Let every witness speak in their own time. 'Thank you, Beth. And do tell Mrs Newson about the pinching.'

At tea, Albert Crosby said to Jemima, 'Her Ladyship extends her compliments, Mrs Flowerday, and requests your company at ten sharp tomorrow morning for a peregrination of the drier paths without.'

Without what? Her confusion must have shown.

'He means a tramp round the walled garden,' Mrs Newson explained. 'Her Ladyship doesn't care to walk out on her own these days. So sad, for she was always out, pottering about the beds.'

'Deadheading,' Jack said, with a dark chuckle. 'Till she found a real one.'

Sara Crosby gasped. Jack looked stricken. 'Sorry, Mrs C.'

Albert Crosby growled at Jack to keep his nasty thoughts to himself.

'Does Sir Finchley enjoy gardening?' Jemima asked, to cover the awkwardness. 'Does he share his mother's passion for asparagus? Oh, I don't mind if I do.' Mrs Crosby was inviting her to help herself to a slice of lemon and ginger cake. She'd thought she could smell ginger earlier. The golden syrup cake was for tomorrow. 'Mm, delicious,' Jemima said. 'Better than Fortnum's.'

Mrs Crosby looked gratified. 'Far be it from me to boast, I've always been considered a light hand with a wooden spoon. Ain't that so, Beth, lovey? You don't mind a beating from me when you spill milk or burn the spuds, 'cause I keep my proper beatings for the mixing bowl.'

Beth, in her customary place at the bottom of the table, lowered her head.

'Not what you'd call a chatterbox, but we'll get there.' Sara Crosby beamed, Jack's misstep forgotten. 'I tell her, if you can bake a cake, you'll never lack for wages, or muscles.' Proudly, she displayed a bicep. 'People will always want to celebrate something, and they'll always want a cake on the table.'

'I so agree.' Jemima's question about Sir Finchley's feelings for asparagus disappeared into the weeds.

For Albert Crosby, taking a basket of the stems from Suffolk to Norfolk had provided him with his alibi for the time his brother had gone missing. He looked less haunted than when she'd first arrived, though that wasn't to say he seemed happier. Rather, he struck her as a man who had accepted that his fate was to be miserable. And why should he not be miserable, potentially the killer of his brother, served cake by the sister-in-law he had made a widow?

Jemima observed her table-companions in turn. Dinah was eating cake as if being forced to swallow birdseed. Grieving for a man who had not loved her one jot. Jack flinched every time Dinah glanced his way in cold indifference. Mrs Newson twitched as though her arthritis was flaring up and Beth never lifted her eyes from her plate.

Misery Buggers Hall indeed, to quote Sara Crosby. Perhaps her first impressions on arrival today had been misleading, Jemima thought. The real and only ray of sunshine was Sara herself.

'Beef dumpling for us lot tonight, best topside for the dining room,' Sara announced, getting up. 'No rest for the wicked.' She swallowed the last of her tea and whistled to Beth. 'Let's be at it.'

Dinah left to collect Lady Hamlash's tea things from the drawing room and Jemima slipped out too, catching up with her in the great hall. 'May I have a word?'

Dinah turned, her expression mutinous. 'What about?'

'Firstly, I want to say how sorry I am that you had to read about Mr Wells's death in the paper.' She wished she could see evidence that the girl's grief was skin deep, but perceived no such thing.

Dinah answered in true fashion. 'Just 'cause he's dead, don't mean I'm going to get sweet on Jack Millar.'

'No. Love isn't a tap. It can't be turned on and off. I understand how it must have hurt that Mr Wells was…' This was delicate. '… full of attention one moment and sharp with you the next.'

'Sharp?' Every inch of Dinah's body issued a denial. 'He never was, not to me.'

'The day I arrived here, you were out on the terrace and he told you to leave him alone. "I'm plumb out of patience," he said. That must have been bruising.'

'Don't know what you're talking about. I never go on the terrace. It's not my place to.' The girl's outrage carried the force of sincerity.

'I must have been mistaken,' Jemima said. 'Could it have been someone else?'

'If it was, it would have been Madame Guyen. She was always lurking outside, in-perturbing Her Ladyship.'

Jemima presumed Dinah meant 'importuning'. 'Bothering Lady Hamlash how?'

'Peering in at the windows,' Dinah sneered, 'tapping her knuckles. "Justice, justice." Mr Wells never cared for that Frenchie, not like he did me. He said so.'

Jemima had lost her appetite for this conversation and retreated to the servants' hall, mulling on what she'd learned. Dinah had not been the target of a telling-off by Wells on the terrace; it was Marie. *She* had been 'lurking', as Dinah put it.

I'm plumb out of patience! Let me do my job. In this new context, Jemima could imagine Wells's frustration with a client who thought she could do better herself. *No, no. It won't happen—* had been his peppery signing-off. Whatever it was that Marie had asked him to do, it had driven him to the end of his tether.

This realisation did not diminish Jemima's belief that Lady Olivia had killed Marie, but it threw a new light on the Frenchwoman's character. Marie had been impulsive, unmanageable as a client and, to the Hamlashes, dangerous.

227

Dinah returned with the tea tray and glowered at Jemima. 'Lady Hamlash invites you to join her and her guests in the dining room tonight, Mrs Flowerday.'

'Really?' Thank goodness she'd bought a smart dress with her. 'What time?'

'Usual.'

'You will have to explain what is usual, Dinah.'

'Seven forty-five in the drawing room for sherry. Now, I suppose, I'd better lug the coal bucket upstairs and light your fire.' Dinah cast a resentful look at the trunk containing Lady Hamlash's dresses. 'Jack won't manage something that heavy and I shouldn't be asked.'

This spurred Jemima to enact her plan. 'It's staying down here. Let's take it and my bag to Marie's old room.'

Dinah looked alarmed. 'We aren't supposed to go in there.'

'The alternative is the stairs and the coal bucket. Come on, be a sport. We all do things we shouldn't.' Jemima invited Dinah to take the other end of the trunk.

They hefted it together and when they set it down in Marie's room, Dinah looked about her. 'I wouldn't want to lie in that bed, knowing what had been on it.'

'The linen's been changed and the blankets. I won't think about the rest,' Jemima said. 'Would you fetch my holdall? As for lighting a fire, fill a scuttle and I'll do it myself. Only, tell nobody I'm in here.'

Within ten minutes, Jemima was stowing her belongings in the wardrobe, handing them alongside Marie Guyen's clothes. Dinah had supplied kindling and a large bucket of coal. By the time on her watch, Jemima had a generous hour in which to get ready for company.

In the kitchen, which was steamy as a bathhouse with a boiling pan on every part of the range, she requested a jug of hot water.

'Supping with the Quality, I hear,' said Mrs Crosby. 'Course you can have your water, Mrs Flowerday. Beth, strain them potatoes over the lady's jug. Waste not want not.' Seeing Jemima's expression, Sara guffawed. 'Only joking! Beth-lovey, fill the kettle and get it on the hot plate.'

When Beth dithered, confused by being given two jobs at once, Mrs Crosby picked up a cast-iron kettle effortlessly in one hand. Protecting her other hand with a thick cloth, she shifted a pan of parsnips and set the kettle in its place.

She could have taken my trunk upstairs, swinging it as she went, Jemima thought. Naturally, it would have been a gross breach of etiquette to ask.

Using the same thick pad, Mrs Crosby opened one of the oven doors to check on the beef. 'That's coming on nice. We'll get the spuds in to roast. Beth, put dripping in a pan, if you please.' She gave Jemima a beetling look. 'What were you thinking of, traipsing outside in the dark just now?'

Jemima had no idea she'd been seen. 'I wanted a breath of air.'

'You must have lungs of leather, then. I've known souls go out in the snow and not come home. Got children, haven't you? You need to watch yourself.'

'I have two, Molly and Tommy, and – yes – I should take care.' Lured by Sara Crosby's open manner, Jemima added, 'I've never made a circuit of the whole house before and I was curious.'

'Curiosity, eh? Remember the cat.'

'True, but what did the cat wish to know?'

'And who killed the blighter?' was Mrs Crosby's answer. She walked to where Beth was spooning pork dripping from a crock, saying, 'Rough them potatoes up a bit when you've done that. Give 'em a little shimmy and they'll crisp up lovely.' Sara performed a dance on the spot to illustrate. 'Let's see you wiggle.'

Beth did her best and the two of them put Jemima in mind of factory workers on a jamboree, clattering in their sparking clogs.

'All right,' Sara Crosby cried. 'That's enough shimmy, get that roasting pan in the oven.'

'Mr Albert Crosby told me you'd settled in nicely.' Jemima's water was taking a while to boil. 'Tell me again, when were you here before?'

'I came the month after I was widowed.'

A mere month?

Sara interpreted Jemima's reaction. 'I know, but they needed someone. The old girl who'd been cooking here since Victoria was Queen legged it and Her Ladyship couldn't get another one to stay five minutes. When Albert wrote about their predicament, I offered myself.'

Jemima recalled the stationmaster at Beggars Heath greeting Mrs Crosby with the words, 'Nice to see you back,' or some such. Clearly, a popular woman. A month after her husband had died though… it must have taken courage.

Mrs Crosby used a long skewer to check the parsnips. 'Ready for roasting. Do me another pan of hot dripping, Beth-lovey and mind it don't spit in your eye.' She turned back to Jemima. 'I'm glad to be here, if I'm honest. I'm not fond of Christmas, not having any children to spoil. I like being busy.'

'Don't your clients mind?'

'Clients?' The sunny smile became a little fixed.

'Your cake customers.' Jemima knew she had blundered again, exceeding her allowable knowledge of this woman's life. 'You mentioned you do a lot of baking. Aren't people clamouring for Christmas cakes?'

Sara Crosby put down her skewer and wagged a finger. 'Now that shows your ignorance, Mrs F. My Christmas cakes are all sitting on pantry shelves, merrily soaking up their brandy and have been for a month or more. Imagine, knocking one up this late! That wouldn't do.'

'This is your less busy time, then?' Jemima's mistake seemed to have slipped through, undetected. 'Weddings aren't so usual this time of year.'

Mrs Crosby's eyes narrowed, the crow-footed skin around them contracting in unexpected displeasure. 'What makes you think I do wedding cakes?'

'I assumed. I beg your pardon.'

'I *used* to. Haven't had a single order since my Roly was killed. You can't blame people not wanting their big day associated with my name.'

'I am so sorry, Mrs Crosby.' But there had been a copy-invoice on the pad in the London kitchen dated quite recently. *Wedding cake, Mrs Blandford and daughter.* Of course, Jemima should not know that. 'Do forgive me.'

'Nothing to forgive, dear. If I'm honest, wedding cakes are a bother. I'll do one for a neighbour if they ask, but frankly all that icing…' Sara Crosby waved the thought away as one might a buzzing bluebottle. 'You can't trust an errand boy, so you have to sit in a cab with three or four tins on your knee.' She grabbed her oven cloth to mop her perspiring face and seemed to find something to stare at. She turned away from whatever it was. 'Beth, lovey, open a window, let the steam out.'

Jemima's eye landed where Mrs Crosby's had a moment before. On a shelf was a cake tin that was very familiar. Except, where had she seen it? Of course. Campden Buildings. Angela Price had taken a cake from a tin of the same design, that of Noah's Ark.

Sara Crosby followed her gaze. 'Tomorrow's teatime, Mrs

Flowerday. My golden syrup sponge is legendary among my neighbours and they're no fools. No piggling, mind, I'll know if you've nicked a slice. Right.' She picked up the kettle and filled Jemima's jug. 'Scuse me if I shoo you out. Horseradish sauce to make.'

When Jemima returned to the room in which she had established squatters' rights, she found Mrs Newson. The good lady's face was a picture of dismay in the light of an oil lamp.

'Who on earth directed you in here, Mrs Flowerday?'

'Nobody.' Jemima explained that she had slipped on her front steps at home. Mrs Newson must have heard her mention it? 'I cannot manage the staircase at any cost and, really, it's far more convenient to Jack and Dinah if I stay at ground level.'

'I'm not sure what Mr Crosby will say.'

'He won't be joining me, Mrs Newson, so why should it concern him?'

'Mrs Flowerday! I mean, to lie on that bed.' The housekeeper clenched her teeth in a shudder. 'After poor Madame was lain there.'

'You're as squeamish as Dinah. At some point, somebody will have to be the first to sleep here so it might as well be me.'

'It's still not right, Mrs Flowerday, to sleep in such proximity to the male members of the household.'

'Mrs Crosby is my near neighbour, is she not?'

Mrs Newson made a resigned gesture. 'Then we'll make sure Mr Crosby never knows. I won't mention it to Mrs Crosby either, as the two of them confide. It's not to be wondered at, as they're kin.' After informing Jemima that she was dining tonight in the company of Dr and Mrs Rushbrook and DCI Bullace, the housekeeper left.

Jemima now had ten minutes before sherry would be served. In her estimation, she had just about time to make a quick search of the room. She wasn't confident Mr Crosby wouldn't find out she was here, and that she'd return later to find the door locked against her.

Pulling up a stool, Jemima took the hatbox down off the wardrobe, placing it on the dressing table. She took the shard of enamel from her purse, where she'd put it for safekeeping, and in the oil lamp's sulky beam, pressed it against the damaged side of the hatbox.

It did not fit. And the colours were not a match, the hatbox being a darker shade of brown. Jemima felt a sweeping relief. She could absolve Marie Guyen of any involvement in the transportation of Roland Crosby's head.

Returning the enamel fragment to her purse, Jemima washed, donned underwear suitable for a soiree, and dropped her evening dress over her head. It was black wool jersey with a modest neck and a beaded taffeta hip belt. Her own design, elegant and un-showy. She combed glycerine cream through her bobbed hair to give it a shine. A lick of lipstick, not too much. She dabbed Chanel behind her ears and picked up her evening shawl. At 7.41, she was sitting on the bed, smoothing on silk stockings. She pushed her feet into the shoes by the bed and immediately felt strange.

Because those weren't her shoes. They were too big as well as being cold, as if they'd been in this room a while. They must be Marie's, though they were not the rubber-soled clogs Jemima had handled previously. Those were still missing, and she had assumed the police had taken them. These must be Marie's spares for when the day's work was done. Jemima balanced one of them in her hand. It was a well-made shoe with a double strap across the front and a low, French heel. 'Rayne. New Bond Street, London' was printed inside. Had Marie gone shopping while staying at The Royal Darnley?

233

Only something didn't mesh. The heel caps had been recently replaced. Marie had not spent enough time in England to wear out a pair of heels. 'Unless she bought them second-hand…' – which did not fit with the image of a monied French-American.

Oops. It was 7.46. She was late for sherry. She found her shoes by the dresser. Having tied the satin bows at the front, she looked for her evening bag.

She hadn't packed one. With an irritable 'tsk!' she turfed the purse, gloves, notebook and pencil from the handbag she used ordinarily. Leaving the powder compact inside, adding a silk handkerchief and draping a shawl around her shoulders, she made her way to the drawing room.

As she did so she was conscious of crossing the invisible divide between realms; leaving the servants' quarters to dine with Lady Hamlash and guests.

Chapter Thirty-Four

Rather to Jemima's surprise, a spritely conversation was taking place in the drawing room. The sherry served by Jack was very decent too. She smiled her thanks, but Jack looked wooden. Very well, she must play her role too. Tonight, she was a guest.

She was introduced to Mrs Rushbrook. 'I hardly need present the doctor and Inspector Bullace to you, Mrs Flowerday,' said Lady Hamlash.

Bullace shook her hand. 'Good evening, Mrs Flowerday. You are intrepid, returning here in the snows of winter.'

'I have no choice, but I'm surprised *you* would venture out.' Mixing business with pleasure, she meant.

'Dr Rushbrook picked me up,' Bullace replied with a dry smile. 'It's his tyres and his radiator fluid that are at risk. I doubt we'll be leaving late,' he confided. 'May I say how fetching you look? What a charming rig-out. Is that the modern slang?'

'Not in Mayfair, but thank you anyway.'

She began a conversation with Mrs Rushbrook. The doctor's wife proved to be a pleasant, intelligent woman. A former school-teacher, reassuringly dowdy and entirely genuine in her admiration of Jemima's dress. Lady Hamlash, clad in what Jemima could only think of as Druidical robes of magenta velvet, explained that Mrs

Flowerday was 'Dragging her into the modern era. Waving a magic wand over my lamentable wardrobe.'

Jemima caught a sardonic twinkle in Bullace's eye as he commented, 'Mrs Flowerday is a lady of many talents.'

Crosby announced that dinner was served.

Dr Rushbrook offered Lady Hamlash his arm. Bullace offered his to Jemima and Mrs Rushbrook, and took them both into the dining room.

The dinner proved excellent. Sara Crosby was no Marie Guyen, but her minestrone soup was flavoursome and her roast beef, if a little well-cooked, was also well-seasoned. The roast potatoes were perfect. Conversation around the table remained hearty, everyone skirting around awkward subjects. This was no great surprise. Jemima had noticed in her social circle that since the end of the war, people steered conversation away from murkier subjects. The chatter was always about books, popular music, and which play was the best on Shaftesbury Avenue. Absurdity and general silliness were encouraged. One need never allude to sons and husbands lost, daughters who might never marry, grandchildren who would remain unborn. An equally careful, choreographed social dance prevailed around this table. The talk was about a new golf course being carved from a sold-up estate near Saxonchurch. Dr Rushbrook offered to put the inspector up for membership. They talked about the state of rural roads, the difficulty of finding reliable help, the probability of the aged local MP stepping down for a younger man. When it was Jemima's turn to grasp the talking-stick, she regaled them on the hostilities between London's horse-drawn transport and the growing dominance of the motor car.

'One can't help seeing it as a release for those poor, put-upon horses,' Jemima expounded, 'but will they be guaranteed a pleasant retirement? Meanwhile, the crossing sweepers are losing their trade, and the straw merchants too.'

The main course was cleared, pudding was served, tinned tange-rines in jelly on a cold rice-pudding mould. When the cheese and port was brought in, Lady Hamlash signalled that the ladies would retire to the drawing room. The gentlemen rose at their departure and the sexes remained separate long enough for the ladies to run out of pleasantries about the cold weather, and the gentlemen – so Jemima speculated – to express their true opinions of the retiring member of parliament.

The men joined them for coffee and Lady Hamlash expressed a desire for some music. 'I have not yet had the pianoforte tuned as per your instruction, Inspector, but I do hope you will again overlook its imperfections.'

'I will overlook them by retuning my ears. What should I play?' DCI Bullace said.

'Something soothing. Will you sing?'

He obeyed, performing an aria and displaying an unexpected counter-tenor voice. After he had finished, he invited Jemima to the piano. 'You have player's fingers, unless I'm very much mistaken.'

'I do play a little, though my sister is the true proficient.'

'Can you duet?'

'"Spanish Rhapsody"?'

They carried it off rather well, Jemima grateful for the hours of practice she'd been encouraged to put in as a girl.

When they'd finished, the inspector leaned closer and whispered, 'Thank you for the letter.'

She pretended not to know what he meant.

'An unusual shade of light mauve,' he continued, glancing towards Lady Hamlash. '"Madam, I write to you in advance of legal action." It seems poor Marie nursed an unfounded claim to be married to a son of this house.'

'Not unfounded.' Dash it, he'd snared her into giving herself away. 'But I don't know about the letter.'

'Well,' he said, 'whoever posted it dropped it into a box in Mayfair...' His pause reminded Jemima that she had earlier mentioned where she lived. 'If the marriage was real,' he continued, 'it offers a motive for murder, even if it is concluded that Madame Guyen's death was accidental.'

'It was not accidental. Didn't I already explain how it came about?'

'You did,' he agreed. 'Acted it, no less.'

Their conspiratorial whispering was attracting attention, and Bullace invited Dr and Mrs Rushbrook to sing a madrigal with him. Jemima removed herself to an armchair to listen. Mrs Rushbrook took the soprano part, the doctor the bass, Bullace the alto. Albert Crosby came in with fresh candles and, with their glow and the firelight, the effect was magical. Jemima detected tears in Lady Hamlash's eyes. Moisture pricked hers too, and she opened her bag to get her handkerchief, pressing it to her eyes.

Albert Crosby, in the act of replacing a guttering candle, bent and picked something off the carpet by her feet. 'Your train ticket, Mrs Flowerday?'

'I don't see how it could be—' Only as Albert Crosby examined it in the light of his candle, and his face changed, did another possibility dawn. The nick in one edge from a ticket inspector's clipper, told her it was the return ticket from Brabberton Manor to London which she'd thought was lost.

It must have attached itself to her glove when she'd dropped it in the tube train on her way back from Finsbury Park. She'd been carrying it around with her ever since. Taking it, returning it to her bag, she tried to think of something to say and nervously thanked Crosby. From his silence she knew he'd seen enough.

The three-part madrigal finished and Bullace next played a slow duet with Lady Hamlash. At 10.40, the doctor went to the window to check the weather. Jemima saw him peering out with one cheek pressed to the glass.

He turned as his hostess played the duet's fading notes. 'Lady Hamlash, have you re-let the gardener's cottage?'

'Certainly not,' said Her Ladyship, peering across at him.

'Odd. I saw a light through the trees.'

They all crowded to the window, but the light, if it had been there, had vanished. Mrs Rushbrook thought her husband must have seen the moon.

'No. It's the dark of the moon at present,' he replied. 'It was a lantern, I'm sure.'

'Then it was my housemaid, Dinah, fetching in tomorrow's coal,' said Lady Hamlash.

That made sense, to Jemima at least, as she could easily imagine Dinah stealing a visit to Wells's cottage to weep over his empty bed.

Dr Rushbrook suggested they should take their leave, it being so dark and the roads slippery. Lady Hamlash rang the bell and coats were brought.

When DCI Bullace bid Jemima good night, she detained him with a touch and pressed the Brabberton-to-London ticket into his hand.

'Find Sydney Deacon,' she whispered, 'formerly stationmaster at Brabberton Manor and ask him who bought it.'

Jemima got back to her room unobserved, quietly locking the door. She undressed in the dark and slipped into bed. She slept deeply, waking just once at some undeterminable hour as a door in the downstairs regions clicked shut. She was awakened some time later, in the sullen dawn, by the noise of the kitchen range being riddled out. Beth was awake and at her chores.

In need of a cup of tea and of hot water for washing, Jemima rose and put on her dressing gown. Her window was the colour of school-room ink, only the faintest thread of sunrise relieving the darkness.

It was Tuesday, 19 December and upstairs at Merry Beggars Hall, somebody lay dead.

Chapter Thirty-Five

By seven, the breakfast table was laid, though only Jemima was seated. Jack was standing by to take Lady Hamlash's tray through to the dining room. From the kitchen came the clatter of crockery, and the mouth-watering smell of frying bacon.

'We're rather depleted this morning,' Jemima said to Jack. 'Where are the others?'

'I heard Mr Crosby in his room when I put his clean shoes by the door,' the footman said. 'He was pacing.'

Tensely? Anxiously? Jemima recalled the butler's face when he'd picked up the fallen train ticket in the drawing room after dinner.

Everyone seemed a little out of sorts this morning. She'd peered into the kitchen a moment ago and seen Mrs Crosby rolling out pastry. The cook had not seen her because she'd been busy complaining to Beth that the butter had been hard as a rock that morning. 'I had to warm it up first, and that's not the way to a good crust.'

Jemima had withdrawn before Beth replied. Assuming Beth had replied. The girl came in now, placing dishes of bacon, mushroom and scrambled egg on the dresser.

'Where's Dinah and Mrs Newson?' Jemima asked her.

It was Jack who said, 'Mrs Newson will be trying to get Dinah out of bed. Dinah's never been one for an early morning. Fill your plate, Mrs Flowerday, or everything will go cold. Ah, I think I can hear Mr Crosby.'

Albert Crosby's entrance a few moments later lacked its usual majesty. He fumbled the closing of the door behind him and, to Jemima's sharp eye, his tie was minutely askew. She was putting food on her plate and because she was wearing a plain dress with a white collar and cuffs, it didn't strike her as entirely surprising when Mr Crosby said sharply in her direction, 'Dinah, has Her Ladyship been served her breakfast yet? And why are you without your cap and apron?'

Putting down the serving tongs, Jemima turned to correct him. The sudden fall of Albert Crosby's face silenced her. Sara Crosby came in with the teapot.

'Albert?' The cook glanced sharply from the butler to Jemima and back again. She seemed to remember then that she was holding a heavy pot and put it down with a bump. 'Mrs Flowerday. Good morning to you.'

Jemima got as far as, 'Good morning to you—' when a scream rang from the direction of the great hall, a cry of animal pain which tailed off into a sustained note of misery.

After a moment's paralysis, Jemima ran towards it.

Jack clumped behind her, shouting, 'Wait, Mrs Flowerday, wait.'

In the great hall, it was obvious the scream was coming from the upper level, the stairwell amplifying the sound. Glancing behind her as she took the stairs, she saw Jack and Lady Hamlash coming too, such dread on their faces, she steeled herself against what she would find.

On the landing was Mrs Newson in her usual black, her hair

tightly bound and her mouth stretched in a continuous scream that paused only for essential breaths.

When Jemima took her arm, she pointed towards the north wing and gibbered, 'Can't wake her, can't wake her!'

Chapter Thirty-Six

Jemima ran. She ran past the housekeeper's room, past the room Dinah shared with Beth. The door of the furthest bedroom, the one she had previously used, stood open. Briefly closing her eyes, Jemima stepped inside. An ice-cold draught hit her immediately. The sash-cord window was raised, a bright trim of snow covering the sill.

'Dinah?'

The girl lay in the bed, her head to one side and her chin raised. There were curl papers in her hair. Jemima went to the bedside. Dinah's face was chalk pale, bluish in the hollows, the skin around the eyes marked with red, freckle-like, spots. The eye that was clearly visible was wide open and when Jemima bent closer, she saw that its white was shot through with spidery veins. A dark bruise marred Dinah's throat and another lay between her ear and cheekbone.

Stepping back, fighting a desire to retch, Jemima noted the impression of knees in the sheets either side of the figure. Something told her she must make a clear, mental record of what she was seeing. Somebody had straddled Dinah as she lay sleeping and squeezed or crushed the life from her throat.

Jack lurched in, and when he saw the bed and the figure in it, a roar of despair tore from him. 'Dinah, no, no, Dinah!'

It was all Jemima could do to stop him cradling the body. She pushed him back. 'This is a crime scene, nothing must be disturbed. Go down and call the police. Jack? Ask for DCI Bullace.'

In the end, she was forced to bundle him out of the room, past Lady Hamlash who stood planted on the threshold, a pillar of shock. Glancing back into the room, Jemima took in the open window, the overset chair, the rumpled bedclothes. She soaked in as much detail as she could.

'Why Dinah?' Jack wailed. He hadn't gone far.

'It wasn't meant to be her,' Jemima said.

It was meant to be me.

Chapter Thirty-Seven

It was midday and the room where Dinah's body lay had been sealed off. The sounds of investigation had not abated since the first PC had arrived at just before nine, followed closely by the men from CID; weighty footsteps, doors opening and closing, the crunch of tyres on the drive.

Jemima had not yet been interviewed. She burned with impatience to give her account, her belief that she was the intended victim.

In the servants' hall, Mrs Crosby served soup to the household, the detectives and to Dr Rushworth who had been summoned in his capacity as police doctor. Rushworth had made a preliminary examination of Dinah's body. A full post-mortem would take place in the mortuary at Ipswich. Pushing her bowl aside, revolted by the idea of eating, Jemima rose and went out into the kitchen garden. She was followed by DS Pretty who had earlier joined them at the table.

'Something troubles you, Mrs Flowerday.'

Her answer was to say distractedly, 'I used that room when I stayed before. In the dark, they wouldn't have realised they had the wrong victim. We're both brunette, and Dinah had curlpapers in, so they wouldn't notice the difference in the length of our hair.'

'They?' DS Pretty echoed.

'I use the term loosely.'

'Are you saying you believe Dinah was killed mistakenly, and that you were the intended target?'

She gave a sharp nod, and then asked, 'Why was Dinah sleeping in that room?'

Pretty sighed. 'The girl changed rooms after Beth crept into the bed with her. Something about Beth snoring and wriggling too much.'

'It was because of me.'

'How do you arrive at that opinion, Mrs Flowerday?'

Jemima shut her eyes, wondering if she would ever rid her mind of the image of a murdered girl, the imprint of something hard and wide on the part of the throat that was exposed. 'I found that room too cold, so I pretended I'd wrenched my ankle, and couldn't climb the stairs.'

Pretty pulled a stem off a crisply frozen sage plant and crumbled it between broad fingers. 'Where did you sleep?'

'In the room Madame Guyen used. Dinah helped me take my trunk in there, and she didn't object because it meant she didn't have to carry coal upstairs…' Jemima's voice tailed off as the cost of that choice swept over her. 'How do you think she died?'

'Too early to say.'

'You have eyes, DS Pretty. You don't have to shield my feelings.'

'Hm. Asphyxiation, but not strangulation. I think she was prevented from breathing by something being held hard to her throat.'

That accorded with the mental notes Jemima had made. 'Do her parents know yet?'

'I can't comment. Who else was aware of your sleeping arrangements, Mrs Flowerday?'

'Mrs Newson and Dinah. Nobody else.'

'Lady Hamlash?'

She shook her head. 'Mrs Newson begged me not to tell anyone because it would cause upset. As a sort of guest, I should sleep upstairs.'

Pretty grunted. 'Why would anyone wish to kill you, Mrs Flowerday?'

'Because of this.' It was DCI Bullace, his approach muffled by the snow on the path. He held up the train ticket Jemima had passed to him the night before. 'Small as it is, it warrants our interest. Take it, preserve it as evidence, Detective Sergeant.'

Pretty took the ticket and gazed on it. 'Brabberton Manor to Liverpool Street. First-class return.' He frowned. 'It's been used.'

'Only one way,' Jemima said, and assured him that it had not been purchased by her. 'DCI Bullace is right, it changes the thinking around Roland Crosby's last movements.'

'Crosby's? How? What d'you know about him, Mrs Flowerday?' demanded DS Pretty.

She took a deep breath. She was stepping into dangerous waters. 'I found it in London, in a wardrobe.'

'Whose wardrobe?' Pretty sounded as though he was halfway to guessing, but unable to believe what he was about to hear.

Jemima detailed the circumstances. 'I happened to be in the vicinity of Finsbury Park.'

'And felt drawn to a particular residence? Strange, that. The coat pocket was that of Roland Crosby, I take it?'

Jemima had no doubt that DS Pretty was soaking in her every syllable and nothing she now said would be overlooked.

'The coat was hanging in his wardrobe,' she confirmed.

Pretty fell silent, while Bullace gave the impression that his deputy's further thoughts were worth waiting for. 'Brabberton Manor,' Pretty muttered to himself. 'Quiet as the grave, except on Sundays when it's quieter. So... whoever sold the ticket might tell us who bought it, and when.'

Bullace supplied a name. 'Sydney Deacon. Lately the station-master at Brabberton Manor. His employment was terminated, but when there's time I'll send a bobby to enquire at his usual haunts. Right now, our priority is that poor girl upstairs.'

They started back towards the house and Jemima heard Bullace saying, 'I must establish how the killer gained entry to her room. Was it from inside the house or from outside?'

'Surely there's no mystery,' Jemima said, catching up with him. 'The open window is an irrelevance. The killer went upstairs, as anyone might, turned left to go along the passage, turned the door handle and walked in.'

This opinion was at odds with that of the first policeman to come upon the scene. That being PC Trowse of Saxonchurch, who on a previous occasion had declared the death of Marie Guyen to be, 'A rum 'un all right.' Jemima had taken him up to the crime scene and opened the door, saying, 'Don't go in.'

After a jolt of shock at the sight in front of him, Trowse had stomped to the window, saying, 'That's how the devil got in.' He'd planted his hand in the unbroken line of snow on the sill. 'He got in from the roof just below.'

'How?' Jemima had demanded.

'Opened the window, of course.'

Jemima had pointed out that pushing up a sash-cord window while balancing on snow-covered and steeply angled roof tiles would challenge all but an acrobat. Add to that that the window squeaked when the sash was raised, the noise would surely have woken Dinah and given her a moment to raise the alarm.

'The window is fifteen feet up from the ground, PC Trowse,' she'd said, adding, 'in my view, it's the least likely means of entry.'

Trowse had been adamant. 'It'll be a prowler, seeing his opportunity. Mark my words.' The discovery of a ladder propped against the side of the tool shed below had persuaded the young constable that his theory was watertight.

They returned to the servants' hall and after stamping the snow off his shoes, DCI Bullace agreed with Jemima. 'The open window and the ladder were a clumsy decoy to throw us onto a different scent.' The footprints at the ladder's base were real enough, but greatly supplemented by PC Trowse who had walked back and forth while checking them out. Two inches of virgin snow on the tool shed roof proved beyond doubt that nobody had climbed into the room from outside. 'My question,' Bullace went on, 'is not how the killer got into the bedroom – I agree it was from inside – but whether he was a resident of this house or a stranger.'

Jemima said quietly, 'I believe I know who the killer is, Chief Inspector.'

Bullace raised a finger. *Not now.* His glance in the direction of the kitchen alerted her to the murmur of voices within. He turned to Pretty, saying in an under voice, 'If it were an insider, the murder weapon will be concealed somewhere in the house or hurled from a window. Have every nook and cranny turned out, every cupboard, every blanket chest.'

'Will be done, sir.' His voice reduced to a growl, Pretty added, 'Anybody could have walked in last night from outside. These doors were open.' He indicated the glazed lobby through which they had just come.

'Unlocked?' Bullace dispensed with whispers. 'Doesn't the damn butler do his job?'

Pretty confirmed that Albert Crosby had insisted that he had locked up last night, as he did every night. 'But the kitchen maid went out first thing to empty the cinders from the range onto the path and says the doors weren't locked then. If we're to believe her,

Crosby is mistaken or lying, or somebody turned keys without his knowledge sometime in the wee small hours.'

Jemima vaguely remembered waking in the dead of night, hearing a door click. 'I went straight back to sleep,' she said. 'It would be worth asking those others who sleep down here if they heard anything.'

PC Trowse came in from the kitchen garden just then. There was snow on his cape and snow to be stamped off his boots. Having done so, he addressed Bullace. 'You sent me out to see if there were any other suspicious footprints in the location, sir.'

'Well?'

'I've found more.'

'Where?'

Trowse pointed to the door they'd all come in by. 'Right outside. Different sizes, all mixed up.'

'They're our prints, you damn fool.'

Trowse flushed. Jemima pretended she had not heard.

'And others, sir,' Trowse persisted. 'Leading into the walled garden, and all around the beds. A woman's shoeprints.'

'They would be mine.'

They all turned to see Sara Crosby standing in the kitchen doorway. She wore the cotton canvas apron that Jemima had picked up from the station platform after the trunk carrying Sara's possessions had spilled open. The rolled, blue sleeves of her dress showed a dusting of flour, as did the knuckles of her hands and the rolling pin she was holding.

'I'm knocking up some cheese flans for later and was hoping to find a few sprigs of parsley.'

'And did you?' Bullace asked.

'No. Had to use dried in the end. I picked some sage from out there, though. That'll be for a sage and onion stuffing later.' She winked at the chief inspector. 'D'you like Bakewell tart, sir?'

'Not especially.'

'Ah. I'm baking one, but I'll do a treacle tart as well, to please all tastes.'

'Thank you, Mrs Crosby.' A nod from Bullace sent the cook back to her domain. He turned to Trowse. 'Where do the footprints go from the walled garden?' he asked patiently. 'Back here to the house?'

Trowse confirmed that they did. 'They'll be the cook's, by the sound of it. But the others won't be.'

'Others?'

'Big ones, leading to the cottage by the park wall. I knocked, but nobody's answering.'

There was a moment of silence as those listening sifted this information.

'You mean the gardener's cottage?' Jemima added for Bullace and Pretty's benefit, 'Kenneth Wells was the previous occupant.'

'Wells?' PC Trowse cut in. 'Him as went under a train?'

Bullace frowned hard, then glanced at Jemima. 'D'you recall, Dr Rushworth thought he saw a light from that direction last night.'

'For a moment,' Jemima agreed. 'But when we all looked, it wasn't there.'

'Hm. Has anyone used that cottage since Wells left, Mrs Flowerday?' Bullace asked.

How could she know? 'Dinah might have mooned around inside, as she is grieving more than anyone for Wells.'

'Not "is", "was",' Bullace reminded her.

Oh, dear heavens. She'd almost walked into another elephant trap. 'I – I really can't say if anyone would have been in that cottage. I've been in town.'

Bullace asked PC Trowse if he'd looked inside.

No, was the answer, only through the window. 'But I reckon someone lit a fire in the grate,' Trowse added.

'I suppose Dinah might have done that, if she'd wanted to sit there for any length of time,' Jemima said thoughtfully.

'It wasn't a young woman's footprints going up to the cottage,' Trowse put in – rather late in the conversation, Jemima thought. 'They came from a workman's boots. Big 'uns and mended a few times, I reckon. I let the traces be, sir,' PC Trowse assured Bullace. 'I haven't walked on them.'

Bullace dispatched Pretty to take a look, while Jemima thought of the boots Wells had acquired from the London hostel where he'd taken refuge. Had he changed his plans, and come back here rather than track down witnesses to Marie and Edgar's marriage?

Bullace proved himself a mind reader. 'Are you thinking what I'm thinking, Mrs Flowerday, that we may be witnessing the gardener's return?'

She met his eye. 'Wells died on the railway track. You were sure of it.'

With Pretty stumping out again into the snow, and Trowse similarly dismissed, Bullace was able to say for Jemima's ears only, 'In a grim way, I hope Wells *is* dead and has no hand in this. The murder of a young woman by a healthy young man is, in my view, a subversion of nature.'

He went to the kitchen and Jemima followed. Mrs Crosby was at the kitchen table, transferring freshly rolled pastry to a circular dish with her rolling pin. She gave a slight gasp as she became aware of being watched.

'I'm baking blind pastry cases,' she said. 'The range is up to heat, so it's a shame to waste it. A nice treacle tart will go down well with your chaps, I'm sure. Lads always have a sweet tooth, don't they?'

'Do they?' Bullace took a long, slow look around.

Sara Crosby carried on pressing her pastry into the base of a dish before adding a disc of baking paper and shaking ceramic beans on top. She took the dish to the range and picked up a pad of cloth, protecting her hands as she opened the oven door. Bullace sauntered to the table, staring into the various bowls of tart filling. Jemima could smell the almond batter for a Bakewell tart and the savoury tang of sage and onion.

Bullace said suddenly, 'Stop.'

Sara Crosby had been about to slide the tart base into the oven.

'Shut the oven door, leave this room, Mrs Crosby. Proceed to the great hall.'

She looked aghast. 'I have to blind-bake this pastry.'

'Leave it. You too, Mrs Flowerday. Go to the great hall, now—' He got no further as PC Trowse hurried in to announce a telephone call for him. A man matching Kenneth Wells's description had bought fuel at a petrol station near Ipswich the previous day. The individual had, reportedly, driven down from London.

So, he's followed me here, Jemima reflected. Like a tolling bell, a single thought chimed in her mind. *Let Dinah's killer not be Wells.*

In the hall, she was joined by Beth and a moment after by Sara Crosby who was visibly upset.

'It wouldn't have hurt to let me put that pastry-case in to bake.'

Dr Rushbrook came down the stairs and went to stand in front of one of the windows looking out on the drive. One by one, the other servants arrived – Mrs Newson, then Jack and Albert Crosby. On his way to the telephone room, without pausing, DCI Bullace asked the butler to have a fire laid in the library. PC Trowse took up a stance in front of the servants' door. A second bobby stood guard at the bottom of the stairs.

None shall pass.

DS Pretty came in. Nobody seemed keen to enact the order to light a fire, and Jemima repeated it to the sergeant. 'It was always Dinah's task, you see.'

Pretty in turn repeated the request to Albert Crosby, who stared back at him, blankly.

'Shall I do the honours?' Jemima suggested. 'I know where the coal and kindling are kept.'

Pretty wouldn't hear of it. 'Trowse can sort it. I want you under my eye, Mrs Flowerday. I've seen footsteps outside to tell me that a man was at large last night. We've got a girl dead upstairs, so let's have no more wandering about, unescorted. Got it?'

The sound of a large vehicle pulling up at the door terminated the conversation. It also brought the butler from his stupor. He hurried to open the front door to admit Sir Finchley and Lady Olivia Hamlash.

'One of you fetch in our bags,' Sir Finchley commanded, his eyes going straight to the stairwell and the policeman standing guard at its foot. It was evident from Crosby's reaction that the pair were not expected.

Jemima saw him gather himself with effort. 'Good morning, sir. I take it that Her Ladyship telephoned you?'

'No – he did.' Sir Finchley indicated Dr Rushworth, who had stepped away from the window to greet him. Sir Finchley ignored the doctor, striding into the drawing room, calling out, 'Mother?' Lady Olivia followed.

Jemima caught a vaguely astonished, 'Finchley, you've come?' in the seconds before the door shut.

Bullace emerged from the telephone room and she went to meet him. 'So – Wells?' she asked in a low voice.

She was answered with a short nod. 'There's no doubting it. Blue eyes and an American accent.' Bullace then asked her something extraordinary. 'Mrs Flowerday, would you be so kind as to lend me a silk stocking?'

Chapter Thirty-Eight

Jemima was allowed to pass into the servants' wing. In her bedroom, she opened a drawer and selected a stocking. Champagne-coloured, five shillings a pair. There'd better be a good reason for her sacrifice. Returning to the great hall, she found Bullace marshalling the entire household into the library. PC Trowse was laying a fire with kindling and coal that must have come from the drawing or dining room.

Choosing a moment when nobody was looking, Jemima passed the stocking to Bullace. He put it in his pocket and promptly left the room, taking his sergeant with him. When they returned, DS Pretty was carrying a small chest from which he removed a box, which, when opened, was revealed to be a fingerprint kit. They were all to have their prints taken.

Sir Finchley flatly refused. 'Nor will I remain in this mausoleum of a room. If you must interview my mother or myself, you will do so in private.'

'Sounds the horn but rarely applies the brakes' had been Wells's summing up of Sir Finchley. Never did a description seem more apt to Jemima.

However, DCI Bullace displayed an equal confidence in his own right of way, informing Sir Finchley that, 'The library not only has seating for all, it has electric light, which I need. As for taking your prints, you may refuse and I may arrest you for obstruction.'

Sir Finchley gaped, and then reminded the chief inspector that his father-in-law was the Earl Rivers, Lord Lieutenant of the neighbouring county and friend of 'significant people'. Bullace answered that he was cognisant of these facts and had the King been present, His Majesty would also have been asked for his finger prints.

On any other occasion, Jemima might have smiled. Rocking the boat? It seemed Bullace was intent on it.

'Oh, for pity's sake, just do it then,' Sir Finchley snarled.

One after the other, they rolled their index fingers across an ink pad and pressed them to white paper. Their names were recorded and the prints placed by Pretty into a sturdy envelope. At this point, the hearse arrived and there was a hiatus as Bullace and the doctor formally released Dinah's body into the undertakers' care.

'How long are we meant to sit here?' Sir Finchley was growing irascible again.

'As long as is needed,' came the reply.

'If you had done your job adequately, Chief Inspector, that girl would still be alive and I would not have had a day's shooting interrupted by my mother's hysterics.'

'I was never hysterical,' his mother objected. 'I was upset and there is a world of difference.'

Bullace's reply was scathing. 'You cannot regret more than I that a killer, or killers, have gone undetected, Sir Finchley. I wish with all my soul that Dinah Pullen's parents still had a living child. If you cannot bring yourself to care for them, at least remember the servants look to you for a lead.' Bullace then closed the library door.

They were all now gathered, and with a frisson of fascination, Jemima counted thirteen in total, including Bullace, Pretty and PC Trowse.

Though the library was a long room, it was a squash getting them all in. It would soon get hot in here. Even so, Jemima noticed that Albert Crosby was shivering. He had revived briefly when Sir Finchley and Lady Olivia had arrived, directing Jack to place their overnight bags beside the stairs. Now, he sat expressionless, his bloodless face under a slick of sweat putting Jemima in mind of cold meat in aspic.

'It'll kill Dinah's parents.' Jack's comment came without any preamble, wrung through with rage. 'She was the apple of their eye.' He added in a mutter, 'Mine too.'

'There now.' Mrs Crosby patted his hand. 'It don't help to dwell.'

'We now have everyone's prints,' said Bullace from his place at the top of the table. 'Fingerprints have been taken from the crime scene and both sets will be compared. If anyone wishes to confess, or speak to me privately, now is the time to do so.'

He waited. Dead silence followed.

'Very well,' he went on. 'I shall start by eliminating those who have an innocent reason for being inside that bedroom, at any time. Mrs Flowerday, you slept there between the night of 11 and 13 December, correct?'

'Correct.'

'Mrs Newson, you regularly went into that room to change sheets and to ensure it was aired.'

Mrs Newson whispered that she did. 'Though not very often, since the nurse who looked after the late master left us.'

'You made the bed up for Mrs Flowerday's use, however?'

Mrs Newson inclined her head. 'The day before she arrived.'

'Naturally, Dinah's prints will be present,' Bullace said. 'Beth

Noaks—' He searched for the kitchen maid who, as always, was hunkered at the furthest reaches of the table. 'Did you ever go into that room?'

Beth shook her head, unwilling to look up.

'There was no reason for her to,' said Mrs Newson. 'Beth belongs down in the kitchen and never came upstairs until recently.'

Bullace said he would like Beth to answer. 'Child, did you go into that room at any time?'

'No, sir.'

Bullace turned to Jack. 'You?'

Jack replied hotly, 'Why would I? I don't go much upstairs, and I wouldn't dream of going along that corridor, where the women-folk sleep.'

'You did this morning, when you followed me in,' Jemima reminded him. 'Please make a note, Chief Inspector, Jack's finger-prints will be on the doorknob, the door itself and likely the bedside table and bedframe.'

'Duly noted, Mrs Flowerday.' Bullace turned to Mrs Crosby. 'You, madam?'

Sara Crosby said she didn't know what room they were all talking about. 'My domain is the kitchen, and my bedroom is right by it. A room on the ground floor is what I asked for, both times of coming here. I start early and finish late, and don't have time to be traipsing up and down stairs.'

Bullace thanked her. 'Mr Crosby?'

The butler shook his head. He couldn't find words.

'Lady Hamlash?'

Sir Finchley answered in her place. 'Why would my mother venture into a servant's bedroom?'

Bullace made a note. 'You, Sir Finchley, did you ever step into that room?'

'Don't ask damn-fool questions.'

'Lady Olivia?'

'Leave my wife out of this.' Sir Finchley was growing redder by the minute.

'Lady Olivia?'

Bullace makes as good a cargo train as Sir Finchley, Jemima reflected, rolling smoothly on. Were she a gambler, her money would be on the detective getting where he wanted first.

Lady Olivia calmly assured Bullace that she had never entered any room upstairs other than the one she used when she stayed and, occasionally, her mother-in-law's chamber. 'You will surely find prints there from servants long departed, Chief Inspector.'

'Undoubtedly.'

'Such as the nurse,' Jemima agreed. 'The one who used the room in the late Sir Rufus's day. And, of course, those of Dr Rushbrook who made an examination this morning.'

Rushbrook cleared his throat, adding that he trusted DCI Bullace would keep that in mind.

A heavy knock at the front door took Bullace away, with an instruction to DS Pretty that everyone should stay in their place. He left the library door ajar and they heard him say, 'Yes, Constable? What is it?'

A snatch of conversation floated in.

'. . . a mile or two away, sir, on the back lane to Beggars Heath. He came quietly.'

'It's our man, you're sure?'

Jemima felt a sick sinking of the heart as she heard this unseen constable say, 'Even if he hadn't admitted to being in the house last night, the snow lies deep in the lanes and his footprints were fresh as a daisy. Only bit of him that is.'

'Fetch him in.'

Bullace returned and confirmed that a man had been caught close by. 'He has admitted entering this house in the early hours.'

'Then you've found your killer!' Mrs Crosby cried. 'I hope he's going straight into the lock-up.'

This was not the plan. 'As mine is the only police car in the vicinity, and I shall need it later, he is being brought here.'

There was consternation, but Bullace was immovable. 'The man is in a state of near hypothermia.'

'Let him perish,' rasped Mrs Newson, 'for what he did to Dinah. I'll go to my grave regretting I was ever cross with her.'

Mrs Crosby now looked very nervous. 'A killer, let loose among us? What if he's still consumed with bloodlust?'

Bullace sought to calm her nerves. 'We don't know if he is a killer as yet and with myself, Pretty, and numerous constables about the place, you have nothing to fear. They're walking him over now.'

'Who is he?' Albert Crosby asked, genuine puzzlement in both look and tone.

Bullace didn't offer a name. 'Suffice to say, the suspect is familiar with the gardener's cottage and with the path leading from there to the servants' hall.'

Perhaps it was inevitable, Jemima thought, that Jack should be the one to voice her own dreadful presumption.

'It's Wells, isn't it? I never really thought he'd died. You've got Wells.'

Chapter Thirty-Nine

There was little luxury for speculation, as within minutes, two thickset constables were half guiding, half lifting, a man over the threshold. Everyone had ignored the injunction to remain seated, jostling to be the first to see the captive. To identify, to condemn.

Only Jemima hung back, pledging that never again would she seek to solve a crime. She was too emotional, too easily gulled. It was indescribably painful.

The policemen hustled their captive into the hall so the door could be closed. One of them said, 'We found him face-down in the lane on account of him being frozen cold and two-parts drunk.'

Wells, drunk? That felt out of character to Jemima, though who could say how a man might medicate after committing a cowardly murder? She moved closer. The prisoner was wearing oilskins, the hood falling over his face. Weren't they the ones that usually hung in the glazed lobby? On his feet were labourer's boots.

Jack Millar's voice cut through the jabber. 'Let me at him. Let me kill the varmint!' He was restrained by DS Pretty.

Bullace, meanwhile, ordered the man to be brought into the library. 'I don't want him expiring from cold. Mrs Crosby, would you brew tea for all? My sergeant will accompany you into the kitchen.'

'Of course, and I'll put that tart in to cook. Lucky for you gentlemen I've already got a cake ready for cutting.' Sara Crosby had regained her sunny nature, perhaps at the prospect of returning to her kitchen, even if under escort. 'Can I take my little Beth along with me?'

Dispensation was given. Sara Crosby beckoned to Beth who went with her, more reluctantly than Jemima might have supposed. Everyone else trooped back into the library. The prisoner was plonked down on a bishop's chair with a high back and armrests that would prevent him falling sideways. He was kept steady by a constable's gloved hands on his shoulders. The second arresting constable placed an object on the table.

'The murder weapon, Chief Inspector.'

Jemima recognised the poker from the gardener's cottage. It was the one Wells had once, alarmingly, raised in front of her. 'Dinah wasn't killed with a poker, was she?' That didn't fit with the marks she had seen on the girl's throat and jaw.

Bullace flashed her a quelling look. 'Where was it found, this poker?' he demanded of the constable.

'Next to him, sir, in the snow. Says he has no idea how it got there, that he must have picked it up by accident. Though how you can walk around with a brass poker and not know it beats me.'

'Let's take a look at him.' Bullace signalled for the unveiling to take place, and Jemima's seasick heart plunged into a trough.

A moment later, it resurfaced in blessed relief.

'Good Lord, it's Sydney Deacon,' she exclaimed, as the pinched, purple-tipped features of the seated man began making sense. 'The stationmaster at Brabberton Manor. Former stationmaster,' she corrected. 'Sacked for intoxication while on duty.'

Mrs Newson found her voice. 'Deacon? You killed Dinah? I knew your mother!' The housekeeper put her hands over her eyes and began to weep.

Sydney Deacon presented as wretched a picture as might be expected of a man scooped out of the snow on the margins of hypothermia, frogmarched two unsympathetic miles to be found guilty by his peers of horrible murder. Even so, Mrs Newson's distress forced an answer from him.

'I wouldn't hurt a fly, missus, other than myself when I fall down. Did I hear mention of a cup of tea? I'm parched. I can't talk till I get one. Four sugars.'

Jemima, feeling the need for air as the crowd in the room had expanded, offered to go see how Mrs Crosby and Beth were getting on. She was granted permission.

'Touch nothing that you do not need to touch,' Bullace warned her.

In the servants' hall, she glanced into the glazed lobby and saw for herself that the oilskins were missing. She was still astonished that neither Bullace nor Pretty had objected to the suggestion that a poker was the murder weapon. The marks she'd seen on Dinah were, to her inexpert eye, made by something broader, though perhaps a poker pressed down in a sustained way would create a wide bruise. DS Pretty had shared his belief that Dinah had died from something 'held hard to her throat'.

She spent a quiet moment asking herself if mild-mannered Deacon could have done such a thing. Sober, she doubted it. If drunk, who could say? He must have come in during the moonless hours of the night. To steal or to find alcohol, most probably. She glanced out into the kitchen garden and saw Beth. PC Trowse was with her, working the pump. It looked like hard effort. The pipes were probably half-frozen.

A cry from the kitchen took her in there and she found Mrs Crosby staring at the kettle. Jemima had the idea the woman had kicked the cooking range with a clogged foot.

'It won't boil if you watch it,' Jemima said.

Sara Crosby turned with a sigh. 'Never a truer word, Mrs F. This range is a stubborn brute, not a patch on mine at home. I've sent Beth to draw water.'

'I saw her, and the constable.'

'With all these folk in the house, a second kettle on the hob won't hurt.'

A moment later, Beth came in. 'There's someone in the walled garden,' the girl muttered. 'That policeman went to look.'

Jemima couldn't help thinking that, if word had got out of another death, there'd be voyeurs arriving from all sides. Perhaps the first gawper was here already.

With the kettle being so slow, Jemima used the time to gather up crockery left from lunch. She took it through to the scullery and noticed two piles of plates on the side, waiting to be washed. One lot was the everyday blue-and-white, the other the dining-room set from which she had eaten last night.

Beth must have been packed off to bed, told to leave the washing up until the morning. Jemima counted up the blue-and-white plates. She counted them again. And once more, to be sure.

When she returned to the kitchen, Beth was arranging cups on three trays. Sara Crosby had taken her tart base from the oven and was shaking her head over it. 'It's not had its time. Still…' She took it to the table, piled treacle-and-breadcrumb filling into it, smoothed the top and returned it to the oven. 'I never got them cheese flans cooked and as for roasting a chicken…' Sara flashed a smile at Jemima. 'First thing I ever learned to cook well was roast chicky-bird with sage and onion stuffing. Be a dear, Mrs F, and refill the sugar.' She held the bowl out to Jemima and gestured towards the pantry. 'Beth, take those cups in a tray at a time. Sniff the milk before you jug it.'

Jemima opened the narrow pantry door and went down the white-painted steps. Curious about the figure Beth claimed to have seen, she went straight to the small window. It was unglazed and covered with wire mesh. By convention, a pantry window faced north to keep the interior chilled. She placed a hand against the mesh and withdrew it at once. Brr!

'You found the sugar, dear?' Mrs Crosby called to her.

'Almost.' Jemima lifted down the box of white cubes and imagined Beth doing the same on the day Marie died, filling the sugar bowl as she was now doing. Adding brown, Demerara cubes from the other box. White for tea, brown for coffee. Jemima paused, the bowl in her hand. She'd said to Bullace that as Marie was the only person drinking coffee at teatime, it was inevitable the adulterated cube would end up in her cup. Jemima pictured the sugar bowl on the table that day, the silver tongs lying across a bed of white cubes and a cluster of brown ones. A cluster, not just one. What wretched luck, then, that Marie had selected the one that killed her.

She replaced the Tate & Lyle box on the shelf above her head, and hearing a faint noise from outside, went back to the window and pushed it open. At once, a figure rose up from below the sill. Though the face was familiar, its sudden appearance startled a shriek from her.

'Wells!' she hissed. 'What—'

He put an urgent finger to his lips.

'Was it you Beth saw?'

'Shh!'

'Mrs Flowerday, who's there?' The question was followed by fast footsteps and then Sara Crosby was peering through the pantry door, past Jemima at the gaping window. Wells had ducked out of sight.

'A mouse,' Jemima stammered. 'It dashed over my foot.'

'Why open the window then?'

'Erm, so it could get out?' She made to close the window and noticed something caught on the sill. It was a leaf, but not ivy, nor from a climbing rose or anything that might live in the walled garden. This one was waxy and ribbed. Hoya. How had it got from the conservatory to the pantry?

Mrs Crosby was watching. 'I didn't have you down as the screeching kind, Mrs F. You must have seen a mouse before, living in London. They're a plague where I live, and their big brothers too.'

'I've seen plenty in my time,' Jemima agreed, recalling the whiff of rat poison at the top of Mrs Crosby's cellar stairs. 'I don't screech, generally. It darted out of nowhere, that's all.'

Sara Crosby hadn't moved. Jemima looked at the woman's feet planted on the top step. The leather uppers of the kitchen clogs were fastened to the sole with small, round-headed nails. One nail on the front of the left side was missing. And another on the right-hand clog, in almost the same place.

'Mrs Flowerday? What's with my feet?'

'Nothing. The sugar.' Jemima looked around for it. She'd put the bowl down when she went to the window.

'Right in front of your nose.'

'So it is.' Jemima reached for it, and realised she was still clutching the Hoya leaf. Dropping it, she picked up the bowl which she handed to Sara. How odd. Her fingers now carried a faint odour of tobacco. Looking down, she spied the leaf on the floor, ducked quickly to retrieve it, pushed it into her skirt pocket, then followed Sara into the kitchen. Beth was absent and one of the tea trays had gone. 'Shall I take the other one through?' Jemima asked, now deeply anxious to get away.

'First, would you do me a little favour,' Sara asked. 'Step up and fetch down a cake tin from the top shelf. That one.' She pointed to the tin with the biblical motif, identical to the one Angela Price had produced during a cosy teatime in Campden Buildings. 'I don't much like standing on stools these days to be honest, Mrs F.'

'Of course.' As she stepped up and reached for the tin, Jemima heard the range door being opened, and Sara Crosby muttering, 'If you want a happy home, promise not to roam. To win 'is heart, it's treacle tart.' She projected to Jemima, 'Do I have time to knock up that Bakewell? Pastry's made. Seems a shame to waste it.'

'I don't know. Where's PC Trowse? You could ask him.' Holding the tin at waist level, Jemima looked at the twin giraffes whose necks were entwined across the lid.

Sara Crosby opened a drawer and began rifling through.

A moment later she was muttering, 'Lost my rolling pin. Blimey, I'm all out of sorts today. We'll have to make one tart and a cake stretch to the five thousand.' She came over to take the tin from Jemima, stretching up her hands for it. 'Pass it down, dearie.'

Jemima had been admiring the naïve decoration. The animals plodded in double-file around the side of the tin, making their way towards Noah's ark. The giraffes were in the queue, their bodies painted on the side, their long necks extending over the lid. One giraffe had a dent in its flank, and – Jemima's breath caught.

'Mrs Flowerday?'

She looked down and knew in that instant that Sara Crosby meant to pull the legs of the stool from under her and bring her crashing to the floor.

PC Trowse chose that moment to come into the kitchen. Seeing him, Jemima dropped the tin.

Mrs Crosby caught it, saving the cake inside. Jemima jumped down and hurtled back to the library.

Chapter Forty

She arrived, shaky and breathless, to discover that Bullace had extracted enough from Sydney Deacon to share Jemima's opinion of him as an unlikely murderer. 'The fact that you were here last night is insufficient grounds to arrest you for murder. However, we will take your fingerprints and I would value the doctor's opinion.' He addressed Rushbrook. 'Could Dinah Pullen have been killed with the implement we found on this man?'

Dr Rushbrook examined the poker, turning it over and over so that its shaft caught the firelight. As Jemima sank into her seat, he said, 'No.'

'Not the murder weapon?' Bullace prompted.

'In my opinion, it is not.'

'Are you sure, Doctor? Much hangs on this.'

'In my professional judgement,' the doctor replied patiently, 'this could not have caused the fatal crushing to Miss Pullen's throat. Its circumference is too narrow. I am not a pathologist, but my initial impression is that the bruises to the windpipe were made by a cylindrical object. Perhaps a chair leg? A bottle was my first thought, laid horizontally with pressure applied evenly at both ends.'

'Then it is him.' Jack Millar pointed aggressively at Deacon. 'He's no stranger to a bottle by the smell of him.'

'The killer would have to be positioned above the victim,' said Bullace, ignoring the interruption. 'Although Dinah's head was turned to the side, you found the bruising was in fact central to the throat, correct Rushbrook?'

The doctor agreed. 'I'd say the killer did his work with a knee either side of her torso, as she lay on her back. At some point, perhaps when she stopped struggling and passed out, the killer turned her face to the side and covered her mouth and nose with their hand, the heel of the hand leaving a further bruise beside the ear.'

Between ear and cheekbone, Jemima elaborated silently to herself. She'd seen that bruise, wondered what had made it.

Bullace asked Deacon why he had stolen a poker. 'Lady Hamlash has identified it as one she discarded from her drawing room some years ago. It was found beside you. You also stole a coat.'

'I took the poker to sell,' Deacon confessed. 'It was lying on the hearth in the cottage, and there's a fellow who drinks at the Wheatsheaf would give me a few bob for it, since it's solid brass. I took the coat because I was cold.'

Bullace said, 'You're guilty of theft, at any rate. And trespass. Any questions, Detective Sergeant?'

'One,' grunted Pretty, with a narrow look at Deacon. 'What were you doing here in the first place, man?'

'I haven't got nowhere else,' Deacon mumbled. 'This time of year, you need a roof. I heard what happened to the last gardener, the Yank, so I came over and tried the door of the cottage. It wasn't locked, I didn't break in.'

'Did you at any time enter this house?'

Deacon's hesitation amounted to an admission. 'I might have.'

'Answer truthfully.'

'I had a bottle of the hard stuff with me last night. It makes you forget.'

'See!' Jack half rose. 'He had a bottle. Proves it.'

'You came into the house in the early hours.' It was Jemima's voice, rousing Deacon, who had put his hands to his head as if to shake memories free. 'I heard a door go. It woke me. That was you, making your way into the scullery. You took a plate of food scraps.' She said to Bullace, 'There will be a blue-and-white plate somewhere. Most likely in the gardener's cottage.'

Deacon slowly nodded his head. 'You've been in and looked?'

Jemima assured him that she had not. 'I can count, Mr Deacon. There should be six used china plates on the scullery drainer, not five.'

Mrs Crosby came in then, carrying a tray. PC Trowse carried another. She said so jovially, 'Well I never, Mrs Flowerday. You're as good as a detective,' that Jemima wondered if she had imagined the woman had wanted to harm her not twenty minutes ago.

The trays were set down. The freshly baked treacle tart smelled delicious.

Sara Crosby said, 'Shall I be mother?' and started pouring milk into cups.

Jemima asked Deacon, 'Did you walk in or break in?'

'Walked in,' Deacon answered. 'The lobby doors weren't locked, I swear it. I'm no housebreaker, just a man down on his luck.'

'What leftovers did you find?'

Deacon answered readily. 'Beef Dumpling, roast potato, cabbage, carrots and a dollop of horseradish. Very tasty.'

Sara Crosby paused in her pouring. 'Condemned himself, hasn't he? Here, in the house, sozzled on hard liquor, armed with a bottle. He crept upstairs and did for that poor girl.'

'I am disinclined to think so,' was Bullace's response. 'Can a drunkard get upstairs in an unfamiliar house in pitch-dark, negotiate passageways, find a particular room, commit murder and get

271

downstairs again without rousing anyone or bumping into something? I'm also convinced that the murder weapon was not a bottle.'

'A moment ago, you were speculating that it was a chair leg,' sneered Sir Finchley.

'A chair leg I can believe,' answered Bullace. 'Dinah struggled before she died and the bruising on her neck was so extreme, it implies the killer used all his weight on the object to crush her windpipe.' He glanced at Jack who had moaned in distress. 'A bottle neck would snap. The bruising would be asymmetric. Embossed lettering would leave its mark. No. Something solid, strong and smooth was used. Any chairs missing a leg, do you happen to know, Lady Hamlash?'

'Not that I've seen,' said Her Ladyship.

'DS Pretty,' Bullace said, 'show the company the last item placed in your evidence chest.'

Pretty opened the lid of the chest and removed an item. It was around eighteen inches long, pale in colour and – Jemima blinked – good heavens – encased in her champagne-coloured stocking. Pretty laid it where everyone could see and Bullace invited them all to look, but not to touch. 'The stocking is to preserve traces of skin or blood that might be present on the surface. Though I doubt anything human remains on it.'

'Is it a cosh?' Sir Finchley asked.

'No,' said Bullace. 'It is far more domestic. Mrs Crosby, do you recognise it?'

Sara Crosby had been staring at the object, the milk jug stationary above a cup. She slammed it down. 'I don't much like games, Inspector.'

Pulling on cotton gloves, Bullace took the item from the stocking. It was a rolling pin. 'Yours? Brought from London?'

Mrs Crosby opened and closed her mouth, but no words came out.

'Let me save you the effort of denying it. The initials SC are etched onto one of the handles. I believe you were using it not two hours ago to roll pastry. A cook has so many things to hand that can harm and be washed up afterwards.' Bullace indicated the plate that had been placed on the table with pride by Mrs Crosby. 'I advise nobody eat that treacle tart.'

Sara Crosby made a dash towards the door, but DS Pretty stopped her. She kicked his shins with her clogs. He lifted her so her feet paddled the air and a clog flew off, narrowly missing Sir Finchley.

DCI Bullace examined the shoe and when Sara Crosby had been passed into the custody of PC Trowse, he asked Pretty to find an item retrieved from Dinah's bedroom. 'The thing we almost missed.'

Out of the chest came a labelled box from which Bullace took a tiny nail, saying, 'It was lodged in the quilt on the bed Dinah was killed in. Near the foot. I am inclined to think that whoever killed her, first straddled her, a knee either side, the more efficiently to press down on her throat. Doctor' – he invited Rushbrook closer – 'would you tell me if, in your opinion, this nail belongs in one or other of Mrs Crosby's clogs.'

The doctor examined the shoe that had come off Sara's foot. 'There's a hole on the side here,' he said. 'A nail is missing.'

'You'll find another missing on the clog she still has on,' Jemima said. 'I have it in my possession.'

It was not the moment to reveal that she had found it in the glasshouse, as DCI Bullace was speaking sonorously.

'Mrs Sara Crosby, I am arresting you on suspicion of the murder of Dinah Pullen.'

'It was him!' Sara screamed, and her body jerked towards her brother-in-law. 'Albert's your killer, not me. All I did was open doors and rest the ladder against the wall, to make it look like an outsider did it. It was him slipped upstairs – only he got the wrong girl. Dinah shouldn't have been in that room. Wouldn't have been if *she*—' Sara's fury veered not towards Jemima, but to Beth. 'If she wasn't such a stupid little muttonhead, having nightmares and wetting the bed!'

Beth did a surprising thing. Instead of crumpling as she had at every other moment of crisis, she got to her feet. 'I can't help having nightmares,' she said. 'You aren't nice, Mrs Crosby, like you want people to think. You pinch me when no one's looking.'

Sara bared her teeth. 'I should have done more than pinch you. I've never been cursed with such a knuckle-brain in the kitchen.'

Jemima took the opportunity to dash to her room. The police constable on guard at the foot of the stairs called to her to stop, but by now, she'd learned how to open the servants' door without fumbling and was through it before he could stop her. At the door of her room, she fished for the key. Was she being pursued? A footstep behind her made her spin round. 'Constable, I—'

'Shh!'

This time, she did not scream, hissing, 'Why exactly are you here?'

'It's not for the weather and surely not for the social scene,' Wells said.

He doesn't know, Jemima realised. How could he? 'Mr Wells, you need to be very calm, and very strong. The most awful, horrible thing has happened.'

Chapter Forty-One

Kenneth Wells followed her into her room and closed the door. 'What's up? Why are there so many policemen around?'

Jemima told him the grim news.

'Oh, God.' He sat down, covering his face with his hands. When Jemima told him about the swapping of rooms, he said, 'Her or you, either would be unsupportable. Oh, poor Dinah. I have to ask, did you reveal what you knew about Roland Crosby blackmailing Sir Finchley?'

'Not intentionally.' She described the moment when the railway ticket had dropped from her bag in the drawing room. 'Albert Crosby saw it.'

Wells took this in, then said, 'He killed Dinah, in your opinion?'

'More likely Sara Crosby, using her wooden rolling pin as the poor girl slept. I thought she was nice, but it's sweet icing over a cake made of razor blades.' She found what she'd come to collect, showing Wells.

'A nail?' was his response.

'It's the twin of one that will convict Sara for Dinah's murder. This one, I believe, will put her in the frame for the murder of her husband. This and other evidence I have. Mr Wells, dare you accompany me to the library? There's quite a gathering there.'

He got to his feet. 'Sure, it's time we gave up our secrets, Mrs Flowerday. I shelved my plans to track down ex-comrades of Sir Edgar Hamlash. In my gut, I felt I ought to be here. And thanks to information you gave me, I can prove Marie's marriage into this family without witnesses.'

'Tell me!'

'Patience. I'll reveal all when the moment's right.'

Jemima emptied the travel bag she had brought with her from London and filled it with different objects. A pair of black shoes, the Hoya leaf from the pantry windowsill, the shard of chocolate-brown enamel and the key from the pocket of Roland Crosby's spare coat. She added her well-read copy of *The Weekend Sleuth* to the haul.

'I'm not sure anyone will listen just now,' she told Wells as she locked her door behind her. 'Finding a murderer in our midst is enough for one day.'

'With respect,' Wells said, 'it's only the start.'

Chapter Forty-Two

Much had happened since Jemima had left the library.

Albert had been placed under arrest and was seated with his sister-in-law in front of the window, flanked by constables.

Sir Finchley was loudly expressing his opinion that the pair should be removed to somewhere more suitable. 'So my mother need not play host to criminals.'

DCI Bullace regretted it was not possible until a secure police van was provided. DS Pretty was currently ordering one by telephone but... 'It comes from Ipswich, and I hardly need remind you of the current condition of the roads.'

'At the very least,' Sir Finchley boomed, 'lock them in another room so we don't have to see them.'

Bullace was having none of it. 'Having everyone together in one place will allow me to ask the questions I need to ask, without requiring you all to remove to the police station. If you would prefer that, I could organise a police escort?'

Sir Finchley made it clear that he preferred an option that wasn't being offered — of being allowed to drive home secure in the knowledge that Dinah's death would be investigated without any trouble to him or scandal to his family. 'I and my wife only came to lend support to Lady Hamlash. If we had known we would be ordered about, deprived of our freedom—'

Bullace cut him off. 'This is a murder investigation and I have a line of questioning that involves every person in this room.'

Nobody had noticed Jemima's return, nor had they noticed Wells so far. When she cleared her throat, everyone looked towards her.

Seeing who was with her, Mrs Newson uttered a sound of horror. 'You're dead!'

'Not so, ma'am.' Wells stepped forward so everyone might determine for themselves that he was very much of this world.

Only Bullace seemed to find his arrival unremarkable. 'Mr Wells, good day to you. As there are policemen in the house, and my sergeant has also manifested behind you, I advise you not to make another dash for freedom.'

'I won't,' Wells assured him. 'I'm done with running.'

'I hope you have sufficient blood left in your veins after your carefully crafted demise.'

'Plenty more where that came from, sir.'

'You fooled me, I grant you that.'

A degree of respect in Bullace's tone encouraged Jemima to believe that Wells would be allowed to say whatever he had come to say. Would she be allowed to speak too?

'So why have you come back?' Bullace wanted to know. 'You could have skipped the country by now.'

'Not really, without my passport. But there's unfinished business, sir, and I mean to see justice done. I am here to accuse, but also to confess.'

Jack could not let that pass. 'I still say he killed Madame Guyen, even if he didn't kill Dinah. Get the cuffs on him, Inspector. Don't let him slip the leash again.'

'I believe I will hear his story,' was Bullace's comment. 'Then I will decide if restraints are required.'

Sir Finchley also objected strongly. 'This fellow has nothing to say to us. He came here under a false name and a fake guise.'

'Kenneth Wells is my legal name,' Wells came back.

Sir Finchley snorted. 'You took money from my mother who thought you were a gardener and chauffeur.'

'Was I not a good driver, and a halfway decent gardener? Lady Hamlash?'

Her Ladyship nodded. 'I found no fault in your work, Wells. You handle the Crossley better than Finchley ever can, and you dug a creditable amount of bramble out of the gardens.'

'For goodness sake, Mother.' Getting no response from that quarter, Sir Finchley directed his attention back to Bullace. 'Not many days ago, you arrested Wells on suspicion of murder. Handcuff him, or I shall make a telephone call to the Chief of Constabulary and after that to the Lord Lieutenant—'

'Yes, yes,' Bullace interrupted. 'I am familiar with your provenance, Sir Finchley, and your remarkable friendships with all the Lords Lieutenant of the region. Make your calls, but none of them will come to your aid for the simple reason that this place is too remote and' – he glanced at his watch – 'it is now a quarter to three, and will be dark in one hour. It is too late.'

'Then I will read you a riot act that will burn your ears,' Sir Finchley thundered.

'Sit down, sir. Or if you must stand, kindly don't strike the table. It upsets the ladies. Mr Wells?' Bullace clicked his fingers, indicating that Wells should take a seat. 'Are you beginning with an accusation or a confession?'

Wells considered. 'I'm beginning with a story, a history. I'm taking you to France, to the fall of 1916, and to a marriage between my friend Marie Guyen and a man who vowed to love and honour her in perpetuity.'

Lady Hamlash interrupted, asking if she might be allowed to fetch a bottle of headache pills. 'It is so stuffy in here.'

She was given permission by Bullace, who sent Jemima with her, muttering, 'Ensure she finds no excuse to absent herself.'

The tablets were found in Lady Hamlash's bureau, in the drawing room. Returning to the library, they met Lady Olivia who muttered, 'Call of nature. I'm being let out like a dog.'

Lady Olivia was once again wearing the light, kidskin shoes. Again, Jemima heard the footsteps that had taken tobacco tincture on a sugar cube to Marie Guyen. A sugar cube wrapped not in a handkerchief or a scrap of paper but, she now suspected, in a Hoya leaf plucked from a conservatory plant.

Re-taking her seat, Jemima discovered that Wells's story had been cut short by Sir Finchley, who was on his feet, issuing threats of court actions. Beth must have been asked to finish pouring out the tea, and was doing it with such a trembling hand, the spout clinked against the cups, creating a sound like cow bells.

Jemima was ready to take the stage from Wells and now placed the bag she had brought in with her on the table. Bullace glanced at it.

'Mrs Flowerday, are you off somewhere?'

She said she was going nowhere. 'But I wish to speak, if Mr Wells is done.'

'He only got as far as telling us that on a fine October day, near the town of Amiens, the late Marie Guyen, then a nurse, married her sweetheart,' Bullace informed her.

Lady Hamlash fumbled one of the headache tablets into her mouth, swallowing it down with tea. 'Why must that woman's name be constantly in my ears?' she complained. 'I do not wish to discuss the war either. Conflict blighted the last months of my husband's life and blights mine still. My only solace is that Sir Rufus did not live long enough to bear the loss of his eldest son.'

'With respect, ma'am,' Wells said, 'I am telling the story of Marie Guyen's marriage, which is germane to your family.'

'The woman was an imposter and a fraud,' Lady Hamlash replied.

'Ma'am, she was no such thing.'

'Indeed she was.'

'And I can tell you—'

Bullace put a stop to the verbal badminton, telling Wells he would take over the story. Mrs Flowerday would have her moment shortly.

Wells objected. 'With respect, sir, you and I are not likely to be telling the same tale.'

'*With respect*, Mr Wells, I believe our threads will overlap.' From his waistcoat pocket, Bullace took an envelope in a shade of lilac.

Lady Hamlash gasped. 'What are you doing with my writing paper?'

'I thank Your Ladyship for identifying it so readily. This letter came to me anonymously.'

Though Bullace did not look at her, Jemima felt a tingle up her spine. The kennelled bloodhounds were pricking their ears at the blare of a hunting horn. There was no going back now. The chase was on.

Bullace requested Sir Finchley retake his seat. 'Let us begin at the beginning, as I see it. I cannot speak to events that may or may not have taken place in France amidst the smoke of war. Let us start in April this year, with the pick of the crop.' A pause gave all a moment to wonder where this was going. 'I refer, of course, to asparagus.'

Chapter Forty-Three

On Friday, 21 April, as dawn broke, Lady Hamlash's gardener had gone into the walled garden. Entering the glasshouse, Old Bilney had filled a basket with sweet and tender white asparagus.

'Sir Finchley Hamlash commanded it,' Bullace explained, 'as he was hosting a dinner party that night at which certain guests – who may not be named – would grace the company.'

'Merry Beggars Hall was famous for its white asparagus,' Lady Hamlash said, her voice drenched in regret.

Jemima suspected the various compounds Her Ladyship had taken for her nerves were now affecting her faculties. There was a reliance on barbiturates, so Albert Crosby had intimated. And now a headache tablet on top. Jemima tried to catch the doctor's eye, but Rushbrook's attention was on the chief inspector.

Bullace continued smoothly. 'There was only one person here able to drive. Only one person able to deliver the asparagus to Sir Finchley in Norfolk.'

Eyes turned towards Albert Crosby whose shoulders were so hunched, his ears were visible only as tips. To Jemima's thinking, he dreaded whatever revelations were coming, and now had his sister-in-law to fear too. Sara Crosby sat with a face of granite.

Bullace asked the butler, 'Did you drive a trug of asparagus to Steeple Court on the morning of Friday, 21 April, Mr Crosby?'

Albert's tongue darted across dry lips. 'If you say so.'

'I am asking.'

'I can vouch for Crosby,' Sir Finchley shot out, his voice suggesting he too was catching the contagion of fear. 'Crosby drove up with the asparagus and went home the next day.'

'I didn't ask what he did the next day, but thank you for supplying facts,' was Bullace's comment. 'Pretty, the ticket please, from your evidence trove. Show it to the company.'

Sergeant Pretty made his way along one side of the table with the rail ticket Jemima had handed over the previous night. He allowed everyone to see it, including Sydney Deacon, who had revived considerably from being given sweet, strong tea.

'That's—' Deacon began, but Pretty quelled him.

'You'll get your moment.' He held the ticket in front of Albert Crosby. 'Did you buy this?' When Crosby shook his head without raising his eyes, the sergeant informed them all that it was a first-class ticket from Brabberton Manor to London Liverpool Street, bought on 21 April and used in one direction.

Jemima frowned. How could Pretty know when it was bought, since the ticket was undated? Then she understood the bluff. Showing it to Albert Crosby, the sergeant's thumb had obscured one side.

Bullace invited Albert Crosby to think again. 'Did you purchase a return ticket from Brabberton Manor to London that day?'

Albert Crosby said nothing.

'In your original statement,' Bullace ploughed on, 'you claimed you went to Steeple Court early on the Friday and stayed overnight, returning home the following day, Saturday, in time for lunch at one o'clock.'

'That is correct,' Albert agreed in a low voice.

'Does the company agree?'

It took a moment for Jack Millar to say, 'That's pretty much bang on. The stable clock had just chimed when he hobbled in.'

'Hobbled?' echoed Bullace.

'Yes, well… he was walking oddly. I'd taken lunch to Her Ladyship with… with Dinah. Coming back, we found Mr Crosby in the passage, taking off his coat outside his room.'

'*Outside* his room?'

'He'd lost his key. I had to find the spare.'

'Taking his coat off in full view. A little undignified,' was Bullace's reflection. To Crosby he said, 'Are you admitting to buying this ticket?'

'I have no memory of it,' rasped Crosby.

Bullace now invited the former stationmaster to comment. Deacon was ready to confirm that, 'It was him bought it. Him, sitting right there.'

'You are pointing to Albert Crosby.' Bullace, with a nod to his sergeant, oversaw the return of the ticket to the evidence box. 'On what day was it issued?'

'The one you said, sir.'

'Please speak only to your memory, Mr Deacon.'

'Friday, 21 April. It's etched in my brain because that was the day of my downfall.'

'You are positive?'

'I am, sir.' Deacon got up, gripping the back of his chair. 'You mentioning asparagus has brought it all back.'

That was the moment when the riddle of the single and the return tickets was solved by Jemima, quietly within her mind. On the Friday, circa eleven in the morning, Albert Crosby had driven into the station yard at Brabberton Manor and bought a return ticket for London. She had later found it in the coat pocket. Why had Roland Crosby bought a single to come into Suffolk? Answer: he had not bought a ticket at all. Dead men do not, generally.

Deacon was still speaking. 'The Lowestoft freight had just gone through, at a few minutes to the hour. Mr Albert Crosby rolled up in the car. I knew who he was, because he'll take a drink now and then at The Bell in Saxonchurch, and when I was respectable, I went in there too. Everyone knows Lady Hamlash's butler. He paid for his ticket and went to the platform, though it was unseasonable-cold that day. I took a crock of salt and sprinkled it along the platform edge, not wanting him to slip.' A sadness crept over Deacon. 'I was at my best then, not drinking much.'

Jemima chipped in. 'What coat was he wearing, d'you remember?'

'Dark brown,' Deacon said after thinking it through. 'His coat was dark brown, tweedy, with a soft collar.'

'Velvet or corduroy?' asked Jemima. The answer mattered. It would cement her understanding of the brothers' movements.

'Velvet.' Deacon sounded certain. 'Seeing as he didn't want to talk, I went out front and took a look at the car. You don't see many around in the winter. There was something thrown on the grass nearby. It was a basket full of – well, you'll have guessed.'

'Asparagus,' stated Bullace.

'Somebody threw away Merry Beggars asparagus?' Lady Hamlash rocked in her seat.

'Mr Crosby?' Bullace invited a comment. 'No? Carry on, Deacon.'

'We all know about the famous Merry Beggars crowns, how in Sir Rufus's day they would be sent up to London, to the palace.'

Bullace asked Deacon what he had done with the basket.

'Gathered the spears up and went straight to The Bell.'

'And sold your haul to the cook?'

'For five pounds, which I proceeded to spend.' Deacon looked down, miserably.

'At The Bell?'

Jemima provided the answer. 'No, at the Wheatsheaf in Beggars Heath. A reasty place, where five pounds goes a long way. A long way towards destroying your life, Mr Deacon.'

Deacon didn't contradict her and she went on, 'You lost your home and job and were forced to take shelter in a gardener's cottage.'

Deacon muttered, 'You have it right. Thought nobody would notice for a few days, since the Yank ran off and got killed. Except, seems he didn't.' He cast Wells a wary glance.

'We'll come to that,' Bullace said. 'Let us consider a different account of Albert Crosby's movements on that Friday and Saturday. Far from driving to Steeple Court and remaining overnight, could he in fact have doubled back and taken a train to London from Brabberton Manor? Sir Finchley.' Bullace switched direction in one of those moves Jemima had occasionally found unsettling. 'In your statement during the investigation into Roland Crosby's murder last April, you corroborated Crosby's alibi. Do you still wish to?'

'Why are you re-investigating an old matter?' Sir Finchley blustered. 'Explain the relevance, or my next telephone call will be to my constituency MP.'

'You seem eager to run up a telephone bill for your mother,' was Bullace's response. A short, confidential conversation with Pretty ended with the sergeant leaving the room.

Bullace appeared to have lost his thread. He next asked Albert Crosby how he had mislaid the key to his room.

When the butler took refuge in silence, Jemima removed a small room key from her bag and showed it to Jack. 'Will this open the butler's private quarters?'

Jack took it. 'Looks very like it. How do you have it, Mrs Flowerday?'

Jemima answered, 'Thirty-seven, Cherry Hall Road, London, N4.'

This cut through Sara Crosby's defiant veneer. 'You've been in my house? That's a crime. That's trespass! You've no right.'

Nobody took much notice. DS Pretty returned and reported that a conversation with the proprietor of the grocery store in Dersingham, the village serving Steeple Court, had secured the information that five bundles of local asparagus had been ordered by telephone on the afternoon of Friday, 21 April for a dinner party that evening.

'Ordered by...?' Bullace asked.

'Lady Olivia Hamlash,' Pretty answered. 'Delivered by an errand boy at a cost of—'

'Never mind the cost,' Bullace said, and invited Sir Finchley to reconsider Albert Crosby's alibi. 'And, indeed, your own movements that weekend.'

It looked as though Sir Finchley would refuse to answer, until his wife gave him a hard prod, saying, 'Your presence in Norfolk that weekend can be vouched for at the highest level.' She sent Bullace a hawkish look. 'The *highest*.'

Sir Finchley cleared his throat and conceded that Crosby might not have got as far as Steeple Court. Might, indeed, not have actually handed over the asparagus.

'No, indeed. He flung it onto the grass outside a railway station. How far did he get?' Bullace inquired crisply.

'To – er – Attleborough,' Sir Finchley conceded. 'He drove there and we met at the station. On that Friday, at around nine in the morning.'

'Attleborough being...?' Bullace, who was not a Suffolk native, glanced at his sergeant.

'Norfolk, sir, halfway between here and Steeple Court.'

'A convenient meeting point. How did you reach Attleborough, Sir Finchley? By train?'

The husband glanced at the wife. Lady Olivia's expression was steadfast yet Jemima detected cracks in the glaze. She refused to pity her. Lady Olivia was not innocent. Not in one important matter.

'I drove the Silver Ghost, how else would I travel?' Sir Finchley had grasped the shield of sarcasm. Always a sign of weakness.

Bullace leaned forward. Jemima felt that, if he'd possessed hackles, they would have risen. 'We have an innocent girl's body in the mortuary,' he said in a low voice. 'Two strides from the body of Marie Guyen. In a mortuary in Ipswich, we have a decapitated head, so this is no time to be plucking at fig leaves. Sir Finchley, when you swore that Albert Crosby was at Steeple Court between Friday 21 and Saturday 22 April this year, were you lying?'

Sir Finchley's mother roused herself enough to declare, 'A Hamlash does not lie.'

The pause afterwards was broken by DS Pretty saying to his superior, 'Your predecessor, DCI Lidney, interviewed Albert Crosby and Sir Finchley two or three days after the head was discovered. I was present. At Lidney's express desire, however, we did not interview any of the Steeple Court staff. I would have liked to, but DCI Lidney felt it… unnecessary.' Pretty loaded that last word with feeling. 'Perhaps we could take a drive over to Steeple Court later?'

'Excellent idea,' said Bullace.

'Outrageous,' Sir Finchley spluttered.

'Or Sir Finchley could save us the petrol and himself the embarrassment,' Pretty suggested, 'and answer the question?'

'Yes, all right. I misremembered in my statement.' Sir Finchley took off his spectacles, wiped them, put them back on. 'I had tried to help a sorry individual by being cautious with my answers.'

'You're saying you lied,' was Bullace's summary.

'Not lied, exactly, no.'

'He lied. He used me.' Albert Crosby tried to get up, but was kept in his seat by the policeman's grip on his shoulders. Instead, his energy flowed into his voice as he denounced the man who owned the room they sat in, who had called him a 'sorry individual'. 'Used me, and he'll throw me to the wolves. They all will, but I won't allow it, damn them to hell.'

'Crosby!' Lady Hamlash sounded shocked.

They will *all* throw him to the wolves? Jemima cast Wells a glance. His response, a lift of the eyebrow.

Bullace cogitated. 'What have we learned? That instead of going to Steeple Court to deliver asparagus, Albert Crosby met Sir Finchley at… erm… Appleborough?'

'Attleborough,' Pretty corrected.

'And then what? Back to Suffolk, a train ticket purchased. First class… you don't like to travel third, Crosby? No. Nor do I.'

Crosby was muttering. Bullace asked him to speak up.

'The asparagus was an excuse,' Crosby repeated. 'Sir Finchley had something to give me.'

'My asparagus, an excuse?' Lady Hamlash glared at her butler, then her son. 'For what, pray?'

'This.' Wells removed something from his pocket; a pale-blue rectangle. 'It's a cheque drawn on the bank account of Sir Finchley Hamlash and made out to Albert Crosby.' He passed the cheque to Bullace.

Jemima leaned closer to Wells. 'I saw you burn that,' she hissed.

'You saw me burn a sheet torn from an invoice pad, cunningly folded,' he whispered back. 'I wasn't going to let you keep it, Mrs Flowerday.'

Bullace studied the cheque and Jemima recognised the moment

the figure written on it impinged on his consciousness. He had his sergeant show it to Albert Crosby, who mumbled, 'It was made out to me, and I was to put it through my account, because Roland didn't like banks. The money was for him. A payoff.'

'It bears your signature, Sir Finchley,' Bullace said.

'Tell the man.' Lady Olivia once again prodded her husband though with her voice rather than a finger. 'Tell him that our finances are our own concern and we may use them to benefit whomsoever we choose.'

'As my wife says,' Sir Finchley agreed in a bone-dry voice. 'The money was a gift to my mother's butler. I don't understand why he mentioned that other name.'

'Roland,' Albert Crosby barked. 'Roland, Roland, Roland. Does it hurt your ears, Sir Finchley? I visited him in London, to show him the cheque so he knew the money was good.'

'"So he knew the money was good",' Bullace echoed. 'We come to the crux. "The money" being the proceeds of extortion?'

'If you want to call it that,' Crosby agreed.

'To be clear, your brother, Roland, was blackmailing Sir Finchley.'

There was an outcry, Lady Olivia's voice the loudest. Sir Finchley Hamlash could not be the victim of blackmail as he had done nothing compromising in his life. 'Is his kindness to this excuse of a butler now to be thrown in his face?'

Bullace was unmoved. 'Let us finish the miserable story of murder, and how it drew in innocent victims and blighted this house. A meeting takes place in Attleborough after which Sir Finchley returns home without the hors d'oeuvre. It is forgotten in the heat of the moment. Albert Crosby drives back to Suffolk and parks at an out-of-the-way station manned by Deacon here. Crosby hurls the asparagus into the hedge and buys a return ticket to Liverpool Street Station. He then proceeds to his brother's home in Finsbury Park.'

Albert did not deny it. A cloud had settled over him. Shame, fear or resignation, Jemima could not decode it. Asked what time he arrived in North London, he claimed he could not recall.

Taking *The Weekend Sleuth* from her bag, she turned to a page she had read through so often, she could almost quote it blind. "'A neighbour reported seeing Crosby come home at two thirty on the Friday as if for a late lunch and return for the night at well-gone eleven." In other words,' she said, 'he appeared to come home twice, but that isn't likely as he did twelve-hour shifts in Central London. I suggest, Chief Inspector, that the neighbour saw Albert Crosby arrive in the afternoon and mistook him for his brother. Roland returned home after his day's work at his usual late hour. The neighbour mis-identified the brothers the following day, seeing a man she assumed was Roland setting off for work at six thirty in the morning. It wasn't fully light.'

'You are suggesting that Albert was impersonating his brother that weekend?'

'I am,' Jemima answered. 'Like everyone else, I could not work out how Roland Crosby could make a journey to Suffolk and simply disappear. But he didn't make the journey at all. There is a coat in the wardrobe at Sara's house which I suspect is Albert's. It has a velvet collar and in her interview with a reporter from this journal' – she held up *The Weekend Sleuth* – 'Sara describes taking a clothes brush to her husband's *corduroy* collar.'

'Velvet, corduroy, they're the same thing,' Sara said tetchily.

'At a distance, they are similar,' Jemima answered. 'But in their manufacture, and their price, they are far from the same. The coat with the velvet collar still hangs in the wardrobe in London and I would expect to find that the one in Albert's wardrobe here, the one he wore to come home, has a collar of brown corduroy. Because Albert left the Finsbury Park house wearing his brother's coat.'

'Is that why he took to tying a scarf round his collar whenever he put his coat on?' Jack burst out. 'The day he drove you to the station, Mrs Flowerday, I saw him fussing at it in his room. I told you, didn't I?'

Jemima remembered that conversation perfectly. 'Albert Crosby donned his brother's coat so he might leave Roland's house unremarked. The brothers' coats were very similar, but not identical, something that was bound to cause comment in the servants' hall when he returned home. Hence the scarf. He'd have done better to buy himself a new garment, but his real mistake was to leave his return railway ticket and the key to his private quarters in the pocket of the coat he left behind.'

'He had to buy a fresh ticket to get home,' Sergeant Pretty said thoughtfully. 'A single. We never could work out why Roland would buy a single ticket.'

'Roland didn't buy it at all,' Wells cut in, 'because he was dead by then.'

Which was precisely what Jemima had worked out a few minutes earlier. I should have mentioned it then, she thought, then chided herself. This wasn't a competition. It was murder.

She took the story back, however, saying, 'Do you recall a detail of evidence, DCI Bullace, of how "Roland" nearly missed his 7.30 train, stumbling as he got on board? It was Albert, of course, realising at the last minute that he must buy another ticket, rushing to the window and tripping because he was out of breath—'

'Wait.' Jack Millar got up. All this time, he had been staring alternately at Albert Crosby and at Wells, as if one of them must be the Devil, but he could not choose which. 'I need to fetch something.' He limped to the door.

DS Pretty was dispatched to go with him, and they returned after a few minutes, Jack carrying a pair of men's black, lace-up

Oxfords. At the sight of them, the last bit of fight drained from Albert Crosby.

'Size nine.' Jack held a shoe in each hand. 'Mr Crosby's a size ten. I should know because I've cleaned his shoes every day since I came here. He had me take them... oh, dear.' The reality of who was the Devil hit Jack then, and he began to shake.

'He had you take them to a cobbler's in Saxonchurch to be stretched?' Jemima suggested. 'Those are Roland's shoes, a size too small for Albert, whose size tens are in the wardrobe in Finsbury Park. In need of a polish, I may add. Jack has solved a mystery. Albert stumbled getting on the train back to Suffolk because his shoes were pinching him.'

Jack was allowed to go and sit in the club chair by the front door to compose himself. Bullace spent the intervening minutes writing notes. He looked up as Jack came back in, then summoned Albert Crosby's attention.

'Friday, 21 April, you travelled to London, going to your sister-in-law's house to await your brother's return from work. You were there to offer him a substantial payoff to cease his blackmailing of Sir Finchley. Closer to midnight than eleven, Roland came home. What happened then?'

Albert Crosby closed his eyes. 'Ask her.'

Sara Crosby stared stonily ahead.

Bullace waited, then rapped out an order. 'PC Trowse, douse the fire. You,' he said to another of the constables, 'open that great window.' To the third policeman, 'Stand in front of the door. Nobody is to leave. If we freeze, so be it.'

'Unconscionable!' Sir Finchley struck the table. 'My mother will not be ordered about in her own home. I'll have your job. I'll have your rank off you, Bullace. D'you really not know who my father-in-law is?'

'Thanks to your mentioning it on every conceivable occasion, I am familiar with his title, his rank in the peerage and his understandable love for his daughter,' was Bullace's reply. 'I retract my order.'

Just as well, Jemima thought, as PC Trowse was struggling to work out how to put out a fire without a bucket of sand or water, and the other policeman was trying in vain to open a centuries old window.

'However, we will not leave this room until I have the truth,' Bullace intoned resolutely. 'Three deaths at Merry Beggars Hall. Three murders.'

Wells spoke up. 'Between myself, Mrs Flowerday and that fellow there' – he pointed to Sydney Deacon, who looked round as if hoping there was somebody else behind him – 'we will tell you how each death occurred. With your permission.'

Bullace looked nettled.

DS Pretty said, 'Pah.'

Jack Millar, who until now had only glowered silently at Wells, smacked the table. 'Let him, give him a length of rope. He might not be a Crosby, but he's not the blue-eyed boy you all think he is either.'

'I'm sure I think no such thing,' said Bullace. 'But, very well, have your say, Mr Wells.'

Wells strode to the window, squeezed behind Albert and Sara Crosby and pulled shut the curtains. He asked for the lights to be switched on. 'Jack, you will hear my confession. I ask you to be patient.'

Chapter Forty-Four

'Imagine,' said Wells, 'a small sitting room in North London, in an ordinary street. Mrs Sara Crosby has spent the afternoon entertaining her brother-in-law who is up from the country. Does she know why he is there?' Wells glanced at Sara, whose steely mask offered nothing. 'Maybe not at first, but I think Albert told her. Her persuasion would be needed. Albert's job, you see, was to strike a deal with Roland. He had been provided with money from Sir Finchley Hamlash and he had a clear mandate: to make the blackmail stop for all time.'

'I still don't understand why Finchley wrote a cheque to my butler,' Lady Hamlash interrupted. 'I pay Crosby very well, for a country position. He has everything all found. How much was it, Finchley?'

Finchley pretended not to hear.

'Until somebody tells me, I refuse to listen.' Lady Hamlash fastened her hands over her ears.

Jemima rose. Wells's theatricality was compelling, but things needed to be speeded up as she doubted either Lady Hamlash or Mrs Newson would sustain this tension much longer. 'The cheque was for three thousand pounds.'

'Three thousand?' Lady Hamlash was incredulous. 'We do not

have that sort of money. Our wealth is in land, as it should be, as it always is for our class. Finchley?'

Her son chose not to elucidate. Lady Olivia's clenched jaw led Jemima to believe that the money had come from her funds.

'One way or another, the money was found,' said Wells. 'Let's stay in the small front room in North London. Albert Crosby is sitting with his sister-in-law, waiting for Roland to return from a long shift at Bright's Club. What is their conversation? I am sure it is accompanied by endless tea and some of Mrs Crosby's excellent cake. At last, they hear Roland's key in the lock. The brothers no doubt shake hands, Albert produces the cheque. "It's all yours, brother-mine, on the condition that you promise faithfully to cease your malignant activities." Does Roland agree?'

'I have never enjoyed fiction,' Lady Hamlash complained. 'Even as a child. One never knows what an author is about to throw at one.'

'I'll do my best to avoid surprises, Your Ladyship,' Wells said sardonically.

As the two people in the room able to say how Roland had responded to that generous cheque remained mute, Wells answered his own question.

'I should think Roland's socks were blown off. He was looking at more money than he'd earn in a decade. What we know is that it didn't end nicely. So… I pass the storytelling on to you, Sir Finchley. Tell the company why Roland Crosby was able to blackmail you.'

Sir Finchley damned his impudence, adding, 'I met some Americans in the war, and did not take to them.'

'I wholeheartedly suspect the feeling was mutual, sir.' Wells removed a letter from an inner pocket. It was one of the slender, transatlantic kinds, weighing no more than a cornstalk. He addressed Sara Crosby. 'I searched your house, ma'am, and found this nailed behind a wardrobe. Why do people always imagine their hiding places are unique?'

Sara Crosby fixed glittering rage on Wells. 'Dirty tea leaf.'

'Tea leaf. Thief, yes? Sure. I broke in.'

'You and her both.' Sara jabbed a finger at Jemima. 'I guessed as much, when you let slip you knew I baked wedding cakes. I don't discuss my business. I could have you both charged with trespass.'

'Maybe so,' Wells conceded, 'though where I come from, there's a provision in the law that allows a minor crime to be committed to prevent a greater one. Lady Hamlash cannot understand why Roland Crosby would wish to blackmail her son. Lady Olivia is similarly bemused. This letter is your answer.' He held it up for all to see. 'Marie wrote this in December of last year from New York.' He proceeded to read it aloud.

Dear Sir Edgar,

I hope you will forgive me writing directly to you, but I have nowhere else to turn. You, I know, cannot deny a marriage entered into willingly, nor the name that marriage has bestowed on me. I must fight for my right to be recognised, and that of my child. Will you not stand up for me with your family? For I have tried everything and my heart is broken.

'The rest is harrowing, and very private.' Wells returned the letter to its envelope. 'There you have it, Lady Hamlash, Sir Finchley, Lady Olivia. The woman known to you as Marie Guyen was, in truth, Lady Hamlash and bore a child in wedlock. A child named Vivyan.'

'Vivyan?' Lady Hamlash echoed. 'A family name.'

Wells trained a severe eye on her. 'That Marie's pleas were ignored, her rights erased, in no way denies the fact that she was legitimately a wife. This letter fell into the hands of Roland Crosby. Roland was supposed to pass it to his brother here at Merry Beggars Hall. Had Roland been a man of honour, that would have happened. He wasn't. He read it and judged for himself that the Hamlash family was sitting on a powder keg and if he held a match to the metaphorical fuse, they would pay. And they did. The evidence is a series of remittances to Roland, and that cheque.'

Jemima spoke up, describing a post-office book in Roland's name that showed a payment of one hundred pounds received a few days after Christmas last year. 'It tells us that Roland lost no time making his first demand. A telephone call came through on Christmas Eve, as you were serving dinner.' She looked to Albert Crosby for confirmation.

He, having nothing to gain now from loyalty, gave a dark smile. 'Bright's Club, supposedly chasing an unpaid bar bill. I fetched Sir Finchley and it was a short conversation. My thought at the time was that this was no mere unpaid account.'

'I remember it, Mr Crosby.' Mrs Newson woke from her shocked state. 'I asked you, didn't I, who on earth was calling so late on Christmas Eve?'

'Blackmailers like calling at inconvenient times,' Jemima said. 'Roland began with that single demand. By January, his secret was earning him thirty pounds a month. It shows up in the post-office savings book.'

Wells produced the very book, passing it to Bullace.

Bullace turned pages. 'January until April, then it stops.' He glanced at Sir Finchley, but said no more.

'Roland could extort what he wished because Sir Finchley had everything to lose. Of course he would pay.' Jemima braced herself for Sir Finchley to threaten her with a lawsuit, but silence greeted her and so she continued, turning to Lady Hamlash. 'On the death of your late husband, Edgar, away fighting in France, succeeded to the title, making his wife, Marie, Lady Hamlash. Marriage is marriage, whatever the social gulf between the couple. And as has been implied already, they had a child together.'

'I won't believe it.' The denial on Lady Hamlash's face was so intense, it could have been peeled off and placed on the mantelpiece.

'What will you not believe?' Jemima probed. 'That your son, Edgar, could have fallen in love and married without your know-ledge?'

'He might have done,' answered Lady Hamlash. 'He was young and ardent and far from home. What I cannot believe is that he would not have eventually told me. I have all his letters still and not one of them mentions a marriage, or a child. Vivyan.' She spoke the name almost with wonderment. 'Edgar was no fool.' Here she glanced at her younger son. 'He was at the Front, in daily danger. He would have made all efforts to ensure that his son was protected, guaranteed his rights and furnished with appropriate guardians. That is why I will not accept it, and why nothing will persuade me that Marie Guyen was anything other than a common swindler.'

'A son,' Jemima continued, holding up her hand to stop Wells jumping in, 'who by all legal precedent is his father's heir. Just as you have stated, Lady Hamlash. Whatever prevented Edgar from acknowledging his marriage and taking steps to establish a trust for his son, I cannot say, though I can speak to the pressure that a family can bring to bear on a son who marries outside his class.' She let that sink in. 'The marriage happened, and I understand that Mr Wells will shortly provide the proof. And what a bind for

Sir Finchley, to discover he has a nephew with a claim that trumps his. What will he not do to keep his title and the prestige that goes with it? Roland Crosby knew. Sir Finchley would pay anything.'

Jemima asked permission to divulge the contents of the lilac envelope that Bullace had earlier revealed but had not yet read out to the gathering. She explained that it had been with Marie's personal papers. 'I am sure others of its ilk were written over many months, but this one was received in November – the one just gone. It was sent from here by Lady Hamlash, to Marie in London.' Jemima opened it up, and read out Ada Hamlash's demand that Marie cease calling herself Lady Hamlash. 'Marie had been asserting her claim of marriage for some time, as Wells has intimated. The family cannot protest ignorance.'

Lady Hamlash would still have none of it. 'The woman was like a tick, burying into my flesh. Coming over from America, taking my name. As if any son of mine would have married an American cook.'

'Indeed no,' agreed Lady Olivia. Two red spots had appeared in her cheeks. 'Edgar always knew what was due his position. In fact, he intended—' She broke off.

'To marry you, Olivia, I know.' Lady Hamlash reached a hand towards her daughter-in-law. 'That is principally why I cannot believe he would marry elsewhere. Had he survived, you and he would have united.'

None of this was agreeable to Sir Finchley who asked his mother to desist from private matters.

'Everybody knows Olivia and Edgar had an understanding,' his mother said impatiently.

Jemima contradicted her. 'Edgar seems not to have remembered it in the autumn of 1916 when he freely married Marie.' She locked eyes with Wells, and what she saw there told her he had something up his sleeve. He would get his turn in a moment. To Lady Olivia she said, 'Your tragedy is to have lost Edgar and made do with Finchley. Lady Hamlash's tragedy is to have lost her son in war and, through her stubbornness, deprived herself of a grandchild.'

Wells butted in. 'Marie's tragedy was that she was left in limbo, unable to prove her marriage except by subterfuge, and paid the price.'

'But that's the point, isn't it?' said Lady Olivia. '*Unable to prove.*'

Wells was growing impatient. 'A cheque for three thousand pounds is pretty good proof.'

Was that it? Jemima wondered. She'd expected Wells to throw down an ace. As tired, tense people shifted on their seats, and cleared their throats, DS Pretty spoke up.

'I was enjoying your story about the Crosbys in the London sitting room, Mr Wells. We had Albert there eating cake, and Mrs C brewing tea, and then Roland comes home. He's given his money, told to stop his blackmail and burn the letter he intercepted from Madame Guyen… which he doesn't, obviously. Then what?'

Jemima ceded the floor and Wells suggested that Mrs Newson and Beth now be allowed to leave. 'What I'm going to tell you is not pleasant.'

'Let them go,' said Bullace. 'In fact, Mrs Newson, you might be inclined to put the kettle on the stove. Please take that cake away with you, and the treacle tart. The idea of eating pastry rolled out with a murder weapon is disturbing.'

'Let the cake stay,' Jemima said urgently. 'It has a bearing.'

Once the housekeeper and Beth had gone, Wells took up his thread. 'I must say, Mrs Crosby, your home is cleaner than a hospital ward before Royalty visits. That's always suspicious because one thing alone makes somebody clean up to that degree. Blood.' He turned to Bullace. 'You've not found Roland Crosby's body. You found only a head displaying no sign of injury. No strangulation, throat-cutting, no blows or blunt force.'

'How would you know that?' Pretty growled. 'We kept that information back.'

'Exactly. When no cause of death is given, it's obvious the police don't know. When you find the body, my betting is you'll find a wound. A single strike and probably here.' Wells patted himself behind the shoulder. 'A knife-thrust behind the collar bone, deep enough to hit the carotid artery. Death inevitably. Blood, lots of it.'

'If you're accusing me,' Sara Crosby said fiercely, 'how could I kill a man? I'm just a woman.'

'A woman with the muscles of a coal-heaver,' Jemima intervened. 'Thanks to a life of beating cake batter and lifting heavy tins in and out of ovens. Certainly, you have the killer instinct. I saw it in your eyes when you were contemplating pulling a stool from under me.'

'No such thing, dearie. You were wobbling, you were going to fall. I was there to catch you.' Sara Crosby appealed to DCI Bullace. 'They're making this up.'

'I am prepared to hear them out,' said Bullace. 'But I need evidence.'

'In which case, may I suggest you send your sergeant to telephone Scotland Yard,' Wells said. 'Have them dig in the cellar of number 37 Cherry Hall Lane. There is a great deal of coal to shift first. Mrs Crosby had three different coal merchants empty several tons down the chute.'

Bullace spoke when the general reaction had died down. 'You're saying we'll find the rest of Roland Crosby in the cellar?'

'Where else would you put a body in a terraced London home?' Wells invited Bullace to think about it. 'The murder took place on the coldest weekend of April, a freak snap in the weather. You couldn't dig a grave in a small garden on heavy, London clay. A body hastily buried under cellar bricks, an order of coal made. The smell of decomposing flesh masked by the heap tipped over it.'

Masked... Something caught at Jemima's memory. 'Peppermint!' she shouted. 'Mrs Crosby has bottles and bottles of the stuff. The armchairs in her sitting room smell of it. I dare say it does a sterling job of covering up the odour of blood.'

DCI Bullace nodded to Pretty. 'Make another call, Sergeant. To the Yard, ask for the head of CID. Don't take no for an answer. Ask him to get a squad of men with shovels to Cherry Hall Road, on the double.'

Pretty got up and cast a glance across the table. 'When I come back, sir, how about we have another cup of tea and eat that cake?'

Was he serious or turning the thumbscrew on Mrs Crosby? Jemima again opened her bag and took out a scrap of muslin. 'I think he won't want to when he sees this,' she said of DS Pretty who went off, whistling, to make his telephone call.

Chapter Forty-Five

Jemima spoke directly to Sara Crosby. 'You told me once that taking wedding cakes in a hansom cab, four of them balanced on your knee, was a chore you didn't enjoy.'

Feeling perhaps that her life and prospects had shrunk to nothing made Sara stubborn in the one thing she could control. She muttered, 'How would you like it?'

'Not much, I suppose. Just as I hate hemming curtains. You love making cakes for ordinary occasions, not grand ones. Easy to carry around, one tin at a time.' Jemima leaned across the table and pulled the brightly-patterned cake tin towards her, removing the lid to reveal the sticky-sugary offering inside. 'Mm. Caramelised golden syrup is irresistible. How long have you owned this tin?'

Sara Crosby made a face. 'A few years, I suppose.'

'I sense you bought it…' Jemima slowed her voice to a mystic drone. 'From a barge woman selling her wares by the Regent's Canal.'

Sara jerked. 'How d'you know that?'

'I have powers,' Jemima said vaguely. 'Give me a moment.' Leaving the library, she went into the kitchen where the air hummed with the coming-to-boil of a kettle.

Mrs Newson, slowly and meticulously laying a tea tray, asked, 'How long is this going on? My poor head is being torn apart.'

'Not long now.' Jemima found a cake slice and returned to the library. It crossed her mind to ask Sara to slice her own handiwork, but she doubted Bullace would allow her to pass anything with an edge to a woman accused of murder.

Wells had advanced the prospect that Roland had been murdered by a downward thrust from a blade, severing the main artery, and that raised the image of Sara creeping in from the kitchen, some kind of knife in her hand, striking Roland as he sat in his armchair. The armchair where she, Jemima, had sat. Could it have been a more subtle strike? For instance, a long skewer, such as she'd seen in Sara's utensil drawer. A perfect murder weapon, that, hiding in plain sight.

Standing at the table, she cut the cake into eight equal pieces. Insufficient for the company, but she doubted that would offend anyone. 'Before anyone takes a piece,' she said, 'there's something I must show you.'

Opening the fold of muslin, she revealed the fingernail-sized flake of dark brown enamel. 'This was stuck in the doorframe of the glasshouse. I discovered it when I first found my way in there and it seemed odd. Yes, it's a colour you see on any garden tool, or jacket button, but intuition told me it had come from something larger, heavier. An hour ago, at Mrs Crosby's request, I climbed on a stool to fetch down this tin.'

Jemima showed the damage to the metal side, where the giraffe's flank was slightly pressed in. A segment of the creature's camouflage marking was missing. The flake she had found in the glasshouse doorway fitted perfectly into the space. Standing on the stool in the kitchen, a mystery had solved itself.

Jemima said with cold precision to disguise her disgust, 'This is how Roland's head was brought from London.'

PC Trowse, who had been staring hungrily at the cake, jerked in disgust. 'In that tin there?'

'Yes,' Jemima said. 'The person carrying it was forced to squeeze through the glasshouse door, damaging it. Somebody had to carry the head from the murder scene in something that drew no attention. The clue I didn't pick up at the time came from the stationmaster at Beggars Heath. When Mrs Crosby arrived at the station a few days ago, he said, "Good to see you again." Nothing odd about that as Sara had filled in at Merry Beggars Hall a month after her husband died. But I had already heard mention that on the previous occasion, she was picked up from Ipswich. Albert Crosby drove the extra miles to save his sister-in-law the distress of travelling on a local train when her husband's killing was in all the newspapers. For the man collecting tickets at Beggars Heath to have welcomed her back—'

'She had to have been there on a third occasion. Merciful heavens, Mrs Flowerday,' DCI Bullace said solemnly, 'are you suggesting this woman brought her husband's head to the glasshouse in a cake tin?'

'Exactly. And when she realised I knew, Mrs Crosby thought to silence me. I'm grateful to PC Trowse for saving me on that occasion. It was Sara's second try,' Jemima added. 'The previous night, she attempted to do away with me and murdered Dinah instead.'

'A cake tin,' Bullace repeated. 'It defies decency, it insults the imagination.'

'I'm not asking you to imagine it,' Jemima replied calmly. 'A woman capable of hacking off her dead husband's head in the cellar of their home will be quite up to the job of travelling by train with it in a tin, on her knee.'

Lady Olivia ran out of the room, her hand to her mouth.

Sir Finchley visibly reeled, saying in a guttering voice, 'Damnation, Mother, she cooked a dinner I ate here last May.'

Lady Hamlash could not speak.

Jemima sensed an air of denial in the room, suspecting that Dr Rushbrook, Bullace, the constables, Deacon, could not square their rose-tinted ideals of feminine frailty with what she was accusing Sara Crosby of doing. It was left to Jemima to remind them of Medea, of Lizzie Borden and her axe, Judith with her tent peg. 'Salome requesting the head of John the Baptist—'

Lady Hamlash begged her to spare them a litany of Jezebels. 'I've endured too much for one day.'

The men who did not look in the least bit sceptical were Albert Crosby and Wells. But then, both had already arrived at the same conclusion about Sara.

Wells congratulated Jemima. 'Brava, Mrs Flowerday. Your talent for detail triumphs again. In America, we have a fine tradition of using violin cases to transport compromising articles. A cake tin. A beaming, modest, friendly cook-lady. Who would ever question her?'

Jemima's control briefly cracked. 'I thought she was so admirable! She bakes so beautifully.'

'Sure,' agreed Wells. 'I also believe Sweeney Todd made excellent pies.'

Jemima suggested to DCI Bullace that he should ask Scotland Yard to peek into Mrs Crosby's kitchen drawer, where numerous skewers, knives and a cleaver suitable for cutting through bone would be found.

'But why?' Lady Hamlash moaned, as if offering up a riddle to heaven. 'Why bring it here?'

There, Jemima's insights hit the buffers. 'I simply don't know.

DCI Bullace, you once listed the five principal reasons for murder. Greed, vengeance, jealousy, passion, fear. Which of those spurred Mrs Crosby?'

Bullace said nothing so they all looked at the woman herself. Jemima expected to meet again with that basilisk stare. But to her astonishment, Sara Crosby answered in a manner that did not in the least fit with the chief inspector's criminal philosophy.

'Why did I chop off Roly's head and bring it here?' She turned to her brother-in-law. 'To give Albert a bloody big kick up the backside.'

Chapter Forty-Six

The first Sara Crosby knew of her husband's blackmailing of Sir Finchley Hamlash was on that chilly April Friday when Albert called unexpectedly. She'd just put ginger cakes in the oven for a christening party the following day, when he rapped at her door. A cup of tea, a nice sit-down in the warm kitchen, and Albert told her all.

'That's how I knew my Roly was pulling a fast one. He was always up to something. Roly would earwig on conversations in the dining room at Bright's, or he'd go through coat pockets, and more than one gentleman member tipped him to shut him up. What he got, he gambled, and then he'd raid my post-office savings to pay his debts. That man had wrung me dry since we got back from our honeymoon. Would I get a share of that three thousand?' Sara asked. 'Is Florrie Forde going to marry the Prince of Wales?'

Florrie Ford being a buxom music-hall star famous for belting out 'It's a Long Way to Tipperary' and already married, the answer was a solid, 'No'.

'Roly told Albert to cash the cheque, thank you very much, and he'd take the money. I knew it would be blown on a card game by the next week.'

'You killed him to prevent that happening,' Bullace suggested.

'That's for you to ponder, Inspector. At some point, Roly had what was coming and he was dead before he hit the floor. I said to Albert, we'll share the money. Fifteen hundred each. Course, I knew Albert had to bank the cheque first and let the funds clear. He promised to do it first thing on Monday. But you know what? Twenty years married to Roland Crosby, I don't trust a man as far as I can throw him. What was to stop Albert keeping the lot, telling Sir Finchley he'd passed it on? So I sprinkled a bit of ginger in Albert's gravy, so to speak.'

'A little kick up the backside,' Bullace suggested grimly.

'That's right. To let him know I wasn't to be trifled with.'

'You brought your husband's head here to Merry Beggars Hall, placing it where you must have known it would be found either by an ageing gardener or a blameless widow.' Bullace betrayed rare emotion, a revulsion felt by every other person in the room except, it seemed, Sara Crosby herself.

'Worked, didn't it? Her Ladyship found it and set up a screeching fit. I'd have given a lot to see Albert's face when he realised what I'd done! Fifteen hundred pounds in cash was in my hand a short while later, when I came here to cook after the previous woman legged it. If you want to know what I did with the money...' Nobody asked but she told them anyway. 'I bought my house off the landlord and gave myself a nice little holiday in Ramsgate. The rest is for my old age.'

I doubt you'll attain that goal, Jemima reflected. She'd had the head arriving in a military campaign box, a deed box and even a hatbox, even thinking briefly it might have been Marie who planted it. Heaven forgive her for that.

Roland Crosby's death had been explained and the killing of Dinah Pullen also. Bullace summed up, saying, 'Dinah was in the wrong place. The wrong bed. The intended victim was Mrs Flowerday because Sara and Albert realised she was on their trail.'

Jemima said, 'My fate was sealed when I dropped that train ticket last night. It was while you were singing at the piano with Dr and Mrs Rushbrook, Chief Inspector. That ticket broke Albert's alibi for the day of his brother's disappearance, which would expose Sir Finchley's motive for paying off Roland. The whole fabrication would come down like a dynamited chimney. I had to die. Though actually' – she struggled to keep feelings in check – 'I gave myself away before then. Mrs Crosby guessed I'd been into her house.'

She turned a blazing eye on first Sara, then Albert. 'They must have blessed their luck when Deacon appeared as a perfect scapegoat.' Jemima produced the nail she had found in the glasshouse. 'It still has a bit of soil on it. There are nails missing from each of Sara Crosby's clogs. It's always the little details that catch us out. Sara killed Roland and Dinah, but Albert Crosby was present both times. He was at Sara's house when she murdered her husband, and he was outside the bedroom where Dinah was sleeping last night. How else would Mrs Crosby have found her way there? You heard her say, she never went upstairs here. Her domain was the kitchen, the rooms alongside it and the kitchen garden. Albert is implicated. However, I don't believe that Sara or Albert killed Marie. That was somebody else's doing, and the person responsible recently left this room.'

Jemima let a second go by for her words to make their mark. 'DCI Bullace, either you name the suspect, or I will.'

Chapter Forty-Seven

The secure van arrived, creating a break in proceedings and giving the unnamed suspect a reprieve. It was now fully dark. The Crosbys were taken off, heading for the jail at Ipswich. Sydney Deacon was given a ride in the front. He would be lodged at a hostel recommended by Dr Rushbrook.

'A dry hostel,' Rushbrook told him gravely. 'You'll want to sober up if only to get out of there.'

All the constables went too and the eleven people remaining in the library could now sit around the table without being pressed like sardines. Jemima and Beth fetched in fresh coal. Mrs Newson asked Lady Hamlash if she ought to see about some dinner.

When Lady Hamlash replied with a vague noise, Lady Olivia said to Jack, 'Well, young man, it seems you are promoted. You must act as butler and steer the household.'

Jack got up and began to collect the crocks, and Beth helped.

'Jack has stopped accusing me of murder, at least,' observed Wells.

'I'm surprised,' Bullace responded, 'since you promised him a confession. We haven't heard it yet.'

Wells, who had got up to open the door for Jack and Beth, flumped down again in a chair. 'I agree, it's time. Lady Hamlash, may I beg a shot of whisky?'

Sir Finchley fetched drinks for all who wanted them. Observing him closely, Jemima saw a man who believed he had to walk across a tightrope just one more time, and then he would be free. Exonerated of murder, and the mere victim of Roland Crosby. Had he so quickly buried the matter of Marie Guyen's violent end?

Jemima had given up believing that Wells had an ace up his sleeve, but when he asked Lady Hamlash if she had the recipe for the tobacco tincture written out by her former gardener, her interest was piqued.

'The one Bilney wrote?' Lady Hamlash said it was in the conservatory. 'In the decoupage drawers, among the empty seed packets and the pieces of string I cannot bear to discard.'

Lady Oliva took it upon herself to fetch it, and Jemima shadowed her, hearing again the familiar clip-clip of the woman's shoes. An hour or so ago, Lady Olivia had rushed away to be sick and had returned in a waft of floral perfume and tooth powder. Jemima watched Lady Olivia open the top drawer of a highly decorated piece of furniture, muttering, 'So much string!' Sensing Jemima, she jerked her head up. 'You again. Haven't you done enough creeping around?'

'One gets a taste,' Jemima said. 'I'd like to ask you a question.'

'Ask, then.' Lady Olivia returned to her search.

'Why did you thieve from Marie Guyen?'

Lady Olivia's face had passed through enough changes of expression already to fill a photograph album, but she found a new one. Contempt. 'I will assume that whisky fumes have affected your reason.'

'If you don't want to tell me here, privately, I will let DCI Bullace loose on you.'

'Oh, for heaven's sake, to be questioned by an uppity dressmaker! It is too much.'

'Lady Olivia, you stole Marie's book, *Delphine*, from her bedside.'

'Borrowed. I borrowed it. One does it all the time.'

'You tore it before throwing it into a hedge along with a little pressed-flower bookmark.'

Lady Olivia had found what she'd come for and closed the drawer, sweeping past Jemima without another word.

Jemima followed, raising her voice so that it echoed through the great hall. 'The shoes you have on are not yours.'

Lady Olivia stopped dead. She turned. It was too dark in the hall to see her features, but Jemima fancied they were a portrait of denial.

'How dare you?' Lady Olivia breathed.

Bullace came out of the library. 'What now?'

DS Pretty, who since making his telephone call to Scotland Yard had been outside getting a breath of air, came in at that moment.

'Were you to take those shoes off,' Jemima said, not softening her voice, 'we would see they were bought at Bergdorf Goodman. A select store in New York,' she added for the policemen's benefit. 'Lady Olivia, take them off.'

'The impertinence!' With her established route for getting her own way – patrician outrage – blocked, Lady Olivia nipped down a reliable byway. 'My father will learn of this.'

'Good,' Jemima volleyed back. 'I will tell him that his daughter stole a dead woman's shoes.'

Something snapped in Lady Olivia Hamlash. She yanked off the shoes and hurled them. They thudded harmlessly against the oak panelling, but Mrs Newson, carrying a tureen of soup heated up from lunchtime, screeched as though a rifle had been fired.

'You may be the same size as Madame Guyen,' Jemima said to Lady Olivia when they were all seated again, and the shoes were in DS Pretty's care, 'but you have a very different foot-shape. You left a pair of your shoes, manufactured by Rayne of Bond Street, in Marie's bedroom, where I accidentally put them on. The day I first saw you, you went into the servants' quarters to fetch a driving coat and were gone a little while. Did you find your way to Madame's bedroom…' Jemima imagined it. 'And opened the wardrobe? Saw the shoes, which were newer and smarter than yours, and couldn't resist making the exchange?'

'Think what you like.'

'Marie had excellent taste and the money to indulge it. You shouldn't have driven home in them though, Lady Olivia. I thought so at the time. Shoes get ruined from driving a car. I knew the moment you walked past me wearing them, who I had heard scurrying across the hall a short while before Marie Guyen succumbed to allergic shock.'

Lady Olivia looked appalled. 'You're accusing me? You think I killed that woman?' She looked to her husband, who clearly shared her incredulity, and then to Bullace. 'Put a stop to this, Chief Inspector.'

'Mrs Flowerday told me her suspicions,' Bullace said thoughtfully. 'I didn't believe her, but now that I know you had an understanding with Edgar Hamlash, I see a motive. Jealousy against the lady he – allegedly – married.'

'Rubbish,' Lady Olivia blustered. 'I was nowhere near here when the wretched woman died. I was at the Courtney-Leveretts with my husband.'

'We've already established that your family provides shaky alibis,' DS Pretty pointed out.

He's got no time for toffs, Jemima thought.

Wells spoke, and his words changed everything. 'Lady Olivia did not kill Marie Guyen,' he said. 'I know who did.' He nodded in response to Jemima's searching look. 'Yes, it's confession time.'

Chapter Forty-Eight

They had removed to the dining room to have their soup. It was quarter to six, early to dine even in the country, but this day had ripped up convention.

Beth and Mrs Newson had been allowed to retire to their quarters. Jack was serving, rigid and nervous in his unlooked-for promotion. Jemima gladly accepted a small measure of whisky.

Wells was telling them about the woman he had known for some years and counted as a friend. 'Marie was allergic to cigarettes and tobacco. She knew it, I knew it. When she stopped me on the terrace and asked if I'd share the tincture I'd brewed up that morning, I said no. Absolutely not.'

'Wait – why on earth would she want insecticide?' demanded Lady Hamlash. 'She didn't grow plants.'

'Her plan was to ingest a little. Because you were throwing her out, ma'am. Following the telephone call with your son, you instructed Crosby to sack her. Her intention was to render herself just ill enough to make it impossible for Crosby to remove her. She was buying time. I told her on no account could she have any. On the third or fourth time of her asking, I lost my temper. Told her to—'

'Go away!' Jemima said over him. 'You said, "I'm plumb out of patience! Let me do my job. *It won't happen.*" Only, I suppose it did.'

'Marie took matters into her own hands,' Wells agreed.

'And later, at her bedside, finding her dead, you cried out, "What have you done!" I thought you were accusing those of us who had carried her to the bedroom.'

'No,' he said.

'It wasn't Lady Olivia who took a sugar cube into the conservatory to adulterate it,' Jemima said slowly. 'It was Marie herself. She found the newly filled bottle and allowed one or two drops of tincture to colour the sugar. I was coming downstairs and heard her scurrying back to the kitchen, on her way to self-poison. I assumed the perpetrator wrapped the sugar cube in a handkerchief, until I found this.' She displayed the hoya leaf. 'Marie must have chucked it out of the pantry window, but it stuck to the sill. Marie wrapped her sugar cube in a leaf and hurried back towards the kitchen in her soft-soled shoes. She would have gone down the servants' corridor, dashing into her bedroom to change back into her working clogs, before finding Beth in the kitchen. Why didn't Beth see her, though?'

'Because Beth when hard at work doesn't always hear, as you and I discovered, Mrs Flowerday,' said Bullace.

'True. Into the pantry Marie went, dropping the cube into the sugar bowl, perhaps adding a few more brown ones from the box. Of course! She would know which one to select later.'

'Wouldn't it have stunk?' DS Pretty asked.

Jemima passed him the hoya leaf. 'No more than that.'

Pretty gave the leaf a sniff. 'It's there but faint, I grant you.'

'There was only Beth's nose to be alerted. Working in a steamy kitchen, with all the different smells including roast garlic, Beth didn't notice. Nor did Albert Crosby when he confronted Marie with her orders to leave.'

317

Bullace consulted the doctor. 'Does it ring true that Madame Guyen could have faked illness by swallowing a tobacco tincture?'

'I don't see why not,' said Rushbrook warily. 'A small amount might bring on vomiting. A mild fit of fainting, or a racing pulse. Enough to look serious without causing actual harm.'

'But harm is exactly what it caused,' Bullace shot back.

Wells took a slug of whisky. He looked suddenly haggard and Jemima knew his confession was on his tongue.

'Oh, Mr Wells,' she said. 'You knew from the beginning. It was you who instructed Beth to launder Marie's apron and her bed sheets. And you burned my favourite cardigan.'

Wells acknowledged, yes, he had.

'Is this your mea culpa, Mr Wells, that you destroyed evidence?' Bullace asked.

'You may take that into consideration,' was Wells's answer. 'I admit, I panicked after Marie's death and appeared more guilty than I was. But I deserve blame.' He had the recipe Lady Olivia had brought from the conservatory, the same list of ingredients he'd recited after Marie's death. He read it out to them again, and finished, '"One quart of water to be added to the neat tincture, after which, bottle it and keep—"'

'Wait,' interrupted Bullace, beating Jemima to it. 'Last time, in the drawing room before you fled, you said, "A quarter-pint of water" and now you're saying, "a quart". There is a deal of difference.'

'I know. Quarter-pint is what it says—' Wells passed the hand-written recipe to Bullace. 'But it should say "quart". Bilney got quarts and quarter pints confused; I realised too late that's what he'd done. He was getting old.'

'Forgetful,' said Lady Hamlash. 'I suspected as much.'

Wells added, 'I made the tincture as written, wildly over-strength.

Of course, on Lady Hamlash's plants it was highly effective. On a sugar cube, stirred into Marie's coffee—'

'It was eight times too strong,' Jemima breathed. 'But she wouldn't have known that.'

Wells nodded. 'I killed her. Not deliberately, through negligence. And I did what I could to hide the truth. I'm done with that. Once I have fulfilled my task in proving her right to her name, I invite you to arrest me, DCI Bullace. First, I need to give you this, Lady Hamlash.'

Wells drew another piece of paper from his inside pocket. 'I went to Marie's hotel room yesterday and collected a few things.' He sent Jemima a wan smile. 'You were right. The folks at the Royal Darnley are most accommodating. They unlocked a bureau for me, and this jumped out. Lady Hamlash, please read it.'

Lady Hamlash squinted at the paper. 'It's a birth certificate.'

'Read it out, Your Ladyship.'

'It refers to "Vivyan Hamlash. Mother, Marie Guyen Hamlash. Father…"' Lady Hamlash stopped, as if the name that came next had stuck in her throat.

Wells explained that the certificate had been issued in New York in January 1918. 'Will you read the baby's given name again, Lady Hamlash.'

'Vivyan… Ada.'

'Your granddaughter, ma'am.'

Jemima gasped. 'Marie had a little girl?'

'She did and gave her Hamlash family names.'

Lady Hamlash gazed at the birth certificate as if it made no sense.

Jemima couldn't quite grasp this turnaround either. 'So – Sir Finchley had nothing to fear. A girl cannot inherit. His brother's daughter could never claim the title.' This must be the ace Wells had kept up his sleeve all this time. But was it an ace? 'Why,' she put to Sir Finchley, 'pay Roland Crosby to keep quiet? Wouldn't it have been easier to accept Marie as your sister-in-law, as the widowed Lady Hamlash, instead of driving her to desperation?'

'Easier' was not the word reflected in Sir Finchley's eyes. He looked everywhere but at her. Nor could he settle on Wells, or his mother. 'Get out,' he abruptly ordered Jack.

Jack, ramrod straight on the far side of the room, gave a jolt, and sought Her Ladyship's eye as if he didn't know what to do.

'Out!' roared Sir Finchley.

Jack made his escape.

'You know what I'm going to say, Sir Finchley.' Earlier, when reading the letter Marie had sent to Sir Edgar at Bright's Club, Wells had skipped the paragraph he'd described as too private. He would read it now, he said, first reminding them that it had been written almost exactly a year before.

'Let me tell you, as I've already told Mrs Flowerday, Marie knew perfectly well that Edgar had died in France, of wounds. She addressed the letter to him at his club having run out of ways to get your attention, Sir Finchley, Lady Hamlash. She figured it would reach one of you one way or another and you'd open it. And she was right, though not at all in the way she imagined.' He read out the rest of Marie's words.

Why have you deserted me, my darling? You have a perfect cherub for a daughter who deserves to know her daddy. Are you ashamed of us? Your father is no longer alive to mind. Your mother will understand, given time. All I ask is that you honour the vows you made to me in the village outside Amiens.

Wells abruptly passed the letter to Bullace who read the rest with slow-dawning understanding.

"'Why have you deserted us,'" Bullace read, "'my darling Finchley?'" He turned to the man, who made a run for the door, only to be prevented by DS Pretty who had positioned himself at that end of the table. 'Sir Finchley Hamlash,' said Bullace. 'She was married to you.'

Chapter Forty-Nine

With a scream, Lady Olivia threw back her chair, strode to where her husband leaned, white-knuckled, against the sideboard, and began hitting him in rage and incomprehension.

Well she might, thought Jemima, because she had just learned that she was no wife. Until nine days ago, he'd been married to Marie. Lady Olivia's privileged existence had received a broadside from which there was no recovery. She continued to rain blows on her husband until DS Pretty intervened, though not perhaps as quickly as he could have.

The ringing telephone was not heard at once, through Lady Olivia's sobs and Sir Finchley repeating 'I'm sorry, dearest,' like a mechanical parrot.

Wells, watching Sir Finchley with granite impassivity, said for the benefit of anyone inclined to listen, 'Lines in the society pages alerted Marie to the betrayal committed on her. We get the British newspapers in New York, albeit two weeks late, and Marie always read the births, marriages and deaths. She called on me one afternoon, bringing a copy of *The Times* that had in it a notice of a marriage. Sir Finchley Hamlash to Lady Olivia Rivers. A cruel way for a woman to find out she's been replaced, wouldn't you say, Sir Finchley? And, oops, Marie seemed to think you were still married to her. What choice did she have but to travel here to seek redress? To find her justice.'

Sir Finchley gave no impression of having heard this appeal to his conscience.

Lady Hamlash heard well enough, repeating, 'I didn't know!' until it dawned on her that nobody believed her, and so she upped the intensity of her defence. 'I *knew* Edgar never married and he was truthful to a fault. Why would I suspect Finchley, who said not a word? Vivyan Ada.' She spoke to her son. 'Is it true, my boy, you denied your own child, *my* granddaughter?'

These words provoked a fresh cry from Lady Olivia.

It was Jemima who finally said, 'Shush, everyone. Isn't that the phone?'

Bullace went to answer it and came back looking very sober. 'Scotland Yard,' he informed them. 'A body has been found in the cellar of Mrs Sara Crosby's home.' He turned to Kenneth Wells. 'We have our suspects for Roland Crosby's murder and that of Dinah Pullen. Marie Guyen's death seems to have been accidental, and I am disinclined to pursue charges against you, young man, for your negligence in leaving a lethal tincture on a shelf in an unlocked room.'

To Sir Finchley, he made the stern point that bigamy carried the penalty of imprisonment. 'However,' he left a pause so long, Sir Finchley could be heard struggling to breathe, 'as your first wife is no more, and Lady Olivia stands in a precarious position, *and* you have a motherless daughter whose welfare must be considered, bringing a prosecution may not be in the public interest. What good would it do Marie now? If you will solemnly undertake to stand up like a man to your responsibilities, Sir Finchley, then my lips are sealed.'

To Jemima, DCI Bullace had the following to say: 'What a pity you already have a profession, Mrs Flowerday, for I feel you would do rather well in mine.'

Epilogue

The morning of 20 December slunk in with grey mist and a distinct thaw. Jemima was up early, helping Beth with the breakfast. She hadn't slept much. Death had slipped inside Merry Beggars Hall with such impunity, she couldn't trust a new day to arrive without tragedy. Only the clinking of crockery and the slam of kettle upon range drove the feeling away.

After breakfast, she knocked on the drawing room door. Lady Olivia and Sir Finchley had repaired to The Bell in Saxonchurch the previous night as the upper floor was still out of bounds. Lady Hamlash had passed the night in her drawing room, on the sofa. The Silver Ghost had drawn up outside a short while ago, and Jemima steeled herself to meet all the Hamlashes at once.

Nobody answered her knock, so she walked in. She interrupted a heated discussion between mother, daughter-in-law and son.

'Mother, it isn't remotely possible for you to stay here for Christmas,' Sir Finchley was saying. 'The press will sniff out the story and you'll have ghouls knocking on the door at all hours and no Crosby to beat them off.'

'I cannot leave my servants – ah, Mrs Flowerday.' Lady Hamlash looked almost relieved to see Jemima. 'Have you come to say goodbye?'

'First, I've come to hand over your dresses, Lady Hamlash. You remember them?' Jemima couldn't help feeling anxious about her commission for which she had yet to be paid.

'Yes, my gowns,' breathed Lady Hamlash. 'I had indeed almost forgotten.'

'There you are, Mama-Hamlash,' Lady Olivia said with forced brightness. Her eyes were raw with extended weeping, and she regarded Jemima as one might a rattle snake among the bread rolls. 'Never mind staying here, come to Steeple Court and knock us dead with your new modes.'

A tight silence fell.

Lady Olivia cleared her throat. 'An unfortunate turn of phrase. I mean, delight us with your new fashions.'

'I don't know,' Her Ladyship quibbled.

'Bring the servants. Give them a holiday.'

Lady Hamlash looked to Jemima as if seeking guidance. Jemima thought of Beth, Jack and Mrs Newson, the huddled remains of a once tight-knit staff. 'D'you know, I think a holiday would be a splendid thing for all of you. May I give you some of my Fleur du Jour business cards, Lady Olivia?'

Lady Olivia accepted one and looked it over. 'Oh, I see. Fleur du Jour. Finchley?'

He grunted. 'Hey?'

'"Fleur du jour", "Flowerday".' His lady waved the card at him. 'It's clever. She's clever.'

'If you say so, dearest.'

Jemima had no desire for praise from that quarter. She said to Lady Hamlash, 'You really must try your dresses before I go.'

Sir Finchley was dismissed, and Lady Hamlash was helped into her new gowns in front of the fire.

Lady Olivia was impressed. 'You are quite good, aren't you?' The brittleness in her tone seemed to say, 'I can't afford for you to be my enemy.'

Jemima accepted the flag of truce. 'Thank you,' she said.

When the dresses were back on their hangers, Jemima cleared her throat. This was always a difficult moment. 'If I might present my account to you, Lady Hamlash?'

Her Ladyship blinked. 'Your... sorry?'

'She wants to be paid, Mama-Hamlash. She doesn't wave her magic wand for free,' Lady Olivia said bracingly.

'Oh, quite. How remiss. Did we say one hundred pounds, Mrs Flowerday?'

Jemima was sorely tempted, but she landed upon the side of the angels, saying, 'Fifty was what we agreed.' She could go home and pay the children's school fees.

As Lady Hamlash wrote a cheque, Jemima glanced out into the gardens where collops of snow melted from the branches. It looked set to be a mild Christmas after all and, tomorrow, Tommy and Molly would be home for the holidays. Lady Olivia sidled up to share the view. She cleared her throat.

'The matter of the shoes...'

'Keep them,' Jemima said. 'You were jealous when you saw the lovely things Marie owned. How dared she reach up from her sphere, be better dressed than you and equally well-read? It made you destructive, but of course that isn't the same as killing and I apologise for thinking you capable of that. I ask one thing of you, Lady Olivia.'

'Ask it.'

'If Sir Finchley's little girl ends up with you, you will be kind? Her mother was a wonderful woman. Give her this.' Jemima passed Lady Olivia the pressed daffodil bookmark and turned away to avoid the other woman's blush.

*

Jemima left Merry Beggars Hall, driven by Wells. He had hired a car in London which, when he'd arrived the previous morning, he had parked a distance away. As he turned into the lane, and they saw tyre tracks from yesterday's traffic, he shot her a searching glance.

'You made quite a conquest of DCI Bullace.'

'Hardly,' Jemima replied repressively. 'Despite his praise, at heart, the chief inspector considers me a meddlesome woman. And if you're suggesting anything else, I am not at all romantically inclined.'

Wells gave her another sidelong glance. 'I've never had the chance to ask, but is there a Mr Flowerday? Or are you, as you often seem to hint, a widow? Forgive me.' Her reaction made him bite back on the words. 'It's not my business.'

'I am neither a wife nor a widow,' she said after a while.

'That's too much of a riddle to solve while driving in fog.'

She told him the truth. Simon had survived the war, but not intact. 'He is in a hospital, permanently. I'm allowed to see him once a month, but he doesn't know me. Actually, Mr Wells, would you after all drop me off at the railway station? I have my return fare and might as well use it.'

He protested, but she was adamant, and at Beggars Heath he bid her a regretful farewell, and a happy Christmas.

On the train, Jemima found a compartment to herself. After a period of sad introspection, she took out her journal, turned to a fresh page, and wrote the day's date, and the words:

Notes on a murder solved

Roland Crosby's movements in the hours before his disappearance and death seemed consistent with a man making an impulsive journey. I now know that appearances were wholly deceiving. He had died in his armchair at home, quite probably at the hands of his wife, and likely from a downward thrust with a meat skewer, finding the unprotected area between the collarbone and shoulder blade.

About the Author

Kay Blythe, who also writes as Natalie Meg Evans, is an award-winning historical author on both sides of the Atlantic, having reached the *New York Times* top 100 list with her debut novel, *The Dress Thief*. Writing crime as Kay Blythe fulfils a long-held ambition. Her dressmaker-sleuth, Jemima Flowerday, follows in the tradition of clever women set free by the social upheaval of the years after the First World War. Jemima combines her skills as a dressmaker and sleuth to solve crime in the crumbling stately homes of Britain.